Doc

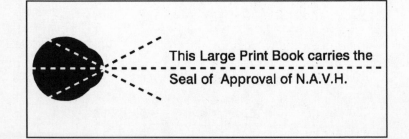

This Large Print Book carries the
Seal of Approval of N.A.V.H.

DOC

MARY DORIA RUSSELL

THORNDIKE PRESS

A part of Gale, Cengage Learning

GALE
CENGAGE Learning™

Detroit • New York • San Francisco • New Haven, Conn • Waterville, Maine • London

GALE
CENGAGE Learning™

LIBRARY OF CONGRESS CATALOGING-IN-PUBLICATION DATA

Russell, Mary Doria, 1950–
    Doc / by Mary Doria Russell. — Large print ed.
       p. cm. — (Thorndike Press large print historical fiction)
    ISBN-13: 978-1-4104-3963-5
    ISBN-10: 1-4104-3963-1
    1. Holliday, John Henry, 1851–1887—Fiction. 2. Earp, Wyatt, 1848–1929—Fiction. 3. Dodge City (Kan.)—Fiction. 4. Large type books. I. Title.
    PS3568.U76678D63 2011
    813'.54—dc22   2011018929

Published in 2011 by arrangement with Random House, Inc.

Printed in the United States of America
1 2 3 4 5 6 7 15 14 13 12 11

For Art Nolan, who told
me what Wyatt knew;
for Eddie Nolan, who showed us
what John Henry had to learn;
for Alice McKey Holliday, who
raised a fine young man;
with thanks to Bob Price
and Gretchen Batton.

This book is fiction, but there is always a chance that such a work of fiction may throw some light on what has been written as fact.
— E. HEMINGWAY, *A MOVEABLE FEAST*

THE GAME

THE PLAYERS

Fictional characters are listed in italics.

GEORGIA

The Hollidays

John Henry Holliday, D.D.S., later known
as Doc Holliday
Alice McKey Holliday: his mother
Henry Holliday: his father
Wilson and *Chainey*: brothers, born into
his family's possession

John Stiles Holliday, M.D.: JHH's uncle
Permelia: his wife
Robert: his younger son, later a dentist
George: his older son; sent to care for JHH
in Texas in 1877
Sophie Walton: his foster child; taught JHH
to play cards

Martha Anne Holliday: JHH's childhood sweetheart

TEXAS

Henry Kahn: a bad-tempered gambler; shot JHH in 1877

Mary Katharine "Kate" Harony: a prostitute; JHH's companion

David W. "Dirty Dave" Rudabaugh: a train robber

George Hoyt: an inexpert assassin

Tobias Driskill: a Texan with a grudge

Billy Driskill: his son, arrested for assault in Dodge

KANSAS

The Earps

Morgan Earp: a policeman; JHH's closest friend

Louisa "Lou" Houston: his girlfriend

James Earp: Morgan's brother, a brothel manager

Bessie Bartlett Earp: his wife, the madam

Wyatt Earp: brother of Morgan and James; a policeman

Urilla Sutherland Earp: Wyatt's wife, deceased

Mattie Blaylock: a Dodge City streetwalker

Lawmen

Lawrence "Fat Larry" Deger: the Dodge City marshal (chief of police)

Ed Masterson: chief deputy to Marshal Deger; deceased

Marshal Deger's deputies:
Morgan Earp
Wyatt Earp
Jack Brown
Chuck Trask
John Stauber

William Barkley "Bat" Masterson: sheriff of Ford County; half owner, Lone Star Saloon and Dance Hall

Dodge City Chamber of Commerce

Robert C. "Bob" Wright: proprietor, Wright's General Outfitting Store; member, Kansas House of Representatives

Isabelle "Belle" Wright: his daughter

Alice Wright: his wife

Hamilton "Ham" Bell: proprietor, Hamilton Bell's Famous Elephant Barn

13

Chalkley "Chalkie" Beeson: proprietor, the Long Branch Saloon

George "Deacon" Cox: proprietor, the Dodge House Hotel

James H. "Dog" Kelley: mayor of Dodge; proprietor, the Alhambra Saloon

George "Big George" Hoover: proprietor, Hoover's Cigar Shop and Wholesale Liquors; leader, Dodge City anti-saloon reform movement

Margaret: his wife; formerly the prostitute Maggie Carnahan

Other Kansas Figures (Dodge and Elsewhere)

Edwin "Eddie Foy" Fitzgerald: vaudeville comedian

Verelda: his girlfriend, a prostitute

Jau "China Joe" Dong-Sing: proprietor, China Joe's Laundry and Baths

John Horse Sanders: a young faro dealer

Charles Sanders: *Johnnie's father, deceased;* a black man killed in Wichita after defending his wife from two Texans

Father Alexander von Angensperg, S.J.: an Austrian Jesuit; Johnnie Sanders' favorite *teacher at* the St. Francis Mission School for Indians, near Wichita

Father John Schoenmakers, S.J.: a Dutch

14

Jesuit; superior of St. Francis

Brother Sheehan, S.J.: an Irish lay brother; taught farming at St. Francis

Father Paul Maria Ponziglione, S.J.: an Italian Jesuit, missionary to the Plains Indians

Captain Elijah Garrett Grier, U.S. Army: stationed at Fort Dodge, Kansas; *owner of Roxana*

John Riney: tollgate operator, Dodge City toll bridge

Mabel: his wife

John Jr., called "Junior": his eldest son

Wilfred Eberhardt: a German orphan

Thomas McCarty, M.D.: a Dodge City physician and pharmacist

Nick Klaine: editor, *Dodge City Times*

D. M. Frost: editor, *Ford County Globe*

The Animals

Dick Naylor: Wyatt Earp's horse

Roxana: an Arabian mare owned by Elijah Garrett Grier

Michigan Jim: a quarterhorse owned by Mayor Dog Kelley

Alphonsus: the Jesuits' mule

THE ANTE

PLAYING FOR TIME

He began to die when he was twenty-one, but tuberculosis is slow and sly and subtle. The disease took fifteen years to hollow out his lungs so completely they could no longer keep him alive. In all that time, he was allowed a single season of something like happiness.

When he arrived in Dodge City in 1878, Dr. John Henry Holliday was a frail twenty-six-year-old dentist who wanted nothing grander than to practice his profession in a prosperous Kansas cow town. Hope — cruelest of the evils that escaped Pandora's box — smiled on him gently all that summer. While he lived in Dodge, the quiet life he yearned for seemed to lie within his grasp.

At thirty, he would be famous for his part in the gunfight at the O.K. Corral in Tombstone, Arizona. A year later, he would become infamous when he rode at Wyatt Earp's side to avenge the murder of Wyatt's younger brother Morgan. To sell newspapers, the journalists of his day embellished slim fact with fat rumor and rank fiction; it was they who invented the iconic frontier gambler and gunman *Doc Holliday.* (Thin. Mustachioed. A cold and casual killer. Doomed, and always dressed in black, as though for his own funeral.) That unwanted notoriety added misery to John Henry Holliday's final year, when illness and exile had made of him a lonely and destitute alcoholic, dying by awful inches and living off charity in a Colorado hotel.

The wonder is how long and how well he fought his destiny. He was meant to die at birth. The Fates pursued him from the day he first drew breath, howling for his delayed demise.

His mother's name was Alice Jane.

She was one of the South Carolina Mc-Keys, the third of eleven children. Fair-haired, gray-eyed, with a gentle manner, she came late to marriage, almost twenty at her wedding. Alice was pretty enough and played piano well, but she was educated in excess of a lady's requirements. She was also possessed of a quiet, stubborn strength of character that had discouraged beaux less determined than Henry Holliday, a Georgia planter ten years her senior.

Alice and Henry buried their firstborn, a sweet little girl who lived just long enough to gaze and smile and laugh, and break her parents' hearts. Still in mourning for her daughter, Alice took no chances when she was brought to bed with her second child. This time, she insisted, she would be attended by Henry's brother, a respected physician with modern ideas, who rode to Griffin from nearby Fayetteville as soon as he received her summons.

Labor in Georgia's wet mid-August heat was grueling. When at last Alice was delivered of a son, the entire household fell quiet with relief. Just moments later, a dreadful cry went up once more, for cleft palates and cleft lips are shocking malformations. The newborn's parents were in despair. Another small grave in the red north Georgia clay. But Dr. John Stiles Holliday was strangely calm.

"This need not be fatal," the physician mused aloud, examining his tiny nephew. "If you can keep him alive for a month or two, Alice, I believe the defects can be repaired."

Later that day, he taught his sister-in-law how to feed her son with an eyedropper and with great care, so that the baby would not aspirate the milk or choke. It was a slow process, exhausting for the mother and the son. John Henry would fall asleep before Alice could feed him so much as a shot glass of milk; soon hunger would reawaken him, and since his mother trusted no one else with her fragile child's life, neither slept more than an

21

hour or two between feedings, for eight long weeks.

By October of 1851, the infant had gained enough weight and strength for his uncle to attempt the surgery. In this, John Stiles Holliday was joined by Dr. Crawford Long, who had begun developing the use of ether as an anesthetic just three years earlier. After much study and planning, the two physicians performed the first surgical repair of a cleft palate in America, though their achievement was kept private to protect the family's good name.

With his mother's devoted care, the two-month-old came through his operation well. The only visible reminder of the birth defect was a scar in his upper lip, which would give his smile a crooked charm all his life. His palate, on the other hand, remained unavoidably misshapen, and when the toddler began to talk, Alice was the only one in the world who could understand a thing he said. Truth be told, everybody but his mamma suspected the boy was a half-wit, but Alice was certain her son was as bright as a new penny, and mothers always know.

So she shielded John Henry from his father's embarrassment and shame. She forbade the house slaves and John Henry's many young cousins to poke fun at his honking attempts at speech. She studied Plutarch on the education of children, and with Demosthenes as her guide, Alice Jane set out to improve her child's diction. All on her own, she analyzed how the tongue and lips should be placed to produce the sounds her little boy found impossible. She filled scrapbooks with pictures and drawings, and every afternoon she and John Henry paged through those albums, naming each neatly labeled object, practicing the difficult words. In that way, Alice taught her son to read by the age of four, and though correction of his speech required years more, their diligence was rewarded. In adulthood, if his difficulty with certain consonants was noticed at all, acquaintances were apt to ascribe it to his lazy Georgia drawl. Or, later on, to drink.

He was quiet and rather shy as a child. Hoping to counter this natural reserve, Alice started John Henry's piano lessons as soon as he could reach the keyboard, and she was delighted to discover that he had inherited from her an accurate musical ear and a drive to master any skill to which he set his hand. Left to himself, the boy would have whiled away his hours reading, or practicing piano, or daydreaming, but Alice knew that was no way for a Southern gentleman to behave. So when John Henry turned seven, she began to encourage the other Holliday boys to spend more time with him. It wasn't long before he held his own in their rowdy, noisy games, riding as recklessly and shooting as well as any of them.

"He ain't big and he ain't strong," nine-year-old Robert Holliday told his Aunt Alice, "but that boy's got a by-God streak of fight in him."

And he was going to need it.

When she was confident that John Henry would not be ridiculed for his speech, Alice enrolled him in a nearby boys' academy. She had taught him well at home; from the start he excelled in mathematics, grammar, rhetoric, and history. Latin and French came easily. Greek was a struggle, but with characteristic determination, he kept at it, year after year, until he could read Homer in the original.

Like all Southern girls, Alice Jane had made a thorough study of the male of the species. She knew the rules by which boys played and wasn't much surprised when her son's diffident aloofness and scholastic success combined to provoke his classmates beyond toleration. The first time John Henry came home bloody, all Alice asked was "Did you win?" Later that evening, she told the story of the Spartan mother seeing her son off to war. "Come home with your shield or on it," Alice reminded him the next morning when he left for school.

His cousin Robert followed that moral lecture with another involving applied physics. "Don't start nothin'," young Robert advised, "but if some ignorant goddam cracker sonofabitch takes a swing at you? Drop him, son. Use a rock if you have to."

John Henry never did make many friends at school, but the other boys learned to leave him alone — and to copy his answers on exams.

And what of Henry Holliday? Where was Alice's husband while their only surviving child practiced phonemes and piano, learned to ride and shoot, and came home from school with bruised knuckles and excellent marks in every subject?

At a distance. Away. At work. At war.

In the 1850s, there was foolishness being talked on both sides of the Mason-Dixon. Throughout John Henry's childhood, the word *secession* had come up in conversations among the men. His cousin Robert thought the whole idea of war was glorious, but John Henry's father and his many uncles were unenthusiastic about the notion, even after the North elected Lincoln in 1860 and as much as told the South, "Secede, God damn you, and be done with it!" When the hotheads of Charleston opened fire on Fort Sumter, his Uncle John remarked, "South Carolina is too damn small to be a country and too damn big to be an insane asylum." That got a laugh, though the Holliday brothers agreed it was unfortunate that a dispute over cotton tariffs had become such a tangle. Still, they expected practicality to win out. Why, the entire nation's economy was based on cotton! Naturally, the Yankees would have to make some token response to the attack on Sumter, but cooler heads would surely prevail. There'd likely be a trade agreement signed by Christmas.

Certainly, nobody imagined that Mr. Lincoln would order an armed invasion over the affair. When he did exactly that, the entire South exploded with defiance and patriotism, cheering the new nation — sovereign and independent — that had just been born.

In April of '61, Henry Holliday and six brothers rode away to join the 27th Georgia Volunteers. John Henry was still four months shy of ten years old, but he was told, "You are the man of the house now." He and his mother were not left alone, of course. The household staff was presided over by the aging brothers Wilson and Chainey, who'd been in the family since their own birth and who would have fought the hounds of hell for Miss Alice and her boy. Even with Henry and a half dozen uncles gone, there were all the aunts and the older Holliday menfolk and the younger cousins near, and Alice Jane's many relatives as well. Hollidays and McKeys never lacked for kin.

Young as he was, John Henry took his responsibility for his mother's safety seriously, and his solicitude warmed Alice as much as it amused her. She was especially pleased by the very great deal of thought he gave to an outing she proposed when he was eleven, with the war well into its second year. The great Viennese virtuoso Sigismund Thalberg was coming to Atlanta to perform Beethoven's Fifth Piano Concerto at the Athenaeum Theater. "Sugar," Alice told her boy, "I wouldn't miss this concert for all the tea in China! And I do believe you are ready to meet the *Emperor*."

"The emperor?" Frowning, John Henry looked up from *The Gallic Wars.* "Did something happen to President Davis?"

"Mr. Davis is fine. The *Emperor* is the concerto's nickname — you'll understand why when you hear it. The concert is to benefit the Georgia Volunteers," she added. "What do you think, shug? Shall we chance it?"

Alice watched her somber, spindly son think the matter through. He presented a number of objections. The weather might be bad, and Alice had not gotten over the bronchitis she'd developed last winter. Griffin was a good distance from Atlanta; twice this spring, the front axle on their ancient carriage had been repaired and it could not be considered reliable.

"You're bein' very sensible," Alice observed. "Well, now . . . We wouldn't have to take the

27

carriage the whole way. We could stay with your Aunt Mary Anne in Jonesboro, and ride the train to Atlanta from there."

A solution to the transportation problem swayed him, but he was concerned about rumors of marauding Yankees and highwaymen, so the discussion went on at some length. Finally, when Alice gave John Henry permission to arm himself with a pair of antique pistols his great-grandfather had carried in the Revolutionary War, the boy agreed to the journey, though he stipulated that Wilson should accompany them as an additional precaution, and that Chainey should remain at home to guard the household in their absence.

"Sugar," Alice told her son, "it is a comfort and a support to have such a fine young man lookin' after me."

It was the sort of thing any Southern woman of breeding might say to flatter a male. What surprised Alice was how much she meant it and how touched she was to see him stand all the straighter for her remark, as though feeling even more keenly a gentleman's duty to protect a lady from whatever insult or danger a barbaric, broken world might present.

He spent days planning their expedition, serious as snakebite about each of his decisions. It was only on the evening of the concert, with his responsibilities temporarily

28

discharged, that John Henry began to relax. He acquitted himself very nicely during an economical supper at their modest hotel's restaurant, and when they strolled down the center aisle of the Athenaeum, he offered his mother a young man's arm instead of a child's hand. They found their seats — on the left, so they could watch Maestro Thalberg's hands — and chatted like old friends while the orchestra assembled. At last the house lights dimmed. The audience fell silent. A commanding figure strode across the stage, ignoring the burst of applause as he took his seat at a gleaming black concert grand.

And then: the first great massed orchestral chord sounded.

From that moment to the end, the boy was caught and held in a grip so tight, his mother could have snapped her fingers in his face and that child would not have blinked. He had never before heard the blended timbres of an orchestra, had not suspected there was such music in the world. At eleven, he possessed no words for what he heard and felt; indeed, it would be years before he could articulate the overwhelming impact of the concerto, with its tumbling, propulsive drive, its kaleidoscopic shifts of mode and mood, its euphoria and gentleness, its anger and urgency. Liszt was more showy and athletic, Chopin more sparkling and luminous. But Beethoven . . . Beethoven was *magnificent.*

The ovation was rapturous. Even the one-legged veteran two rows up struggled to stand along with everyone else in the theater. John Henry applauded until his shoulders ached and his hands stung. Only when the maestro left the stage did the boy come back to earth.

"Mamma, please," he begged, turning toward her, "can we get the score? Mamma?"

He rose on his toes, searching the faces around him. He must have looked distraught, for an old gentleman in the row behind him leaned over to pat his shoulder. "It's all right, son. She was havin' a little trouble with a cough and didn't want to disturb anyone. I imagine she's out in the lobby."

John Henry pushed through the crowded aisle. When he found his mother, she was waiting for him calmly, her dark blue taffeta skirt fanned out over the little bench on which she rested. One hand rested gracefully in her lap. The other clutched a lace-edged handkerchief, stained pink.

"This terrible old cough," she complained smilingly. "I just don't know why I can't shake it!"

For the first time, the boy saw how small his mother was, how thin. The relief at finding her was shattering and he was shamed by the single sob that escaped him, but his pride was saved when Alice Jane let them both pretend it was the emotion of the music that had unmanned him.

"Oh, John Henry, I just knew that you would love it," she cried, gray eyes shining at him from a pale oval face. "The *Emperor* is pure virile beauty! It is everything I want *you* to be, sugar. Elegant, and strong, and full of fire!"

They ordered sheet music for a solo piano transcription the next day and began work on the piece as soon as it arrived in the mail. Alice had taught many children to play and she was realistic about her son's talent. John Henry was good, but not a prodigy. What made him unusual as a student was his capacity for obstinate labor, and she was confident that he would make this music yield to his persistence.

In the beginning, he was still so small that some stretches were impossible. As his reach lengthened, Alice made him play with pennies on the backs of his hands to level them and train his fingers to strike the keys more cleanly. At twelve, he'd have practiced trills and turns for hours if she hadn't cautioned that too much repetition could injure him and stop his progress. By his thirteenth birthday, he was shooting up like a sunflower, already taller than many full-grown men, his wrists and forearms as flexible and strong as steel springs, his hands easily spanning tenths. His attack improved noticeably from week to week. He began to understand when to linger between the notes to expand the

31

elegance and grace of a phrase.

Never in all that time did he or his mother speak of her illness directly.

He continued to study other compositions, but the *Emperor* was their common cause and their great shared passion. It was serene assurance within gnawing anxiety, splendor in defiance of deprivation and creeping poverty; as the drumbeat of incomprehensible Yankee victories grew louder, it became a bulwark against raw fear. By the spring of 1865, he could play the entire concerto without pause, executing the tense flying arpeggios with accuracy and authority, making low chords thunder and high chords chime like silver bells. Alice herself gave less and less instruction as the months passed but never tired of listening to him play, even as her own fate, and the Confederacy's, came closer.

The war that was to have finished by Christmas of '61 lasted four catastrophic years. More than 625,000 combatants were dead of wounds, starvation, or disease, with a million more bodies and spirits damaged beyond fixing. Nearly everyone in the South was bankrupted by the collapse of the Confederate currency and the postwar inflation. In this, the Hollidays were no exception, though the clan was more fortunate than most. Its menfolk bore their share of danger and hardship, but they all came back alive and relatively whole.

In the end, it was not Confederate veterans but his mother who taught John Henry Holliday that there are wars that cannot be won, no matter how valiantly they are fought. Consumed by fever, weakened by privation and by the terrible hunger that followed Sherman's march to the sea, exhausted by the violent cough that all but shook her to pieces, Alice McKey Holliday died, day by day, before her child's eyes.

He was barely fifteen when the great blow fell. Until her coffin closed, they had never been separated longer than a school day.

More mature members of the family were not surprised when John Henry's father remarried a scant three months after his first wife was laid in her grave. In the view of Henry Holliday's many brothers, he had shown admirable restraint during the long years when Alice was no true wife to him, for it was not only the war and her illness that had come between them. No one would have said as much, but everybody knew. On the day his little boy was born, Henry Holliday became superfluous in his own household — displaced as decisively as King Laius by the returning Oedipus, who made Queen Jocasta his own.

Equally unsurprising: Henry's son did not see matters that way. Like the defeated, devastated South, in deep mourning and

33

groaning under Yankee occupation, the grieving boy was outraged by the sudden appearance in his home of a young and pretty pretender to his mother's throne. Relations between father and son quickly went from indifferent to cold to worse.

There are a thousand ways for a boy of fifteen to go wrong. The most gently reared will lash out, battered by gusts of mindless fury. The brightest can be swamped by black despair. The sweetest may turn sullen and withdrawn. The most rational are quick to anger. Add the antagonism of a stepmother hardly older than the boy himself, and not one whit wiser. Pile on daily humiliations in an occupied country where the only things available in abundance are guns, hard liquor, and provocation . . .

Well, something had to be done.

Nearly two dozen aunts and uncles came together to discuss John Henry's future. The consensus was to put a little distance between disconsolate son and newlywed father. That might be enough to mitigate the current discord and keep the breach from widening.

John Stiles Holliday, who'd attended John Henry's birth and repaired his cleft, had always taken a special interest in his namesake nephew. During the occupation, Dr. Holliday had quietly accepted a few Yankee patients who could pay in greenbacks; this was an economic extremity he concealed as effectively as he could, but he soothed his conscience by looking for discreet ways to share the income with destitute relatives and friends. He and his wife, Permelia, had already fostered the young mulatto daughter of a Charleston friend, and if little Sophie Walton could become part of the doctor's family, why not take John Henry in as well? The more the merrier, and the good Lord knew that poor boy could use some cheering up! He could continue his studies at the Fayetteville boys' academy, and there'd be shoals of cousins about — better companions than he might otherwise fall in with, and mindful of his sorrow.

To everyone's relief, John Henry himself agreed to the proposal with gratitude. He had always admired his Uncle John and felt at home in his Aunt Permelia's household, where dinner conversations were enriched by lively discussions of philosophy and literature, of progress in technology and advances in the natural sciences. He would never truly get over the loss of his mother; nightmares of the war and her death would haunt him all his life. Still, the change of scene and company did him good.

Fostered alike, and both of them motherless, John Henry and Sophie Walton quickly became close, though she was only ten and he was five years older. Sophie taught John Henry one card game after another, and they spent countless hours in the cookhouse, playing for buttons and small change, computing odds on the fly, competing to see who could be craftiest in stacking decks, shaving edges, and dealing off the bottom.

Among the dozens of John Henry's cousins, Robert and Martha Anne had always been especially loving and beloved. Robert was the boisterous older brother the quiet, bookish John Henry never had: outgoing and full of fun. And John Henry thought the world of Martha Anne. Everyone did. Sweet as a peach, that girl.

All the aunts had reason to recall that John Henry and Martha Anne were dear to each other even as small children, before the war. And since marriage between cousins was common in their set . . . Of course, they were young yet. And Martha Anne had been brought up a Roman Catholic. That presented difficulties. Even so, there was always something special about the bond between those two.

And you just never know, now, do you?

John Henry's desire to follow his Uncle John into medicine seemed natural enough. The boy was interested in biology and, early on, he asked to observe a surgery. Soon he was assisting his uncle; before long, John Stiles Holliday permitted his bright young nephew to perform some of the simpler procedures.

And yet, when John Henry began to talk about becoming a physician, his uncle advised against it.

Training standards had fallen, his uncle declared. Licensing had disappeared. Medicine had become a haven for quacks and charlatans hawking patent medicines and fake cures to the unsophisticated. Which was just about everyone, by his Uncle John's lights. Now, dentistry, by contrast, had far surpassed medicine as a scientific discipline and a respectable profession for a gentleman. That was the field John Stiles Holliday recommended. After some thought, his nephew came around to the idea, even though it meant going to school up North.

Uncle John would pay the boy's tuition. The other uncles scraped together money for his travel and living expenses. The aunts provided John Henry with the best wardrobe they could fashion from hand-me-downs and hoarded fabric. His cousins threw a festive farewell party, and the next morning everyone went with him to the depot. Even his father came to see him off, although his stepmother had the sense to plead a headache and stay home.

At the age of nineteen, determined to do his family and his state proud, John Henry Holliday left Georgia for the first time in his life and traveled alone to Philadelphia. There, he matriculated at the Pennsylvania College of Dental Surgery, a progressive school with a fine national reputation. He quickly gained distinction as a serious student — and a good thing, too, for the curriculum was demanding. There was course work in chemistry and metallurgy, gross anatomy and physiology, dental histology and microanatomy. There were long hours of practicum, during which he gained surgical experience with operative dentistry.

Fifteen years of piano practice had given him the strength of grip and attention to technique needed to pull teeth quickly and cleanly. His gold-foil fillings were the envy of his classmates, some of whom never mastered that most difficult of dental procedures. Indeed, all of his handwork — creating and fitting bridges and dentures — was judged exceptionally fine by his instructors. In the spring of 1872, he wrote his graduate thesis on dental pathology and passed his faculty examination easily. That summer, he returned to a bustling, rebuilding Atlanta with the degree of Doctor of Dental Surgery. Upon arriving home, he immediately secured a position with the city's most prominent dentists.

Atlanta society sat up and took notice.

At twenty-one, Dr. J. H. Holliday was a slim, ash-blond six-footer with high, lightly freckled cheekbones and a fashionable mustache that concealed his slightly scarred upper lip. His grace and sophistication made him a sought-after partner at Atlanta's many dances, while his serious demeanor at dinner parties made his droll, dry commentary all the more amusing. And, mercy! Didn't that boy play piano beautifully!

Not only was John Henry a fine young man himself, Society noted, but he was turning out to be a good influence on his cousin Robert, who had always been a little wild. Impressed by John Henry's successes, Robert announced that he, too, would be going into dentistry. The cousins planned to form a joint practice in the city just as soon as Robert finished his own degree up there in Philadelphia.

Everyone in town agreed: young Dr. Holliday would make quite a catch for some lucky gal. His proud family did not dispute the assessment but quietly discouraged speculation, for they knew whom John Henry loved and who loved him in return. Martha Anne had gently discouraged several potential beaux while John Henry was away. The cousins were well matched in intellect and temperament. It seemed only a matter of time before their engagement was announced, now that John Henry had come home.

Night sweats. A low, persistent fever. Those were the first signs that the Fates had begun to circle him again.

But it was summer in Atlanta! Everyone suffered from the humidity and heat, so John Henry didn't take much notice. The weight loss was subtle as well, for he was slender to start, but there came a day when he realized uneasily that no clothing he had owned for more than six months still fit.

That winter, a brutal chest cold left him with a deep and painful cough that interrupted examinations and made handwork increasingly difficult. Success was proving too much for him; he simply could not keep up with the hectic schedule of patients. No amount of sleep made him feel rested. He was exhausted from the moment he awoke.

In June, he made the clinical diagnosis himself. Even before his uncle confirmed it, John Henry *knew.* Advanced pulmonary tuberculosis, the disease that had killed his mother. Two foci in the inferior lobe of the right lung, another developing high in the left. He might survive one or two more summers in Atlanta's soggy heat.

Six to eighteen months — that's all the Fates had left him.

He was not quite twenty-two.

His horrified family gathered to discuss this fresh disaster. Once again, however, Dr. John Stiles Holliday was able to say of his nephew's condition, "This need not be fatal." Growing evidence suggested that the dry air, warmth, and sunshine of the North American West could effect remarkable results among consumptives. There were stories of remission and even cures — some undoubtedly exaggerated, but others that sounded legitimate. With rest, a nutritious diet, and moderate amounts of healthful wine, convalescence in that climate seemed possible.

After much anxious consideration and a flurry of letters, a plan developed. John Henry would accept a partnership offered by a Dallas dentist. While his cousin recovered his health in the West, Robert Holliday would finish his studies with a different preceptor. Just before John Henry left, the boys purchased an office building together so that Robert could establish their Atlanta practice in his cousin's absence. The sign above the door would bear both their names, in anticipation of John Henry's return.

Aunts and uncles and cousins came together for another farewell party, but this time their confidence in John Henry's prospects seemed glittery and artificial, their cheer more resolute than giddy. He himself spent most of the evening sitting at the piano, playing Chopin.

At the depot the next morning, Martha Anne wept.

John Henry promised to write.

He boarded the train.

And his life cracked in half.

■ ■ ■ ■

The journey soon took on a wearisome rhythm, for the country was a patchwork of independent short-haul railways in those days. Atlanta to Chattanooga. Find a room. Change trains. Chattanooga to Memphis. Find a room. Change trains. Memphis to Jackson. Find a room. Change trains. Jackson to New Orleans. Find a room. Change trains . . .

At first, he passed the time with game after game of solitaire, laid out on the travel case he kept in his lap. Watching every penny, he'd buy a stale sandwich and an apple from the newsboy, and make them last all day. When the train stopped to take on coal and water, he would get a cup of tea at the railway house. If he could charm a waitress into finding a little honey in the kitchen to sweeten the tea and ease his cough, he'd leave a generous tip.

He sent his first note home from Jackson. It was to Sophie Walton, in care of Aunt Permelia: *I play cards by the hour and imagine myself with you, sugar, sitting at the cookhouse table back in Fayetteville.*

The cinders and smoke were inescapable. By the time he crossed the Mississippi line, his throat was raw and his chest ached from coughing. He ran out of rails in Louisiana, but learned that there was a ferry to Galveston and looked forward to the fresh air of a crossing. When he got to the dock and found how expensive it was, he could only sit on the luggage with his head in his hands, trying not to cry.

Spunk up, he told himself, but every breath hurt and his chest felt strangely hollow. He was uncertain whether the sensation was physical and genuine or merely morbid imagination mixed with memories of the cadaver he had dissected in dental school. He could sometimes see that body as clearly as if it were still beneath his hands: its cavitated and fibrous lungs laid open, its belly concave, its limbs wasted to ropy muscle and bird-thin bone . . .

The stagecoach to Beaumont, Texas, was far cheaper than the ferry; it was also two hundred miles of jarring, bruising, dust-choked punishment. Waiting for the train from Beaumont to Houston, he mailed a second note, this one to the elderly brothers Wilson and Chainey Holliday, in care of his Aunt Martha. *I wish that I had been sensible enough to accept your kind offer of help on this journey,* he wrote. *It would have made all the difference.*

Too late now, he thought. In any case, the expense of three travelers would have been ruinous. And from what he'd seen so far of

43

Texas, it was no place for colored folks.

There was one last stretch of track from Houston to Dallas. He found a telegraph office, intending to wire his arrival time to Dr. John Seegar, the dentist who had offered him a position. While John Henry was writing out the message, the telegrapher announced to the room that one of the big northern railways had just gone bust.

"After what them damn Yankees done to us," someone remarked, "it serves the sons-abitches right."

John Henry was inclined to agree with the sentiment, but railroad trouble didn't concern him as long as the Houston train still went to Dallas. He submitted the form, paid for the wire, and gathered himself for another effort. He had sent his baggage on ahead, but simply walking unencumbered to the platform now seemed herculean.

Dr. and Mrs. Seegar were waiting for him at the Dallas depot. He had done his best to make himself presentable, but judging from the looks the couple exchanged, a good first impression was not in the cards. His throat was so raw, he could hardly be heard above the noise of the crowd when he introduced himself.

Appalled by what eleven days and sixteen hundred miles had done to a boy who'd been sick when he'd started the trip, Mrs. Seegar clapped little gloved hands to plump, pink cheeks. "Oh, honey, don't even try to talk!" she cried. "You look ready to drop, child! See to his things, darlin'," she ordered, and her husband did as he was told.

Her accent was balm. John Henry wanted to tell her so, but he could only gesture at his neck, grimace an apology, and croak, "You're from — ?"

"Georgia, honey. You can tell, can't you! I grew up in Lovejoy, just down the road from Jonesboro. Your mamma had kin there, didn't she?"

He tried to say something about his father's sister Mary Anne, but Dr. Seegar told him brusquely to be quiet and insisted on examining John Henry's throat, right there in the street.

"I thought so. Completely ulcerated — all that damn coughing! Our buggy's right around the corner," Dr. Seegar said, gesturing to a porter to bring the bags.

"Are you hungry, honey?" his wife asked John Henry. "You must be perishin'! Our girl Ella has a ham and greens and biscuits waitin' for us at home. You are gonna eat your fill, and then go straight on up to bed. Don't you dare argue with me! I won't hear a word!"

The final leg of the journey was a short drive to the Seegars' home, during which Mrs. Seegar did the talking for all three of them, naming friends in Lovejoy and kin in

Macon and acquaintances in Decatur, hoping for a connection. She was thrilled when John Henry whispered that he had indeed met a lady she knew in Atlanta.

"Why, she is my second cousin!" Mrs. Seegar cried. "Do you know her husband, too? Oh, but he was a handsome man when they married!" Her voice dropped to confide, "He was disfigured in the war, poor soul. Dreadful, just dreadful . . ."

When he was able to slip a word in, Dr. Seegar spoke a little about the practice ("Thriving, my boy! Thriving!") but allowed as how he could wait for some relief from the workload until young Dr. Holliday had recovered from his travels.

"Say! Did you hear the news?" Seegar asked as they pulled up to a large frame house on a treeless lane called Elm Street. "Jay Cooke's bank went bust!"

"Oh, now, don't you go botherin' the poor boy with all that money nonsense," Mrs. Seegar said breezily. She led the way up a boardwalk, waited for her husband to open the door, and hung her hat by its ribbons on a hook in the center hall. "Tote his bags upstairs for him, darlin'. Dr. Holliday, you sit right there, honey. Ella, bring Dr. Holliday something to drink! Just tea, honey? You sure you don't want something stronger? Children! Y'all come and meet Dr. Holliday!"

There were four ambulatory Seegar offspring and a two-month-old babe in the arms of the oldest, a girl who looked to be about twelve. All of them were excited, vying for the attention of the newcomer. Dr. Seegar begged pardon for the uproar his children made, but John Henry waved the apology off and hoarsely conveyed to the flattered parents that the sound of their children's voices was music to him, so much did he miss his own young cousins.

Ella, tall and dark, approached shyly with a cup and saucer. He accepted the tea, swallowed carefully, and, clearly as he could, told her how much he regretted that his throat was too sore for anything more, promising that he would do justice to her cooking after he had some rest.

He allowed himself to be put to bed in a state very near prostration.

As awful as the trip had been, he fell asleep believing he'd made the right decision to come to Texas. In a few days, when he felt strong enough to sit up and write, his first note to Martha Anne would tell her that the Seegars could not have been more welcoming. To Robert, he reported that if the Seegar home and its furnishings were any measure, business in Dallas was good.

Otherwise, he hardly stirred and certainly never gave "all that money nonsense" a second thought. Dr. Seegar provided a bottle of good bourbon and prescribed small doses to quiet the cough. Mrs. Seegar and Ella carried light meals up to him: tepid soups, and applesauce, and custards to soothe his throat. When he awoke on the morning of September 19, he had the energy to look at the newspaper Ella brought upstairs with his breakfast.

Later on, he would be grimly amused by his naive bewilderment upon reading the headline that morning, for it made no sense to him at all.

How can a *bank* panic? he wondered.

The economic collapse began in Europe, but financial markets were intertwined around the world; when Jay Cooke's bank crumbled, America's postwar railroad bubble burst. Fortunes quickly made were even more quickly lost in the Panic of 1873. Sham prosperity — built on debt — disappeared with shocking suddenness. The resulting depression dragged on year after year, crushing dreams and wrecking lives, John Henry Holliday's among them.

Robert and Martha Anne continued to write faithfully, their letters full of family news and encouragement. Martha Anne did her best to provide perspective when Dr. Seegar let John Henry go, just a few months after he arrived in Dallas. *Even in times of abundance,* she pointed out, *visiting the dentist ranks low as a form of entertainment. During a Depression, dentistry — along with everything beyond daily bread — becomes a luxury. You must not blame yourself, dear heart.*

She was right, of course. It certainly wasn't John Henry's fault that he couldn't make a living at his profession. No reasonable person would have thought so, but who is reasonable at twenty-two? What prideful Southern boy could acknowledge his own frailty and admit that his prospects of employment in a place like Texas were severely limited?

Gradually his livelihood came to rest entirely upon lessons learned at a cookhouse table from that little mulatto card sharp Sophie Walton. By the end of 1874, John Henry Holliday was dealing faro and playing poker professionally.

He was also drinking heavily.

A conviction of his own disgrace had taken hold of him. He had begun to live down to his opinion of himself. His mother's devotion, his aunts' faith, his uncles' money, his professors' respect — all that had come to nothing. Worse than nothing, really. There wasn't a family in Georgia that didn't own up to at least one male who'd gambled away money, houses, land, and slaves, but John Henry Holliday had done the unforgivable. "A man could gamble himself to poverty and still be a gentleman," his second cousin Margaret would one day write in her famous book about the war, "but a professional gambler could never be anything but an outcast."

In letters home, John Henry made comical stories of occasional arrests and fines for gambling, as though these were the result of informal Saturday night card games, but there were hints of his frightening new life. *At the risk of descent into unscientific generalization, I must report to you that ninety percent of Texans give the other ten percent a bad name,* he told Martha Anne after an exceptionally unpleasant encounter that he left undescribed. To Robert, he wrote, *In Texas, rocks are considered inadequate weaponry during school yard scuffles. Dallas children carry a brace of loaded pistols, a concealed Deringer, and a six-inch toadsticker in one boot. That's the girls, of course. Boys bring howitzers to class.*

Had John Henry been more forthcoming about the sporting life, Martha Anne's concern for his safety would have increased, but she might not have been quite as scandalized as he feared. Standards of conduct had loosened some, after the war. Martha Anne had learned to play poker from little Sophie Walton at John Henry's side, and she herself could be ruthless at the table. The Hollidays had always maintained a fairly cavalier attitude toward weapons, liquor, and high-stakes gambling.

A murder indictment, on the other hand . . .

Well, John Henry never mentioned that, not

50

even indirectly. Several witnesses agreed: the other man drew first. The charges were dropped. John Henry was badly shaken by the event, but he never would have worried the folks at home about such a thing.

When the Fates took their next shot at him, it was in the guise of a bad-tempered gambler named Henry Kahn who sat down at John Henry's faro table in July of 1877.

Coughing and irritable, young Dr. Holliday caught Mr. Kahn monkeying with the discards and suggested twice that he quit it. Sweating and belligerent in the Texas heat, Mr. Kahn was disinclined to do as he was told. Dr. Holliday, perhaps unwisely, widened the scope of his remarks.

Mr. Kahn left the table, apparently chastened. Ten minutes later, he returned with a pistol. Someone shouted, "Holliday! Behind you!" Before the dentist could fully rise to face his assailant, a shot was fired, and John Henry lay bleeding on the floor. Kahn walked out of the saloon without a word and left town before he could be arrested.

A friend in Dallas telegraphed word of the assault to the Atlanta Hollidays, informing them that newspaper reports of John Henry's death were inaccurate but that the wound was very serious and might yet prove fatal. John Stiles Holliday wanted to travel west immediately to attend his nephew, but the aging physician was talked out of it by his son George, whom the distraught family sent to John Henry's bedside in Texas.

George was shocked by his cousin's pallor and thinness; these he put down to the terrible wound until John Henry admitted that he'd rarely seen the curative western sunlight or breathed the fresh dry western air since leaving Atlanta four years earlier. Far from home, living among uncongenial strangers on the rawest edge of the American frontier, John Henry had allowed his habits to deteriorate. He had become accustomed to playing cards all night in smoky gambling halls. In lieu of the nutritious meals and healthful wine his uncle had prescribed, he lived on saloon snacks like boiled eggs, and tried to calm his worsening cough with immoderate amounts of bourbon. He was not well even before Henry Kahn tried to kill him.

The howling Fates were sure they had him this time.

By December, however, after five long months of rest under Cousin George's watchful eye, John Henry was back on his feet, though he would need a walking stick, off and on, for the rest of his life. He was not robust — never had been, never would be — but the leaden tubercular fatigue had lifted. His appetite returned. He put on a little weight and had more energy. The chest pain had eased and his cough was drier, not so deep or exhausting.

The economy, too, was showing signs of recovery, the cousins noted. The idea of a part-time dental practice no longer seemed unrealistic. If John Henry were not quite so dependent on dealing faro and playing poker, he could at least diminish the dangers and debilitation of the sporting life.

He recognized that he'd been given another chance and resolved to change his ways. When the New Year turned, 1878 seemed as good a time as any to reform. He'd already given up tobacco, almost, and was hardly drinking at all. He would continue to eat decently. Get out in the sunshine more.

He began to think that maybe he could beat this thing after all.

Hope smiled, and the Fates laughed.

Waiting at the Dallas depot for the train that would take George back to their family in Atlanta, John Henry promised his cousin that he would regularize his routines and build upon the gains he'd made. But for all his resolution, he lost heart when the train pulled away, leaving him alone again in Texas.

He went back to his room and tried to read, but the silence was too loud. He needed company, and a drink. He found a poker game, and Kate.

"Cito acquiritur, cito perit," she murmured when he lost a $700 hand.

Without thinking, he heard the phrase as plainly as if she'd said it in English. Easy come, easy go. Leaning back in his chair, he gazed at a small, fair-haired whore with eyes the color of Indian turquoise. He'd seen her before. She liked to watch the gamblers when she wasn't working.

"Game's not over yet. *Si finis bonus est, totum bonum erit,*" he remarked experimentally.

Astonished, she said, *"Lingua Latina non mortua est!"*

"Latin's not dead yet," he confirmed, adding in a soft murmur, "and neither am I. What's your name, darlin'?"

"Mária Katarina Harony," she said, coming closer. "Americans call me Kate."

He rose and brought her hand to his lips. "John Holliday," he told her. "Miss Kate, it is a pleasure to make your acquaintance."

Two hours later, up by almost a grand, he gathered his money. Eyes on Kate, who had stuck around, John Henry addressed the table. "*Tempus fugit,* gentlemen, and I believe I have found a better use of my time."

What force brought them together? Dumb luck, the Fates, or Fortune's whim? All John Henry knew was that he was a little less lonely after he met Kate, not quite so starved for conversation in a land that seemed to him peopled by illiterate barbarians. In a voice sanded down by cigarettes and whiskey, Kate spoke excellent French and Spanish as well as her native Magyar and German, all in addition to the crude but fluent bordello English she had learned in adolescence.

And she could quote the classics in Latin and in Greek.

"Doc, what's half of three hundred and fifty thousand?" she asked over breakfast a few days later.

From the start she called him Doc, as though that were his Christian name. Soon others did the same. He found he didn't mind.

"A hundred seventy-five thousand," he told her. "Why?"

"What's seven times a hundred and seventy-five thousand?"

Frowning, he made the calculation. "A million and a quarter. Why?"

"What's eight times a hundred and seventy-five thousand?"

"A million four," he said. "Will we be movin' on to spellin' next?"

"Dodge City expects three hundred and fifty thousand head of cattle this season," she said, tapping the newspaper spread out before her on the table. "Seven dollars a heifer, eight for a steer . . ." She looked up. "How much is that, total?"

"Two million, six hundred and fifty thousand," he said. *"Why?"*

55

Those turquoise eyes were half-closed now in dreamy speculation. "Two million, six hundred and fifty thousand dollars in five months' time . . . We should move to Dodge," she decided.

We? he thought.

"Kansas?" he said, as though she were mad and that settled it.

"That's where the money is."

"Suit yourself," he told her, "but I am not goin' to Kansas."

"Sera in fondo parsimonia," she warned.

Seneca! he thought. Thrift awaits at the bottom of an empty purse.

Her Latin was always a treat.

"This town's played out," she told him on the way back to their hotel room, a few weeks after they met. They had already separated twice by then; Kate could be hell to live with, but they were good together, too. "You didn't win nothing last night."

"I did all right," he objected.

He'd cleared almost $400 at the game. That was more than most men made in a year, but most men didn't have his expenses. Kate did not present herself as tastefully as she might have; that reflected on him. He'd bought a new wardrobe for her just before they left the city.

Kate was genuinely mystified by his reluctance to try Kansas. "Fort Griffin is even worse than Dallas!" she cried. "Doc, why are we wasting time in a dump like this? You could be pulling in thousands in Dodge!"

"No, and that's final," he muttered. He wasn't even sure why he didn't want to go. He just didn't like being pushed.

Then a few days later, Kate's enthusiasm for Dodge was endorsed during a chance meeting in a Fort Griffin saloon with a deputy federal marshal named Wyatt Earp.

With their brief conversation concluded, John Henry rose carefully and hobbled outside, leaning on his stick. For a good long while, he stared at the featureless, scrubby desolation around him.

Kansas can't be worse than this, he thought.

In the spring of 1878, John Henry Holliday sent word to his cousin Robert, informing him of another change of address.

Thanks to your brother George, my health and spirits are considerably improved. I have made inquiries about opening a practice in Dodge City, Kansas. The town appears to have escaped the worst of the Depression and is prosperous now. In any case, I believe I have enjoyed about as much of Texas as I can stand. Give my love to your parents, and to George and to Sophie Walton. Tell Martha Anne I will write

57

as soon as I get to Dodge.

YOUR COUSIN JOHN HENRY

First Hand

THE DEAL

As far as Wyatt Earp knew, it was not illegal to beat a horse.

In the past few years, he'd worked as a part-time policeman in a string of Kansas cow towns. Each time he was sworn in, he made an effort to study the ordinances he was supposed to enforce, but he wasn't much of a reader. In Ellsworth, he asked a lawyer for some help. "Wyatt," the man told him, "the entire criminal code of the State of Kansas boils down to four words. Don't kill the customers."

Most of the time, it seemed sensible to keep things just that simple.

It was, after all, a long way from the cattle roundups in south Texas to the railheads of Kansas. There were dozens of ways for a cowboy to prove his mortality before he got that far. He could be trampled in a stampede or get himself gored by a cranky longhorn. He could be rolled by a spooked horse or break his neck falling off one. He could get snakebit. He could drown crossing a river. He could die of ptomaine poisoning or bloody flux. A cut could go bad. Sometimes that's all it took.

Once they got their herd to town, drovers collected their accumulated pay and it was "Whoop it up, Liza Jane!" After three months of relentless labor — enduring bad weather and worse food, sleeping in their clothes, unsheltered on the ground — when they thundered into Wichita or Abilene or Ellsworth, Wyatt guessed that those Texas boys could be forgiven for presuming that such places existed for no other reason than to show them a good time.

Certainly, Kansas businessmen did nothing to discourage the illusion, what with the "Longhorn This," and "Alamo That," and "Lone Star the Other" on every sign on every saloon and whorehouse north of the Arkansas River. Dodge City's leading men were especially ardent about conveying the splendid reception Texans would receive, should they elect to follow the Great Western Trail to the southwest corner of the state. All winter, there were advertisements in Texas newspapers to that effect. Bob Wright's General Outfitting Store offered to send supply wagons south to provision cattle companies along the trail — for a small fee, of course — and Bob himself was so accommodating, he'd take a cattleman's word as bond for payment.

When the long, hard drive was done and the herds were delivered to Dodge, weary cowboys would find clean, comfortable rooms at the Dodge House Hotel and enjoy excellent dining at the Delmonico Restaurant (Deacon Cox, proprietor). Big George Hoover declared his intention to reduce the wholesale prices of liquor and tobacco during the entire cattle season, just to make those fine young Texans feel right at home in every saloon in town. Mayor James "Dog" Kelley assured them that the attitude of the townspeople toward high spirits was tolerant and friendly. Dog himself was a veteran of the Confederate Army, and his recent election to Dodge City's highest office was proof that Southerners would receive fair treatment there — not like in those east Kansas towns where unbearably victorious Yankees would likely cheat those Southern boys every chance they got.

Some of that was even true, mostly, but it wasn't comradely fellow feeling that accounted for the welcome Dodge extended.

The facts were these. Dodge City did not invent or manufacture goods. Dodge did not raise or educate children. It did not nurture or appreciate the arts. Dodge City had a single purpose: to extract wealth from Texas. Drovers brought cattle north and got paid in cash; Dodge sent them home in possession of neither.

Dead men don't pay for baths, haircuts,

meals, or beds. Dead men don't buy new clothes, or ammunition, or saddles. Dead men don't desire fancy Coffeyville boots with Texas stars laid into the shank. They don't gamble, and they don't spend money on liquor or whores. And that was why, when the Texans got to Dodge, there was really only one rule to remember. Don't kill the customers. All other ordinances were, customarily, negotiable.

So Wyatt was pretty certain it wasn't illegal to beat a horse. It was just stupid and mean. Dick Naylor was proof of that.

It was August of '77 when Wyatt first laid eyes on Dick. Overridden and underfed, the horse was a ewe-necked, long-backed, club-footed three-year-old whose coal-black flanks were marred by weeping spur sores. He was shaking like he had a chill and his eyes were white-rimmed with fear, but they were set well back on a good broad head with a tapered muzzle. There was quality to be noticed, if you had the sense to look.

The Texan who owned him was shouting and hauling on the lead, trying to drag eight hundred pounds of bony horseflesh where it didn't want to go. Wyatt hated to see that.

"Halter's too tight," he called. "Loosen the strap behind his ears. He'll stop pulling."

"Go to hell," the Texan replied, and since no law said you couldn't wreck your own property, all Wyatt could do was watch.

Scrawny as the animal was, he had that cowboy scared, for the fella backed away every time the animal bobbed his head and snapped. It's all show, Wyatt wanted to say. He could've reached your shoulder if he wanted to. You're scaring him, is all.

The Texan didn't see things that way. Sputtering curses, he pulled a gun out of his coat pocket and declared, "Why, I'll shoot you, then, you worthless no-good bag of shit!"

The shot went wild when the horse jerked on the lead. A moment later, Wyatt had disarmed the idiot and bashed him with his own pistol.

"Discharging firearms inside city limits is a misdemeanor. Fine's five dollars," he informed the Texan, who had crumpled to the ground, stunned but conscious. Wyatt dug into his pocket and counted what he had. "You can go to court or you can sell me this horse," he said, dropping $2.15 onto the dirt. "I'll let you off with a warning."

"Take him and be damned," the Texan muttered, gathering up the coins. "I hope he kills you."

"What do you call him?" Wyatt asked.

"Besides sonofabitch? Dick Naylor," the Texan told him.

He didn't seem inclined to explain how a horse got his own last name.

Two months later, Dodge laid Wyatt off

again. Cattle towns needed all the law they could hire during the season. When the weather cooled off, toward the end of October, the streets went quiet. Didn't matter how well he did his job, Wyatt was always out of work come winter.

He had harbored some hope that things would turn out different in Dodge. He'd worked there with his brothers Virgil and Morgan for two seasons running, and they got a grip on the town when it was still making national news for being the most violent and lawless place in the country, even counting Deadwood and New York City. When the Earp brothers were hired in '76, their boss was Larry Deger. Fat Larry was already close to three hundred pounds, too big and too slow to do much more than file the charges when somebody else made an arrest. By the end of '77, everybody knew Wyatt was running the Dodge City police department. He honestly expected to be appointed city marshal at the end of Larry's term.

Which just goes to show you how dumb Wyatt was.

Sure, he'd heard that jobs in Dodge were passed around from one insider to the next, but hearing things is not the same as understanding them. Morgan tried to explain what happened, but Wyatt had no talent for politics and could not keep the shifting alliances and factions straight. All he knew was Big George

Hoover lost the mayor's race to Dog Kelley by three votes. Suddenly the Earps were on the outs, for no reason Wyatt could fathom.

Mayor Kelley promptly reappointed Fat Larry as Dodge City marshal, which was a good joke, what with Larry weighing upwards of 320 by then. Wyatt thought he'd get chief deputy at least, but Dog settled on Ed Masterson for that.

Wyatt asked why. Dog told him, but it didn't make any sense.

"Everybody likes Ed," Dog said.

Which was true, Wyatt acknowledged, but kind of beside the point, in a marshal.

Ed Masterson was personable, Dog said. He made a good impression on important people. He was chatty and had a winning smile.

Wyatt had not smiled since 1855, and didn't like to say much more than six or seven words in a row to anyone but his brothers.

That same election, Ed's younger brother, Bat, got voted in as sheriff of Ford County. Wyatt had done the Mastersons some favors over the years, like hiring Ed and Bat as buffalo skinners back in '72, when they were just a couple of kids who needed work. Seemed reasonable to expect that Bat would return the favor now and hire Wyatt as undersheriff, but that job went to Charlie Bassett instead.

So. There he was. Out of work again.

Disgusted with the situation, Wyatt's older

brother Virgil packed up and moved to Arizona with his girl, Allie — they had some kind of ranch down there now. But his younger brother Morgan got himself an off-season job as bailiff for the Ford County Court, serving papers on the side, so he was staying in Dodge. Their older brother James managed his wife Bessie's bordello, and there was enough local trade to keep them open year-round. They were staying, too.

Past winters, Wyatt had gone back to driving freight or cutting firewood for a dollar a cord but that was getting old, and so was Wyatt. This time he asked around more and landed an appointment as a deputy federal marshal. That sounded good, but it was really just another temporary job. For the space of six months, from November of 1877 to April of '78, Wyatt S. Earp was empowered to follow David W. Rudabaugh across state lines, to arrest him for a train robbery, and to return him to Kansas for trial. To sweeten the deal, the Santa Fe Railroad was offering a big reward for Dirty Dave, a thief whose personal hygiene was notoriously unwholesome and whose notion of personal property consisted of, "If I can take it, well, I guess it's mine."

Wyatt aimed to collect that reward, just on general principles, and because he was almost broke. On top of his regular expenses, he had a bill for stabling Dick, and decent feed cost extra. That salve did a good job on the horse's spur sores, but it wasn't cheap. And before Wyatt could chase after Dirty Dave, he had to buy a pack mule and outfit himself at Bob Wright's store for a winter ride south, because Dave had headed for Texas after the robbery. Which left a little under five bucks in cash money after an entire season of risking his neck in Dodge.

That was the story of Wyatt Earp's life. He'd get ahead a little, something would happen, and the money'd be gone again.

On his way out of town, he saw an army officer approaching from the direction of Fort Dodge, riding a mare like nothing Wyatt had ever before beheld.

Even at a distance, the captain saw Wyatt's jaw drop and he laughed, though kindly. "Roxana has that effect on folks," he called as they closed on each other in the road. He reached across and offered his hand. "Elijah Garrett Grier," he said.

"Wyatt Earp. She's something, all right."

"Arabian, bred for sand," Grier told him. "Tremendous endurance."

"What would you take for her?" Wyatt asked, thinking of the reward he stood to collect when he brought Dave Rudabaugh in. "I'd go two hundred."

The officer looked at Wyatt's clothes, and his gear, and his horse, none of which was impressive. "You'd have to add a zero to that figure, I'm afraid," the officer said, friendly but firm.

They spoke for a time about the mare's exotic bloodlines and her temperament. Wyatt wondered if Grier had raced her. The officer admitted that her performance was uneven. "She's a three-miler by nature," he said. "Shorter contests don't do her justice."

She was restive, standing there when she'd expected to run.

"Best we move on," Grier said.

Raising his hand in a half salute, the officer leaned forward slightly. The mare took off, and she was a sight: her body perfectly balanced, her timing beautiful. She had a lovely floating stride that made you forget she had muscles at all. Fast, but you almost didn't notice it, dazzled by how effortless the movement appeared.

Roxana, Wyatt thought. Pretty name.

He wheeled Dick southward, and kicked him into a lope.

For the rest of the day and most of that night, Wyatt fought the thoughts, but he had a tendency to ruminate on the trail, and there was no quieting an idea once it took hold. At dawn, he doubled back toward town and rode all day, arriving in Dodge by late afternoon. When the mule was unpacked and Dick was settled into his usual stall at the Elephant Barn, Wyatt went looking for Johnnie Sanders.

The boy was a newcomer in Dodge, but he already had half a dozen small jobs around town. Johnnie was responsible and pleasant, so people mostly overlooked that he was colored. Bob Wright had hired him to restock shelves at the store, but then Bob found out that Johnnie was real good with numbers; now the boy was helping with the account books, which were always a mess because Bob did a lot of bartering and carried debtors for a year at a time. Johnnie got another job sweeping up at the barbershop, which led to cleaning the floors at a couple of saloons. Then he showed how he could cover at the faro tables when regular dealers needed to take a piss or something. So now he did that pretty regular, too.

Wyatt found him at the barbershop and motioned him outside.

"Mr. Earp," the boy said, leaning his broom against the wall. "I thought you was goin' to Texas."

Almost ashamed, Wyatt explained what he had in mind. Listening carefully, the boy started to smile, and the smile turned into a wide gap-toothed grin.

"You can count on me," Johnnie told him. "We'll get that mare for you, Mr. Earp. And I'll be careful, I promise." For the first time, the boy offered his hand, man to man. "Thank you for lettin' me do this, sir. I didn't think I'd ever be able to pay you back for

71

your kindness."

He was so pleased to be trusted. So eager and grateful. It would haunt Wyatt later on, that gratitude.

Wyatt walked across the tracks to the bordello and went inside. Bessie started to welcome him. Then she realized who he was.

"You'll be wantin' James," she said.

Wyatt nodded, not meeting her eyes.

"Have a seat," she suggested, and left him alone in the vestibule.

Perched on a horsehair sofa, Wyatt waited for his brother. He was doing the sums in his head again and gave a little jump when James said, "I thought you was going to Texas."

"Loan me three hundred — Hell. Make it three-fifty, to be safe."

"It's yours if you need it," said James, but he didn't hide his surprise.

Wyatt took a dim view of his older brother's business and an even dimmer view of his older brother's wife. "Wyatt, what have you got against Bessie?" James had asked him once. "Well, James . . . she's a whore." "Yes, she is," James replied with perverse pride, "and a hardworking one, too." Wyatt had never reconciled himself to the situation and thought the brothel money was tainted. But here he was, asking for a good-sized pile of it.

James counted out the cash and handed it over.

"Pay you back," Wyatt said, and left to finish his business with Johnnie Sanders.

Dawn, the next morning, he headed south again.

He kept back enough of the money to have Dick reshod every five weeks. Usually Wyatt tried to get at least three months out of each set of shoes for a horse, but it's important to keep a clubfoot leveled. He needed to equalize the work of the shoulders and hindquarters, so Dick's gait stayed balanced during the long ride south. Morning and evening, Wyatt stretched out that leg good, too.

Dick's mouth was ruined, so Wyatt had taken him off the metal bit and used a *bosal* instead. Treated with kindness, filling out, the horse appeared to appreciate that his situation had improved, but Wyatt had come to understand why that Texan had hated the animal. There was just no give in Dick. He had heart and smarts, but even when his halter fit right, he'd balk when you tried to lead him and just about pull your arm out of the socket. Or he'd move up and snap at your back to let you know he could take a chunk out of you if he cared to. On the other hand, Dick enjoyed being groomed. He was the first horse Wyatt knew who really liked to have his face brushed. Afterward, Dick would lean his muzzle into Wyatt's shoulder and they would just stand together quietly. It was a sign of growing trust and made a nice end to the day.

The long, steady rides that winter served two purposes. They were the best thing you could do for a horse hard done by in his youth, and they kept the pressure up on Dave Rudabaugh.

In February, Wyatt almost caught up with his man at Shanssey's Saloon in Fort Griffin, Texas. When Wyatt asked about Dirty Dave, John Shanssey directed him to the table of a thin, ash-blond gambler from Georgia who'd played cards with Dirty Dave a few days earlier.

About Morgan's age — twenty-six or so, Wyatt guessed. Dressed nice, but not flashy. Nickel-plated pistol, cross-draw shoulder holster. No other weapons visible.

"Forgive me, sir, if I do not rise," the Georgian said, using a silver-headed walking stick to tap a chair in invitation. "I am still recoverin' from an unfortunate injury."

He offered Wyatt a drink. Wyatt turned it down. The Southerner's brows rose coolly above slate-blue eyes. An explanation seemed both courteous and wise.

"Methodist," Wyatt told him.

"Ah. My mother was a Methodist, sir! In her memory, I, too, have taken the pledge. Twice, in fact," the Georgian said. "Lately I have found it necessary to deviate from the path of rectitude in the name of health. Chest complaints run in the family, and bourbon is effective for a cough. You look weary, sir! May I offer you a coffee?"

"Sure. I guess. Thanks," Wyatt said, disarmed.

Shanssey brought a mug over for him and put a bowl of sugar on the table. Wyatt dug in, adding three big spoons of it before the coffee tasted right to him.

The Georgian's eyes widened.

"I like it sweet," Wyatt admitted. "Rudabaugh?"

"He was here three days ago, braggin' that he had recently taken out an unsecured loan from the Santa Fe Railway. I must say, I applaud your determination to bring that man to justice, sir. If you were to hang him accidentally, it would be a mercy to his future cellmates. His habits would shame swine. He already smells of the grave." The Georgian's voice got gravelly, and he paused to clear his throat. "David Rudabaugh rates himself clever," he continued. "That is a delusion. He is confident but stupid, as are most thieves. He was headed to Galveston but knows you are on his trail, sir, and believes it might make a fine joke if he were to circle back into Kansas again."

The Georgian had used more words in five minutes than Wyatt had spoken during 1872 and '73, combined. It took a moment to get his thoughts together, but Wyatt thanked him for the information.

They spoke briefly about Dodge.

"Bigger'n Wichita now," Wyatt said. "Thousands of drovers. Money to throw at the birds."

"Any dentists in residence, sir?"

It was a strange thing to ask, but Wyatt answered, "Not when I left."

"Well, now, that sounds promisin'," the other man said. "My companion and I have been discussin' a move to that city, which is to say Miss Kate will not take no for my answer and I am bein' worn to a nubbin on the subject. I have begun to think of reopenin' my practice. From what you say, the plan is not unreasonable —"

It was only after a short spell with an ugly hacking cough that the gentleman lifted the shot glass to his lips. He took a sip of bourbon, eyes on Wyatt's mouth, and set his glass down. With a slowness that signaled no ill intent, he drew a flat silver case from his inside pocket. From this, with long, slender fingers, he extracted a pasteboard card and reached across the table to offer it to Wyatt.

"J. H. Holliday," Wyatt read aloud to make sure he got it right. "Doctor of Dental . . . Sugery?"

"Surgery," Holliday corrected gently. "I am a dentist."

Wyatt's hand went to his mustache, to

smooth it, and to make sure it covered his lips.

"I can help you, sir," the dentist said quietly. "Look me up when you get back to Dodge, y'hear?"

They shook hands. Holliday didn't look sturdy enough to stand up in a stiff wind, but his grip was surprisingly strong.

Wyatt sent a telegram to Bat Masterson, alerting him to the rumor that Rudabaugh might return to Kansas. Wyatt himself continued to pursue the fugitive toward Galveston, in case Dirty Dave was as stupid as the dentist thought and proved it by staying in one place more than a night or two. Then, after three bone-chilling months of chasing Rudabaugh across Texas and into Missouri as far as Joplin, Wyatt got word that Dirty Dave had been arrested a little east of Dodge, near Kinsley, Kansas, where he'd tried to rob another train.

The reward would go to Bat and the Kinsley city marshal.

It was hard not to feel bitter about that.

With little else to occupy his mind, Wyatt found himself brooding about how Ed and Bat Masterson had managed to get so far ahead of him in life. Just five years ago, those two kids were doing Wyatt's scut work, wrenching the skins off thousand-pound buffalo carcasses from dawn to dusk. Stinking of blood and filthy for months at a time, Bat and Ed would banter and josh all day, and compete all winter to be the first to get Wyatt Earp to smile. He paid them no mind and concentrated instead on dropping bison for them. They were young, of course, and game, but Wyatt didn't think either of them would amount to much.

Now Bat was sheriff of Ford County at twenty-four, and Ed was only twenty-six when he made chief deputy in Dodge. Wyatt himself was about to turn thirty, with nothing to show for it. That was starting to eat at him.

At least Ed Masterson was earning his salary running the city police force for Fat Larry; as far as Wyatt could see, Bat was paid to sit around in bars, telling stories to his cronies. Bat was a good man in a fight, but he won sheriff mostly on the strength of being "the hero of Adobe Walls," as if there weren't twenty-seven other men right there with him, shooting at those Comanches. And the way Bat told it, you were sort of invited to believe he'd been wounded while rescuing two little girls from the Indians, even though Wyatt knew for a fact Bat got himself shot in a fight over a dance hall girl, down in Sweetwater. After he got elected, Bat started dressing fancier than a Kansas City hooker. Brocade vests, silk sashes, embroidered shirts. He even designed himself a big gold badge, special, so it would look nice with the gold top of his fancy walking stick. Wyatt himself hardly ever carried a sidearm, even on duty, but Bat had a pair of chrome-plated, ivory-handled .45s and wore them all the time, prominently displayed in a heavily tooled, silver-studded gun belt that must have cost what Wyatt made in a month.

What Wyatt couldn't work out was how a county sheriff like Bat could be making so much more money than a city marshal. Dodge was dangerous day and night, all season long. Ford County covered a lot of territory, but it was empty apart from a few German farmers who worked like mules and minded their own business. They'd drive into Dodge every month or so to buy supplies from Bob Wright. Their idea of blowing off steam was going to church and treating their wives and kids to some pie. Then they'd climb into their buckboards and head home. All Bat ever had to deal with was horse theft now and then. And maybe bill collecting or something.

How could a man do so well by doing so little? That's what Wyatt wanted to know.

Some folks just had the knack of making money, he guessed, the way some could sing nice or read. Now, you take Bob Wright, just as an example. Bob didn't look like much, with his pale eyes and that big mustache hanging over his little chin, but everything he touched turned to cash. Wyatt shot buffalo and the Masterson brothers skinned them, and they did well while the herds held out, but Bob? He got richer than Croesus, selling the meat to railway crews and mining camps and army garrisons, and shipping the hides east.

Like pretty much everybody in the country, Wyatt lost what he had in the crash of '73. Next thing you knew, the buffalo were gone, too, and then the grasshoppers and drought were killing off the crops in Kansas. People were going bust left, right, and center. That was when Bob Wright got the notion of paying bankrupt farmers to go out and collect buffalo bones off the prairie. Wyatt thought he was crazy, but Bob sold the skeletons to factories back East, where they were ground up for bone china or burned to make carbon black for printer's ink. Only Bob Wright would have thought up something like that. Now Bob had that big store, and the post office, and a bank, almost. Nicest house in Dodge. A pretty wife and real good kids . . .

Wyatt had worked like a full-grown man since he turned thirteen — ever since his older brothers went off in '61 to fight for the Union — but he never seemed to see the payoff himself. His father got the good of it, or men like Bob Wright, who owned things: freight wagons, and stores, and livestock, and land.

You needed money to make money, that was the trouble. You had to get a leg up, somehow.

There was no hurry about getting back to Dodge. When he heard Fort Worth was hiring a deputy, Wyatt turned Dick in that direction. He started to think that if he got year-round work in Texas, he would wire Johnnie Sanders, tell him to pay James off, and forget the whole thing about Roxana. It was a half-baked notion from the start, Wyatt decided. He never should have involved the boy.

Along the way to Fort Worth, he got into the habit of stopping in towns and settlements to ask about local races. It was curiosity, really. He just wanted to give Dick a chance to test his speed. The stakes weren't real high, but it was easy to get a few riders together, and the results were encouraging. Even when they lost, the finishes were close. Short races seemed to suit Dick best. Anything over half a mile just gave him time to get into trouble. If another animal drew even, Dick would pin his ears and bare his teeth and snap. He lost a couple of contests that way and was more bad-tempered than usual afterward.

Wyatt applied for the Fort Worth job, but — no surprise — it went to somebody local. By that time, though, he knew what a bargain he got with a pocketful of loose change the summer before. A season of conditioning and experience was all Dick Naylor had needed. The bony ewe neck had muscled up into a stallion's crest tied to a good sloping shoulder. After months of patient stretching and frequent reshoeing, the clubfoot didn't seem to hold him back a bit. By spring, Dick Naylor had developed into a stocky little sprinter with a wide, deep chest and powerful hindquarters, all drive and push.

If he was just a hand taller. Maybe shorter in the back, and less inclined to bite . . .

Once again, Roxana filled Wyatt's thoughts. She was leggier than Dick, delicate-looking but larger, all elegance and speed. Breed his scrappy little quarter-miler to a fine long-distance mare . . . Why, you could just see the colts! They'd have Roxana's endurance and her lovely gait. They'd have Dick's heart and desire to win, but without his stubborn malice.

Nights, by the campfire, Wyatt would scratch out calculations with a stick in the dirt. He was as good as anyone with numbers and odds, though reading gave him headaches and made him feel resentful. Morgan was the reader in the family, but Wyatt could do sums in his head, easy as Morg could read.

No matter how he figured it, $2,000 was a lot of money. Even when Wyatt was working regular, he got a dollar and a quarter a day. You couldn't get ahead on that. At some point, he told himself, you have to take a chance. You have to make your move.

So, as much as he hated debt, and hated the way his brother James made his living running girls, and hated asking Johnnie Sanders to work for him that way . . . Well, every time Dick Naylor won a race, Wyatt's conscience got a little quieter.

Whenever he found a town with a telegraph office, Wyatt let Morgan know where he was. All the brothers did that — wire Morg and wait around for a reply, to be sure the rest of the family was all right. In early May, a return telegram arrived within the hour, and this one was a shock.

ED MASTERSON KILLED STOP DODGE
HIRING REPLACEMENT STOP COME
BACK STOP MORG STOP

Wyatt certainly hadn't wished Ed ill and was sorry to hear of his death and disliked to profit by it. Even so, this was a stroke of luck, and Wyatt headed back to Dodge feeling pretty good about his prospects.

This time, he'd get the chief deputy job Ed had vacated. That would mean a lot more money. He'd held on to every dollar Dick had won and counted it out often. Add that to his salary and . . . Well, it still wasn't enough, but with Johnnie's help, it wouldn't be long before he could buy Roxana. If the timing was right and she wasn't already in foal this year, Dick might sire a colt that could begin to race by '81. In a few years' time, Wyatt would have a string of horses that would run the legs off anything west of St. Louis.

And then, by golly, he could quit the law and finally get somewheres in life.

There were no towns, the last long stretch of the ride. No houses, no fences, no sign of human life, let alone a place to send or receive telegrams. Until you got to Dodge, there was just grass and sand hills and silence, day after day.

That was why he didn't get the news. See, Dick's right foreleg felt a little hot and Wyatt decided to give him a couple days' rest and grazing on good grass before they started the final push into the city. But the leg wasn't that bad. If he'd known, Wyatt could have reached Dodge in time for Johnnie Sanders' funeral.

A day late, he would think when he finally stood staring at the boy's grave.

Just like always: a day late and a dollar short.

DOWN CARDS

The body was charred. It could have been anyone, in Morgan Earp's opinion. On any given night during the cattle season, as many as fifty drunken cowhands might bed down in the loft of Hamilton Bell's Famous Elephant Barn. Could have been one of them.

Morg kicked at a chunk of smoking wood. "You sure, Doc? It's Johnnie Sanders?"

It was an innocent question, and Morgan didn't mean anything by it. Doc Holliday was, however, a man of ardor and conviction as regards matters of personal dignity, and the dentist was already at a social disadvantage, kneeling next to the corpse as he was, peering into its gaping jaw and studying its teeth.

Doc looked up over his shoulder at Morgan. "Which is in doubt?" he asked. "My competence or my veracity?"

"I was just hoping maybe you was wrong, is all."

"Help me up," Doc muttered.

Morgan offered an arm.

When he was on his feet, Doc brushed the ash off his trousers, wiped his hands on one of those white cotton handkerchiefs he always carried. "There is a diastema between the upper central incisors, and I can palpate a raised lingual margin on those teeth as well. The left eyetooth is slightly twisted. I filled the lower right six-year molar myself, two weeks ago."

Morgan didn't know what any of that meant, except: Yeah, Doc was sure.

"Hell," Morg said. "Wyatt's gonna take this hard."

"When's he due back?" Bat Masterson asked.

"I thought he'd be here by now."

Legally, Bat had no standing in this matter. The fire was inside Dodge City limits, so it wasn't in Bat's jurisdiction. On the other hand, Morgan Earp had never dealt with a death like this one. This would be his third season as a deputy, but he was used to working with his brothers. Without Wyatt or Virgil around, Morg didn't mind having Bat there to back him up.

"Poor soul," Doc murmured, looking at the corpse. "Seventeen years old . . ." He straightened and declared by way of eulogy, "John Horse Sanders was the second best faro dealer I ever met."

"Who's the best?" Bat asked him. "You, I guess."

There was fame to be had and money to be made writing dime novels about the Wild West. Bat Masterson hadn't published anything yet, but he was on the lookout for salable material. He already had a good title for his first story: *Doc Holliday, the Killer Dentist.* Or maybe *The Deadly Dentist.* He hadn't decided which was better.

Morgan had heard the rumors about Holliday, but he already suspected Bat was making some of Doc's exploits up. Bat didn't lie, exactly, but he never told a story that didn't improve some, over time. Far as Morg knew, the dentist's only crime was rivaling Bat Masterson as the best-dressed man in Dodge.

"No, sir," Doc was telling Bat, "best I ever saw was a little bitty gal name of Sophie Walton. My Aunt Permelia took Sophie and me in, after the war. Sophie taught all us cousins to play cards, but she didn't teach us everything. She'd clean up four times out of five. Young Mr. Sanders was near as good."

"Johnnie don't belong on Boot Hill," Morgan said. "We should take up a collection. Bury him right."

Bat shrugged. With his brother Ed barely cool in the grave, it was probably hard for him to summon the feelings he'd need to give a damn about this death. Mostly Bat seemed angry with the barn's owner, Hamilton Bell.

Ham was friendly to a fault — same as Ed, who got himself killed by being nice to a drunk.

"I knew something like this was going to happen," Bat muttered. "It was only a matter of time 'til this place burned down."

Morgan nodded to the mortician's boys, who were waiting at the edge of the smoking timbers. It was gingerish work, moving a burned body. They had just tipped it onto a stretcher so they could carry it to the coffin shop when Doc Holliday stopped them.

"You see something?" Morg asked.

Leaning on his cane, the dentist took a closer look, coughing again when the smoke and smell got to him. The back of the corpse was unburned, and he felt through the dark hair, moving his fingers systematically over the skull, stopping behind one ear. His hand came away sticky, and he held it out to the lawmen before wiping the mess off on his handkerchief.

"Blow to the head," he said. "*Ante-mortem,* in my judgment."

Morg was going to ask Doc what he meant by that part about his auntie, but Sheriff Masterson wasn't willing to look ignorant.

"Probably got hit by a barrel," Bat said.

Somebody'd had the idea of hoisting empty whiskey casks onto Dodge's rooftops. The notion was that the rain-filled barrels would tumble over as a burning building caved in, thus extinguishing the flames. From the looks of the Elephant Barn, the heavy casks had simply compounded the generalized destruction.

"No barrels near the body," Doc noted.

"Might've rolled," Bat said.

"Can we take him now?" one of the mortician's boys asked.

"Sure," Morg said. "I guess."

A crowd had formed just beyond the smoldering ruins of the barn. Standing a little apart from the others, Edwin Fitzgerald hugged himself morosely. The black-haired Irishman had a body blessed by the gods — lithe and superbly coordinated, capable of acrobatics and grace — but it was topped with a rubbery, comical face and a head full of sarcasm and mockery. The combination would make his fortune, for young Mr. Fitzgerald had recently taken the stage name Eddie Foy, and he had a stellar future in vaudeville ahead of him. One day there would be a movie and books about his life, as there would be about so many men who lived in Dodge that year: Bat Masterson, and the Earp brothers, and Doc Holliday, to name a few. For a good long while, Eddie's fame would shine most brightly, though it would fade the soonest.

That afternoon, he stood by himself and waited for Doc Holliday to make his slow and careful way out of what remained of the barn.

"Johnnie Sanders," Doc told him quietly.

The mobile face crumpled. "No!" Eddie cried. "Ah, Christ . . . Now, that's a pity."

Hats off, they watched silently as the crisped and blackened body was carried past. A few yards away, Bat Masterson had returned to his earlier theme for the edification of the assembled citizens.

"I told Ham Bell this would happen! I said, One of these days, Ham, some drover's going to pass out with a cigarette in his hand and set the whole damn barn alight. You just wait and see, I told him. Only a matter of time 'til that barn goes up in smoke!"

"Lucky it didn't take the whole town with it," Eddie muttered.

He had survived the Great Chicago Fire as a boy. Now twenty-two, Eddie Foy retained a morbid anxiety about such things. It was a concern John Henry Holliday shared, as would anyone who'd seen what Sherman did to Georgia. Like old Chicago and antebellum Atlanta, Dodge City was all wood. Wooden walls, shingle roofs, wooden floors. Plank sidewalks and galleries. Everywhere you looked: wood, waiting to burn.

"This burg could use a fire brigade," said Eddie.

"Could've used one last night," Doc agreed.

■ ■ ■ ■

Morgan went back to the jail to make his report to Fat Larry. Bat headed for the newspaper offices to be sure his name got into the stories. Eddie stuck with Doc, though he had to slow down considerably to match the gimpy Georgian's pace. Usually Doc contrived to give the impression that he was a gentleman in no particular hurry who enjoyed a leisurely stroll through town. Today he was winded and limping before they'd got to the corner of Bridge and Front.

Eddie had more sense than to rag the man about that. If you were going to be friends with Doc Holliday, there were things you did well not to notice. That raw Christ-awful cough. His weight, what there was of it. The lameness. Doc had accumulated a fair number of infirmities for a man so young, but insisted he was in better health than he'd enjoyed in some time. That told you a lot, right there.

The two of them were recent arrivals in Dodge. Eddie had just landed a good gig headlining a song-and-dance show at the Comique Theater, twice nightly during the cattle season. Doc Holliday sometimes ran a faro game there; it was a temporary arrangement — just something to tide him and his lady friend over until he could get a dental

91

practice going. Doc enjoyed Eddie's act. Eddie liked that Doc got all the jokes.

"Look at them, now, will you," Eddie said, stopping so Doc could rest. "Shameless, I call it."

Driven out of the barn by the fire, Hamilton Bell's little rat terriers were roaming the town. One of them had taken a shine to Dog Kelley's brindle greyhound bitch, who was standing in the middle of Front Street, bemused by the attention. The terrier tried several approaches without achieving much in the way of satisfaction.

"It would appear that his reach has exceeded his grasp," Doc observed, keeping his breath shallow.

"Ah," said Eddie, "but you have to admire the ambition, now, don't you."

The greyhound got bored and wandered away, leaving a deeply disappointed terrier to reconsider his aspirations.

"Don't wait on me," Doc told Eddie. "I've got errands."

"See you tonight, will we?"

"Depends. I'll have to see what Miss Kate has planned."

Eddie grinned. "Give my love to herself, then, won't you!" he called, and did a little jig step before he set off briskly, grateful as a child let out of school early.

To anyone watching for the next few moments, the town's new dentist would have appeared to be enjoying the spectacle of Eddie Foy's sprightly progress down Front Street. In point of fact, John Henry Holliday was absorbed by a kind of calculus that had become second nature to him: plotting the shortest route from where he stood to China Joe's Laundry and Baths, the post office in Bob Wright's store, and on to his hotel room at Dodge House.

The wind shifted, adding dust, blown ash, and lingering smoke to the equation. Laundry first, he decided.

It wasn't far, objectively. Nothing was. Front Street was just a dirt road three blocks long, with a row of buildings on each side of the railroad tracks. The Atchison, Topeka and Santa Fe ran straight west through the center of a town that consisted primarily of saloons, saloons with gambling, saloons with dance halls, and saloons with brothels. The saloons were mostly south of the rails, a district they shared with China Joe's Laundry, the remains of the Famous Elephant Barn, and the lower class of girls who worked in the cribs out back. More respectable commerce took place on the other side of the tracks. Bob Wright's General Outfitting Store. The barbershop and a pool hall. The hardware and gun shop. A few of the fancier bars and bordellos. George Hoover's Cigar Shop and Wholesale Liquor Store. The Dodge House Hotel and the Delmonico Restaurant.

That was the sum total of the town. Naming this place Dodge City was pure bluff. It barely amounted to a village.

Back in April, there were more stray dogs than people on the street. In early May, the herds had begun arriving from Texas. Now Ford County's nine hundred permanent residents were outnumbered three to one by the drovers who came into Dodge to enjoy themselves while their cattle fattened on the grassland south of the Arkansas River.

By midnight tonight, Front Street would teem with carousing cowboys but at the moment, the town was relatively quiet and small as Dodge was, everybody had seen the fire last night. The big news was that Morgan Earp had found a body in the ruins and the dentist said it was Johnnie Sanders. Word of that spread faster than Doc Holliday could walk.

Even Jau Dong-Sing had heard.

Most people thought Jau was Dong-Sing's personal name. China Joe, they called him. Doc addressed him as Mr. Jau, and he had even tried to reproduce the rising tone in Sing correctly. "F to F-sharp," Doc said, listening hard when Dong-Sing taught him how to say it. Dong-Sing had no idea what that meant, but the dentist came close to getting it right. Dong-Sing appreciated the courtesy. He always made a special effort for

Doc, a good customer who had three baths a week and who liked his pastel shirts boiled, starched, and ironed after a single wearing. Dong-Sing had done some alterations for Kate. Taking up hems, adjusting darts. He did tailoring for Doc as well. It was a pleasure to work on the dentist's suits. They were beautifully constructed of fine English broadcloth.

In Jau Dong-Sing's opinion, Doc's *chi* was seriously unbalanced. That was making him sickly. "Doc! You too damn skinny!" Dong-Sing always told him.

"A man has no secrets from his tailor," Doc would reply.

"You come by, I cook you noodles," Dong-Sing always offered. "Make you fatter! Give you long life."

"Mr. Jau, that is a handsome offer," Doc always said. "I believe I'll take you up on it one day."

Today when Doc came in to pick up his shirts, Dong-Sing leaned over the counter to confide, "I know why that nigger boy dead."

"Do you, now?" Doc said.

"Kill chicken. Scare wolf."

"Well, now, Mr. Jau, that is an interestin' theory," Doc said, "though I shall have to think it over before I can subscribe to it. When do you suppose that pair of trousers might be ready?"

"Two day more. Very busy. Hotel trade

pickin' up."

As always, Doc asked about Dong-Sing's family back in Kwantung and about the business prospects of Dong-Sing's nephew, who had recently opened a laundry in Wichita with Dong-Sing's backing. Nobody else took the time to help Dong-Sing with his English, and he enjoyed these conversations.

They served John Henry Holliday as well, for listening to Dong-Sing's news allowed him to rest up before he continued his journey. That accomplished, he bid Mr. Jau a good evening and walked on, stopping once to catch his breath and to watch the Kansas sunset for a while.

Spring was lovely back in Georgia this time of day. A thousand miles away, lilac and pine and honeysuckle scented the air in the stillness that followed short, soft afternoon rains. When the sun went down on an afternoon like this, it glowed scarlet in a pink-and-orange sky, turning the red clay fields coppery. Fresh green shoots of new cotton shone as though they were lit from within, and everywhere there were magnolia and dogwood and peach blossoms, delicate as angel wings . . .

Five years in September, he thought.

Five years since he'd seen home.

"Afternoon, Doc," Bob Wright said when the dentist came in. "Lot of mail for you today.

96

Philadelphia Inquirer. The *Scientific American.*
Dental supply catalog. I can place the orders
for you, you know. The *Atlanta Constitution,*
and — wait, now! — a parcel from Atlanta,
too."

Bob found the package and laid it on the
counter before he cleared his throat. "That
was a shock, about Johnnie," he said sincerely.
"Real sad. He was a fine young man."

"And a daisy with a deck," Doc said, but
he was looking at the package. One finger
lightly touched the handwriting on its return
address: *Miss Martha Anne Holliday.* "If you
would be so kind, Mr. Wright, I'd appreciate
the use of your scissors."

Bob handed them over and watched Doc
cut through the neatly knotted string. Many
years later, as a very old man, Robert Wright
would tell people about that day. "Bat
Masterson always claimed Doc Holliday was
a cold-blooded killer. I never saw that in Doc,
myself. He was quiet. Soft-spoken. My first
wife — God rest her soul — Alice always used
to say that Dr. Holliday had beautiful manners and that he was a gentle dentist who
never made the children cry."

Not to quibble, but it was Bob's daughter
Belle — God rest her soul, too — who always
said that. Of course, the elderly do sometimes
mix things and the rest of Bob's story was
fairly accurate. He would go on to tell about
the slow way Doc unwrapped the book Miss

Martha Anne Holliday had sent, and how the dentist's eyes filled with tears that did not fall.

"I asked him, 'What is it, Doc?' And he said, '*The Aeneid.*' The book was all in Latin. Doc was a real educated man."

John Henry Holliday turned away from the storekeeper and stared out at the dirt and raw gray wood of Dodge, at the treeless prairie, and at the empty sky beyond. The cattle season had only just begun, but already the air was heavy with the odor of manure, monotonous with the buzz of swarming flies, loud with cowpunchers' shouted curses and the bellowing protests of cattle being run up wooden planks into the railway cars that would haul them off to Chicago for slaughter.

"Doc just stood there," Bob Wright would recall, "looking outside, you know? And then he said — real soft, his voice was always real soft — he said, 'I am in hell, but my Beatrice has sent me Vergil to be my guide.'"

When Doc Holliday left the store, Bob's daughter Belle emerged from the back room, where she had listened to all that passed between the dentist and her father.

"Oh, honey," Bob said when he saw that she'd been weeping. "Don't cry!"

"Why not? Somebody ought to cry!" she snarled, glaring at him with angry, red-rimmed eyes. "Johnnie deserves *that* much, at least!"

At fifteen, Isabelle Wright was a small, slender, dark-haired girl who ordinarily carried herself with the grace and dignity of a young woman. The Belle of Dodge, people called her, and she was as justly celebrated for her beauty as for the charity work she did among impoverished Ford County farmers. In form and face, Belle was fortunate to have taken after her pretty little mother and not her gangling, chinless, homely father. Bob never ceased to marvel that he had sired such a pretty child, but now her lovely lips were swollen and her porcelain skin was spoiled by the purple blotches that had always spread across her face when she cried, ever since she was a baby.

" 'A fine young man,' " she mimicked sarcastically. "You didn't even like for me to *talk* to him, Daddy!"

Bob Wright prized this daughter above all else on earth, but lately nothing he did was right in Belle's eyes. Sometimes it seemed that she held him personally responsible for every bad thing that had ever happened in Kansas.

"Odd, wouldn't you say, Daddy?" Belle remarked in a voice far too cold for a girl so young. "Why, there must have been two dozen drunken drovers asleep in that barn last night. They all woke up and got the horses out. Johnnie Sanders didn't drink, but he was the only one to die."

"Honey, it's not —"

"It's not your fault," she finished for him, though that wasn't what he'd meant to say. "It's never your fault!" she sobbed. "Nothing is ever *your* fault!"

Three blocks away, catching his breath in the lobby of the Dodge House Hotel, John Henry Holliday rejected the notion of leaving *The Aeneid* behind the front desk, having concluded that such an act of cowardice would only postpone Kate's reaction.

Arriving in their second-floor room, he tossed the book, his shirts, and the other mail on the bed. Kate glanced at Martha Anne's gift before returning her gaze to the game of solitaire she had laid out on the small table in the corner.

"That girl again," she observed. "You said you'd break it off."

He didn't deny it.

Kate's Magyar accent was noticeable only when she spoke English. Her Latin was elegant when she continued. "Your behavior is dishonorable. I consider it an injustice to her."

"Red jack on the black queen," he said.

She went back to her game. This was a considerable relief to him.

"So," she said, in English again, "was it

someone you worked on, that body?"

"Johnnie Sanders."

Her hand stopped, a seven of spades hovering above the table. "You're sure?"

"I never forget a smile, darlin'."

"Oh, Doc." She set the deck aside. "I'm sorry."

Kate could be kind. It always caught him off guard.

He stepped to the open window, bracing his right hand high against the frame while he recovered from the stairs. The posture opened up his intercostals and gave his diaphragm more leverage with which to work. Anyone out in the street who happened to look up would have seen a slim, well-dressed young man lounging, not a sickly boy grieving.

It was surprising, really, how much he felt the loss. It wasn't as though he and Johnnie were close, though they might have become so. He'd admired Johnnie's skill dealing faro, recognizing some of the mechanics and suspecting others. He was impressed by Johnnie's cleverness and curious about his unusual education, that was all.

As much as anything, it was the boy's accent that had drawn him. Johnnie Sanders himself wasn't from Georgia, but his paternal grandmother was. Her legacy of absent *r*'s and gerunds with no terminal *g* had been passed down intact for two generations. For

101

John Henry Holliday, Johnnie's voice was like a visit home.

Johnnie had recognized the kinship as well. "I can always tell Southerners," he told Doc at the barbershop. "Northerners'll tell you where they're goin', not where they're from. Southerners're like Indians. They'll ask who your relatives are until they find out, oh, my mother's sister married your father's uncle, so we're cousins!"

When Doc inquired about the boy's own background, Johnnie thanked him for being polite about it.

"I confuse people," Johnnie admitted. "They look me up and down, and then it's 'What in hell are you?' "

"Prairie nigger," Texans called him. *Un pardo,* Mexicans said, or *un moreno.* He'd heard the term *grif* or something like that, once or twice. Johnnie didn't know what that meant. "Couldn't find it in my dictionary," he said. All by itself, the idea of that boy owning a dictionary was enough to endear him to Doc Holliday.

"*Half-breed*'ll come to mind for some, but *breed* usually means Indian and white," Johnnie said. "My Granny Sal was half white, but that don't show a whole lot in me."

What in hell are you? That's what everyone wanted to know, and Johnnie would try to tell them sometimes but it was complicated and hardly anybody wanted to listen that

102

long. Course, listening was the pleasure of it for Doc and to make it a fair exchange, he had offered some of his own background. A youth in the South. An education in the North. Bred for life in the East. Trying not to die in the West.

"You're a map," Johnnie said judiciously. "Me? I'm a mixed multitude."

His family had an interesting story, and Johnnie thought it was true. His daddy had told him over and over, "Don't you forget this, boy. You tell your children and granbabies every word I say." So Johnnie listened hard every time, though the story was always the same.

"Daddy was a Black Seminole," he told Doc. "Seminole ain't a tribe. It's a word. It means 'runaway' in Indian. Seminoles was rebel Creeks, and Muskogee and Yuchi, and some was fugitive slaves. None of them would bow down. Daddy said that was important: the ancestors wouldn't never bow down. Seminoles lived way off deep in the swamps of Florida. Florida is a jungle, like Africa, with deadly snakes and gators. Gators're big lizards," he informed Doc helpfully, "longer than a man stretched out."

Johnnie's grandaddy was named Yusif and he came from Africa, so he knew all about jungles and wasn't scared. "Yusif could read and write Arab, Daddy said. I don't know if readin' Arab is the same as bein' Arab. What do you think, Doc?" he asked, and he was a little disappointed when "Not necessarily" was the best the dentist could do.

"Granny Sal was a Georgia slave what run off," Johnnie told him. "Her daddy was white and he tried to get her back because she was worth a lot of money, but she joined up with the Seminoles." Sal married Yusif and taught their children the English that Johnnie learned from his father, which accounted for the boy's accent. Johnnie said he'd cleaned up his grammar at St. Francis, a mission school near Wichita that he'd attended until recently. Time spent among the illiterate here in Dodge had evidently undermined the improvement some.

"My daddy didn't get no schoolin'," Johnnie told Doc, "but he could talk Mexican and Creek, and some Arab from Grandaddy Yusif. Daddy always told me, 'You come from educated people. Don't never believe white folks tell you Africans was ignorant.'"

The Spanish and the English and the Americans all sent armies into Florida to fight the Seminoles. Georgia slave owners sent militia in, too, hunting fugitives like Yusif and Sal. "Didn't matter a lick who they sent to Florida," Johnnie said. "White folks'd get lost, or die of sicknesses, or get killed by Seminole warriors."

"Remember the names, boy," his daddy always said. "They had Andrew Jackson and

General Gaines and General Jessup and
Zachary Taylor, but we had Billy Bowlegs and
Osceola and Wild Cat and John Horse. And
we was always tri-*un*-fant."

That's how his daddy said it. Tri-*un*-fant.

At some point, Wild Cat and John Horse
led their people from Florida to Mexico.
Johnnie was a little hazy about that part, but
he was sure that Texas hunters started raid-
ing into Mexico, thieving livestock and dragging Black Seminoles back to sell them for
slaves in America.

"They was a war about it," Johnnie told
Doc. "Daddy said Seminoles fought twenty
battles 'longside the Mexican army and
whipped them Texans every time."

As far as Johnnie knew, the only thing that
ever beat the Seminoles was smallpox. Smallpox carried off his Granny Sal and two of his
uncles and his aunt, who Johnnie never got
to meet, and it had marred his daddy's handsome face.

When slavery was done in the United
States, it was John Horse who led the Black
Seminoles into Fort Duncan in Texas, where
the menfolk joined the United States Army.
"They was called the Seminole Negro Indian
Scouts," Johnnie said, head high. "They was
four thousand of them, Doc! They could
track anybody, they could fight anybody, and
they was —"

"Always tri-*un*-fant," Doc finished with

105

him, smiling.

The Scouts patrolled the Rio Grande borderlands, and they took on all comers. Comanche, Apache, Kiowa. Confederate renegades. Cattle rustlers — Mexican and Texan, both. The Scouts wore uniforms, like white soldiers, but they didn't much care for their West Point officers, who wanted them to line up straight and do as they were told.

Johnnie was of the opinion that the Scouts had more in common with the cagey desert Indians they fought. His daddy would always wink when he said, "Sometimes we'd get together with them Indians. Your mamma's people was crazy gamblers — all them Indians was. They'd bet what buzzard'll fly off first! Stake their horses and wives and tents on any kinda race. I won your mamma that way. Her Indian husband was a damn fool to gamble her."

Which is how Johnnie came to be.

"See? I am a mixed multitude all by myself," he told Doc. "African, and white, and Indian, and maybe Arab, too."

"That is a wondrous story," Doc said. "Somebody should write it all down. I could help you with that, if you like."

"Oh, I can write," Johnnie assured him. "I can read and write better than most white folks. I learned myself before I got to St. Francis, but Father von Angensperg made me better at it."

Doc asked how the Sanders family wound up in Kansas after being down in Texas, and that was when Johnnie realized he didn't know. And he had his own questions, too. Like: How did his daddy get the name Sanders? And was there some special reason Johnnie himself was named after John Horse?

"You could ask next time you visit," Doc suggested.

"Too late now," Johnnie said. "My folks was killed when I was twelve."

He went quiet for a while.

"All them ancestors," he said thoughtfully. "And I'm the only one left to remember."

SHOW CARDS

That evening Doc tried to put the boy's dead, burnt body out of his mind, but circumstance conspired against him. Kate had found him a moderately interesting poker game and he sat in, but all anybody talked about was the fire. Much of the commentary centered on how capacious the Famous Elephant Barn had been. Word was, Hamilton Bell had already ordered lumber and a crew of carpenters, and he intended to rebuild, bigger than ever. There was a good deal of speculation as to what Ham might name the new stable. What was bigger than an elephant?

Nobody seemed inclined to inquire into Johnnie's death. It wasn't that folks didn't care. Everybody seemed to have liked him, but Johnnie was just a colored kid, after all, and kin to no one. Bat Masterson was telling everyone that it was an unfortunate accident. That quickly became the common wisdom.

There was no mention of how much money the boy had taken at his faro table in the past few weeks. Apparently no one else had noticed how steadily those winnings had accumulated. Even Doc tried to forget his suspicions that first night. None of my affair, he thought. Why borrow trouble?

Two hours into the game, Kate leaned over to whisper *sotto voce* into his ear, *"Viens coucher avec moi, mon amour."*

Her arms were wrapped around his shoulders. Her voice was throaty. Her French required no translation. The other players nudged each other, looking down her dress. This was the desired effect, for she was giving Doc an excuse to cut his losses. He knew she was right. His concentration was shot and he was playing poorly, but he waved her off.

She straightened. "You don't want me? You want that girl back home? I ain't good enough?"

When he failed to rise to that well-chewed bait, Kate cursed him roundly and declared, "All right, then. One of us has to make some money tonight! I'm going to Bessie's."

"Suit yourself," he said.

He played three more hands, lost two, and quit the game. Back at the hotel, he tried to read, but *The Aeneid* was no better than the poker game as a distraction.

Beloved Troy is in flames . . . The roar of the fire grows louder, the seething flood of flame rolls closer . . .

He skipped ahead to Carthage. That was

more successful.

Here Aeneas dares to hope he has found some haven and, after all his hard straits, to trust again in better times . . .

On John Henry Holliday's best days — when he'd slept well; when a freshening breeze from the northwest cleared the air; when his cough was just a nuisance he could almost ignore — on those days, his mood lifted and soared. On one such day, he had written to Martha Anne, *Western Kansas appears to have a good climate for me. Tell Cousin George that I feel quite well most of the time and take regular meals in a restaurant with a good Austrian cook.* To Robert, he reported, *Dodge isn't much yet, but the town looks to grow. There are no dentists closer than Wichita, so the work will not be split among competitors, as it was in Dallas.*

He needed capital to set up an office. For that, he could rely on a summer's worth of cowboys who thought faro was easy and cattlemen who believed they knew how to play poker. It would take time to develop his practice, but he was already getting referrals from Tom McCarty, a decently educated physician who'd read up on consumption, now that John Holliday was his patient.

"No crackle in the lungs," Tom had told him last week, "but you've got a thirty percent loss, is my guess."

That was just an estimate, of course, but if

it was accurate, John Henry still had 70 percent of his lungs left, and that was better than he had imagined. If he could hold that line, he'd manage just fine. Maybe next spring, he'd be healthy enough for a visit home. In the meantime, he was starting to make some friends here in Dodge. Morgan Earp was a cheerful young man who liked books and would sometimes talk about them. And Eddie Foy was always good for a laugh. All told, things were looking up.

Except for what happened to Johnnie.

Drunk and defiant, Kate waltzed in just past dawn, fully intending to pack her bags and tell Doc to go to hell. Instead, when she saw him, she closed the door quietly behind her.

He was sitting in the upholstered chair next to the window. Kate waited while he wiped his face, and blew his nose, and coughed, and got a grip.

"That boy was clubbed from behind," he said, rough-voiced. "Some coldhearted sonofabitch rolled him over to go through his pockets. John Horse Sanders was robbed, and he was killed, and nobody gives a damn."

Sometimes Doc seemed so young to her. So innocent. "Take it from me," she said wearily, sitting on their bed. "Nobody gives a damn about anybody."

Hoping to cheer him, she changed the subject. "There's a high-stakes game tonight.

111

Turner's your man. He won last night and thinks it was skill. Time to put on a show, *mon amour*."

He turned his face from her, the muscles in his jaw hardening. She had learned by then that it was better not to push, so she let the idea drop for now. Leaning over, she took *The Aeneid* from his lap, riffled the pages, and set it aside.

"That girl," Kate said with something like pity, but her hands were moving now, around his neck, down his chest. "She don't know you. Not like I know you, Doc. Vergil is all wrong. She should have sent you Homer."

They rang the bell for room service when they awoke, dressed at leisure, and left Dodge House at about eleven-thirty that night, in no great hurry to arrive at the Green Front Saloon. Bets, Doc had observed, become increasingly ill-considered as games progress, when losers try to win everything back in one hand. That's when patience paid.

A cool spring shower was just tapering off. The stockyard dust had settled out of the air. The temperature had dropped as well. Kate could feel a slight tremor when she took Doc's arm.

"You want to stop for a drink?" she asked. "Warm up a little?"

"I'm not cold."

Stage fright, she thought, but he had agreed

with her strategy. Drive the stake into Cyclops' eye early. Word would get around. Her Greek was better than Doc's, but she knew he'd recognize the quote. *"Enter fearlessly,"* she recited. *"However foreign a man may be, in every crisis it is the high face that will carry him through."*

"Brazen it out," he translated.

"Words to live by," she told him.

"Easy for Athena to say."

Front Street was alive with young men. Sauntering, staggering. Laughing, puking. Shouting in fierce strife or striking lewd whispered bargains with girls in bright dresses. They were giddy with liberty, these boys, free to do anything they could think of and pay for, unwatched by stern elders, unseen by sweethearts back home, unjudged by God, who had surely forsaken this small, bright hellhole in the immense, inhuman darkness that was west Kansas.

"You see, Doc? Dodge is where the money is," Kate reminded him as they passed saloon after saloon, each filled with tables where months of wages and a year of profits were at hazard. And the season had barely started! "Stick with me," she told him, squeezing his arm and dancing a little with her own excitement. "I'll make us rich."

Johnnie Sanders' daddy had told no lies. The Indians were crazy gamblers. For numberless centuries and uncounted generations, the Choctaw, the Zuni, the Crow, the Arapaho, the Navajo, the Dakota, the Mandan, the Kiowa, and a hundred other tribes had whiled away countless days and nights playing a thousand games, betting on anything with an outcome that was not assured. Blame boredom. Blame the timeless, unrelieved monotony of land so devoid of trees that owls burrow in the ground for want of better accommodation. Blame vast herds of ceaselessly chewing ruminants who walked with the unsyncopated beat of a Lakota chant. However you explained it, never and nowhere else on earth had gambling occupied the attention of so many for so long as in this flat and featureless land.

Then in a geological instant — just five years' time — the American bison had been replaced on the prairies by European domestic cattle. Dead red Indians made way for live white bankrupts lured west by the promise of a fresh start on land free for the grabbing. Kate had watched it happen and felt no pity. The Indians all but wiped out? Good riddance. A danger eliminated, nothing more. Millions of buffalo rotting on the plains. Who cares? They were filthy brutes, huge and stupid.

Tout casse, tout passe, tout lasse. That was the lesson Kate learned in childhood. Everything breaks, everything passes, nothing lasts. Revolution was the way of the world, the only constant in life. The question was how to survive it, how to make it pay. Now Kate had her answer: she had Doc. Because, from the Mississippi to the Rockies and beyond, everything had changed, except gambling.

Freighters, hunters, railroad crews. Soldiers, miners, cowboys. Homesteaders, merchants, traders. Con men and thieves. Lawyers, physicians. Judges and journalists. White and black and brown. Male and female. Children and gray-haired elders. Hookers and farm-wives.

Everyone gambled. Everyone.

They bet on cockfights, prizefights, dog-fights. They bet on horse races, dog races, foot races. They shot craps and played euchre, seven-up, pitch, brag, and all fours. Monte, both three-card and Spanish. Roulette, *vingt-et-un,* faro, keno, crown and anchor, *rouge et noir,* and whist. Many of the games were blindingly fast. You'd have thought the money must be burning the hands that held it, so quickly was it thrown down and lost.

In every boomtown and mining camp she'd worked, Kate had watched the gamblers. She was fascinated by the way they tossed the meager return from backbreaking, soul-killing work onto the tables. Their stoic, unmoving faces were a marvel, for she could smell the frantic, feral fear hidden behind those masks. Often such men would turn to her next, hoping to bury their despair in a woman's body. There was a special satisfaction in telling them, "Go to hell, and don't come back 'til you got ten dollars."

She had noticed Doc before he noticed her, back in Texas. Kate still didn't know quite what to make of him. "Short-term loan," he'd warn punters who won their first few bets at his faro table. "Quit while you're ahead," he always advised. Of course, no one ever listened. Two minutes later, the fools would be broke flat.

If you could find an honest faro game, and if you bucked it sober, and if you could concentrate on the cards, Doc claimed, the odds of beating the dealer were just about even. In practice, the house always won, for faro had no logic discernible by a drunken miner or an ignorant dirt farmer or a witless young cowboy.

"It's a game for imbeciles! They all play until they lose," she'd said back in Dallas. "Take their money and be done with it. Why do you warn them?"

Doc sat up, and coughed, and moved to the edge of the bed, where he reached out for the makings and rolled himself a cigarette. He was quiet for a while, smoking and watching the dawn through the window of her room above the bar. She could have counted the bones of his spine, prominent beneath the light linen shirt.

116

"Because," he said finally, "they break my heart."

Startled, she barked a laugh. "They don't break mine! I like to watch the fuckers get fucked."

He turned to stare at her, appalled by her coarse language and her callousness. "What an *ugly* thing to say."

She was ashamed and so she was belligerent; their first night together ended with their first fight. She threw the skinny, smug, high-hat bastard out of her room. But when the hangover wore off, she found herself remembering his hands. And how clean he was. And how gentle. The next night, she sat down near his table again to watch him deal.

Like Kate, Doc had made a study of gamblers and had theories about the breed. "A game like faro gives men the power to stop time," he told her when they'd been together for a week. "That is the appeal, in my observation."

He was lying on his back with his hands behind his head. She thought he was staring at the ceiling, the way some men will when they've rolled off. Later she learned that lifting his arms that way helped him breathe.

"When the bet is placed," he said, "a moment is carved away from the past and the future. In that enchanted moment, anything is possible. A man's debts and regrets and limitations disappear. He is buyin' the chance

117

to imagine — for one moment at a time — that the next card I deal will make him rich."

Speaking, Doc had begun to shiver. Falling silent, he rolled away from her in bed. He's cold, she thought. A Southerner with no meat on his bones. She came up close behind him, putting an arm over his shoulder, warming his bony back with her own small, soft body. She tried to remember the last time she had listened to such a thoughtful man. Not since her father died, most likely.

"I hate it," Doc muttered. "Makes me feel like a thief."

Faro was the means to an end for Doc, something to which he resorted when he needed to accumulate cash to play poker. Kate found that mystifying. Why give up a sure thing for a game you could lose? If it had been up to her, Doc would do nothing but deal faro night after night, raking in money from one idiot after another. Drovers, farmers, soldiers . . . Every damn one of them would bet his eyeballs out if you gave him odds.

"Who cares how hard they work?" she cried. "Nobody puts a gun to their heads!"

They argued their way through Texas. Nothing she said about faro made any difference to Doc, but she'd won the battle over moving to Dodge. Now that they were here, she would make it her business to find him high-stakes games.

After years of watching gamblers, she was a good judge of poker players. Doc himself could be astonishing. He didn't cheat, as far as she could see, but he was impossible to predict, and that could be just as effective. He'd play tight and slow all evening and then destroy an opponent in twenty minutes. Raising and reraising, jacking the game up, betting like a tyrant until his baffled competitor folded or lost. Once she saw him win nearly $3,500 with a pair of nines that way and the biggest loser hardly knew what had happened to him. Two hands later, sure that Doc was bluffing, the table lost another grand to him because that time Doc had the goods. Then he played small for the balance of the night, driving the others crazy.

This evening, she had the perfect mark: a South Carolinian named Estes Turner, a consistent, aggressive player who expected the same from others. Last night in a private game at Bessie Earp's bordello, Turner tossed a grand into a $315 pot to chase another player out. He ragged the man about it for the rest of the night, and then — sitting on thousands of dollars — he argued about the brothel tab! It was going to be a real pleasure to watch Doc take that bastard down a notch.

Just as she and Doc reached the Green Front's door, he stopped short and whistled his admiration for a fine dapple-gray mare tied to a rail out front. "That might be the prettiest head God ever put on a horse," Doc remarked to a pair of troopers who lounged nearby, smoking and complaining.

Kate turned back and frowned. Doc was broad-minded, but he usually drew the line at uniformed Yankees. These boys were too young to have been in the war. Maybe that made it possible not to hate them on sight.

"Take a look, darlin'," he said, gesturing with his cigarette. "Unless I miss my guess, she is one of Anthony Keene Richard's fillies."

"Naw," a stringy corporal told him. "She's Captain Grier's horse."

"I stand corrected," Doc said with a slight but courteous bow. "I should have said that Captain Grier's mare carries the bloodlines of Mr. Richard's horses. One must choose one's words carefully among scholarly Yankees."

Kate rose on her toes and breathed, "Turner," into his ear.

Ignoring her, Doc asked, "Now, why aren't you two gentlemen enjoyin' the city's hospitality this evenin'?"

"Goddam barn burned down," the corporal told him. "So we're guarding this goddam horse all night."

"All night, or until the goddam captain goes bust," a private added, lifting a blunt chin toward the Green Front.

"The captain would not be *Elijah* Grier,

120

would he?" Doc asked.

The soldier nodded. "That's him."

"Well, now . . ." Doc drew on the cigarette and coughed a little: dry and shallow. "It is an unexpected treat to see such a mare right here in Dodge. My understandin' was that all Mr. Richard's breedin' stock was lost durin' Mr. Lincoln's war."

Stolen, he meant.

"Horses bore me," Kate said with a calculated sullenness, tugging at his elbow.

"Can't have that, now, can we?" Doc told the troopers. "If you'll excuse us, gentlemen?"

Doc turned and held the saloon door open for her. Stepping inside, she smiled up at him, pleased to demonstrate her own acumen. The Saratoga was more plush and the Long Branch was much bigger, but the Green Front clientele was more serious about both drinking and gambling. There was a piano, badly tuned and poorly played, but the predominant sounds were the slide and slap of pasteboard cards, the clatter and chink of chips and coins, the clicking of a roulette wheel. Around the saloon, the low male mutter of conversation was punctuated by crisp professional calls.

"Are you all down, gentlemen?"

"Eight to one on the colors."

"Keno!"

Around the room, customers and bar girls

alike paused to take note when Doc Holliday and his woman arrived, for they made a handsome couple in silver gray and pale shimmering pink. Noticing the hush, Bat Masterson rose from his table at the back and approached with a friendly smile. He spent most nights at the Green Front, taking a percentage of the house for making sure the rougher element in town didn't smash the place up. It was his custom to greet newcomers to the saloon as though he owned the place, and then say, "A word to the wise" about not starting any trouble.

"Evening, Kate. Nice to see you again, Doc," Bat began, but before he could say more, the dentist's admiring gaze rendered him mute.

"Why, Sheriff Masterson!" Doc said. "I never before noticed how intensely blue your eyes are. That waistcoat sets them off a treat! You should wear the color more often, sir."

Kate had both hands around Doc's arm and tightened them a little, but kept her face carefully composed. The sheriff of Ford County was built like a chunk of wood: short, solid, cylindrical. That evening, Bat's burly body was resplendent in a lavender suit and a pale yellow shirt. A vest of midnight blue and gold brocade set off his silvery pistols.

"Vestis virum reddit," she observed.

"Clothes make the man," Doc told Bat. "Marcus Fabius Quintilianus. Isn't she a daisy?" Eyes on Kate's, Doc brought one of her small hands to his lips, then seemed to remember that Bat was still standing there. "I apologize, Sheriff. You were about to say something?"

"Welcome to the Green Front," Bat said tightly. "First drink's on the house. I'll be at the back table if you need anything."

If you start anything, he meant.

Kate almost laughed. She hadn't planned on that little joust, but it didn't surprise her either. Doc could be patronizing and snide, and cocky little bastards brought out the worst in him. As for Bat . . . Well, sure as henna hates a natural red, Bat Masterson would always think the worst of Doc Holliday. Bat told stories; Doc was a wit. Bat was false; Doc was wily. Bat was ambitious, but Doc had a sense of his own superiority so deep in him, he didn't even know it existed. Most galling of all, both men had physical limitations they worked hard to conceal, and neither liked being reminded of that.

Vanitas partita, vanitas aperta, Kate thought. Vanity shared is vanity exposed.

Or, in more practical terms, one redhead to a whorehouse.

Doc ordered a couple of shots and handed one to Kate, who set off on her own toward Turner's table, where she would watch the action until he himself could join the game.

123

He trusted Kate's judgment in these matters and felt no need to second-guess her. In the meantime, sipping at his bourbon, he went looking for the Arabian mare's owner.

There were several cavalry officers in attendance, but Captain Grier was easy to pick out. Yes, he thought. The same man . . . Older, naturally. In his early twenties when he was stationed in Atlanta during the occupation. Somewhere around thirty-five now. Career officer, but still only a captain. What went wrong? Tailored uniform, some shine on the cuffs. Expensive boots, heels worn down. Grier played scared, looking at his cards too often.

The pot was upwards of a grand and a half, with three players still in: Grier, the storekeeper Bob Wright, and Big George Hoover, the man who wholesaled liquor and cigars to all of Dodge City. As befitted the husband of an ardent Prohibitionist, Big George did no drinking — in public, at least. That made him circumspect. He played sober. That made him formidable. And as homely and artless as he appeared, Bob Wright barely glanced at his own cards, paying more attention to what was on the table.

"That is a fine-lookin' horse you have outside, sir," Doc remarked, to see how Grier would take an interruption.

"Yeah," one of the others at Grier's table said, "and if he keeps betting her, one of these

124

days he'll have to pay off."

"But not this evening," Grier said. "Full house, kings over jacks."

Big George groaned good-naturedly. Bob Wright smiled, ever so slightly, eyes satisfied. No question. He knew he was going to lose that hand, but . . . It was tuition! Bob didn't mind paying it, either, for he had just learned precisely how much money Grier had, and he knew now how the captain reacted, going that close to the edge.

Which made Bob Wright a *very* interesting man.

"Peach of a hand," Doc remarked as Grier took the pot. "Your mare is Baghdad stock, is she not? Crockett's Arabian and May Queen, is my guess."

Grier looked up. "That's her line, all right. By Pasha, out of April Princess. You have a good eye, Mr. — ?"

"Dr. John Holliday," he said, watching Grier's eyes. There was no flicker of recognition. "I trust you enjoyed your stay in Georgia?"

Grier looked puzzled. "Have we met, sir?"

"No, though you may recall an uncle of mine by the same name."

"Goddammit, Grier, you gonna talk or play?"

Doc bowed slightly, hand on his heart. "My apologies, gentlemen. I will let y'all get on with your game," he said, but he stayed to watch a while longer. Grier's tells were obvious. He tended to lean forward slightly when he was bluffing, and often sat back when he had the goods. Big George was more difficult to read, but one thing was certain. The bar girls didn't like him. They got a percentage of every drink they sold, and there was no profit in a customer who didn't drink. And Bob Wright was a puzzle. If you watched carefully, you'd swear he was throwing money in Grier's direction — betting when Grier had a good hand, folding a little late.

Across the room, Kate beckoned. Doc strolled to her side.

"Dealer's a Chicago meatpacker," she told him, voice low and intimate. "On the dealer's right: Estes Turner. From Charleston, touchy about the war. Owns a ranch in Texas now. To his right, a banker from Topeka. Then two more cattlemen. Both flush. Banker'll drop out in a hand or two."

"Thank you, darlin'. Find out what the girls have to say about George Hoover. And what is Eli Grier to Bob Wright?"

It was easy enough to put Grier out of his mind. Ignoring the piano was harder. He studied the action at Turner's table, waiting for the banker to go all in and lose. It wouldn't take long. Five-card stud is a fast game, and there was a $20 ante. The meatpacker was almost sober and very good. The two cattlemen were dulled by drink. Turner

126

was loud, and reckless.

When the banker left the game, Doc stepped up. "Gentlemen," he inquired, "may I join you?"

Kate returned to the table, sitting behind Doc so nobody could accuse her of signaling an opponent's cards to him. Her job was to roll cigarettes and keep his shot glass filled with tea from the bar girls' "bourbon" bottle, occasionally substituting the real thing if he started to cough.

For a couple of hours, Doc stayed small, playing quietly, folding a good hand now and then, to see how Turner would react. With every win, the man sat easier, talked more, and had another drink. Money was tossed into the center of the table with an insouciant flip of the wrist — *cito acquiritur, cito perit* — but it was a carelessness as yet untested by any significant loss. Turner was drunk on winning. He was drunk, period.

In the fourth hour of play, one of the cattlemen dropped out, leaving nearly all his money in front of the meatpacker, Doc, and Turner.

Doc began to work his man. It was nothing flashy, just playing hands he'd have quit earlier. He took three big pots in a row, betting heavily. Then, when he had Turner on his back foot, Doc let him win with a sudden fold. Kate held her face still, but it was hard not to smile. Turner couldn't make out what was going on: suspicious when he lost, bewildered when he won.

"Goddammit, Holliday," Turner complained. "You don't make any sense at all!"

"It is wrong to have a ruthless, iron heart," Doc recited, squinting through smoke at his cards. *"Even the gods can bend and change . . .* Your five hundred. A thousand more."

A crowd began to gather. Side bets were being made. Doc took the pot and turned the talk to war. Tinder for Turner's spark. A few hands later, he drew the spade he needed and gave a sign to Kate, who left to get Bat Masterson.

This was when things could go all wrong. After what happened in Denison, Doc wanted a witness with a badge. "There's trouble at Doc's table," Kate would tell Bat, knowing that there would be soon and trusting that Bat would leave his own game, for she'd been priming him for weeks with tales of Doc's bad temper and readiness to attack.

"Why, ten minutes after I got off the train in Philadelphia, I knew why we had lost," Doc was saying in his laziest drawl. "The North had iron mines. Foundries. Shipyards. Munitions factories, mills . . . Your grand and another."

The meatpacker and the cattleman folded. It was just him and Turner now.

"The South?" he continued. "We knew how to produce two things, my friend. Cotton and

128

aristocrats. Only thing left is the cotton, and the weevils are gettin' half of that. What've you got?"

Turner had a king-high straight. When Doc caught sight of Kate and Bat, he laid out his flush and took the pot, letting the sweep of his arm go a little wide, as though drink had made him sloppy.

"The cause was lost," he said, pulling the money in, "before you ignorant goddam Carolina crackers fired the first shot at Sumter."

For years afterward, Bat Masterson would tell people about that night.

"I arrived too late to hear exactly what Doc said to set the fracas off, but there was no question about what happened next. Turner hollered that Doc was a goddam liar and reached for his gun."

Along with everyone else in the saloon, the South Carolinian went motionless a heartbeat later, paralyzed by the sight of a short-barreled, nickel-plated Colt .38 leveled at his chest.

"Think about how much practice a move like that takes! Hours and hours," Bat would say. "I never saw a hand quicker than Holliday's. And I'll tell you something else," he would continue. "A serious gunman was always a little deaf in one ear — pistol practice, you follow? Doc always turned his right ear toward you when you talked. He was left-handed, y'see?"

"I step aside to no man in my love for the Southland," Doc said softly in the sudden silence, "but I speak the truth. You will do well to apologize for suggestin' differently, sir."

"Doc's voice never rose much above a whisper," Bat would tell people. "Course, his lungs were so bad, I doubt he could've shouted if he wanted to, but that man could put a by-God whiplash into his words."

"*Say it,* you white trash *chicken*shit sonofa*bitch.* John Holliday speaks the truth, or I am a lyin', Yankee-lovin' yellow dog."

Eyes wide, Turner swallowed hard. "John Holliday speaks the truth."

Doc waited.

"Anyone says different is a yellow dog," Turner finished.

The gun was holstered as quickly as it had appeared.

"I accept your apology, sir," Doc said graciously. He rose to address the room. "And I offer my own for the unpleasantness, gentlemen."

Nobody moved, not even Turner, who was white beneath his drunken flush. Doc and Kate were heard to speak briefly in a foreign language. Doc ambled out into the night, leaning on his cane. Kate swept their winnings into her carpetbag. Turner looked down. He still had some money left and he wasn't dead. He shook his head and started to laugh: half nerves, half relief.

"No harm done," Bat said with a shrug. Holliday was all talk, he decided, though he would not have said so aloud.

"Bartender!" Kate called, holding up a fan of cash and tossing it into the air. "Doc says the drinks are on him!"

The tension broke and there was a cheer as Kate sailed like royalty through the crowd. She stopped at the bar before she left, dropping five dollars on the polished walnut.

"Bourbon. A bottle," she ordered. "The good stuff, too, not that piss you sell cowboys."

There was one last stop, this time at the piano. It was foolish, but Doc had insisted. Kate pulled a gold piece from the carpetbag and offered it. When the startled player reached for the coin, she whipped it away, holding it just beyond his grasp. "Doc says bring somebody in from St. Louis and get this goddam piano tuned. Savvy?"

The piano player nodded. He'll be gone on the morning train, she thought, but she handed him Doc's money.

She found Doc out behind Dodge House. To anyone else, he would have looked a picture of nonchalance, leaning against the clapboards.

"Bravo," she said when she was close. "They won't forget that, Doc!"

He was rolling a cigarette in the starlight, or trying to. Kate took the makings from him and tapped the tobacco into line.

"We tripled the stake," she told him, "and the story'll be all over town by morning. You wait and see. Nobody's gonna bother you from now on."

She licked the edge of the paper cylinder, lit the cigarette for him, placed it between his lips. There was the usual little choking cough on the first puff. Nothing to worry about. It was the cheap tobacco they'd been reduced to lately. She'd stop by George Hoover's shop tomorrow. If he didn't have any decent North Carolina leaf in stock, she'd order some, special. They had plenty of cash now.

"Let's go to the Comique," she suggested in French, pronouncing the theater's name properly, not the way the locals did. Commie-Q, they called it. Ignorant louts. "We can catch Eddie Foy's last show."

He shook his head and went on smoking. For a time, they stood together silently, listening to the night sounds. Clanging pianos. Accordions and fiddles. Inebriated shouts of laughter. The hollow clatter of horns in a cattle pen south of the tracks.

Kate took the cigarette back, pulled the last long drag on it, and flicked the butt into the dirt.

Doc was a tall man. She liked that about him. She liked the feel of stretching up to put her hand on the back of his neck, bringing his face toward hers — pulling him down to her level. She kissed him on the mouth, then stood on tiptoe to bring her lips closer to his ear.

"Come to my bed," she said in English, the language of the brothels. "I can make you forget all those bastards."

And that little bitch back home, she thought.

"Come to my bed," she said, voice low and harsh and foreign, "and I will fuck you blind."

Later, after, he lay beside her, hands linked behind his head. He'd hardly said a word since they left the Green Front, but Kate was used to that. When Doc wasn't talking a streak, he dummied up entirely.

She got out of bed and poured them each another drink. "Which reminds me!" she said. "He won't give the girls his empties."

Doc looked at her, blank.

"George Hoover?" she reminded him. "Cheap sonofabitch makes the bar girls *buy* the empty whiskey bottles for their tea. And they hate his wife — reformed hooker."

"Grier?" Doc asked.

"Nobody knows." Kate smiled. "But trust me: I'll find out."

SECOND HAND

BAD BEAT

The former prince and present priest Alexander Anton Josef Maria Graf von Angensperg had been warned about Johnnie Sanders. "Don't get your hopes up," Father John Schoenmakers told him. "These children will break your heart."

Twenty years on the Osage reservation had taught Father Schoenmakers to temper his expectations. So many obstacles had hindered the spiritual and educational progress of the Indians. The scarcity of Jesuit missionaries and the miserable conditions under which they worked. The violence and dislocation of "Bleeding Kansas," and of the civil war that followed. The American government's policy of deliberate neglect. The rapacity and corruption of Indian agents. The fear and intransigence of the Indians themselves.

"The work of bringing the Osage from barbarism to civilization and thence to Christianity is a labor not of years but of centuries," the stolid Dutch priest told Alexander von Angensperg when the Austrian arrived at St. Francis School in 1872. "Mere decades are too brief a time to yield significant effects."

The younger priest did not argue with Father Schoenmakers, but neither did he accept what his superior said. Alexander von Angensperg was a man in his prime. Energetic and fit, his hair still cropped cavalry short, his bearing still military, he was an aristocrat accustomed to achievement, eager to serve Christ among the red Indians and prepared to charge through enemy lines when necessary. Father Schoenmakers was not the enemy, of course, but Alexander believed it was important to resist the older man's weary pessimism. To do this work, it was imperative to keep a high heart and even to believe in miracles.

In that spirit, Alexander had allowed himself to imagine a glowing future for Johnnie Sanders. Finishing his secondary education with the Jesuits in St. Louis. Going on to university. Conversion to the True Faith. Perhaps, one day, even a call to the priesthood, for it was plain to Alexander that the young man would have made a good Jesuit. *John Sanders is a natural teacher,* Alexander wrote to the Missouri Provincial, outlining the boy's potential and inquiring about the possibility of a scholarship. *He is at home on the borderlands between races, languages, and religions.*

The letter was posted just a day before Johnnie disappeared, last autumn.

They did that, Indian children. They disappeared. You had to be on guard all the time. Father Schoenmakers was usually able to detect the signs. "Keep a close eye on Paul Little Dog," he'd say at breakfast. Or "Joseph Two Birds is going to turn rabbit soon."

Sometimes, they'd find the runaway before he made it off the mission grounds. Sometimes, they would never see him again. They might hear that a boy had gone back to his tribe; a few days or months or years later, they'd learn that he had been shot dead by a frightened settler west of Wichita, or that he was killed in a skirmish with the cavalry, or that he'd died of alcoholism on the edges of Kansas City. Once boys left St. Francis, their chances of survival fell like stones dropped from a high tower.

Some Indian parents understood that grim fact. They insisted that the runaway return to the mission school, often with a younger brother in tow. Small, skinny children would arrive all but destitute of clothing, and what little they wore was fit only to be burned. The boys themselves had to be dosed for ringworm, bathed with yellow soap, their heads shaved and their bodies rinsed in kerosene to kill their fleas and lice. When that ordeal was over, they were shown how to put

on the school uniform and escorted —
stumbling in their unfamiliar shoes — to the
classroom. Scrubbed, shorn, and shod, they
sat on wooden benches, wary as deer. If they
spoke English at all, it was a poor and
ungrammatical pidgin. Most seemed almost
mute.

When Alexander von Angensperg walked
into the classroom his own first day, he was
nearly as overwhelmed as the newest boy at
St. Francis. All the children were dark-haired,
dark-eyed, dark-skinned, and they seemed to
him as indistinguishable as the dark little
chokecherries that grew on bushes near the
school. On any given day there might be fifty
students in his class, though their numbers
were often thinned by illness, for scarlet fever,
colds, whooping cough, mumps, and chicken
pox spread easily in the close quarters of the
dormitories. Each had been given a short,
plain Christian name — easy to spell and
write, but not memorable, not individual.
Daniel, Thomas, Paul, Joseph. Matthew,
Mark, Luke, John.

"Me, I'm not named for the Evangelist,"
Johnnie Sanders told Alexander. "I'm named
for John Horse. He was a Seminole general.
My daddy fought at his side in Mexico and
Texas." The boy looked thoughtful for a mo-
ment and added, "Course, could be John
Horse was named for the Evangelist."

Everything set Johnnie Sanders apart. His

140

fluency in English. His looks: the curling hair, the flaring nose, his pride in bearing. His responsiveness and immediacy in class. His curiosity and openness to learning. He was only twelve when he came to St. Francis, but he was calm, not wary. Self-possessed, not speechless. He had been orphaned in June of 1873, but told Alexander that he'd already gotten through the worst of his sadness while staying with Wyatt Earp, a Wichita policeman who'd brought the boy to the mission school that September.

During his four years at St. Francis, John Horse Sanders absorbed lessons as good soil takes in rain. "I'm here because my parents were killed," Johnnie said when Alexander praised his hard work. "I don't want to waste the tears."

In addition to English, Johnnie spoke his mother's tongue, not the Osage of his classmates, but he was good with new boys, patiently showing them how to work door latches and pump handles, how to button shirts and tie shoes. Before long, he could communicate with the others in their own language, and full-bloods would tell him things they'd not been willing or able to tell the Jesuits. It was Johnnie who explained why they resisted looking adults in the eye. ("They don't want to be disrespectful, Father.") And it was he who helped Alexander understand why cutting the boys' long hair was so distressing to them. ("Indians cut their hair for mourning, Father. When you cut their hair, they think someone in their family died, but they don't know who.") Alexander came to rely on Johnnie as an interpreter and as an informal assistant teacher. Working together, they had many of the new boys reading reasonably well and writing a good hand by the end of each school year. And Johnnie invented ways to teach arithmetic with card games, an unorthodox but effective method that was enormously popular with the other students.

John Horse Sanders was the last one Alexander expected to turn rabbit. Even Father Schoenmakers was surprised.

For the children's own good, punishment for running was severe. One winter, a boy attempted to walk back to his parents and froze to death in the snow. His body was found the next spring, and Father Schoenmakers took no chances after that. Those who were recaptured were made examples, to discourage further attempts at escape.

Just before he disappeared, Johnnie had been involved in a serious altercation with Brother Sheehan, the massively muscled Irishman who managed the mission farm and taught the boys to plow and plant. Brother Sheehan was generally indulgent with the Indians, except when their conduct deserved stern treatment. In Johnnie's case, Alexander had counseled leniency, if the prodigal returned.

Brother Sheehan was not too awed by a priest's authority to argue. "Father, you've led that kid to believe he's as good as anybody. Well, he's not, and he never will be, not while he's living on God's green earth! If a boy like that bucks me in here, he gets a beating. If he bucks men out there, they'll kill him for it. That's a lesson the little shite needs to learn, and when we catch him, by God, I'm going to teach it."

Too late now, Alexander thought, the flimsy yellow paper of the telegram crackling softly in his hand.

REGRET TO INFORM YOU OF THE
DEATH OF JOHN HORSE SANDERS STOP
DETAILS TO COME STOP WILL YOU
CONDUCT SERVICES STOP REPLY PAID
STOP JH HOLLIDAY DODGE CITY STOP

Alexander took word of the tragedy to Father Schoenmakers, asking for and receiving permission to travel to Dodge. He exchanged additional telegrams with J. H. Holliday, who promised to make all the arrangements and to delay the interment until Friday. On Wednesday, an envelope arrived with a round-trip train ticket, first class, to Dodge. The note inside was on good rag paper, written in a precise copperplate hand.

Johnnie had died in a barn fire. The promised details were conveyed with tact, but Alexander read the truth between the lines. J. H. Holliday suspected that the boy had been assaulted and robbed before the building burned down.

On Thursday at first light, Brother Sheehan drove Alexander through a soaking rain to the train station in Wichita. The Irishman hardly spoke a word, but there was no need. All the way to town, the mule's hooves clopped out a rhythm. *I told you so, I told you so, I told you so . . .*

Hours later, still damp from his dawn drenching, Alexander von Angensperg stepped down onto the railway platform and learned a lesson of his own: you needn't be a mixed-blood boy to experience mortal and moral danger upon leaving St. Francis and arriving in Dodge City.

The first shot passed closely enough for him to feel the breeze of it near his ear before the bullet went pinging off a brass train fitting. The second shot was high, but if Alexander had not jumped aside quickly, he'd have been run down by a panicky riderless horse a moment later. Before he could react to any of that, a glassy-eyed girl with a painted face roped her arms around his neck, planted a wet kiss on his lips, and declared with exuberant hospitality, "Welcome to Dodge, Father!"

144

Decidedly *cognito* in a Roman collar and black soutane, Alexander tried to preserve some crumb of dignity while peeling the intoxicated prostitute off his chest. To the amusement of the station crowd, the task proved impossible, and the best Alexander could do was to feign serene indifference and address the assemblage more generally.

"Can anyone tell me, please, where is J. H. Holliday?" he asked.

A familiar-looking young man wearing a deputy's badge pushed toward Alexander through the crowd, though his eyes were on the whore. "Clear off, Verelda," he ordered. "Show a little respect, will you?"

"He ain't here to pray, honey. Nobody comes to Dodge to pray, f'crissakes!"

"He's here for Johnnie's funeral."

"Oh." Verelda stepped back and dropped a simpering little curtsy. "Bless me, Father, for I have sinned," she said piously, adding with a boozy laugh, "and sinned and sinned and sinned!" Enjoying the laughter around her, the grinning girl spotted a prosperous-looking salesman and moved with blurry enterprise toward her next target.

Of his single meeting with Wyatt Earp, Alexander retained a clear recollection of a natural horseman who'd have done well in the imperial cavalry. Lean. Fair, with a heavy chevron mustache. An overall impression of calm command. The lawman before him matched that memory, and Alexander offered his hand.

"Deputy Earp, it is good to see you again, though in sad circumstances."

"You know my brother, not me, Father. I'm Morgan," the young man said. "Wyatt ain't back from Texas yet."

"My apologies! I met your brother once only, when he brought Johnnie Sanders to St. Francis."

"Folks mix me and Wyatt up all the time. All us Earps look alike," Morgan told the priest genially. "Here, lemme take your bag."

Alexander hesitated. "I was supposed to meet a J. H. Holliday at the station —"

"I know. Doc sends his regrets. He's with a patient and couldn't get away."

There was another volley of gunshots and the sound of breaking glass nearby. With an indifference worthy of a hussar, Morgan ignored a pack of cowboys thundering by on horseback, their leader holding high a pair of lacy pantaloons in a drunken game of capture the flag.

"We put you up at Dodge House," he said, striding across a muddy street toward a large two-story hotel. "I hope that's all right with you."

"Usually I stay with a Catholic family," Alexander said, trying not to sound ungrateful. "We must be careful about expense."

"Oh, don't worry about that none. Doc's

taking care of everything — Watch your step, Father." The deputy grabbed Alexander's arm, pulling him back before he could put his foot into a pile of horse dung. "Your English is real good. You German?"

"Austrian, but I have lived in America since five years already."

A few doors down, three boys tumbled out of a bar, singing with an enthusiasm undiminished by rare agreement regarding melody and lyrics. Suddenly, one of them bent double and vomited into a puddle. The other two leaned against each other, laughing so hard that they fell to their knees in the mire, helpless with *Schadenfreude.* None of them looked older than sixteen. In Wichita, Alexander was the youngest priest at forty-five. In Dodge, he was a good deal more than twice the average age of those around him.

"Sorry about all this," Morgan said. "We got three herds coming in all at once. Town's been wide open since Ed Masterson was killed. The office is pretty shorthanded." He reached past Alexander and pulled the hotel door open. "Deacon?" he called. "Guest for you!"

The hotel seemed hushed, Front Street's cacophony effectively damped by heavy window curtains in sun-faded maroon velvet. The wooden floor was carpeted in mud-stained bilious green, the lobby furnished with a suite of dusty furniture upholstered in blue plush with yellow floral figuring. Several vivid chromolithographs decorated walls papered in a red-flocked geometric pattern.

Morgan whispered, "Doc says temperance ladies decorated the place to punish hungover guests."

Alexander stared.

"Joke, Father!" Morgan said, with a remarkably sweet and open smile. "Deacon Cox just has bad taste."

The hotelier appeared a moment later, dressed as soberly as his decor was flamboyant. There was a flurry of welcome, and an explanation of his title ("George Cox, Father. Folks call me Deacon, but it's just a nickname."). This was followed by assurance that Dodge House was the best hotel in town, confirmation that all of the priest's expenses were covered, information about a Chinese laundry and the possibility of getting a bath, and the location of the privies.

In the midst of it all, another deputy stuck his head in the door and called, "Morg? Some idiot just rode a horse onto the second story of your brother's cat house. We can't get the damn thing to come back down."

Morgan excused himself to deal with the emergency, leaving Deacon Cox to show Alexander up a steep staircase.

"We expanded last year. Fifty rooms now," Deacon told the priest. "Best billiard parlor in the city. Restaurant, bar — no charge to you, sir. Doc says everything's on him. That's Doc Holliday for you! First class, all the way! You can come down to eat or I can send your meals up. Just ring the bell. We got room service, same as St. Louis. Oh, and the preacher says you can use the Union Church tomorrow for the funeral. Ten in the morning, we told people. Drovers'll be sleeping it off that time of day — more peaceful for the burial, follow? Some of the Germans are coming in from the farms for your service. Mass, it's called, right? Mostly Methodists here in the city, although the majority of the populace is as heathen as China Joe. Still, you should have a pretty good crowd. Folks thought well of Johnnie."

Deacon opened the door to a room at the end of the corridor, then stepped back with a sweep of his hand. Alexander entered and crossed to the window, pulling a coarse lace curtain aside, hardly listening as the hotelier pointed out amenities. The room was on the far side of the building, away from the street and the railroad and the stockyards, overlooking an expanse of buffalo grass that stretched northward into Canada. It was quiet, apart from the occasional report of a pistol shot and Deacon Cox's chatter.

"We told people you'd be hearing confession this afternoon. That's how you say it, right? Hearing confession? Four o'clock, we told them. That's when the dago priest always does it. Father Poncy — ? Damn, I can never say that fella's name! Something Eye-talian —"

"Ponziglione." The room was generously sized, with an ornate woven wicker screen to divide a sitting area from a bedroom with a washstand and a dresser. He could use the screen to shield penitents. "Thank you. This will do very well. Four o'clock will be fine."

There was more talk, including a promise to knock on the door at three forty-five, but at long last, the hotelier bid him a good afternoon and left.

Staring dumbly at the door, Alexander listened as Deacon Cox's footsteps retreated down the corridor. Belatedly it came to him that he should have asked about Dr. Holliday and why he was being so generous.

Too late, too late, too late . . .

With a long, shuddering sigh, Alexander von Angensperg stretched flat on the bed, exhausted and empty. Since Tuesday morning, when he'd stood in the mission doorway and read that awful telegram, each passing hour had required all the self-discipline he could muster.

Placing one foot before the other.

Going through the motions.

Getting himself to this moment: when he could be alone at last, cover his face with his hands, and cry.

■ ■ ■

As promised, the knock came at a quarter to four. "I hope you got some rest," Deacon Cox said through the door. "You got quite a line out here."

Alexander straightened the bed linens and left the room to use the privy, keeping his eyes down so he would not recognize anyone waiting in the hallway. When he returned, he rolled up a blanket, put it on the floor as a kneeler, placed a purple stole over his shoulders, and settled himself in the chair behind the dressing screen.

"We may begin now, if you please," he called out quietly.

For the rest of his long and eventful life, Alexander von Angensperg might have topped just about any war story told in a Jesuit residence. He could have listened, and nodded, and acknowledged each man's most colorful adventure, and then achieved an awed, respectful silence with just six words: "I heard confessions in Dodge City."

The seal of confession imposed silence, so he never told a soul. Had others tried to imagine the litany of violence, greed, deceit, and debauchery, they could not have come close. The average priest would rarely hear in all his days what Alexander did in a single memorable afternoon.

Everything but sloth, he realized afterward. Dodge was diligent in sin.

Nearly all the women were whores, most of them Irish girls hardly more than children. "A hooker's never worth more than she is on her first night," a tired young voice began. "I told my pimp I'm thirteen. Sure, if he finds out the truth, I'll be working the cribs that much sooner, then, won't I. So I lie."

"And what was I going to do with a baby? I'd be out of work for months, wouldn't I! It was get rid of it or starve. So I got rid of it."

"He drug me out here all the way from Ohio, and then the sonofabitch died on me! There I was, with three little kids to feed. I tried to work honest, Father. I tried being a dressmaker, but I can make so much more money this way!"

"So he fell asleep, and I by God stole every penny he had. After what that bastard made me do, I reckon I earned it!"

"You have to drink, then, don't you, Father? It's so much easier if you're drunk, now, isn't it."

On, and on, and on . . .

The sins of the men were more varied, if no less dismal.

"I swear: the gun just went off. I only wanted to scare him. It was an accident!"

"I was winning all night long, and then the sonofabitch drew a jack. I lost it all, Father. I can't go home. I just can't face her and the

152

kids. They think I'm dead."

"We knew he stole them horses, so we had to hang him, but Jesus! The way he looked at me . . . Did we do murder, Father? If we was pretty sure he done it?"

"I didn't mean to hurt her so bad, but she wouldn't shut up, and I couldn't stop hitting her."

"We only did it twice, Father. We was so damn lonely, see?"

On and on and on . . .

A few *vaqueros* provided variation. God alone knew what those Mexican cowboys said, for Alexander understood no Spanish.

And then there was the German who simply sobbed for five agonizing minutes before choking out the words *"Est tut mir Leid. Ich bitte tausendmal um Verzeihung."* I'm sorry. I am so dreadfully sorry.

In the end, there was an Irishman who announced his presence with a cheerful greeting. "Buck up, Father," this voice said. "I'm your last, and I'll be quick about it. I've broken all the commandments except murder, theft, and worshipping false gods. I've done more'n me share of whoring, but you know how it is yourself, then, don't you, what with Verelda throwing herself at you, same as she does me. She's not a bad girl, Father. This's a terrible hard country for women. Anyway: no time for a rosary before me first act! Whaddya say? A few Hail Marys, and we call it square!"

Without waiting for an answer, the Irishman rattled off an Act of Contrition. Alexander was too benumbed to argue.

"I'll be on me way, then," the lilting voice said, but a hand snaked around the screen. In it was a liquor bottle, a shot glass perched upside down over the cork. "Here you go, then, Father. It's from himself. 'Something to wash the taste of transgression from your mouth,' says he. There's a note on your dresser. We're after having a wee wake for sweet Johnnie tonight."

The stationery was rag, the handwriting copperplate. *On occasion,* the note read, *a good Kentucky bourbon may be considered therapeutic. If you'd rather not drink alone, please join the friends of John Horse Sanders at Delmonico's, 7 P.M. — J. H. Holliday*

He had hardly finished reading when there was a knock on the half-open door. Alexander looked up and saw a stocky middle-aged Chinese carrying a large tin bathtub, accompanied by two helpers with buckets.

"You want wash up?" this person asked. "Doc say bring you plenty hot water."

Whoever Dr. Holliday was, he seemed to have thought of everything. A good stiff drink, a reviving hot bath. Even a clean shirt, trousers, and a set of underclothing had been provided — a little too large, but not a bad fit — with a promise from the laundryman that the priest's own things would be returned by morning: "I brush, no wash. No time for dry. Doc say make 'em nice for funeral."

Freshly bathed and freshly dressed, hungry for the first time in three days, Alexander went downstairs at the appointed time. Deacon Cox directed him to the restaurant a few steps down the boardwalk. The entrance to Delmonico's was shut, and there was a handwritten sign in its window: *Private Party This Evening*. Alexander knocked and waited to be let in. He meant to stay a short while only, just long enough to express his thanks for his host's generosity and to have a bite to eat.

A small, neatly made woman opened the door and waited, brows up.

"I am Father von Angensperg," he told her. "I was invited —"

"Hochwürden! Willkommen," she said with warmth and dignity. *"Ich bin so froh, das Sie sich durchringen konnten, sich uns anzuschliessen."*

Her German was cultivated, though charmingly accented by Magyar, and her voice was wonderful — low and husky. "Please," she urged, "do come in. I am so pleased you decided to join us — we had feared you might be too fatigued." She offered her hand, still speaking his own mother tongue. "I am

155

Mária Katarina Harony. Americans call me Kate."

She was handsome, not beautiful, but she had a creamy complexion and flaxen hair, and her eyes were perfectly matched by the aqua watered silk she wore. To find such a creature in such a wilderness! His response was courtly and automatic: to straighten, heels together, to incline his head and bring her hand close to his lips. Only then did the astonishment hit him.

"Harony? But I know that name! There was a Michael Harony, a physician — he served at the court of Maximilian in Mexico, yes?"

"My father."

"I met him twice, though I doubt he would remember me. My grandmother was his patient. How is Dr. Harony?"

Her head remained high. "He died some years ago."

"I am so sorry to hear it," he began. "*Ach!* The revolution, of course!"

Before he could say more, Kate turned and, with a practiced smile over her shoulder, led him inside. She was the only lady in attendance. The restaurant was crowded with men eating, drinking, talking, smoking, none of them startled by the intermittent gunfire in the street as gangs of horsemen charged by, whooping like savages.

Speaking English now, Kate began to introduce him, and those dazzling eyes sparkled with mischief, for she had recognized his family name, as he had hers. As she expected, the arrival of Prince von Angensperg created a minor sensation.

"Can a priest be a prince?" someone asked.

"I was rather a small prince, and for rather a short time," Alexander said modestly. "Our lands are less than a county here in Kansas. The title is now my nephew's."

Names came at him from every side and, once again, Alexander was struck by the youth of everyone around him. Few appeared beyond thirty, and most were a good deal younger. Only one among them was approaching forty: Mr. Robert Wright, an unimposing man with an ill-considered walrus mustache that only made his receding chin look weaker. He was, however, the owner of the biggest store in town, the city's postmaster, and a recently elected Kansas state representative who talked at length about his admiration for Johnnie's gumption. ("Reading all the time," Bob said. "That boy was trying to make something of himself. Real admirable, sir. Real admirable.") A Mr. Hamilton Bell was also important in some way having to do with elephants. He seemed to feel responsible for Johnnie's death somehow.

Before Alexander could ask about that, a man named Chalkie Beeson introduced himself. ("It's really Chalkley, sir, but nobody

157

says it right.") He owned the Long Branch, whatever that was, and talked about a brass band that would have played for Johnnie's funeral, except that the instruments hadn't arrived from St. Louis yet. "I ordered the kind with silver trimmings," Chalkie confided. "Cost me over two hundred dollars!"

Each of these worthies had handed him a drink. With no food to buffer the alcohol pressed upon him, Alexander was already working hard to appear unaffected when he was cornered by the town's mortician, whose poorly fitted glass eye was almost as distracting as the moistness of his palms when he grasped and held Alexander's hand between both of his own. "Thank you for coming so quickly," the undertaker said earnestly. "I did what I could for the body, but it's not easy to embalm remains when they've been burned. We put him on ice, but the weather's getting pretty warm, and —"

A barber, whose name Alexander didn't catch, mercifully interrupted the undertaker before additional detail could be supplied. The barber, too, had many nice things to say about Johnnie Sanders, as did everyone who'd known the boy, one way or another.

It was heartwarming but all rather overwhelming, and Alexander was relieved when Kate reappeared at his side and steered him through the crowd toward a table covered by a variety of aperitifs, spirits, and wines.

"And Dr. Holliday?" Alexander asked, pulling out her chair. "Am I correct in believing that J. H. Holliday is also the 'Doc' to whom I owe so many thanks?"

"Ja, das ist mein Mann," Kate said comfortably when Alexander sat across from her. "He's going to be a little late."

Mein Mann. The term meant "husband" in German, but Kate had introduced herself as Harony, not Holliday. The discrepancy registered, though his curiosity remained focused on his host. *"Und so,* Dr. Holliday is a physician, as your father was?"

"A dental surgeon." She lowered her eyes, adjusted her skirt, and folded small hands in her lap. The rustle of silk took Alexander back to his days at court, as did the impact of her eyes when she slowly raised them to his own. The effect was slightly diminished when she added in English, "A cowboy got shot in the face at the Bon Ton this afternoon. Doc's doing the surgery. He'll be here soon."

When they were settled, a stout blond waitress pushed through the crowd to provide Alexander with a menu. The selection was amazing, and he frowned at it in a mighty effort to focus on what might best counter the liquor. Iced oysters, broiled salmon, turbot in lobster sauce, fillet of sole, trout. Roasted beef and lamb and venison. Spring chicken, duck, and quail. Potato dumplings. Green peas. Six kinds of cheese. Strawberries.

Compote of cherries. Ice cream. A Neapolitan cake, charlotte russe —

"Doc had most of it brought in, iced, on the train. I recommend the pork tenderloin," Kate said in German, smiling. "It's Doc's favorite. He's from Georgia, and Southerners like pork almost as much as Austrians do! The cabbage strudel is quite good, as well. Sweet and buttery, savory and crisp in just the right proportions. Those are made right here. Delmonico's cook is from Straubing, the widow of an immigrant farmer."

Alexander was silently pleased to know that at least one woman in this town had found honest work with which to support herself. "I shall rely on your recommendations," he told Kate, and smiled vaguely at the waitress as Kate translated the order.

The meal was as good as Kate promised, as was the bottle of wine she ordered and the brandy she selected after the dessert. There was an excellent cigar at the end of the meal, but still no sign of their host. To pass the time, Alexander offered his hostess amusing if rather dated court gossip. Guests came and went around them, ordering dinners, taking full advantage of the freely available liquor. Every few minutes, someone would raise a glass and call out, "To Johnnie!"

With each round of drinks, the room got noisier. Conversation with Kate grew difficult, then ceased. Alexander had always found small talk somewhat enervating; small talk at the top of his voice was even less pleasurable, and he was becoming aware of the fatigue beneath an alcoholic fog.

With every new arrival, Kate turned toward the door. Over and over, her look of eager anticipation was replaced by a disappointment that was hardening into unconcealed anger. Rolling cigarette after cigarette, she was drinking now with alarming steadiness, no longer pretending that this was in response to the toasts. Alexander was concerned, if not shocked. He had, of course, witnessed indiscretion among ladies at court who embarrassed themselves and others with overindulgence, but Kate's mood was like the crackle in the air just before a lightning strike. While he pitied the poor man upon whom this matrimonial storm would soon be unleashed, he felt no desire to witness the event. Indeed, he decided, it might be considered an act of charity and a sign of respect to remove himself from what might well turn into an unpleasant public scene.

Sliding to the edge of his chair in careful preparation for departure, he suggested loudly, "Perhaps Dr. Holliday has been drawn into some other medical emergency. I'm afraid I'm no longer used to such late hours, so with your permission?"

Fingers drumming on the table, Kate shrugged. With some relief, Alexander rose, but before he could withdraw, he saw Deputy Earp pushing through the crowd.

"Doc's on his way," Morgan reported to Kate, "but he went over to China Joe's to clean up first. He was bloody to the skin —"

The first curse was like the thunderclap that heralds a cloudburst. In quick succession Kate called down the wrath of God on drunken Texans, on someone named Tom McCarty, who "should do his own goddam surgeries," and on Doc himself for "wasting his time with that shit when he can make so much more at the tables!"

Wincing at her language, Morgan took Alexander aside. "I know how you feel," he said quietly, glancing at Kate, "but Doc's really looking forward to meeting you. Educated people are kinda scarce around here. If you can stay a little longer, I promise he's worth the wait." The deputy must have noticed that Alex was impaired, for he added, "You should probably sit down, Father."

A graceful exit effectively blocked, Alexander took his seat once more. Morgan tried to raise Kate's spirits a little but gave up when she snarled at him, leaving uneasy silence at their table amid the general din. Suddenly, the restaurant door was flung open to admit a loudly dressed young man with a mop of curling black hair, who made his entrance to a round of applause and came straight to their table. For a disorienting mo-

162

ment, Alexander thought this might be Doc, but with an impish grin, the fellow dropped into a chair and introduced himself as "Eddie Foy, headlining at the Commie-Q Theater, I'll have you know!"

Alexander recognized at once the voice of the Irishman who'd handed him the bottle of bourbon that afternoon.

"I decided not to bring Verelda tonight," Eddie said in a stage whisper, leaning over to nudge the priest in the ribs. "I'd hate to have to fight you for her, Father."

For the next half hour, Kate drank steadily, fuming and smoking like Vesuvius, while the Irish boy tucked into a thick steak, told jokes, sang snatches of song, and complained about the paucity of imagination American mothers employed when naming their sons.

"Watch this," he told the priest before yelling, "Hey! John!"

At least a third of the men in the room turned around.

Eddie waved to them happily, pointing as he listed, "John Riney, John Tyler, John Mooar, John Pope, John Morgan, John Reynolds, John Mueller . . . And that doesn't count Doc or Johnnie Sanders, let alone all the Jacks. Texas Jack, Jack Belmont, Missouri Jack — Ah, Christ, look who's coming, will you? You've heard of mountain men, Father? Well, here's a man worthy of the title! That boyo's suit must have been stitched from a whole day's output at a Massachusetts mill, without taking a bit of his shirt into consideration!"

Alexander turned to see a giant approaching. Easily two meters tall, almost half that broad, with a nearly square head sitting on massive sloping shoulders, this colossus slowly made his way through the room on a circuitous course that would eventually lead to the table at which Alexander and Kate and Morgan and Eddie sat.

"Big George Hoover," Eddie said, leaning sideways and speaking close to Alexander's ear. "Reform Party, and he'll shake every hand in the room. Watch, now! Grasp the hand firmly! Grip the elbow! Yes . . . Gaze into the eyes . . . Ah, the sincerity! If a politician can fake that, he's got it made. Damn few votes for him in this room, but he's a grand hopeful optimist, our George. That speck behind him is the former Maggie Carnahan. Not a bit better than Verelda, but all dignified she is now."

When the couple arrived, Eddie hopped to his feet and did the introductions. "Father von Angensperg, may I introduce Mr. George Hoover?"

The hand firmly grasped. The elbow gripped. The sincere gaze applied.

"Very pleased to meet you, sir," Hoover said in a startlingly high voice. "And welcome to our community. It's an honor to have a man of learning and religion in our midst. Until just last year, I was the mayor of Dodge City, and I hope to serve the public again —"

"George Hoover has always served the public," Eddie declared in a burlesque of civic pride. "Served the public bourbon. Served the public rye."

"You are the proprietor of a drinking establishment?" Alexander asked politely.

"Long ago, sir —"

"Four years," Eddie noted. "Everything in America is done double-time, Father."

"I am in wholesale liquors, wines, and cigars now," Hoover said, "but my wife and I yearn for the day when Demon Rum is driven from our community and I am reliant on tobacco alone for a modest but honest income —"

"Hypocrite," Kate muttered.

"To be put out of business, sir, that is my ambition," Hoover continued smoothly. "What a blessed day that will be! And what a tragedy young Sanders' death was, sir! The second dreadful loss to our community in less than a month, and all on account of drunkenness!"

Alexander stared. "Am I to understand that Johnnie was a drunkard? Because he had never touched liquor when —"

"No, sir. No, you mistake me! While young Johnnie did not take the pledge, neither had he fallen to the depths of so many of his kind.

Nonetheless! He was the victim of drink, sir —"

"We don't know that," Morgan said, but Hoover didn't even pause.

"— just as our late chief deputy Edward Masterson was, and that, sir —" There was a small noise behind the massive Mr. Hoover, and he paused in his stump speech to look behind him. "Goodness! Margaret, my sweet. I forget my manners! Permit me to introduce my wife, Father."

Hoover reached down and took the tiny hand of a tiny woman whose head barely topped the middle button on her husband's waistcoat. Emerging from his considerable shadow, this miniature brunette dropped a well-tutored curtsy, her eyes downcast.

"Pleased to meet you, I'm sure, Father," she said, Ulster still audible in her voice.

"The lovely Margaret," Eddie announced, "and isn't she a picture!"

Eddie said something in Gaelic then, and the lovely Margaret shot him a defiant look, as though accepting a dare.

"I'm a Methodist now, Father," she said, chin tilted upward. "And didn't I leave the Church because Rome refuses to join the battle against intemperance! German Catholics have fought Prohibition every step of the way in Ford County, and aren't *you* a fine example! If I were a betting person, I'd wager you heard this afternoon how many drink has ruined. Lives blighted. Pay pissed away, wives in despair, sons thieving, daughters on the street!"

Kate moaned with boredom and tossed back another shot.

"The church will be free tomorrow by half past twelve," Eddie told her helpfully. "Come back then, and you can preach all you want, Maggie."

"Not afraid to speak her mind, my little Margaret!" George declared, putting a huge square hand on Maggie's shoulder. He pulled her toward him with affection and not a little pride, but with a slightly better idea of how their audience was taking her remarks. "You came in from Wichita, I understand," Hoover said, and turned the conversation toward weather. "We had quite a rainstorm here last night! It must have reached you by this morning!"

Appointing himself host, Mr. Hoover inquired then as to the comfort of the priest's journey, his satisfaction with his hotel room, his enjoyment of the meal, and his possible desire for anything additional to eat, or to drink, or perhaps to smoke. ("Those cigars are Cuban, sir! The very finest in the world!") The interrogation stopped only when Kate demanded, "Who in hell do you think you are? It's Doc's party, not yours, you arrogant sonofabitch."

"You see, Father?" Margaret Hoover asked.

167

"You see the depths to which liquor has brought this woman?"

Kate was on her feet. An instant later, Morgan Earp was between her and Maggie, who was shouting now about walking with Gentiles in lasciviousness and lust and excesses of wine, while Kate cursed in three languages. Big George lifted his wife off the ground and deposited her behind him, concocted a credible excuse for leaving early, and promised to attend the funeral in the morning. Before the Hoovers were halfway to the door, Alexander found himself refilling his glass.

"You see, Father?" Kate mimicked triumphantly. "You see the depths to which that woman has driven you?"

"The pair of them don't bear thinking of, now, do they, Kate?" Eddie remarked. "She must ride that bull or risk being squashed flat!"

Kate hooted. Morgan snickered. Alexander choked on his drink.

Eddie clapped his hands and pointed at the priest. "Got you good with that one, now, didn't I, Father!" Just then, the comedian's eye was caught by the tall and sparely built young man entering the restaurant. In the voice that filled the Commie-Q twice nightly, Eddie Foy announced, "And here's himself at last!"

Kate's face lit up, only to darken in a mixture of wifely concern and fury. Like

168

everyone else in the room, Alexander had turned toward the door.

The newcomer was in his mid-twenties, slim in well-tailored silver-gray. Freshly barbered, with a neatly trimmed imperial mustache, he was also visibly fatigued and leaned on a walking stick that was not merely a fashionable accessory. Shaking hands, murmuring greetings, he occasionally paused in these brief conversations to cough into a square of fine cotton cloth.

When he came even with Mr. and Mrs. Hoover, he learned that they were leaving. His disappointment at this news might have been just a shade too sincere. When he glanced at Kate, one eye twitched ever so slightly in what might have been a wink.

Uncharmed, Kate snarled, "Just look at him! He's exhausted, goddammit."

Alexander tried for diplomatic neutrality. "So! This must be your husband at last!"

"That's Doc," she confirmed, but her tone implied correction. With drunken hauteur, Kate lifted her head and chose High German. "My husband left me the day that he discovered I was pregnant, *Hochwürden.* Oh, the baby wasn't his," she admitted breezily, speaking now in the language of the brothels, "but the bastard didn't know that when he left me high and dry." She looked at the priest, and then at the other two — the Irishman and Bessie's brother-in-law — and

169

laughed at their dismay. "And that makes my *husband* a no-good goddam lying sonofa-bitch! Doesn't it!"

"Kate, darlin'," Doc said, now standing just behind her. "What a remarkable line of conversation you have opened!" He leaned over to kiss the back of her neck and spoke into her ear. "Is there *any* of Kentucky's finest left? I was hopin' for a drink myself."

Slightly breathless, the young gentleman then reached across the table to offer his hand. "Father von Angensperg, I presume. John Holliday. An honor, sir. Johnnie Sanders spoke highly of you."

ROUGHING THE EDGES

Alexander stood. "Dr. Holliday, you have been far too generous, but I am very grateful for your thoughtful —"

"Don't mention it, sir! It was the least I could do for the man who educated John Horse Sanders." Doc straightened and glanced toward the noisy crowd. "Would y'all mind, I wonder, if we were to move to a quieter table? I am happy when my guests enjoy themselves, but it has been a longer day than I anticipated. I don't have a lot of shout left in me."

Naturally, everyone agreed. Doc nodded to the manager, who hurried off to ready a table that was tucked into an alcove in the back, where the clamor of the party would be muffled.

"Dr. Holliday," Alexander urged, "please, sit while we are waiting."

"You are very kind, sir, but if I go down now, you'll have to winch me out of the chair," Doc admitted with weary good humor. Kate started to say something tart. Like a man calming a skittish horse with a touch, he ran his fingers lightly down her neck until his palm rested on her bared shoulder. "Miss Kate tells me the Angenspergs are from the Ansfelden region. Bruckner was born there, was he not?"

"Why, yes! I'm astonished that you have heard of him, or of Ansfelden!"

"My mamma insisted that I study some of his work, but Bruckner was one composer upon whom we disagreed." Doc took the cigarette from between Kate's lips and brought it to his own. Squinting through smoke, he said, "I hope I will not offend you when I say that I keep waitin' for that man to get to the *point,* myself, but he never seems to arrive."

"Yes," Alexander agreed. "As a Viennese critic once put it: a Bruckner symphony is like *coitus interruptus.* All the work with none of the joy." He blinked. *"Mein Gott,"* he said, horrified. "Forgive me . . . I have had too much of your good brandy, I fear!"

Doc had coughed in surprise, but a slow, appreciative smile emerged, mainly visible in his tired eyes. "Mamma would've skinned me for sayin' such a thing," he murmured, "but the observation is apt, sir! Very apt. Now, Brahms — perhaps you have heard, sir! I read recently that Brahms has finished a second symphony. Any truth in the rumor?"

172

Morgan looked at Eddie, who shrugged, palms up.

"Music," Kate hissed, rolling her eyes.

"I am afraid we are quite isolated at St. Francis, but I will write to a friend in St. Louis who will know this," Alexander promised, attempting to sound sober. "I shall certainly inform you when I hear from him."

The manager reappeared and led them to their new table. Waving the others on, and looking ready to drop, Doc brought up the rear. Morgan got to the table first and gave one of the heavy wooden chairs a shove with his boot, trying not to make the move look too solicitous. Doc flicked a glance at him, acknowledging the assistance, and lowered himself carefully.

"I trust y'all will forgive my late arrival," he said, returning a hollow-eyed gaze to the priest. "I speak no German myself, but I had hoped for the pleasure of watchin' Miss Kate enjoy the sound of one of her cradle languages. Instead, I have spent the evenin' in the unedifyin' company of a Texan who disliked bullets so much, he tried to damage one with his face."

"Your work must be rather like that of an army surgeon in a town like this," Alexander suggested.

"Beginnin' to look that way. Days, it's general dentistry, but after dark . . ." Doc shook his head and leaned over to stub out

173

the cigarette butt on his boot heel. "Roll me another, will you, darlin'? I treated facial trauma back in Philadelphia, and there were plenty of barroom brawls in that fine city, but nothin' like this gunshot wound! Cracked ascendin' ramus on the impact side. Molars shattered, tongue torn up. Mandibular body blown apart on the way out —"

"Jesus, Doc!" Eddie cried. "We just ate, now, didn't we!"

"When do you sleep?" the priest inquired.

"Still figurin' that out," Doc said, ignoring the little sound of annoyance Kate made.

"I got the night off," Morgan pointed out, "but the doctors are on call all the time."

Without being asked, a waitress delivered a tray laden with clean glasses and a full bottle of bourbon, along with a cup of tea and a little pot of honey.

"Why, thank you, Miss Nora. You are very kind," Doc said, smiling up at her. She poured the first round, and Doc lifted his glass. "To John Horse Sanders," he said, and they repeated the toast. More quietly, Doc added, "And to the nameless young fool from the Lone Star State who has just entered eternity with half his jaw shot off."

"So he died anyway! After all you did for him!" Disgusted, Kate lit the cigarette, took a pull herself, and handed it to Doc. "And now who will pay you?" she demanded, shooting a plume of smoke upward.

Doc's wheezy laugh became a dry cough that eased when he took a sip of bourbon. "I doubt the boy expired just to avoid his dental bill, darlin'." He paused to stir some honey into his tea before addressing the priest. "Not countin' Johnnie, the tally this week is one dead, three others shot up, and two knifed — one of whom has no more than a fair prospect of survival. And it is only Thursday, sir." Cigarette between two fingers, Doc lifted the cup with both hands and breathed over the surface of the tea to cool it. "Healthy young men, throwin' their lives away," he said softly, eyes unfocused. "Sometimes the sheer waste is more than I can bear."

From his vantage at the end of the table, Morgan smiled a little, watching Father von Angensperg try to make out what he'd just heard. Before Morg himself met Doc a few weeks ago, he'd hardly ever spoken to anyone from the South, excepting Texans, and about the only thing he ever said to them was, "Shut up. You're under arrest." Tonight, Doc was whipped, and that must have made his accent even harder for a foreigner to understand.

Sometimes th' sheah waste is mo'en ah kin beah . . .

You could see the Austrian's wheels turning, but by the time he began to say something back, Kate had started in on Doc again.

"You look terrible! You'll make yourself sick

175

again! And for what? For nothing!"

"I am beat hollow," Doc admitted, "but there is no fever or chest pain, darlin'. And paid or not, there is considerable satisfaction in the exercise of a hard-won competence. For example," he said, trying to head her off, "the good father here was not materially recompensed for the time he spent teachin' our young friend Johnnie, but I believe he must have found the effort rewardin'. Am I correct, sir?"

"Indeed," von Angensperg said quietly. "He was an extraordinary student."

"An unusual and intriguin' mind," Doc said. "One night, we were havin' a smoke outside the Alhambra and he remarked that the Greeks and Romans named the heavens — Venus, Mercury, Mars — but Indians named the ground beneath our feet. Kansas, Iowa, Nebraska . . . It was a moment of poetic metanoia, sir. I had never thought of things that way."

Doc pulled out a pocket watch and checked the time. It was a nice enough piece, Morgan noticed, but not extravagant, as you might've expected, given how freely he was spending money on this affair. Morgan had heard about Doc's win the other night — walked away with fifteen grand and damn near killed a cattle boss, according to Bat. There had to be some truth to the story. Patching up Texans and pulling teeth for farmers wouldn't

176

hardly pay for the priest's train ticket and hotel room, let alone this kind of shindig. The liquor alone . . .

Doc returned the watch to his pocket and caught the waitress's attention with a wave. "Nora, honey, I am perishin' for a dish of peaches in cream. Will y'all join me?" he asked the table. "Father von Angensperg, I calculate there is plenty of time yet, sir. As I recall, the rule is nothin' after midnight when you are going to say Mass in the mornin' and —"

"All this is costing us a fortune," Kate muttered.

Doc slowly turned his gaze toward Kate. "Us?"

"Yes, us! I bring money in, too. I staked you —"

"A loan, darlin', repaid with interest six hours later." Doc stared until Kate's eyes dropped. Then he smiled at his guests. "I assure you, gentlemen, peaches in cream will not bust the Holliday bank."

As much to spite Kate as to please Doc, Morgan and Eddie accepted the offer, as did von Angensperg.

"You know the rules for the fast," the priest observed with some surprise. "Are you a Catholic, Dr. Holliday? I have thought Catholicism rare among Southerners."

"It is, outside of New Orleans. My people are Presbyterians and Methodists for the most part, but our clan does hold in its wide embrace a few lace-curtain Irish —"

"Does it now!" Eddie cried. "Is it possible we're family, then?"

"Why, Eddie Foy, you miserable shanty bog rat," Doc said affably, "kindly give my kin credit for *some* taste."

Eddie took it for the joshing it was, but Kate said, "Even if you have none, I suppose? Is that what you're saying?"

There were a dozen things about Doc Holliday that Morgan didn't understand, but this was the most baffling: why did he put up with Kate? She was not bad-looking and she was nice enough when she was sober, but at least once a week, she'd tie one on and try to pick a fight with him.

"— so I am not unfamiliar with the customs of the Church of Rome," Doc was telling von Angensperg. "My dearest cousin prays for my conversion nightly, I am given to understand."

"That girl!" Kate said with a dismissive wave of the hand. "Poor Penelope! Still weaving . . ."

"And shall your cousin's prayers be answered?" the priest asked.

They were following Doc's lead now, pretending Kate wasn't there.

"After the war, the Lord God in his *infinite* wisdom," Doc said with sudden hot sarcasm, "saw fit to take my *mother* — who was as fine

178

an example of Georgia womanhood as ever walked this earth — while electin' to leave that vile, murderous Yankee barbarian William Tecumseh Sherman alive and —"

As often happened when Doc's blood got up, he started to cough, and this time it was pretty bad.

"You see? I told you!" Kate said, sounding satisfied. "You're killing yourself, damn you!"

Father von Angensperg didn't seem to mind profanity or cursing, but he was beginning to realize that Doc was a lunger. Concerned, the priest started to say something. Morgan caught his eye and shook his head, for in Morg's opinion, the best policy was to wait things out and let Doc finish whatever he was saying, after he got his breath. Eddie, by contrast, usually tried to fill in.

"Vile, murderous Yankee barbarian . . ." the Irishman recited dreamily. "Miserable shanty bog rat . . . Ignorant goddam Carolina cracker . . . I collect them," he told the priest brightly. "Georgia poetry, that is! An artist with an insult, our Doc."

"*— alive and well,*" Doc repeated with hoarse insistence, still holding a handkerchief over his mouth, "a state that despicable —"

"*Goddam,*" Eddie supplied joyfully.

"Yankee —"

"Sonofa*bitch!*" Eddie cried with a happy grin.

"— continues to enjoy to this very day."

Doc drained the bourbon in his shot glass and cleared his throat before finishing. "The Almighty and I have scarcely been on speakin' terms since the sixteenth of September 1866."

Nora delivered the peaches just then and Doc thanked her prettily, his voice genteel once more. "I must say," he told the priest, "that the opportunity to listen to Latin regularly constitutes Catholicism's most considerable temptation. Johnnie felt the same way."

"He never found his way to the Faith," von Angensperg said, but the priest looked a little dazed, and Morgan sympathized. He'd never known anybody to get as mad as Doc did, as quick as he did, but he got over it fast, too. That could be just as startling if you weren't used to it.

"Nevertheless," Doc was saying, "Johnnie told me that he was always pleased to attend the Mass. He said that the prayer book had Latin on the left and English on the right, and he enjoyed followin' the ceremony in both languages. I recall one day when he asked if I knew offhand what *turb* meant. 'Has to be Latin,' he said. He was tryin' to work out a derivation, you see: perturb, disturb, turbulence, turbid."

"Turbare," von Angensperg said. "To stir."

"Yes, indeed, sir! And when I told him that, you'd have thought he'd struck gold. That boy had a mile-wide smile. Did my heart good to see it. Do you happen to know, sir, who taught Johnnie to deal faro?"

"Pharaoh?" The priest blinked, trying to follow. "From Exodus, do you mean?"

"I'll be damned," Doc said. "Never thought of that! Could well be the origin of the name . . . No, sir, faro is a game of chance, a variation on a slave game called skinnin'. I learned from a freed slave myself, after the war, and I wondered who had taught Johnnie to play."

"Johnnie was gambling? I thought he worked for the barber."

"He did that as well," said Doc, "and helped Bob Wright with his accounts, too, I understand. Johnnie was a hardworkin' young man, sir, but he was also a mechanic of the first water."

"A mechanic?"

"Sleight of hand, clipped edges, cold-decking," Morg explained.

When the priest looked blank, Doc said, "Let me put it this way: Johnnie was dealin' faro, but the way he played? It wasn't gamblin'."

"I won't believe that," von Angensperg said, offended now. "Johnnie was an honest boy."

"Yes, sir. Yes, he was, fundamentally," Doc agreed. "But a dealer generally gets a percentage of the house, so there is every temptation to cheat, and a thousand ways to do it. John

Horse Sanders knew more of them than I do, and that is no small statement."

Doc raised his handkerchief again and turned away. He coughed hard — deliberately and only once. Everyone could see that it hurt him and they kept quiet while he sat still.

"A dealer needs three, four hundred dollars to bank a small-stakes faro table," he continued a moment later. "I have asked around Dodge a bit, but nobody seems to know how Johnnie got his game started. Do you have any notion from whom he might have obtained that kind of money, sir?"

"I'm quite sure I have no idea," von Angensperg said. "Certainly no one at St. Francis had such a sum, and we would not have encouraged gambling."

"Just as well, for whoever staked him may have placed him in the line of fire, so to speak. Dealin' faro is a dangerous occupation. I myself have learned to avoid it when I can," he added, tapping his cane lightly with an index finger. "I wonder if Johnnie mentioned any kin to you. I understand that he was born in Texas, though the family was livin' in Wichita when he was orphaned. Perhaps there is someone who should be informed of the boy's passin'."

"We do not encourage our students to keep their ties to the past," von Angensperg said, shifting in his chair when Doc's mouth opened in astonishment. "It can only hold them back."

"I do not believe that is the case, sir," Doc said. "Johnnie was knowledgeable about his family and their traditions. He took considerable pride in them, as I do in my own, and as I expect you do in yours. Tell me, sir, how did his parents die?"

"I never asked." Von Angensperg was starting to sound a little huffy. "Many of the children come to us after a tragedy," the priest explained. "We try not to allow them to dwell on their sadness."

"I can tell you, Doc," Morg offered, glad to take some pressure off the priest. Doc could be pretty relentless when he was riding down an idea. "See, Johnnie's mother was a squaw and his father was a buffalo soldier."

"A Seminole Negro Indian Scout," Doc said.

"The Indians call them buffalo soldiers, Father," Eddie told him, "because Negro hair is curly, like a buffalo's."

"Anyways," Morg said, "Charlie Sanders — that was Johnnie's father — his regiment moved up from Texas to Fort Sill during the Indian wars. Charlie brought his family up north, too. They moved to Wichita after he mustered out. This was a few years back," Morgan told the priest, "when the cattle drives all went to the Wichita railhead. And you've seen what these cow towns are like!

183

Wichita was almost as bad as Dodge, in its day. Charlie was working as a hod carrier in the city and when he got home one night, he found a couple of drovers interfering with his wife. Beat the tar out of 'em."

"I expect the Texans came back with their friends," Doc said. "To even the score?"

"Murdered Charlie and his wife, both," Morgan said.

"Don't never bow down . . ." Doc said, eyes closing. "Charles Sanders had more courage than wisdom. It is a trait I fear he passed on to his son."

"I blame myself," von Angensperg confessed. Everyone looked at him. "I was too lenient with Johnnie. He argued often with Brother Sheehan, and I interceded, but I was wrong to do so . . ." He looked away.

"Sheehan. Now, there's a name I know," Doc said, narrow-eyed. "Tried to thrash the devil out of Johnnie a couple of times, I was told. Any truth in that?"

"Johnnie, Johnnie, Johnnie!" Kate muttered.

"Yes, and I see the reason for it now!" the priest told Doc. "There are many men in this country who would kill an Indian or a Negro who is disrespectful, or who is simply better than they —"

"Who is Johnnie Sanders to you?" Kate demanded suddenly. "Why do all of you care so much about some nappy-haired —"

"Kate!" Doc was working on the tea again, staring at her over the rim of the cup. "Say another word," he warned softly, "and you will regret it."

"These are excellent," von Angensperg said of the peaches.

He's learning, Morgan thought. And he was sobering up a little, too.

"They are canned," Doc pointed out apologetically, "but they are a taste of home, and a comfort to me."

"Ah! Georgia peaches — of course!" the priest said, his tone changing slightly. "You are a most gracious host, but I must confess, Dr. Holliday, that I am somewhat surprised by your kind regard for a boy like Johnnie, and by your keen interest in his life."

Doc's brows rose slightly. "And why should that be, sir?"

"Well, you are a Southerner, and . . . of a certain class."

"Why, Father von Angensperg," Doc said, "whatever do you mean?"

Morgan shifted uneasily. Doc's voice always took on a peculiar musical quality when he was about to go off on someone. "Come on, Doc. Don't take it like that. He didn't mean —"

"The hell he didn't," Doc snapped, not even glancing Morgan's way. His eyes remained steadily on the priest's. "Twenty dollars says Father von Angensperg has read

185

Mrs. Stowe's little book and now he knows all . . . about . . . Southerners. Any takers?"

"Ah, Father," Eddie cautioned happily, "you're in grave danger of learning a lesson, so you are!"

"I have offended you," the priest said.

"Yes, sir, you have."

"C'mon, Doc," Morgan said, "let it go."

"No, Morgan, I don't believe I can do that," Doc replied with that eerie musical malice. "If the good father and I are goin' to be friends, this is a topic worth explorin'. I am curious to know what he means by 'a boy like Johnnie.' I am reasonably certain I understand 'Southerner of a certain class.' Father von Angensperg is callin' me a bigot."

The priest blinked. "Not at all —"

"I beg to differ, sir," Doc said politely. "I believe you are callin' me an idle, vicious, slave-ownin', nigger-beatin' bigot."

Von Angensperg looked stunned. "I assure you: I never meant — I said no such thing!"

"Not in those words, but that is most certainly what you meant to imply, and I will thank you not to deny it." Doc leaned forward suddenly, the anger open now. "I was thirteen years old when the war ended, sir. I myself never owned a slave. It is true that my father had seventeen hundred acres under cotton before the war. He owned slaves who worked his fields. It is also true that I was served by slaves in my childhood. I was born to that

186

life, sir, as princes are born to theirs."

"Let it go, Doc," Morgan said again, but the priest shook his head. He seemed willing to hear Doc out, which was just as well, because Doc didn't even pause.

"Of course, we are told in Scripture that the sins of the fathers are visited upon the sons. Do you believe that, sir?" Doc asked. "Or perhaps there is somethin' about my *own* behavior or my conversation that strikes you as bigoted?"

"No, of course not."

"And yet you are surprised by my regard for John Horse Sanders. Earlier today, I took my noon meal with a Chinaman. Morgan here is a Republican. Why, at this very moment, there is an Irishman at my table!"

"Which is as low as any gentleman in Dodge is willing to go," Eddie noted proudly.

"And I'm a whore," Kate declared. She was really skunked now.

"Miss Kate's marital status cannot be regularized," Doc said in her defense, "which places all her associations beyond the pale, but I must point out that in many social circles, sir, Jesuits are considered the very worst that the Great Whore of Babylon has to offer in the way of papist idolaters. And yet: you, too, are my guest, sir. Where, then, do you suppose I might draw the line?"

Eddie was grinning his head off and even Kate seemed entertained, but Morgan felt bad for the poor damn priest, who only wanted to know something Morg himself had wondered about, because it was kind of strange how Doc was doing all this for a kid he'd only known a few weeks.

Doc's voice was getting roupy again and he turned away, coughing hard into his handkerchief to clear some obstruction. "I admit," he said a few moments later, "that I might not have an equal regard for other boys *like* John Horse Sanders. Then again, I have never met anyone remotely worthy of the category. In fact, I am inclined to argue that anyone who imagines that such categories exist should be considered a bigot himself."

"Your points are taken, Dr. Holliday," von Angensperg said.

"Then perhaps you would like to reconsider your words," Doc pressed.

"All right, that's enough, Doc," Morgan said. He meant it, too, because John Holliday was — bar none — the most educated man Morgan Earp had ever met, and he could be the most courteous and kind, but there was just no quit in him when he got like this, and he was stupid sometimes about how long and how hard he pushed. Morgan himself had made a study of this sort of thing. You didn't have to be chummy like Ed Masterson, and you didn't have to bash heads with no warning, the way Virgil did. You could give an order and make it stick, like Wyatt did, but you had to leave a man some pride to walk away with. That's what Doc just never seemed to see.

To Morgan's surprise, the priest thought it over and replied, "Yes. I believe I would like to correct myself." He straightened, looked directly at Doc, and declared, "There was only one John Horse Sanders. He was worthy of respect. I am pleased and grateful that he had yours, as he had mine."

There was a considerable silence.

"Sunt lacrimae rerum," Doc said finally, "for he is gone now, and that is a pity, and I offer you my hand on it, sir."

"No victor, no vanquished!" Eddie cried.

Doc poured them all another round. "To Johnnie," he said, "and to men who won't bow down. *Requiescant in pace,* by God. They ever catch the killer, Morg?"

Morgan put his glass down and frowned. Doc could pivot like a stock horse sometimes.

"Johnnie's parents," Eddie prompted.

"Oh! No, but everybody knew who done it. Fella name of Ramsey rode through town right after, shooting his mouth off about how he pulled the trigger. My brother Wyatt, he wanted to ride after Ramsey, but the city marshal called him off."

"Nobody wanted trouble with the cattlemen," Doc guessed.

"Bad for business," Eddie agreed with a shrug.

Morgan nodded. "Anyways, Wyatt was just a part-time deputy and he —"

Kate, who had drifted off into her own world, suddenly turned to von Angensperg. Her eyes were teary when she asked, "And what could Penelope offer Odysseus but illness and death if he returned to Ithaca?"

Baffled, Eddie and Morg looked at each other and then at the priest, who seemed about to say something, except Doc answered her instead.

"Calypso was offerin' Odysseus immortality, darlin'. Penelope offered him endurin' love. I myself just wanted some company." Kate's mouth opened, and she looked like she'd been slapped, but Doc turned to Morgan. "You were sayin'?"

"Yeah, well . . . Wyatt don't hardly ever get mad but when he does, look out! He told Marshal Smith off, and they got into it some. The town ended up putting Wyatt on full-time, but Ramsey was long gone by then."

"And that's why your brother took Johnnie into his home, after the boy's parents were killed?" von Angensperg asked.

"Wyatt took Johnnie in?" This was news to Morgan.

"Yes, that is what Johnnie said."

"I'll be damned! Wyatt never said anything about that part —"

"I don't need you," Kate told Doc, defiant now. "I never did!"

"Darlin'," Doc said, weary of her at last, "the door is behind you and to the left."

"Go to hell," she muttered, getting unsteadily to her feet. She flounced off through the main room, staggering against a table, knocking over some bottles. "To hell with all of you!" she shouted. "I'm going to find myself a Texan! With some meat on his bones!"

In the alcove and in the big room, forty-some men watched Kate go, then turned uneasily toward Doc Holliday to see how he would take it. For a while there was no sound in the room but the thrum of moth wings as the big white insects thumped against glass lamp chimneys.

Eddie was the first to speak. "Hellion and a half, our Kate," he said. "You're a better man than I am, Doc."

Doc seemed distant, his face expressionless. When he spoke again, it was with that quiet, careful thoughtfulness that Morgan Earp liked best in him.

"When I am sick," he told them softly, "she fears that I will die, and she will end up on the street. When my health improves, she fears that I will go back to Georgia, and she knows I will not take her home to my family." He glanced at the others. "Strikin' a balance eludes me."

Nobody said anything. Apparently unperturbed (unstirred, Morg thought), Doc fin-

191

ished his tea and set the cup down carefully before taking a shallow, careful breath. "Not Calypso," he decided. "Athena. She is a warrior."

"And she is fighting wounded," Alexander said, pouring the next round.

Their eyes met. Doc tossed back the liquor and began to recite.

"Desire with loathin' strangely mixed . . . On wild or hateful objects fixed . . . To be beloved is all I need . . . And whom I love, I love indeed."

"Deny it, if you will, but there's an Irishman revealed!" Eddie accused, thumping his emptied shot glass on the table. "Make him sad, get him drunk, and on to the poetry, it is!"

Doc unleashed a sudden charming, crooked smile. "Morgan!" he cried with theatrical good humor — loud enough for the others in the restaurant to hear. "What ever happened with that horse up in your sister-in-law's bordello?"

THREE GRAND GONE

With Kate's departure, the mood cleared the way prairie weather does after a short, violent summer storm. Doc called for more bourbon, and cigars all round, and the crowd began to gather.

"You sure?" Morgan asked, because Doc was tired hours ago.

"Hell, yes," Doc insisted. "Why, the evenin's hardly begun!"

"Well, all right, then," Morg began, "you know how narrow Bessie's second-floor hallway is —"

"I most certainly do not, sir," Doc insisted amid howls of disbelief, "and I hope you will never again suggest such a thing in polite company."

"Polite company?" Eddie asked innocently. "And what would that be, then?"

"Any gatherin' without an Irishman," Doc replied.

"What's the difference between a Chinaman and an Irishman?" Eddie asked, shouting above the laughter. "Either one'll sell you his granny, but the Chinaman won't deliver!"

"Narrow," Morg yelled, trying to take back the floor. "The hallways are narrow! Anyways, this dumb sonofabitch decides to ride up the stairs to visit his temporary best girl, right? And the horse is fine going up, but once he's on the second floor, he can't turn around. Now, James — that's another one of my brothers, Father — James wants to shoot the animal, but Bessie — that's James's wife — she says it won't be any easier getting a dead horse out of the building —"

"To Mrs. Earp, a levelheaded woman," Doc said, raising his glass, and every man in the place joined him.

"— so me and John Stauber climb in one of the windows —"

"Spoiling some poor Texan's fun," Eddie noted mournfully.

"Right," Morg said, "and we apologize for the interruption, and go on out into the hallway, and there we are — looking at this horse, who's looking at us like he wants to say, 'I hope *you* got a plan, because I'm fresh out.' So we decide to take him into Dora's room, down at the far end of the hall —"

"Christ, Morg," Eddie cried, "you're lucky Lou's not here! 'And how would yourself be knowing that was Dora's room,' she'd be asking you!"

" 'Lou,' I'd swear, 'I only know because

Stauber told me,' " Morgan said, ignoring the hoots. "Lou's a girl I've been seeing, Father. Anyways, Dora's not in her room because she's singing down at the Bird Cage —"

"And," Alexander offered sagely, "it is easier to ask forgiveness than to obtain permission."

There were cheers for this useful notion, and the priest inclined his head.

"— so we open up her room and lead the horse inside, figuring that we'd have enough play to head him around, but the stirrup gets hung up on the damn doorknob. So, now, I'm inside Dora's room, and the horse is halfway through the door, and Stauber's down on his knees trying to reach the girth and the horse gets nervous —"

Everyone moaned.

"Yeah, well, Stauber can take a bath, but the carpet in that hallway'll never be the same," Morgan told them. "So, me and Stauber get the saddle off, and we get the horse turned around, and we're leading him back out into the hallway, and now he's headed toward the stairs, but when we get there, the animal just will not budge. Stairs are fine going up, I guess, but he's not having any part of going down. I'm hauling on this horse's head, and Stauber's pushing from behind because — hell, he already reeks, and I've been a deputy longer than he has. But it's just no use, and —"

"Wait!" von Angensperg cried, to everyone's surprise. "You found a mare in season?"

"Yes!" Morgan yelled, and there were shouts of laughter. "The horse caught the scent and damn near ran over me trying to get to her! How did you know?"

"I served in the imperial cavalry in my youth," the priest told them, adding, "Dodge City is not the first town to be invaded by unruly young men on horseback." He waited for the reaction to die down before noting with a sly grin, "And narrow hallways are not unknown in Europe."

Eyes widening seraphically, Doc poured another shot into von Angensperg's glass. "Do tell, sir! We are agog with anticipation."

Alexander's own stories came first. These were matched, then topped by a variety of other tales. The laughter was raucous and good-natured, the cigars were very fine indeed, and there was no bottom to the bottle. Dressed as he was in a soft cotton shirt, without the nudge of a starched Roman collar to remind him of who and what he was, Alexander relaxed into the general conviviality. For the most part, however, he found himself talking to John Holliday, whose accent became more familiar as the evening progressed, and whose opinions were as strong and undiluted as his bourbon.

Before long, their conversation made Alexander think of two starved men falling upon a banquet table laden with richer food than either had tasted in years. The Chinese labor question, Dodge City politics, Mr. Darwin's proposal. ("The notion explains a great deal of natural history," in Doc's opinion, "but considerin' the presidency from George Washington to Rutherford B. Hayes, I believe we can dismiss the case for evolutionary progress.") The electrical principles underlying telephony. Strategy in poker. The Schliemann excavation of Troy, and Lucian's satires, which they both loved, especially *The True History.* Homer's "Wrath" reminded Doc of Saint John's "Logos," and he asked if Alexander thought the beginning of that Gospel reflected the philosophy of Heraclitus. "Quite likely" was Alex's answer, which led them on to biblical criticism and the work of Hermann Reimarus, and somehow that wandered into a discussion of German versus Italian opera.

They only noticed that the room had emptied out when the manager came to the table, asking if he could lock up. There was a short, whispered discussion. Doc counted out what must have been over three thousand dollars and made one last purchase of cigars and a final fifth of bourbon. Cane in one hand, bottle in the other, Doc led them around to the north side of the building, away from Front Street's all-night carouse. There they sat on kegs and packing crates, smoking and drinking under the stars, and talking about home.

By that time, only four men were left: Doc himself, Morgan Earp, Eddie Foy, and the former Prince Alexander Anton Josef Maria Graf von Angensperg, who was just plain Alex by that time, drunker than he'd been in fifteen years and long past noticing how late it was or how soon he would be saying Mass.

Many hours later — when the funeral was over and Johnnie had been buried — on the train back to Wichita, Alexander should have been preparing himself to confess gluttony and public intoxication and a failed fast. Instead he found himself trying to remember everything he'd said to Doc in the deep dark before dawn when, for the first time since leaving Europe, Alexander had felt — suddenly and fully — how homesick he was, how much he missed his mother tongue, and his brothers and sisters and friends, and skiing and parties, and simply having a good time. He had the uncomfortable feeling that he'd become rather maudlin at one point, and suspected that Doc had saved him from making an ass of himself.

"Yes . . . Kin and conversation," Doc had agreed before deflecting the talk delicately. "And good music — played *well*," he emphasized, for somewhere out on Front Street, a Strauss waltz was being hammered *approximento.* "At my last count, there are nineteen saloons in this town. Seven have pianos, not a single one of which is in tune. I cannot bear to put my hands on any of them."

"You are a pianist, then?" Alex asked.

"*Thalberg* was a pianist, sir, but I do love to play."

"Thalberg! So you have been to Europe?"

"Regrettably: no. The maestro toured the South when I was a boy."

"I heard Liszt in Paris," Alex said, like a man laying aces on the table.

"They say he changed pianos the way another man might change horses," Doc said, "to keep from wearin' the beasts out."

"And that he played so intensely the very keys would bleed! I can testify that he drove women to frenzy. A young lady sitting next to me wept so, she fainted during a sonata. I preferred Chopin's performance, frankly —"

"You heard Chopin?" Doc fell back against the clapboards. "I am prostrate with envy, sir!"

"He played at a private salon one night. I was young, but the evening was unforgettable . . . He played the Polonaise in A-flat, and some truly magical variations on a Bellini aria. Such delicacy! His *pianissimo* was like angel's breath! A selection of mazurkas — those were remarkable, as well, his left hand always in strict tempo, but the right *rubato:* ahead of the beat, behind it. And when we thought he had nothing left, an encore! The

G-flat Waltz. It was such a demanding program, and the poor man was half dead from consumption, but somehow he got through the whole —" Alex stopped. "Forgive me. That was thoughtless."

"Yes," Doc said coolly, but he waved the moment off. "Apart from Miss Kate, you are the first person I have spoken to since leaving Georgia with the slightest notion of who Chopin was. We, sir, are an atoll of culture on this godforsaken ocean of grass," he said, lifting a hand toward the vast darkness around them. "Kate loves the mountains, as you do, but my own eyes are schooled to a gentler landscape. Rollin' hills. Curvin' roads. No vista entirely untouched by human hands . . ." Doc looked at Eddie, who'd been strangely quiet all this time. "How do you stand this wilderness, after Chicago?"

"It's a job, then, isn't it, and that's more than I could find at home," Eddie snapped, his brogue deepening. "It's a bed to sleep in and a roof over me head when the show is over, and don't that beat a traveling carnival all hollow, now? And I don't mind the wilderness one wee bit. It's being trapped in a burning city gives me the cold creeps, and if any of youse so much as breathes the name O'Leary, I'll have your guts," he promised. "Changed my name from Fitzgerald to get out from under the curse — they blamed all us micks for that damn cow. I tell you true,

Father: when I shuffle off the mortal coil, I'm going straight to heaven, for I've served me time in hell. Run for miles, I did, me sister's small boy in me arms, and there was us standing in Lake Michigan, watching the whole city go up, not knowing if there was anyone left alive at home. There's nothing worse than burning, that's the lesson I learned from Chicago! At least in Dodge, there's a fighting chance you could get away from a fire —"

Silence fell. They were all thinking the same thing. Finally Eddie asked the question that had gnawed at him since he'd smelled Johnnie's charred remains as the mortician's men carried the body out of the ruins.

"Doc, do you think he was dead, then? Before he burned, I mean."

"No," Doc said, "but I believe he was unconscious. He would not have felt the flames."

"Christ," Eddie said, holding his hand out for the bottle, and speaking for them all. "That's a mercy, then."

They listened to the pianos, and shouts, and drunken laughter, to the wind in the grass and to the crickets. A few yards away, a vixen's eyes caught a bit of light from a saloon, then darkened again as she turned her head; presently, they heard the whir of wings — a prairie chicken, flushed by the fox and caught to feed her kits.

201

"And you, Morgan? Where is home for the Earps?" Alex asked.

"You know, I been sitting here wondering about that," Morg said. "I don't guess my family stayed anywheres long enough to call it home. Illinois. Iowa. Missouri. California. Pa always had some reason for moving on. New opportunities, he told us, but there were debts . . . And trouble with neighbors, usually. It was hard on my mother. And my two sisters hated losing their friends over and over, but there was six of us boys, and we didn't need anybody else. We're all grown now, even Warren, but we keep moving. Utah, Nevada. The Dakotas. Colorado. Kansas. Arizona. I guess wherever my brothers are, that's home. When we're scattered, like now? I guess missing them is like being homesick for you and Doc."

"The early Church," Alex said. "Wherever two or more of you are gathered . . ."

"Yeah, well, Earps seem to need at least three or four brothers to feel right. It's just me and James here in Dodge, and that's still pretty lonesome . . . I wish Wyatt would get back. I keep hoping he'll show up for the funeral, but we're running out of time."

Roman Venus was climbing. Greek Eos — saffron-frocked and rosy-fingered — had begun to show herself over the gray-green Kansas prairie. Alex stood and stretched and groaned.

"I think I must turn in, gentlemen, and get a few hours' sleep before Mass. Dr. Holliday, this has been an extraordinary experience. Nothing in Vienna could compare! Thank you again for all you've done."

Doc was slumped over, elbows on his knees. Head cocked to look up at the priest, he raised a hand to accept the one Alex offered. "My pleasure, sir. Next time: happier circumstances, I hope."

Alex shuffled off, and Morgan told Doc, "You should be in bed, too," but the dentist remained where he was.

Eddie asked, "Would you like me to go find out where herself has fetched up, then?"

"Check our room. If she's not there, I don't need to know more."

"Sure, Doc," Eddie said, exchanging a look with Morgan before he left.

"I can ask Deacon Cox if he's got a different room for you," Morg offered.

Doc's wheezy laugh ended with a cough. "Can't afford it, son. Spent my last two dollars on those Cuban cigars," he said with a lopsided grin.

So much for the fifteen grand. Morgan made a note to divide anything Bat Masterson said by five. "You can bunk with me. If you need to."

"I 'preciate the offer, Morg, but Kate usually stays at Bessie's."

"Doc, I probably shouldn't ask this —"

"Then don't."

"It's not about Kate."

Doc didn't say anything, but he didn't tell Morg to shut up, either.

"I just wondered — and it's not 'cause you're Southern or anything — I just wondered about why you did all this tonight. I mean, I don't know how much a piano costs, but it seems like you could've bought a nice one with what you spent on the wake. I liked Johnnie, too, but you seem to care so much . . ."

Sudden, slanting light broke the horizon and made the dew glitter. Doc sat silently for a time, watching the short grass ripple in the breeze, listening to the red-winged blackbirds down by the slough, and to the meadowlarks and the quail.

Morg was about to apologize for asking when Doc spoke at last.

"Oh, it was selfishness, I expect."

Which didn't make any sense at all until Doc finished.

"That poor boy died all alone," he said softly. "He has no kin to bury or remember him . . . So I took him for my own."

Eddie came back. The room was empty. It was safe to go to bed. Half-amused by the situation, Doc let Morgan haul him to his feet. Anyone watching would have thought he'd drunk himself bandy-legged.

"I fear I shall not be able to attend the funeral," he told Morg and Eddie as they walked him back to the hotel. "I may have overplayed my hand."

He refused to let them accompany him to his room, insisting that he was fine now, and demonstrating it by taking the staircase with a sudden show of energy. He had discovered a few years ago that if a thing could be accomplished quickly — between one breath and the next — it could be done with a brief but serviceable burst of strength, though there was a price to pay. The ache in his hip became a sharper pain and he was winded when he got to the second floor, but no matter. For a few moments, he looked and felt healthy and unimpaired.

In case Kate had returned with someone in the meantime, he knocked on their door. No one answered. He let himself in. The sun was climbing, and he pulled the curtains closed.

Sleeping was somewhat easier this time of day. Dodge roared in the darkness, but it was quiet in the early morning light. He thought, We live like bats in this burg, and wondered idly if the habit of being up all night had given Sheriff Masterson his nickname.

Undressing seemed almost more trouble than it was worth, but in that way lay degeneracy and ruin. Feeling pleased by his own resolve, he slipped out of his coat and by-God hung it up. Carefully removed the

205

diamond stickpin that Uncle John had given him and returned it to the small velvet-lined box. Unknotted his cravat. Folded it neatly. Placed it on the chiffonier. His boots proved more of a challenge. He sat down, intending to take them off, but gave the project up and laid his head against the high-backed chair.

He was learning to doze while sitting up. Sometimes it was easier to breathe that way. The chair was upholstered and reasonably comfortable, but when he woke, he wouldn't feel rested, and that would make him short-tempered. Still, when he was tired enough, it was possible to drop off for a few hours.

Soon he would have a better alternative. Last week, he'd fallen asleep while getting a shave. Upon awakening, it came to him that barbers and dentists had the same basic requirements for working on people's heads. A reclining chair that could be raised to a comfortable level would reduce the muscular effort expended while leaning over during examinations, and he could nap in it between patients. That afternoon, he'd telegraphed an order to a supplier in St. Louis and asked Bob Wright to transfer the money.

Tom McCarty had been generous about sharing his clinic space, accepting no payment apart from occasional help with injuries of the face, teeth, or neck. Still, it would be good to have a proper office of his own again, and Deacon Cox had given him very reasonable terms on No. 24, Dodge House.

Jau Dong-Sing was surprisingly distressed by this good news when told of the new office. Mr. Jau had peculiar ideas about numbers. "Twenty-four no good! Bad luck for you," the Chinaman had insisted with strenuous conviction. "Number nine much better."

Too late now. The lease was signed.

In any case, he himself did not believe in lucky numbers. He did not believe in luck at all, good or bad. Gamblers believed in luck, and he was not a gambler. Never had been, never would be. John Henry Holliday believed in mathematics, in statistics, in the computation of odds. Fifty-two cards in a deck. Make it easy. Say it's fifty. Any card has a 2 percent chance of being dealt from a full deck. Keep track of what's out. Adjust the probabilities as the hand progresses. Observe your opponents. Be aware of the chemistry of the table, the nerves, the tells. At his best, he played poker with the same combination of informed artistry and complete concentration he had once brought to the keyboard, and yet . . .

There is always something else — something uncontrollable — at work in every hand. The most cold-blooded card counter knows that, though he might not name it luck.

Moera, the Greeks called Mother Fate, the ancient apportioner of lots. Her decisions were unalterable and made long before a mortal's birth, rendering human striving valueless and vain. Fortuna was the Romans' answer to that grim Grecian goddess. Not everything was settled before a babe drew breath, but Fortune ruled over half of life; her caprices could explain why a man might prosper one day and come to ruin the next, without a single change in his habits or his character. Providence, Christianity countered. Destiny is divinely dictated, but influenced as well by our decisions and our deeds. Providence, moreover, holds out the promise that, one day, a just God's plan will be made known to his puzzled people.

John Henry Holliday believed in none of them.

He did not imagine that Moera had decreed before his birth that he would die as soon and as wretchedly as his young mother had. He could not accept that Fortuna might smile on him for half of his short life, only to watch pitilessly while his lungs gave out, leaving him to suffocate slowly. He refused to bow before a Providence determined to deliver him to an unmarked pauper's grave in Colorado, fifteen hundred miles from the home he would never see again.

John Henry Holliday believed in science, in rationality, and in free will. He believed in study, in the methodical acquisition and accumulation of useful skills. He believed that he could homestead his future with planning and preparation: sending scouts ahead and settling it with pioneering effort. Above all, he believed in practice, which increased predictability and reduced the element of chance in any situation.

The very word made him feel calm. Piano practice. Dental practice. Pistol practice, poker practice. Practice was power. Practice was authority over his own destiny.

Luck? That was what fools called ignorance and laziness and despair when they gave themselves up to the turn of a card, and lost, and lost, and lost . . .

An hour later, he woke to Kate's fingers on his buttons, to her lips, to her voice, to her breath, whiskey sweet, smoke sour.

"Viens au lit," she was saying. *"Viens t'allonger près de moi, mon amour."*

"Darlin', please," he mumbled. "I am beat flat. I can't —"

"You don't have to do nothing, Doc. I'll do it all," she said. "You'll sleep good."

"I *was* sleepin'." His voice sounded fretful and peevish, even to himself, and he tried to spunk up. "You have to let me rest, Kate."

"I'm sorry. I'm sorry, Doc. I was drunk last night, that's all. I'll make it up to you. I'll make it right."

The vulgarity. The exaggerated, theatrical, lascivious carnality. All that was gone. In its place was this fearful, earnest, pathetic need to please. He fought to open his eyes, too tired to lift a hand and stroke her hair.

"Let me make it up to you," she said. "You'll get some rest, you'll feel better."

He was consumptive and exhausted; he was male and twenty-six. And Kate, too, was practiced in her trade.

"See how good that is?" she whispered, lifting her skirts now, straddling him, lowering herself. "That's good, isn't it, Doc?"

She watched his face as she worked, saw the growing tension, the rigidity. She slowed her rhythm, deepening her hold, smiling when she saw release, triumphant when his breathing caught, and stopped, and then went on, without any coughing at all.

"That's my man," she said softly. "That's my loving man . . ."

The doctors said this was bad for him, but she knew that they were wrong. They all said something different. He should rest. He should exercise. He should go to the mountains. He should stay on the plains. Get plenty of fresh air. No, stay inside. They said the smoking was bad for him, the drinking, the all-night games, but he could make so much money at the tables, and it was so easy for him! It was this day work that was killing him, anybody could see that. And it didn't pay!

Doctors don't know nothing, she told herself. They said he'd be dead by now, but

I'm good for him. He don't cough with me.

She waited until he slipped from her, then lifted herself and backed away. Leaving him asleep in the chair, she lay down on their bed and watched his thin chest rise and fall, rise and fall, regular and even.

Well, a little shallow, a little labored . . .

Don't mean nothing, she told herself, but he looked so pale in the sunlight, his skin as colorless as his ash-blond hair.

"Ne meurs pas, mon amour. Non morais," she whispered in the language of love, and the language of prayer. "Don't die on me, Doc," she whispered, over and over, watching him until her own eyelids drooped and closed. "Don't die on me. Don't die . . ."

When Wyatt Earp rode across the Arkansas River toll bridge into Dodge the morning after Johnnie's funeral, it was not quite noon and the city was still pretty much asleep. Apart from a few hungover cowpunchers who'd drawn the short straw and had to work the stockyards, the only things moving were cottonwood fluff, dust, and Dog Kelley, who was crossing Front Street with half a dozen skinny greyhounds.

Dog knew what was coming, and waited. "Wyatt," he said. "Welcome back."

"You still mayor?" Wyatt asked.

"Reelected in April," Dog confirmed.

"Still looking for a chief deputy?"

"Job's open yet."

"If you'd hired me in the first place," Wyatt said, "Ed Masterson would still be alive."

Dog squinted up toward a clouding sky, scratching at the three-day beard on his stretched-out neck. "Wyatt," he said peaceably, "you're probably right about that."

Wyatt Earp was the most fearless man Dog Kelley had ever met, and Dog had known a fair number of truly brave men in his time, for he had ridden under the Stars and Bars in the late war, and courage was commonplace among his comrades. That said, Wyatt Earp was not *quite* the most arrogant bastard Dog had ever met, for Sergeant James H. Kelley had also served in the U.S. Cavalry after the war, scouting for General George Armstrong Custer. It was, in fact, a direct result of Custer's unwavering, unflappable belief that he was something awful damn special in the eyes of God and man that Dog Kelley had inherited his former commander's pack of coursers and wolfhounds, acquiring a nickname into the bargain.

No doubt about it: George Custer took first prize for arrogance. But give the devil his due, Dog thought, watching Wyatt ride on. That prissy goddam sonofabitch comes in a real close second.

Just then Bob Wright appeared outside his store with a broom. "So," Bob said to Dog, sweeping up the boardwalk, "Wyatt's back.

That's good news for the town."

"Could be," said Dog.

"Say, Dog! You suppose the town oughta hire Wyatt again?" Bob asked.

Like he hadn't already decided.

"Maybe so," said Dog.

"Let's talk about that at the city council meeting," Bob said.

Like it was a suggestion.

"Whatever you say, Bob," Dog replied, but his eyes were on Wyatt, who was halfway down Front Street now.

I'll take honest arrogance over fake humility any day, Dog thought.

"See you at council," he said.

Bat Masterson was sitting in front of the Green Front. He was dressed like he was going to a wedding except for a black mourning band around his arm for his brother. Wyatt drew up.

"Hey, Wyatt," Bat called. "You finally shoot that two-dollar horse?"

"This's him. You spend all your money on clothes, or just most of it?"

"Appearances count, my friend. Appearances count."

"I was sorry to hear about Ed. What happened?"

"Drunk shot him."

"Hell. You get the drunk?"

Bat looked like he was deciding something.

213

Then he said, "Damn right I did."

"Good." Wyatt glanced over his shoulder at the Elephant Barn. "When'd that happen?"

"Monday night," Bat told him, and looked away.

It wasn't until he found Morgan that Wyatt learned the rest.

The first time a man was killed in Dodge, the corpse just lay around all day until, toward evening, somebody decided to dig a hole in a scrubby little hill northwest of Front Street. The deceased was buried as he'd died: with his boots on and without the dignity of a coffin.

Boot Hill received sixty-two more bodies in the next three years — mostly killings, though smallpox took a few one season. At that rate, it wasn't long before Dodge outgrew its makeshift cemetery. On top of the crowding, there was the additional problem of where to bury townspeople whose friends and families didn't want to plant their dearly departed next to some overconfident fool who'd picked a fight with the wrong stranger in a bar. So Bob Wright opened the Prairie Grove Cemetery down by the Union Church. It was prettier than Boot Hill, but you had to pay to get in.

Leave it to Bob, everybody said. Damn if he didn't find a way to make money off you, even after you was dead.

"It was a real good funeral, Wyatt," Morgan told him. "Almost as handsome as the one for Ed Masterson. That priest — Alex? He came in from Wichita. The service was real pretty." Wyatt was staring at the plank with Johnnie's name and dates. "Wasn't sure about his birthday . . . Did I get it right?"

"Near enough, I guess."

"Alex said you took Johnnie in. After his parents."

"Owed him that much. Ramsey got off clean." Wyatt ran a hand over his face. "I shoulda known better'n to let him stay in Dodge. He was doing good in school. I shoulda taken him straight back to St. Francis."

"Wyatt, I been wondering . . . Why'd you pick a Catholic school for Johnnie?"

"White school wouldn't have him." Wyatt frowned and looked away. "I don't guess there was any money in his room."

"Nope. Just his clothes and some books."

A wilted bouquet was lying on the mound. Wildflowers, purple and yellow and pink, but tied with a thin black ribbon. "Who left those flowers?" Wyatt asked.

Morgan shrugged. "Hell if I know."

Wyatt bent over and picked up a playing card half-shoved into the dirt near the bouquet. Ace of hearts. There were some words written on it. "*Mix forever with the . . . elements, brother to* — What's that word?"

215

"Insensible."

"*Brother to insensible rock.* Make any sense to you?"

"Sounds like some kinda poetry," Morgan said. "Must have been Doc left that. He couldn't come to the funeral, but he threw a hell of a wake for Johnnie."

Wyatt looked surprised. "Why would McCarty do that?"

"Not Doc McCarty. Town's got a dentist now. John Holliday. He says he met you down by Fort Griffin."

"Skinny? From Georgia?"

"Yeah, that's him. Bat says Doc's real dangerous, but —"

"Bat's full of it. Always has been. But there's talk about Holliday."

"No trouble here. Couple of fights with his woman. Kate's registered as his wife at Dodge House, but about half the time she's over at James and Bessie's."

"Working?"

Morgan smirked. "I don't think she's there for the uplifting conversation."

"His idea?"

"Doc puts up with it. More like Kate pimps him, the way she finds poker games for him."

Wyatt looked at the card in his hand once more before pushing it back into the dirt where he'd found it.

With anyone else, Morgan would have known what to do next. Take him to a bar or a brothel, or both. Get him drunk, get him laid. Wyatt might have been a happier man, and better liked, if he developed a taste for the commoner vices, but he didn't drink and he didn't fornicate. Didn't even curse. Worst word he ever used was *hell.*

"Jake Collar opened up a soda fountain in his place this spring," Morgan told him. "How 'bout I buy you an ice cream?"

They walked back into town. It was getting hot. A gang of drovers came rumbling over the bridge, hollering and waving their hats and shooting into the air. One of them rode up onto the boardwalk and straight into the Long Branch.

Wyatt watched, indifferent. Wasn't his job to deal with them, not yet.

He looked down the street toward where the old Elephant Barn had stood. The debris had been shoved off to one side. New walls were already framed up. A crew boss was yelling orders as two dozen men hoisted a truss into place. Wyatt would pasture Dick out by Anderson's for now, but he could move the horse back into Ham's by next week, looked like.

For a long time, he said nothing at all but he was thinking hard, grateful that Morgan left him alone as he worked out what was bothering him.

What business did Johnnie have in the barn that night? he wondered. Why would he go

there at all? Johnnie Sanders didn't have a
horse.

STACKING THE DECK

One by one, the Dodge City fathers assembled around the poker table on the second floor of Wright's General Outfitting. Cigar smoke climbed the walls, pooling in the ceiling, filling the room like a fog.

"Anybody know where Dog's at?" Bob Wright asked, half an hour into the game. "I'll raise, I guess."

"Start without him," Deacon Cox suggested. "Call."

"Can't do that, Deacon. Dog's the mayor."

Chalkie Beeson folded. "Why ain't you mayor, Bob?"

"I'm awful busy these days, what with being representative and going to Topeka all the time. Anyways, it was Dog's turn. Deacon?"

"Pair of jacks."

"Well, all I got's a pair, too, but they're ladies," Bob said, sounding apologetic.

"Damn," said Deacon. "Your deal, Chalk."

Several hundred dollars circulated. A great deal of detail about Chalkie Beeson's new brass band was conveyed and ignored. A bottle's contents disappeared. Finally the click of nails and the ropy thump of a long, nearly hairless tail announced the arrival of a bony harlequin hound hauling its narrow carcass up the stairs, a few steps ahead of Dog Kelley.

" 'Bout time, Dog," Bob said quietly.

"That is the ugliest animal I ever seen," Chalkie said, just like he did every damn time the council met. "He ain't got enough room in that skull for a prairie dog's brains."

"Don't have to be smart to be fast," Dog said, sitting. "Told you not to bet against him Sunday. What's the ante?"

"Sawbuck," Deacon told him. "Bob? Let's get started."

"Well, all right, then," Bob said. "I call to order the Dodge City Council meeting of June fourth, 1878, at" — Bob pulled out his pocket watch — "at nine forty-five P.M. Let's begin with a prayer. Mayor Kelley?"

Placing his palms together just like his dear old mother taught him, James H. Kelley aimed his eyes heavenward. "May the saints preserve us, the Blessed Mother protect us, and the Lord Jesus Christ save us from honest men and Methodists."

"Amen to that," said Chalkie. "You don't drink? Fine, but don't tell the rest of us to go dry. Deacon! Ante up."

Deacon Cox tossed ten dollars into the pot.

"And may God damn George Hoover to

eternal hellfire while he's at it," Chalkie added. "Tell me that jackass ain't putting together a Reform ticket to run against us again."

"The man is an opportunist," Deacon said.

"Know what an opportunist tells you?" Dog asked, looking straight at Bob. "Tells you who's winnin'."

Takes one to know one, Bob thought.

"Raise you twenty," Dog said.

Bob folded. "You fellas see who's back in town?" he asked. "Wyatt."

There were groans around the table.

"He wants chief deputy," Dog told them, and the groans got louder.

"Newspaper's on his side, too." Bob reached down for a copy of the *Dodge City Times* lying on the floor by his chair. "Says here, *Mr. Wyatt Earp, who served with credit on the police force last summer, arrived in this city from Texas on Saturday last. We hope he will accept a position on the force once more.*"

"That teetotaling killjoy," Chalkie muttered, tossing twenty into the pot. "Jesus. Business fell off something terrible when he was cracking heads last year. Call."

"That was mostly his brother Virgil," Dog pointed out.

"James and Morg're good people, though," said Deacon, folding.

Chalkie had two pair, kings and tens.

221

"What've you got, Dog?"

"Deuces," Dog said, but there were three of them.

"Damn," Chalk said. "Deuces! Is that all?"

"Good enough to beat you," Dog told him.

"I'll give odds George Hoover gets Wyatt to run against Bat Masterson on the Reform slate," Chalkie said. "Any takers?"

"No percentage in a sure thing," Dog said, scooping up the pot.

Bob Wright could have argued that point with Dog, for he had grown wealthy dealing in a sure thing. The men at this table represented half a million dollars in gambling, prostitution, and liquor, but Bob could match them — on groceries alone. It was only a month into the season and Bob had already cleared more than $12,000. Drovers ate on their way north. They ate while their herds grazed and fattened on the grassland south of Dodge. They continued to eat until the cattle were sold and loaded onto the trains to be shipped east. Occasionally, they even made time to eat while they were in the midst of drinking, whoring, and playing cards. There was money to be made, as well, supplying groceries to townspeople and to restaurants like the Iowa House and Delmonico's, where cattle buyers and railroad officials dined. And then there was the Fort Dodge trade, and the railroad crews. Even lawmen and prostitutes had to eat. Nobody seemed inclined to legislate against the selling of canned goods, coffee beans, and soda crackers, so Bob Wright didn't stand to get hurt all that much if the Prohibitionists took hold in west Kansas, the way they had in the eastern part of the state.

It was that steady stream of morally unobjectionable cash that allowed Bob to admire the iron self-control George Hoover needed to keep a straight face while he talked about putting brothels and gambling dens and bars out of business.

Big George aimed to be on the right side of Front Street when civilization arrived, and that was smart. Any day now, the politics and the economy of Dodge City were going to shift from one side of the tracks to the other. And when they did, there'd be no going back. Saloon owners like Chalkie and Dog considered it the cost of doing business when they replaced window glass shot out by drunken cowboys, but there were families moving into town now and random gunfire scared them. Local grangers feared the Texas longhorns would infect their own stock with tick fever, and local farmers complained that the drovers cut their fences and let the herds trample cropland. Soon, settlers like that would hold more votes than those who served the cattle interests. When they did, old-timers like the men at this table — who'd built towns up from the bare ground — they'd be on the outs. It had happened in Abilene, Ellsworth, Wichita, Caldwell. It was going to happen in Dodge, too, and soon.

Chalkie Beeson was right about half of it. George Hoover intended to run for mayor on a Reform ticket again, and this time he'd have the railroad men behind him. The Atchison, Topeka and Santa Fe had a lot invested in the roaring hell that was Dodge, but its owners had begun to back Reform demands to close the saloons and dance halls on Sundays at least. Eastern visitors were disturbed by the open drunkenness that offended George Hoover's birdy little wife, Maggie, and by the same brazen prostitutes who annoyed Bob's own wife, Alice.

Even Bob was starting to be concerned. He tried to keep his daughter inside when the drovers were in town, but Belle had a mind of her own. He couldn't watch her round the clock or keep her locked up half the year. Short of posting an armed and gelded guard in the hallway, there wasn't much more Bob could do, apart from getting her married off before she got out of hand.

Ignore it, deny it, or fight it, change was inevitable. "The smart man doesn't just wait for the future," Bob often told his children. "The smart man shapes it." His whole life was proof of that.

He had come west alone in 1856, a boy possessed of nothing but a fierce desire to better his condition. He was still driving freight for the Mexico trade when he saw the commercial potential of a site where the Santa Fe Trail crossed the Arkansas River just west of Fort Dodge. It was spang in the middle of the buffalo range, but it could have been a fine homestead, with a trading post, maybe. There was a spring-fed creek nearby. Geese and duck, three seasons out of four. Fish year round. Otter, beaver, and muskrat for the fur trade.

Bob kept his eye on that piece of land, especially after he got himself appointed sutler to Fort Dodge after the war. In those days, the fort was just about the only thing on the prairie between Kansas City and Denver. Soldiers had no recreational alternative to standing at the bar in Bob's store, spending all $13 of their monthly pay on drink. Given the fort's atmosphere of general boredom, simmering rancor, and the assiduous cultivation of grudges, manly moments of indignation or disagreement were liable to get physical. Bob insisted it was no extra trouble to deliver whiskey to combatants who'd been hurt badly enough to require a stay in the post hospital. Didn't even charge extra for the service!

When the medical officer complained about drunken brawls breaking out among convalescents, the fort commandant prohibited liquor on the post. Bob considered this an infringement on his constitutional right to sell whatever he wanted, wherever he wanted, to whoever had the cash to buy it, but there was no sense paying a lawyer to argue the point. The solution was to ride five miles west, stake out that creekside site on the bluffs above the Arkansas River, and invent Dodge City.

Bob knew what men saw when they looked at him. They saw a scrawny fella with a weak chin — the kind that was supposed to be a sure sign of mental inferiority and a feeble character. He hated mirrors, but Bob made himself study his reflection every morning when he shaved: to see what others saw and daily renew his determination to turn that disadvantage to his benefit. Let 'em believe what they like, he'd tell himself as he trimmed the luxuriant mustache that overhung his little jaw like a mountain crag.

All his life he'd made men pay for their slights and disregard. In Topeka, the legislative big bugs in the Kansas House of Representatives had taken one look at the storekeeper from Dodge and dismissed him as a good-natured, slightly simpleminded rube. And yet after two years in office, the Honorable Robert C. Wright had deftly blocked a boneheaded farmers' relief bill, and then cornered the southern cattle trade for Dodge by getting the Texas tick quarantine line moved to the eastern boundary of Ford County.

Let 'em sneer, that was his motto. Stupid sonsabitches.

He was only thirty-eight, but he had already exceeded his boyhood dreams of wealth and power. In the six years since he drove his first stake into the ground, while the rest of the whole damn country was going bust, he had made himself quietly, securely rich, and groceries were the least of it.

Millions of dollars changed hands in Dodge each season and every penny of it passed through the massive safe Bob Wright had in his back room. Cattlemen, shippers, meat processors, the army, freight companies, the railway. They all had payrolls. They all needed transfers, checks, credit. They all paid fees and interest. No matter what it was or who was involved, Bob got a slice of every transaction. It all added up, and every single dollar was revenge for the snickers and jests of lesser men.

Of all the men Bob hated, and that was just about every man he knew, only Big George Hoover had ever taken Bob's true measure. In a few months' time, George might well take the mayoralty. Worse yet, he had applied for a license to open a real bank. There was only one conclusion: George Hoover was aiming to beat Bob Wright at his own game. And Bob would sooner sell his daughter to white slavers than let that happen.

So when the time was right, Bob brought

the poker conversation back around to politics, and when it was his turn to deal again, he laid the cards aside. "Seems to me, Chalk, what you're asking is, how do we cut the legs out from under Reform and make a buck doing it?" He looked around the table and saw no bright ideas waiting to be expressed. "How about if we don't wait for the reformers to outlaw vice altogether? How about if we regulate it some, and tax it?" he suggested, like he was offering an idea that just occurred to him.

"No taxes!" Deacon cried.

"Well . . . All right, then, we could *fine* it."

"Same thing," Dog said, shrugging.

"But it's not a tax," Bob said innocently. "And then, see, we could use the fines to pay the men we hire to enforce the regulations. Wyatt Earp, for instance."

"Oh, hell!" Chalkie cried. "Not that prig!"

"Well, see, I've been thinking —"

Deacon snorted. "Don't hurt yourself, now, Bob."

Bob joined in the laughter at his expense, but it was right then and there that he decided to open a hotel and put the Dodge House out of business.

"Well, see, Deacon, when I heard the *Times* might back Wyatt for Ford County sheriff, I thought, How about if the city appoints him chief deputy? It would make reformers who read the *Times* happy, and it would make

Wyatt beholden to us, not George Hoover. What do you fellas think?"

"If Wyatt's enforcing the laws," Deacon admitted, "he'll think he's on the side of the Lord."

"And he'll be makin' money off the fines," Dog observed. "Which means you don't have to pay him much."

You, Bob thought. Interesting choice of words . . . It was time to shorten up on Dog Kelley's leash.

Chalkie grinned. "The bastard's bought — and he's bought on the cheap. I like it!"

By the end of the poker game, the new ordinances had been discussed and written up. Public drunkenness was prohibited. Why allow cowboys to wander the street when they could be corralled inside, drinking and gambling and whoring? Disorderly conduct — understood to mean prostitutes soliciting during daylight hours — was also banned. Everybody knew where to find the girls anyway. *No riding on the sidewalks* passed without quibble. *No horses above the ground floor of any building* took longer.

"Don't need that," Dog argued. "Can't get a horse to the second floor without ridin' up on the sidewalk. That's already illegal."

"I don't put anything past a drunken cowboy," Deacon said darkly.

"Two ordinances means two fines," Bob

pointed out. "Better for the city treasury."

"Maybe we should make it *No livestock above the ground floor,*" Deacon mused.

"That include dogs?" the mayor asked, leaning over to pat his greyhound's bony haunch.

"Oh, for crissakes!" Chalkie cried. "Dogs ain't livestock. Any fool knows that."

There was already an ordinance against the discharge of firearms within town limits. Dog made a motion to start enforcing it. Chalkie suggested they make an exception for the Fourth of July and New Year's. The resolution passed. Then Bob proposed that they outlaw the carrying of guns within town limits.

All hell broke loose.

"Well, see, George Hoover has people all stirred up about Ed Masterson," Bob told them. "You fellas don't mix with the locals much, but I hear a lot of talk down at the store. A city marshal, gunned down on Front Street! Where's it going to end? What's it going to take to get a little law and order around here? So I thought, well, how about if we put gun racks in *our* places, the way they did in Abilene, right? We write the law so's the first place they go into, they have to hang the guns up when they get there and they get a claim number. And then when they're ready to leave —"

"They gotta come *back* to our places to get

their guns!" Chalkie said. "One more opportunity to sell 'em a drink 'fore they leave town!"

Bob smiled happily. "You're right, Chalkie! I never thought of that!" Before last year . . .

"Texas boys won't like Yankees disarmin' them," Dog pointed out.

"Aw, hell. You're right, Dog," Bob said, sounding abashed. "Why, just telling them to take off their guns'll be dangerous. Arresting them if they refuse'll be even worse. After what happened to Ed, we can't ask the police to take chances like that. Forget the whole idea. Sorry I mentioned it."

"Well, now, not so fast, Bob," Deacon Cox said. He was dumber than shit, which was to say, almost dumber than Chalkie, but Deacon thought he was real sharp. "I believe that a fine, upstanding lawman like Wyatt Earp would do his duty, no matter how dangerous it is."

"And if the sonofabitch gets killed like Ed did?" Chalkie asked. "We'll give him a fine funeral. Fifty bucks says he's dead before the Fourth!"

"I'll take that," Dog said comfortably. "I don't like him, but Wyatt gets the job done."

"How much should we pay him in the meantime?" Deacon asked.

Bob said, "Ed got a hundred a month, and three bucks for every arrest."

Chalkie said, "Make it seventy-five salary,

231

and two bucks for the arrests. The lower the fee, the more chances he'll take."

Dog shook his head. "Can't see cuttin' the pay like that."

Bob let them argue a while before suggesting a vote on Wyatt's salary. Dog lost. Deacon Cox made a motion that the meeting be adjourned. Chalk seconded. The men stood. Dog's greyhound rolled off his bony back and rattled himself all over in preparation for departure.

"What do you think, Dog? Will that horse of yours win on the Fourth?" Chalkie asked as they made their way toward the stairs.

"Fastest quarter-miler in Ford County," Dog said.

"I lost money on him last month," Bob lied.

"Like hell you did," Dog said over his shoulder, without even doing Bob the courtesy of glancing back. "You never lost a nickel in your life, Bob."

"Hey, fellas?" Bob called, before they got down the stairs. "I heard something else at the store you might be interested in."

This time, they turned to look up at him, and Bob Wright knew exactly what they saw. Good ole Bob. Simple, uncomplicated Bob.

"There's probably no truth to it," he said, "but people are saying maybe George Hoover paid somebody to start that fire in the Elephant Barn."

"Why in hell would he do that?" Dog asked.

There were a few more of his damn grey-hounds circling at the bottom of the staircase, and Bob sighed inwardly.

"Well," Bob said, "I guess maybe he couldn't wait to get elected fair. Maybe he figured if Reform couldn't close the businesses south of Front legally, he could burn 'em out. Maybe he figured the fire would spread on that side without touching his place on this side of the tracks."

"Why start a fire in Ham Bell's place?" Chalkie objected. "Ham's Reform, too."

"Throw off the suspicion," Deacon said shrewdly, and Bob almost laughed.

They clomped down the staircase and patted Dog's hounds, who whined and curled under their hands. Bob let them out, cleaned up some dog shit and a puddle of piss, locked the store doors, and went home satisfied by the evening's accomplishments.

Nobody even noticed that he'd won close to $800.

"How was the game, Daddy?" Belle asked when Bob got home.

"Fine," he said. "You didn't have to wait up, honey."

"Oh, but I wanted to, Daddy."

The words were nice as pie, though there was something about the niceness that seemed false. Like father, like daughter, Bob thought. The notion did not please him.

"How much did you win, Daddy?"

"Oh, more than I lost, I reckon."

She laughed, a shimmery musical sound. Like crystal: brilliant and brittle. It broke his heart, the chill between them now. Why, just last year, she was happy to be his little angel.

"Did you hear the news?" Belle asked. "Mr. Eberhardt killed himself."

Bob stared.

"His son Wilfred — you remember Wilfred, Daddy. Eight years old? A little towheaded boy? So serious at his mother's funeral, taking such good care of his sisters while his poor father sobbed! Wilfred heard the gunshot and found his father's body in the barn. He walked the girls down to the Krauses'. Poor things, all that way, crying . . . Mr. Krause rode over and buried the body. Isn't it sad, Daddy?" Belle asked, but she seemed almost . . . satisfied, somehow. "Mr. Eberhardt was about to go bust, I guess. He just didn't have the gumption to go on, after his wife died. I suppose he never should have come out here. Kansas isn't quite the agricultural Eden all those advertisements make it out to be."

"You can't blame me for that, Belle! It's not my fault when —"

Her large, dark eyes widened. "Why, Daddy! I never said it was your fault," she protested. "What would I blame you for?"

"Go to bed, Belle," Bob said.

"Of course, Daddy. Whatever you say, Daddy. Good night, Daddy."

She started up the stairs, then paused and turned, one delicate, perfect hand on the carved oak newel post he had shipped in from St. Louis, special.

"Mother and I said we'd take the Eberhardt children in," Belle told him. "That's all right with you, isn't it, Daddy?"

She didn't wait for his reply.

In the *Dodge City Times* of June 8, 1878, it was reported that the regular meeting of the city council had been held the prior Tuesday from seven to nine P.M., Mayor James H. Kelley presiding. Councilmen Colley, Anderson, Straeter, and Newton were listed as present. The minutes of the previous meeting were said to have been read. Some new city ordinances had been approved. A salary of $75 per month was allocated for the new deputy marshal, Wyatt B. Earp. There was no mention of Bob Wright, Chalkie Beeson, or Deacon Cox.

"Look, Wyatt," Morgan said. "Your name's in the paper. Spelled right, too."

Morg handed the *Times* across their breakfast plates and pointed out the notice. The waitress brought the coffeepot over and refilled their cups. Morgan smiled at her. Wyatt glanced his thanks.

When he finished reading a while later,

Wyatt said, "Charlie Bassett's getting a hundred as undersheriff for the county, and he does even less than Bat. What're you making, Morg?"

"Seventy-five. Same as you."

"So why does Charlie get a hundred?"

"Politics, Wyatt."

It was late afternoon. They were expecting Richard Rasch's Flying-R crew to come across the river this evening. Wyatt wiped up the last of his eggs with a piece of toast and finished his coffee. "Well," he said, "we're all going to earn our pay tonight."

"Sworn in yet?"

"I'll stop by Dog's on the way to the bridge."

Wyatt was about to hand the newspaper back to Morg when he noticed the advertisement headlined DENTISTRY.

"*J. H. Holliday very respectfully offers his —* What's that word?" Wyatt asked.

"Professional."

"*— professional services to the citizens of Dodge City and the . . . surrounding county —*"

"Country," Morg said quietly. "See? There's a *r.*"

"Country," Wyatt said. *"Office at Room No. 24, Dodge House. Where —"* He pointed to another word.

"Satisfaction."

"Where satisfaction is not given, money will be re . . . refunded." Wyatt looked up. "What's

that supposed to mean?"

Wyatt had a good memory and he wasn't stupid by any stretch, but he had a hell of a time reading. The words never seemed to add up for him.

"It means," Morg told him, "Doc knows he's so damn good, you won't mind paying. You should go see him," Morgan urged then, because what had happened to Wyatt was Morg's fault, really, and he still felt bad about it, all these years later. "Doc fixed a tooth for me a few weeks back. Didn't feel a thing!"

"Gone is gone, Morg. Some things can't be fixed."

"Just ask, is all I'm saying."

"Maybe." Wyatt stood and dropped fifteen cents on the table. "Wake up John Stauber and Jack Brown and Chuck Trask," he told Morg. "I want everybody on tonight. Bat and Charlie, too. Meet me at Dog's in half an hour."

It is human nature to notice differences. Mothers are only human, so it's not unusual for one child among many to be a mother's favorite. Commonly a woman will favor her youngest: the babe in arms who reminds her of the others when they were small and milky sweet and sleepy, before they walked and talked, and made noise and trouble. On the other hand, the oldest is often appreciated for being a sort of vice-parent, providing companionship and practical help in raising the younger children.

Wyatt and Morgan were middle kids, the fourth and fifth of six sons and not special like Martha and Adelia were, just for being girls. Ordinarily, those two boys would have been lost in the shuffle, unnoticed amid the growing tribe of Earps crammed into a series of small houses or an even smaller Conestoga wagon. And yet, Wyatt and Morg were especially dear to their mother.

Virginia Cooksey was the second of Nicholas Earp's two wives and stepmother to Newton, his oldest boy. The family moved a lot and often settled far from any school, so Virginia herself taught all the kids to reckon and to read. Most of the children were competent, if impatient, at their lessons, but poor Wyatt struggled from the alphabet on up, though he was good at sums. Morgan — four years younger — took to books like a foal to running. That was what distinguished those two boys from the others in Virginia's heart. Wyatt's earnest, frowning effort. Morgan's pure joy in reading.

Even when he was little and just listened, Morg loved the feel of a book in his hands, loved the pictures books drew inside his head, loved even the smell of paper, and leather binding, and glue. Lord, but it did Virginia's heart good to watch that child with a book, his solid little body almost motionless while his mind traveled. And she admired the way Morgan helped Wyatt with his lessons instead of making fun of him, like the older boys did.

Morg was as unruly and active as any of his brothers, but from the start he had a sunnier and more tolerant nature. Morgan was able to get along with folks, able to imagine that somebody else might have a different notion of things without that person being wicked or wrong. Morg wasn't slack or morally adrift, but he wasn't so rigid and hard-minded as the family Virginia had married into.

Bless his heart, Virginia always thought, Morgan is a Cooksey.

Morgan loved stories, and Virginia herself saw no harm in reading them, but her husband was dead set against the practice. Nicholas approved of reading so long as it was confined to the Bible and the newspaper; stories he considered not just a waste of time but close to sinful, for they were make-believe and akin to lies. In Virginia's opinion, stories were simple amusements at worst and windows into other lives at best. The way people talked in stories was a source of freshness and novelty after a stale day of listening to the boys' squabbling, the girls' complaints, and her husband's stream of demands, instructions, and orders. Reading about people in stories was like having visitors.

The Earps seldom had real visitors, let alone guests. When people dropped by to see

Nicholas on business, he never said, "Stay to supper," though Virginia would have liked to have someone new at the table now and then. Nor did Nicholas ever call on others. Earps didn't do such things. They were sufficient unto themselves. Of all the boys, only Morgan ever made friendships beyond the family. The rest were solitary in a crowd, reticent among strangers.

At home, the boys would josh and tease Virginia, and torment their sisters, and argue and scuffle amongst themselves — unless Nicholas was in the house. Their father's presence was like the lid on a pot, hiding the simmer, bringing things to a sudden boil. Nicholas had a temper and there was no knowing what would set him off. An opinion ventured. Spilled food. Crying. His was often the only voice during meals. Sometimes Nicholas would read aloud from the newspaper, pointing out corruption and folly and wrongheadedness. More often he lectured the children on their own shortcomings and warned them about the consequences of their failings.

The girls kept their heads down. The boys became respectful and obedient to Virginia, but there was an edge to it. The older ones — Newton, James, and Virgil — made a show of their quick responses to Virginia's quiet requests, doing willingly for her what they resented and resisted when Nicholas snapped commands like he was back in the army, ordering recruits around.

Wyatt was born after his father got back from the Mexican war and had never known him to be any different. Of all the boys, Wyatt was always the most conscientious. From the time he was small, he made it his business to stay ahead of his father's orders. Asked about his chores, he'd look Nicholas in the eye and say, "Done it, sir." Quizzed about the details of the job, Wyatt answered briefly. He was always polite enough, as far as Virginia could see, and he never shirked, but that just seemed to make Nicholas hot up more. All of the boys took their beatings, but Wyatt always caught it worst.

When Morg was little and things got tense, he would climb up into Virginia's lap, too young yet to be directly involved in these hushed skirmishes but braced, like his mother, for the moment when his father would explode because Wyatt didn't say "sir," or because Wyatt hadn't answered quick enough, so Nicholas could accuse him of thinking up a lie to tell.

"Say sorry!" Morgan would plead, speaking Virginia's mind. "Say sorry and he'll stop!" But Wyatt was pure Earp. Even when he was a boy, there was something stern and resolute about him, something that could absorb his father's anger and draw strength from it, something that would not bend and could

241

not be broken.

Wyatt wasn't more than seven when he first took on the full fury of his father's rage, and he did so not on his own behalf but on Morgan's. Morg was only four, but he'd snuck off to the barn to look at a picture book instead of going out to pick berries like he'd been told. When Nicholas went out looking for him, there was no doubt in anyone's mind. That child was about to be thrashed.

Wyatt was on his father's heels. Without thought or hesitation, he darted between his father and his little brother, and gave Nicholas back the language Wyatt himself had heard from earliest childhood.

"Leave him be, you worthless goddam pile of shit!"

It took Virginia and three of the boys to drag Nicholas off Wyatt. When they did, the child was bleeding from the mouth and almost senseless, but that afternoon Wyatt won for life what Nicholas had lost forever: the respect and ferocious loyalty of James, Virgil, and Morgan Earp.

It wasn't the last time Nicholas beat the daylights out of one of the boys, but it was the first time he felt ashamed. He never admitted it was wrong for a grown man to do that to a little kid, but a couple of days later he came home with a book for Morgan.

For the next few weeks, all Nicholas got from any of the children was "Yes, sir" and

"No, sir." He didn't even get that much from Wyatt, whose battered, swollen, unmoving little face was a wordless rebuke.

Go ahead, those calm, steady, ancient young eyes said. *Go ahead, old man. I can take your worst.*

Dodge didn't have a city hall. Generally, the saloon owned by whoever was mayor served that purpose, which made the Alhambra the seat of government for now. The Alhambra wasn't as big as the Long Branch and the bar didn't offer as many drinks as the Saratoga, which served everything from straight whiskey to milk punches, but Dog Kelley's bartender was said to be the best damn billiard player in the by-God world, and a lot of men came there to test Jake Schaeffer's claim to the title or to bet on the outcome of such competitions.

"Raise your right hand," Dog told Wyatt. Frowning at the piece of paper on which the oath was printed, Dog said, "Repeat after me: I, Wyatt Earp, do solemnly swear that I will support the Constitution of the United States and the Constitution of the State of Kansas . . ." Dog waited.

"Go on," Wyatt said.

Dog shrugged, finishing, "And that I will faithfully and honestly discharge the duties of deputy marshal of the City of Dodge durin' my term of office, so help me God." The crack and roll of ivory balls stopped, as did the conversations at the gambling tables. Dog looked up from the paper. Wyatt was just standing there with his brother Morgan and the rest of the police force. Waiting. Sometimes Dog thought Wyatt might be a little slow. "You want me to read it again?"

"I got it the first time. I want to get something straight," Wyatt said. "Somebody breaks the law, I don't care whose friend he is, I'm taking him in."

"Sure, Wyatt. That's fair," Dog said.

"That goes for everybody," he said, glancing over his shoulder at the other men. "Not just me and Morg."

"You bet."

"I want Bat and Charlie sworn in as city, too."

"I'm not sure that's necessary," Bat told Dog. "Dodge is inside Ford County, so I'm thinking maybe we have jurisdiction in town, too."

Wyatt shook his head. "City police have jurisdiction inside town limits. Sheriff's department covers unincorporated territory in the county. I don't want somebody getting off because Bat or Charlie made the arrest."

"I'll swear them in as city," Dog said, "just in case. Anything else?"

"Shotguns. One for each man. An extra, loaded, in every saloon, behind the bar."

"Bird or buck?" Dog asked.

"Bird. I want a bang, not bodies."

Dog nodded.

"It's two dollars for every arrest, right?"

"That's right, Wyatt. I tried to get you three, but —"

Wyatt turned to the other men on the force. "We work in pairs. Point and backup. Morg and Stauber, Bat and Charlie, Jack and Chuck. I'll circle. We pool the fines. No money for dead men. End of the month, we split the cash up even."

Nobody objected.

"All right, then." Wyatt picked up the Bible with his left hand and raised his right. "I, Wyatt Earp, do solemnly swear that I will support the Constitution of the United States and the Constitution of the State of Kansas, and that I will faithfully and honestly discharge the duties of deputy marshal of the City of Dodge during my term of office, so help me God."

He got it word perfect, too, Morgan noticed, which was better than either Bat or Charlie did when Dog swore them in. By that time, everybody in the saloon was watching as Wyatt pinned the badge on his shirt and drew a map in the beer slops on a table.

"The river," he said, making a wavy line. "The bridge." A straight line over the wavy one. "Tollbooth." A dot, and then a T-shape. "Bridge Street. Front."

He looked up. The deputies nodded.

"Morg and Stauber: north end of the bridge, here and here. Bat and Charlie, south end. Jack and Chuck, down at the corner, second-floor windows of the Green Front and the Lady Gay. Street's mine."

Wyatt looked at each one of his men in turn, for that was what they were. His, and no argument about it.

"Everyone carries a shotgun, every night. You need help, fire it. Rest of us'll come on. You see any weapon at all, bash whoever's carrying it. Don't argue. Don't explain. Don't wait."

He looked away and then at each of them. Bat. Charlie Bassett. Chuck and Jack. John Stauber. Morgan.

"Last time I saw a lawman gunned down, the drunk who did it walked away for a twelve-dollar fine." Wyatt fell silent. No one moved. When he spoke again, he seemed to be talking to himself. "Nobody dies tonight," he said. "We all go home in the morning."

In the back of the Alhambra, at a table as far from the noise and dust of the street as possible, John Henry Holliday shuffled and reshuffled a deck with absentminded precision, watching as the policemen left the saloon — all except for Morgan, who had noticed Doc and Kate there and stopped by their table briefly.

"Hey, Kate. What're you reading?" Morg asked.

"*Crime and Punishment.* Translated from the Russian."

"Sounds interesting. Can I borrow it when you're done?"

She shrugged.

"Twenty bucks says Wyatt don't even raise his voice," Morg offered, "and the Texans do as they're told."

Doc reached over to lift Kate's hand to his lips. "You're on your own with this one, darlin'. I wouldn't take that bet."

"Make it ten," Kate told Morgan. "We're short."

■ ■ ■ ■

Third Hand

■ ■ ■ ■

THE RIVER

Winters in Kansas could fool you, John Riney always warned newcomers.

A man would come west in the springtime, and it would be just like the newspaper said. Homesteads weren't free anymore, but they were sure enough dirt cheap. There were no trees to clear nor swamps to drain. No rocks to dig out before you could break ground. First day you got up and ran your eyes over your land at sunrise, you'd be so glad you came to Kansas, you'd think, Damn, how'm I gonna know when I'm in heaven after living someplace this good?

Couple months later, you knew just how tough that grassland was, and how hard you and your wife and kids and the mule had to work to bust through it — and not a particle of shade for five hundred miles, sun beating on you like a hammer. Still, you'd get your crop in, and when that first summer passed, you'd have a pretty good harvest, even after the cyclone that one time and a long stretch

251

of dry in August.

And anyways, you could get bad weather back East, too. Farming's the biggest gamble there is. Ask the man who's tried it.

With no trees, you wouldn't even notice so much that it was getting to be autumn, but then nights would cool off a lot. You'd tell your wife, "Well, it's hot as hell, summer, but when the heat breaks, the weather's real pleasant." There'd be cold snaps and frost in October and you'd think, Oh, Lord. Here comes the snow! But that was squaw winter, and November would surprise you. The air would turn mild and sweet, and the light was soft and golden, slanting in low as the days shortened.

The first sign of what you were in for? Just a shift in the wind. Right before Christmas, usually. Huge clouds the color of spent charcoal would pile up on the far horizon. Suddenly the temperature would drop like a rock, and the first blizzard of the season would roar across the plains and hit you like a damn train. Men would get caught outdoors — fixing a fence, maybe — no coat, just wearing what seemed sensible that morning when the sun was shining and it looked to be another pretty day. Happened so fast, you didn't hardly know what to think.

That's how it was the year John Riney took over a farm from a Dutch fella, out north of Dodge. The Dutchie had a run of bad luck and went bust, what with the drought and the hoppers and the depression, but John reckoned him and Mabel and the boys could make a go of it, and by December he could see his way clear to proving up on the land.

Then one day — mid-December — John was out in the shed working on a broken harness when the breeze came up. Before he even thought twice, the wind was so strong, the whole little building started to shake and the snow was coming down like nothing he ever seen in north Arkansas. Can't last, he told himself and went back to the harness, figuring he'd wait it out, but the storm just got worse and worse, and next time he peered through a gap in the siding, he couldn't see the house anymore, nor hear his own voice above the wind when he hollered.

Before long, it got so bad, he said to himself, "Damn if this shed ain't gonna come down around me." So he crawled in between a couple of bales of hay he'd used to prop up a workbench, hoping they'd break the fall of the roof.

He never knew until that day how cold a man could get. He was shaking like anything, but all he could do was wrap his arms around himself, curl up like a babe and wait for the storm to blow itself out, except it didn't. It just went on and on like that, and then the air started crackling, and there was lightning and thunder — in a snowstorm! — which seemed against nature.

"By God, it's the End," John cried, and gave himself up to Jesus and prayed for salvation. Sure enough, he felt strangely warm after a while and finally stopped shivering. In the peacefulness that followed, he believed he was dying, and though he regretted leaving his family, he was happy that the Lord was coming for him.

Later, the *Ford County Globe* reported that the temperature hit sixteen below, and that the plains surrounding Dodge were littered with the carcasses of antelope and deer and livestock and coyotes and birds. Several farmhands froze to death, but John Riney had always been a lucky man, and the proof of it was that Mabel and the boys got to him before he died, digging through the snow with their hands and an iron fry pan. They slid him out of the shed and drug him back into the house, where the door faced southeast and could still be opened, even though the snow on the northwest side reached the roofline.

It was the Lord's mercy that John only lost parts of his feet and most of his fingers instead of his life, but there he was: a cripple, and no farmer anymore. And you'd have to call that bad luck, except that very year, Dodge City got itself a committee and built a bridge over the Arkansas.

In those days, the river was swimming-deep

and too fast to cross without danger most of the time. Freighters needed to double up their ox teams to pull the wagons through it, and that meant a lot of extra work, unyoking and yoking and what all, and then their merchandise got wet because the wagon beds weren't high enough to stay above the waterline. Or let's say you were trying to take a herd through the river. Some of the cattle you drove all the way up from Texas would get pulled downstream and be lost, just before you got them to market. Now and then, somebody on your crew'd drown, too. That was a hell of a thing.

So it was pretty bad until Bob Wright figured out that a bridge would make Dodge more attractive as a railhead for the cattle trade. Bob's old partner Charlie Rath knew how to build bridges, from during the war, so they got together with a finance man from Leavenworth and ordered in a lot of wood, special, and construction began.

Then Bob had the notion that folks would be willing to pay to drive across the only bridge between Hutchinson and the Colorado line just to avoid the trouble of crossing that damn river for free. Which they were. And *that* meant there had to be a tollbooth, and someone to be there all day and all night to collect the tolls, and you didn't hardly need more than four fingers, total, to do a job like that.

See? That's how lucky John Riney was, and he defied anyone to tell him different.

There was a nice tollhouse for him and Mabel and the kids to live in, fairly large and built real tight against the storms, and the boys swam all summer in the river, and John himself could just sit there and let the world come to him. He collected $1.50 for a two-horse team and wagon, $2 for a four- or six-horse hitch, and two bits a man, mounted. Pedestrians were 25 cents, too, but since 1874, John Riney had never once seen anybody walk across the bridge, until this very day.

"Official business," Bat Masterson told him, ducking under the gate.

"Me, too," said Charlie Bassett.

They were both carrying shotguns and wearing two pistols apiece. So were Morgan Earp and John Stauber, but those two didn't cross the bridge. They just waited on either side of the end nearest the tollbooth.

Morgan said, "John, you might want to send Mabel and the kids down to Jake Collar's for an ice cream or something."

"Why?" John asked. "What's going on?"

"Probably nothing, but it might get kinda noisy around here. Better safe than sorry."

Morg's brother Wyatt was down at the corner, talking to Jack Brown and Chuck Trask, who were sitting in the upstairs windows down at the Green Front and the Lady

Gay, one leg in, one leg out, shotgun stocks resting against their thighs on the outside.

Charlie Bassett let loose a shrill whistle. John Riney swiveled in his chair and saw the dust rise from a crew coming in from the pastureland south of the river.

"Mabel!" he yelled. "Git the boys and git into town!"

"Why?" she yelled back from the kitchen.

"Do as you're told, woman!"

A crowd was forming on either side of Bridge Street. Whores and gamblers, and Bob Wright, and Dog and Chalkie, and Deacon Cox, and some kids galloping theirselves around on stick horses, hollering and waving their hats like drovers, and Hamilton Bell and Big George Hoover, and a big bunch of off-duty soldiers from the fort, and gamblers making book on what would happen next. Pretty much everybody in town was standing around like they were waiting for a parade to pass by, but it was only Morg's brother Wyatt, walking toward the bridge down the center of the street.

Mabel came out, drying her hands on her apron. "What's going on?" she asked. "Wyatt, nice to see you again."

"Afternoon, Mrs. Riney," he said, touching the brim of his hat when he drew even. Wyatt leaned his shotgun up against the north wall of the tollhouse, where it was handy but out of sight. "You best go back inside, ma'am.

John, keep the gate down 'til I tell you different."

With Dodge getting closer, the drovers got noisier, and you could hear them whooping now and shooting off their guns. Wyatt waited until the first bunch of them banged onto the bridge. Then he stepped out to stand just behind the center of the tollgate.

A moment later, eight barrels of four shotguns went off like cannon at the corners of the bridge. The next instant, forty-some horses were rearing and squealing, with their riders yelling and trying to check up those ponies.

Wyatt stood quietly during the general uproar and confusion, paying no mind to the curses and demands, just waiting until the cowboys shut up and started to get scared. Which didn't take long because the bridge was pretty beat up after being crossed by ten million longhorns and Lord knows how many thousands of freight wagons loaded high with buffalo hides before that. When they finally stopped hollering, those Texas boys could hear the groan and creak of a wooden trestle that was none too sturdy anymore, and the roar of the river beneath it. They could see how the roadbed planks were kind of rotten, and they could smell the gun smoke that came drifting out of those street howitzers when Bat and Charlie and Morg and Stauber broke, and tossed shell casings aside, and reloaded.

An older fella pushed his mount through the crowd that was bunched near the tollgate. He pulled up when he saw Wyatt and looked at him, hard.

"Afternoon, Mr. Rasch," Wyatt said, polite as you please. "I don't know if you remember me from Ellsworth, sir."

"I remember you, Wyatt," Rasch said.

John Riney heard Morg mutter, "Probably still has the headache."

"I wonder if you'd mind having a word with me before your crew goes into town," Wyatt said. "John, let Mr. Rasch through."

John hauled on the counterweight from where he sat, then let the gate drop down again before anyone else could pass. Rasch rode through but didn't dismount, and Wyatt didn't ask him to.

"I expect you heard about Ed Masterson," Wyatt said.

Rasch nodded. "Good man, but out of his latitude."

"Yes, sir, I agree," Wyatt said. "Dodge is open for business, Mr. Rasch, but you and your men should know we'll be enforcing the laws. They can wear their guns into town, but they don't ride in shooting. First place they go into — livery, bar, store, hotel — they rack their hardware and leave it. They can call for the weapons on their way out of town, but they don't ride out shooting, either. Anything gets out of hand, we're busting heads and jailing 'em. Fair warning, sir. It's twenty dollars apiece to get them out in the morning —"

"Twenty dollars!"

"Yes, sir, and I know you don't want that expense. This'll carry more weight if they hear it from you. I'm giving you a chance to talk to them."

Richard Rasch sat a bit, chewing it over. Then he nodded to John, who lifted the gate for him again. Rasch's crew formed up around him, listening to what he had to say. When he got to the part about their pistols, there were a few protests and a lot of unchristian remarks. Rasch cut off the backtalk with a look, and waited for shrugs and nods and Yessirs before returning to John to pay the toll.

The crew rode over the bridge and Rasch steered them toward Ham Bell's corral, where they could leave their horses and their guns.

Down at the south end of the bridge, Charlie Bassett looked at Bat, who shook his head in dumb amazement. They walked across the bridge, joining Morg and Stauber.

"That was the easy part," Wyatt told them. "Watch for trouble with the troopers."

Mabel Riney retrieved Wyatt's shotgun from next to her kitchen door and handed it to him. "Take care, now," she told him.

"Yes, ma'am," Wyatt said. "We will."

"Damn if that don't beat all," John Riney said, watching him go.

Mabel said, "Don't curse, John," and went back inside to finish making supper.

A few yards down Bridge Street, Doc and Kate waited for Morgan to pass by. Doc took off his hat and bowed. "Achilles and his Myrmidons!" he declared in his soft-voiced way. "If your brother is wise, he will keep his heel well-armored, sir."

Morg had no idea what that meant, but he could tell it was a compliment somehow. "I told you he was something."

"It was neatly done," Doc agreed.

Like everyone else in Dodge City, John Henry Holliday was still working out what he had just witnessed. There was an admirable element of *sangfroid,* but something else as well, visible but unspoken. A deferential civility, he decided, combined with . . . a physical insolence that subtly welcomed a challenge. It was an interesting approach.

"Lord," he cried suddenly, "but I do enjoy a display of professional proficiency! You owe the gentleman money, Miss Kate. Pay up."

Kate counted out ten dollars and handed them to Morg, who was grinning ear to ear. Kate made a mouth at him and looked away.

"Don't sulk, darlin'," Doc said, offering his arm. "Make him buy that Dostoevsky."

"I can make the money back in five minutes," she said. "Let's go milk these Texas cows."

Rasch's crew left the New Famous Elephant Barn's corral and headed for Front Street on foot. Gamblers and whores laughed and waved and dispersed to the saloons, ready to start the night shift.

As Wyatt approached Wright's General Outfitting, Bob called, "Nice work!" Wyatt acknowledged his praise with nothing more than a slight lift of his chin, which was strong and square and chiseled, and which silently proclaimed his strength of character and moral rectitude to anyone who looked at the bastard, which was everybody in town at the moment.

How in hell does he do it? Bob wondered.

Wyatt's brother Morgan was well liked and respected, but didn't draw the eye the way his older brother did, even though they looked so much alike. Wyatt didn't holler or throw his weight around like Fat Larry used to, back when he was still able to get out of the marshal's office. Bat Masterson's clothing account was damn near enough to keep Wright's General Outfitting in the black all on its own, and the sheriff cut an impressive figure for a man so short he wore lifts in those high-heeled boots of his, but Wyatt dressed simply. A cheap, collarless shirt. Dark trousers. Scuffed shoes. Bob wasn't even sure that

Wyatt owned a sidearm; if he did, he rarely wore it. And yet six deputies — each of them Wyatt's equal or better in experience — simply accepted that he was running things. And forty Texas cowboys rode into town like they were on their way to church.

As though reading Bob's mind, Chalkie Beeson said, "Jesus, I hate that sonofabitch. Goddam. I thought they'd plug him where he stood, just for asking."

Dog laughed. "Chalk, you're gonna owe me fifty bucks on the Fourth."

Bob Wright waited to comment until Wyatt was well out of earshot.

"Naw . . ." he said then, like he was talking himself out of thinking something. "Probably just a coincidence . . ."

"What?" Dog Kelley asked.

"How he got them to leave their guns at Ham's."

"Kickback," Chalkie said darkly, wishing he'd thought of it before Ham.

"Well," said Deacon Cox, always reasonable, "makes a certain amount of sense to corral the horses first thing and leave the guns at Ham's instead of letting them come through town heeled. We should've written the ordinance that way in the first place."

"Golly, Deacon," Bob said, "you must be rolling in money. Me, I could have used the extra business when they came back to the store."

"C'mon, Bob," Dog groaned. "You're pullin' in boxcars of cash, and everybody knows it."

"I got expenses, too," Bob pointed out. "Why, shipping costs alone can kill a merchant out here! Anyways, I better get back to the store."

By then the saloons were getting noisy. Bridge Street was almost clear, except for Nick Klaine, who was leaning against a hitching rail, still scribbling notes for the *Dodge City Times.* Bringing up the rear, Bat Masterson came even with the newspaperman and told Charlie Bassett to go on ahead and start the patrol without him. It wasn't much of a chance to take. Rasch's boys wouldn't be drunk for at least twenty minutes yet, and Bat wanted to make sure Nick got the facts right — especially the part about how he and Charlie were deputized to work within city limits, but the sheriff's office still had jurisdiction in the county. So this was not a demotion but an expansion of responsibility.

Nick listened, and nodded, and wrote a few words. When he looked up from his notes, Wyatt was already dragging a dazed and weakly protesting young Texan to the jail. "Doesn't waste time, does he."

"Nope," Bat said. "He was like that even back when me and Ed and him was hunting buffalo. Size up a herd. Move downwind of the animal most likely to be a troublemaker.

264

Drop that one first. See, now, here's the difference between me and Wyatt and these cowboys," Bat continued, warming up. "Drovers are tough, but if you're with a cattle crew — why, there's always thirty, forty other men nearby. You got a trail boss. You got Cookie driving a chuck wagon, making meals for you like he was your mamma. Each man's got eight or ten horses at least in the remuda. Something goes wrong — say, your horse breaks a leg or you do? Why, there's always help near. Now, buffalo hunters? That's a different story. You hunt buffalo, you're the only thing on two legs for four thousand square miles. Jesus! Wet, sick, thirsty, starved, trampled — you'd just handle it or die trying."

Nick Klaine nodded, gazing at Wyatt.

"Yep. Do or die!" Bat said. "Most I ever had was a three-man crew. Just me and Ed and Wyatt —"

"Bat!" Wyatt yelled.

"Doesn't waste words, either," Nick observed. "Guess you better get to work."

All that night, when Bat and Charlie weren't settling things down before an argument turned into a fight, or backing up a faro dealer whose customers suspected fraud, or making sure a whore got paid, Bat was going over and over in his head how he'd have written the confrontation at the tollbooth if he were working for the newspaper. RASCH AC-

265

TIONS, he'd have headlined it, and he thought that was pretty clever. Or maybe NO RASCH ACTIONS. He couldn't decide which was better. He was particularly pleased with his analysis of why cowboys weren't near as tough as the self-reliant ex–buffalo hunters who wore the badge. That was what you called "a good angle," and as the night went on, Bat regretted more and more that he hadn't saved it up for D. M. Frost instead of giving it away to Nick Klaine, because the *Ford County Globe* reached more constituents than the *Dodge City Times*.

The next morning, same as always, Bat bought both papers and read them before he went to bed. Being an elected official and not an appointee like a city marshal, he believed it was important to keep up with local politics, and he was eager to see how the toll bridge story had been told.

The *Globe* didn't cover it at all, which was dismaying. The *Times* concluded its brief account with Nick's laconic observation: *Our new deputy, Wyatt Earp, has a quiet way of taking matters in hand. He gives the impression that the city will be able to enforce her mandates and preserve her dignity this summer.*

Hell, Bat thought, climbing into bed. If you want something written right, I guess you just have to do the job yourself.

Still, even he had to admit that the story lacked a dramatic climax. Maybe that was

266

why it didn't get much ink . . .

Unless his brother Morgan pointed out something of interest to him, Wyatt Earp never read the papers and, unlike Bat, he finished the night with a sense of satisfaction. He'd jailed five of Rasch's men before the trail boss made it clear to the rest that he was taking the fines for drunk and disorderly out of their own pay. The Texans still got loaded, and they still gambled, and they still whored, and they still spent their last dime in Dodge before they were done, but nobody got killed. And all the deputies went home in the morning — excepting Wyatt himself, who ate a couple of boiled eggs at the Green Front and then shuffled over to Ham's.

The new barn smelled good. Fresh wood, fresh straw, fresh manure. Down in the last stall, Dick Naylor snorted, and nickered, and looked at Wyatt as if to say, "About time. Where you been?"

"Busy," Wyatt told him, offering a couple of carrots from a bucket Ham had hung on a spike in the wall. "I been busy."

He gripped Dick's halter and made a move into the aisle. Being Dick, the horse gave him an argument about it. Wyatt got a brush out of the tack room, which changed Dick's mind about the desirability of staying put.

"Getting fat," Wyatt noted, sweeping dust and bits of straw off Dick's back with long, firm strokes. "You're done with oats. Cost too much anyways."

When he got a rhythm going and Dick relaxed, Wyatt started working out the numbers. Five arrests a night, $2 apiece, pooled, made $10 divided by seven deputies. A little over $1.40 a night, on top of his salary, which was barely enough to live on. At that rate, it would take months to pay off the loan from James, especially if Larry Deger demanded a cut of the fines because he was the city marshal, even though all he did was sit in the office eating and doing paperwork.

Course, it was pretty quiet last night, with just Rasch's gang new in town. There'd be more arrests when they had two or three fresh crews coming in all at once. For the next few weeks, every outfit approaching Dodge would be laboring under the impression that Ed Masterson's laxity still obtained. The new ordinances and enforcement standards would have to be explained repeatedly, and every crew would have a few idiots who needed to be knocked cold to get their attention. Eventually, as the cattle outfits returned to Texas, word would filter back along the trails that Dodge was no longer tolerating any nonsense.

Which meant there'd be fewer arrests as the season went on.

The better Wyatt did his job, the less money he'd make, and the sooner the town would let him go, come cool weather. "Dick," he said, bending over the horse's near front foot to clean out around the frog, "I can't win for losing."

Another man might have considered bashing a few extra cowboys a night, just to run the fines up. In the past, Wyatt himself had indulged in the practice, along with a few other habits involving more enterprise than integrity. That was exactly why he didn't anymore: he knew from experience that his conscience bothered him a whole lot longer than the time it would take to pay James back legitimately.

He finished with Dick's hooves and got him saddled.

"All right," he said, swinging up. "Let's see what you can do."

With the sun low behind them, he struck west and took Dick out to the county racetrack, half a mile beyond the city limits. This time of day, the place was deserted, so Wyatt let the horse get used to the surface, alternating easy with quick laps. The track was harder than Dick was accustomed to, but he did fine.

"Best win on the Fourth," Wyatt told him, slowing to a walk. "If I have to sell you back to some cowboy, you'll have to work for a living."

When he spoke to Dick now, it was just to amuse himself. Most of the time, Wyatt didn't so much as *think* what he wanted. Dick would know his intentions from a little shift in weight or a slight tightening in the reins, even before Wyatt himself noticed what he was doing. This morning, for instance, Dick left the track and started off north toward the farms, like he knew they were due for some real exercise for the first time since getting back to Dodge.

It struck Wyatt as interesting how close you could get to an animal and how much you could have in common with a dumb brute. He recalled Morg reading somewheres that when the Indians first saw a Spaniard on horseback, they thought they were looking at one animal with two heads. Wyatt found that easy to understand. Watch a stockman on a cutting horse, say, and you'd come to the notion yourself. A cow would get ready to turn tail and change direction or bolt for the herd. The horse would see what she had in mind, slide to a chest-deep stop, pivot, and beat that beeve every time. A good rider just slacked the reins and kept out of his horse's way, but he had to anticipate the action and adjust his own balance or be thrown for his inattention.

There was beauty in that wordless partnership, and Wyatt could never watch such a marvel without feeling moved. He came closest to it himself when he was on Dick at the line, waiting for the start. Dick didn't need spurs or a quirt any more than Wyatt himself.

They felt the same tension, reacted at the same instant, working the field together, driving for the inside or spotting a break and muscling through to a lead. Man and beast were one thing during a race.

In Wyatt's opinion, Dick would have the advantage on the Fourth of July. Dog Kelley's gelding, Michigan Jim, was the favorite in local races, but Dick would get long odds, for he would take the bookmakers by surprise. Until they'd seen him run a few times, nobody would expect "that two-dollar horse" to be anything much.

"They're underestimating your cash value by a good fifteen cents," Wyatt told Dick, who flicked an ear at him but otherwise minded his own business.

The sun was well up when they turned back toward Dodge. Wyatt was occupied with calculating how much he should hold back from James in order to put together a bet on Dick in the race, and what the payoff would be at thirty to one, when he saw another rider to the east, about five miles out.

Didn't take but a glance at the lovely, floating gait to know who it was. That army captain — Grier, his name was — riding Roxana.

It was his father's voice that Wyatt heard then. As always, an indictment.

It's your own damn fault, you stupid worthless goddam pile of shit.

All them dreams . . .

Trying to get about yourself, dragging an innocent boy down instead.

Shoulda been you dead, not Johnnie.

Dick snorted and jogged sideways a few steps, and tossed his head. Distracted, Wyatt needed a few moments to work out why the horse had lost his stride.

"Hell," he said, disgusted, when he realized that he was crying.

"Easy, now," he told Dick. "Easy. Settle down."

In all his life, he had wept only twice before that he could recall. Once was back when he was ten and his sister Martha passed. The second time, he was twenty-two, and his wife had just died of typhus.

He was visiting his grandparents in Lamar, Missouri, when he first saw Urilla Sutherland. She was on her way to church, dressed up real pretty but still modest and sweet-looking. In that very first moment — before Wyatt drew his next breath — he decided that it was time to quit drinking and quit drifting and settle down so he could be near Urilla and see her twice a week at church.

Before he even spoke to her the first time, he made himself break the habit of cursing and swearing, and that wasn't easy for a son of Nicholas Earp. After years of driving freight to wide-open towns like Deadwood and Cheyenne and Yuma, Wyatt decided he

272

should get a decent job. As much as he disliked his Grampa Earp, he became determined to study law with that cold, old man.

To win Urilla's favor and to gain her family's consent to a marriage, Wyatt made a dogged yearlong effort to read an entire law book, but the words just wouldn't stick. Reluctantly, he lowered his sights and got a job as the Lamar town constable. It was not close to what he had hoped to offer Urilla, but it was enough. When she agreed to marry him and her parents gave their blessing, Wyatt felt it proof that he'd made something of himself at last. He didn't even have time to get over his amazement that such a good Christian girl had married him when Urilla came down with typhus.

"Don't begrudge the Lord what is his own to give and to take."

That's what Urilla told Wyatt when they both knew she was dying, and that she would take their child with her, too: one who hadn't even lived long enough to quicken and who would never see the light.

Wyatt tried to accept it like Urilla did. When the fever and sickness got worse, he was almost willing to let her go, if only to put an end to her suffering. Then — at the very end — she was lucid again.

He had just enough time to think, The fever's broken. She's going to live.

For the space of those few moments, he saw

it all: how he'd nurse her, and how she'd be stronger every day, and how the baby would come and be joined later by a pack of rowdy brothers and pretty sisters. He could *see* the home they'd have, and he started to weep because the vision of their future was so clear, because he was so grateful and happy that they weren't going to lose everything they'd meant to be to each other when they made their vows a few months earlier.

"Don't cry, Wyatt. I'm going to a better place," Urilla told him.

Then she was gone. Just like that. And he was left to stare at the husk of that dear girl, and to hear his father's voice.

It's your own damn fault, you worthless pile of shit.

If you made more money, you coulda got a doctor.

Shoulda been you . . .

For a good long while after Urilla's passing, Wyatt lost his way. He only started going to church again when a Wichita preacher suggested that he honor Urilla's memory by honoring her faith in the Lord. It was never easy and it was sometimes impossible, but Wyatt kept trying, though he did not fear God so much as he feared Urilla's disappointment, for he felt her eyes upon him whenever he did what he knew to be wrong or failed to do what he thought was right.

The dead are in a better place. That's what

274

Urilla had told him. That's what Wyatt Earp wanted to believe, but this is what he knew. Gone is gone. Some things can't be fixed.

Shoulda sent him back to school . . .

Wyatt wiped his eyes with his sleeve.

Could be, it's better this way, he tried telling himself, for in his experience, not many were improved by age. People generally got meaner and harder and sadder. So maybe it was a blessing to die before life could compromise and coarsen you, and twist you into someone you didn't hardly recognize. Johnnie was a good kid, but who knows what kind of man he'd've been?

"Hell," Wyatt said, aloud. "I shoulda sent him back to school."

He wanted to make himself hear his own regret, and to see if his voice was steady.

He was almost back to town before Dick Naylor settled down.

LADIES HIGH

Dime novelists worked hard to make a city marshal's job seem thrilling. They told stories about showdowns and shoot-outs and so on, but they mostly made it all up. Even in a frontier hellhole like Dodge, policemen spent a lot of time replacing boards in the wooden sidewalks, controlling packs of stray dogs, and trapping skunks or raccoons that made nests under buildings. Nights could be lively, what with the bar brawls and so on, but the allure of that excitement faded the first time a drunk puked all over you. Oh, there were shootings and occasionally a theft, but by the time you got there, the deed was done and the criminal long gone, unless he was drunk enough or stupid enough to get caught red-handed.

So there wasn't really all that much drama in the job, except for what police always called "family" fights. Wyatt hated them. Given a choice, he'd take fifty drunken cowboys over two drunken lovers. Ask him,

"What kind of call do you hate the most?" and he'd tell you, "Family fights. Family fights are always the worst."

And they were always the same.

Somebody'd come running up, hollering, "They're killing each other next door!" Get there, and the woman's screaming that she's being murdered, so you go in after the husband or the boyfriend or the pimp. But the minute you try to arrest him, the woman would be on your back, pounding on you with her fists, yelling, "Leave him alone, you sonofabitch! I love him!"

Nine times out of ten, she wouldn't let you press charges, and you'd be back again a couple of nights later. It was unrewarding work, and you could get hurt doing it. Wyatt was laid up for a week one time, not drawing pay, and he got ragged for months about the lamp that whore busted over his head.

Everything about a family fight was a misery, and he avoided those calls when he could, but he appeared to be the only officer around when Deacon Cox came out of the Dodge House, yelling about a pair of his hotel guests who were fighting.

Wyatt shrugged and nodded and crossed the street, feet dragging some after a long night. The argument became more distinct as he climbed the Dodge House stairs and scuffed down the corridor. A female voice, heavily accented, dominated. Her themes were perfidy and abandonment. As proof of her opponent's faithlessness, she loudly offered his desire to save money so he could return to an old girlfriend. A soft answer turneth away wrath, and that was evidently the gentleman's policy. Then the term "bastard" entered the conversation. Wyatt reached their door in time to hear the unmistakable sound of a solid slap delivered to a face.

"You speak of my mother again," said a soft Georgia voice, "I will shoot you where you stand."

"Son of a *bitch!*"

Wyatt raised a foot to kick open the door and prevent the murder. He nearly fell, off balance, when the door was flung open.

"Get out," the gentleman suggested, without looking into the hallway. "And this time? Don't come back."

"I don't need you! There are men lining up for me. I pick and I choose! What I do is less disgusting than looking into stinking, diseased mouths," the woman snarled, stuffing clothing into a carpetbag. "Be damned to you!" She snapped the bag shut and pushed past Wyatt. "And you can go to hell with him!" she shouted over her shoulder.

For a few moments, both men stood in the hallway, watching as she stomped down the corridor muttering curses under her breath.

"I apologize, Morgan," the gentleman said. "I swear: this time, it wasn't my fault —" He stopped and stared.

"I'm Morg's brother," Wyatt told him. "People mix us up all the time."

"Wyatt! Of course. Just last evenin', I was admirin' your work from a distance." The gentleman offered his hand. "John Holliday, sir. I don't know if you remember me."

"Fort Griffin. You gave me your card."

"You ever find David Rudabaugh?"

"He circled back to Kansas, like you said. Thanks for the tip."

"And Dodge is everything you said it would be . . . Well, sir, if you will excuse me, I am late for office hours. If, however, you are here to arrest me for creatin' a disturbance" — the dentist stepped back into his room and pulled a frock coat on over his shirtsleeves — "I shall not dispute the charge, unless you intend to put me in a cell with that *insufferable woman!*"

He shouted the last two words toward the window, apparently hoping his whore would hear him out in the street, but it was poor judgment. The effort set off a hellacious coughing fit.

"No harm done," Wyatt said.

It seemed rude to walk away while the man was hacking like that, so Wyatt waited. That was when he noticed a copy of the *Dodge City Times* on the bed. "I saw your ad in the paper," he said, when the coughing eased.

"You mean it? About giving the money back?"

Watering blue eyes narrowed above the handkerchief Holliday held over his mouth while he was getting his breath back. "Why would I extend the offer, if I were not in earnest?" He cleared his throat fiercely. "Which is it you are callin' me, sir? A cheat or a liar?"

"Maybe it's different in Georgia," Wyatt said. "Out here? Pretty much anything in a newspaper is a cheat or a lie."

Holliday blinked. "I had not thought of it that way," he said. He appeared to consider the notion before deciding, "Fair enough. Yes, I mean it. If you are not satisfied with my work, I will not charge for it."

"So, how much would it be, to . . . ?" Wyatt waved vaguely at his mouth. The dentist must have known that he didn't make much money. His salary was right there in the same paper, for everyone to see.

"The examination is performed *gratis*. If you become my patient, we can arrange for payment over time."

"*Gratis* means free, right?"

"You are a scholar, sir!"

"I read a law book once. Part of it, anyways." Wyatt thought the offer over and nodded his assent. "You don't have to 'sir' me. Wyatt's fine."

"Wyatt, then," Holliday said. "Most people call me Doc."

■ ■ ■ ■

No. 24, Dodge House was dustless and orderly, furnished with exactly what a dentist required for his work and nothing more. There was a glassed-in bookcase and a small oak table for a desk. A washstand, with its china bowl and pitcher, stood next to a closed and locked enamel cabinet. Near the window, where the light was best, a new barber's chair was screwed into the floor for stability.

The deputy hung a well-worn flat-crowned hat on a peg by the door and watched uneasily as the dentist laid a clean towel on the table, unlocked the cabinet, and selected a few chromed instruments, some of which were alarmingly pointed.

"How much is this going to hurt?" Wyatt asked, still on his feet, half-ready to call the whole thing off.

"Unlike physicians, sir, veterinarians and dentists are aware that our patients can and will bite. We are, therefore, diligent about the mitigation of pain. Today I merely wish to assess the accumulated damage. If we agree on treatment, I have ether, which is administered with a Chisholm inhaler. You won't feel a thing during the procedures, but I must warn you that your mouth will be sore when you wake up. Now, before we begin: this is a toothbrush," he said, handing one to Wyatt, "and this is Larkin's Dentifric. A tooth-cleanin' powder."

The patient showed no sign of recognition, which was typical. In his first five weeks of practice in Dodge City, Dr. J. H. Holliday had encountered precisely three patients who had ever before used a toothbrush.

"Sprinkle a little of the powder into your palm," he instructed, while pouring a glass of water from the pitcher. "Wet the bristles, dip them in the powder, and brush your teeth. Start on the bottom. Inside, by your tongue . . . Do every surface, like you're cur-ryin' a horse," he said, watching. "Good," he said. "Now rinse your mouth. Don't swallow. Just swish the water around and spit into the basin."

Finished, the deputy wiped his lips on the back of his hand and tried to hand the brush back.

"That's yours to keep," the dentist told him, returning the Larkin's to the cabinet. "A gift."

Wyatt put the brush down on the washstand and backed off with a look so hard, John Henry Holliday could almost feel the pres-sure of it. "I'll be damned," he said softly. "Oh, that's funny . . . Diogenes could've found his man in Dodge!"

The idea of someone being bribed with a toothbrush was almost beyond belief, but when Wyatt got his hat to go, Doc changed his tone. "I buy inexpensive brushes by the dozen and provide them free of charge to *all* my patients," he said firmly, adding, "It makes my own work more pleasant."

Wyatt thought this over. After a few moments, he retrieved the brush and put it into the breast pocket of his shirt.

Inclining his head with respect, Doc resumed his instruction: "You should brush your teeth at the end of every day —"

"I work nights," Wyatt pointed out. "You mean — ?"

"Before you go to bed, then, whenever that might be," Doc amended. "You can get Larkin's at Bob Wright's, or you can use plain bakin' soda if it's handier. Either way, don't swallow the water when you rinse." He gestured toward the barber chair. "Please. Make yourself at ease."

Wyatt climbed into the chair. He tried to relax, but it was hard with somebody poking around inside his mouth, even if the dentist was only looking with a little mirror on a metal wand.

"I see you've had some amateur work done," Doc said. "You knock that molar out yourself?"

"Ed Masterson did it."

"A sweet-natured man. Open again, please . . . Deputy Masterson's death was a lamentable loss to the community. His dentistry, on the other hand, was notably lackin' in finesse. You are lucky to have lived through the procedure."

There was a silence for a time.

"We all have our vices," the dentist observed, his voice low and near. "Sugar is yours. I encourage you to moderate your habits . . . Rinse and spit."

Doc handed Wyatt the glass of water and held the basin for him.

"Lie back again, please," Doc said. "Not quite finished . . ."

Wyatt opened his mouth again, trying not to be ashamed.

"This injury to the front teeth," the dentist began gently. "It took place when you were about seven, I'd say, before the roots were fully formed. Am I correct?"

"Uh-huh," Wyatt said.

"There is ridge resorption naturally. . . . Some mesial drift, but I can get around that . . . I've noticed that you have some slurrin' of the letters *s* and *f,* but you have compensated remarkably well. Did someone work with you on your diction?"

"Nuh-uh."

Doc murmured, "Almost done," and changed the subject. "It must be a comfort and a support to you to have your brothers Morgan and James so near, but the Earps are spread out some, I understand. A half brother, Newton, back in Missouri . . . An older brother, Virgil, down in Arizona?"

Wyatt grunted affirmation.

"A younger one, Warren, still livin' with your parents out in California. And a married sister. Adelia. Lovely name. A-*de*-li-a . . . Very musical."

Doc's drawl was calm and soothing. The chair was comfortable. Wyatt had worked a tense fifteen-hour night, followed by three hours out riding with Dick. Light poured through the window. He closed his eyes against it.

"I am an only child, myself," Doc told him, "though I grew up with a battalion of cousins. I miss them very much. Morgan reminds me of my cousin Robert, back home."

Lowering his hands, the dentist slid off his stool and backed away noiselessly.

"Home," he said softly. "If there is a more beautiful word in any language, I do not know it."

He put his instruments down, careful not to let them clank.

"Poor soul," he whispered when he was sure that Wyatt was sleeping. "Rest now. Do you good."

Wyatt woke with a start about an hour later and sat up, feeling like a fool. Doc was at his desk, writing a letter, it looked like. "Monologue: the dentist's vice!" he declared before Wyatt could apologize. "I fear I bored you straight to sleep."

The dentist laid his pen aside and showed Wyatt a chart with little drawings of teeth on it. "You have two molars, here and here, that should come out, and soon, I'm afraid. The decay is deep, but you're luckier than most. I calculate you have a little time yet before the rot breaks through to the nerve. When it does . . . Well, you know what an abscess is like."

Wyatt nodded, trying not to shudder.

"There are significant cavities in two other molars, here and here. You also have a pair of mandibular bicuspids in serious trouble. I may be able to salvage them and I urge you to allow me to try — always better to preserve the integrity of the arch, in my opinion. It is possible to do some of the restorative work without anesthetic, but I do not recommend it and the additional expense is not great. I use silver-mercury amalgam to fill teeth and gold for crowns."

"What about . . . ?" Wyatt pointed toward his lips.

"For the incisors — your front teeth — I can make you a partial denture that will give a very natural appearance. If you decide to go ahead with the work, I shall write to my cousin Robert. He is now secretary of the Georgia Dental Association and will obtain materials for us. After the denture is in place, new habits of tongue placement will be required. I can help you with that as well."

"How much?" Wyatt asked. "For all of it? With the ana—"

"Anesthetic. It'll take quite a bit of time. The materials are not cheap, but I will cut no corners on quality and my work is durable. . . . Call it thirty dollars."

"You're not just trying to scare me? About the toothache?"

Doc stared.

"That, sir, would be un-pro-fessional," he said, his drawl more pronounced, the last word drawn out in emphasis. "Is there anything about my demeanor or my procedures that strikes you as un-pro-fessional?"

"No! I don't know!" Wyatt said, startled by the sudden hostility. "It's just — Look, that's a lot of money. Can I think it over?"

"Of course," Holliday said evenly. "You know where to find me. Good day."

Dismissed, and embarrassed, Wyatt had his hat in hand and was halfway into the corridor when the dentist's voice stopped him.

"I beg your pardon, sir. I forget my manners as well," Doc said in a conciliatory tone. "I understand from your brother Morgan that condolences are in order."

Wyatt blinked. "Morgan told you about Urilla? My wife died . . . almost eight years ago," he said, a little surprised by that himself, "but thanks."

"You are a widower? I am truly sorry, sir. I did not know. My sympathy for that terrible

287

loss as well, but I was referrin' to the untimely passin' of our mutual young friend, John Horse Sanders."

It was Wyatt's turn to stare.

"I participated in the investigation of his death," Holliday told him. "Now, if you wish to speak of unprofessional procedures," he said, hot again, "I would direct your attention to the local authorities, sir! In my opinion, the inquest could have been considerably more thorough."

Wyatt was stupid with the need for sleep. "What're you talking about, Doc?"

"Well, as you may know, I sometimes supplement my income with games of skill and chance. I was in a position to have observed young Mr. Sanders at similar employment in the weeks prior to his death. I calculate he was at least eighteen hundred dollars to the good when he died and —"

"Eighteen hundred dollars!"

"In my estimation, yes. I have only resided in Dodge since the end of April. He may well have won more prior to my arrival. There was no mention of the money in the local press. I would like to call your brother Morgan a friend of mine, and I would never wish to question his competence, but it seems to me that someone in authority might have at least considered robbery as a motive for assault and arson! I told them there was every indication that the boy sustained an *ante-mortem* blow to the back of the head before the fire, but Sheriff Masterson decided the death was an accident and that was the end of it. Justice was not well served, in my opinion."

Wyatt shook his head. The man never used one word when twenty would do the same job. "Make it simple for me, Doc. You're saying somebody killed Johnnie for the money and set the fire to cover it up?"

"Yes —"

Wyatt turned on his heel and strode away without another word.

Mouth open, John Henry Holliday watched until the lawman had disappeared down the hallway. Then he went back inside No. 24 to ready the office for the next patient, if and when such a one might arrive.

"About time somebody took this seriously," he muttered, cleaning out the basin so he could rinse the instruments in carbolic. "That boy deserved better than he got."

Isabelle Wright was just entering the lobby of Dodge House with little Wilfred Eberhardt at her side when Wyatt Earp brushed past her looking like thunder.

This was the first time Belle had seen Mr. Earp since he left Dodge in the autumn to track down David Rudabaugh. Ordinarily, she would have welcomed him back to town, and told him how glad she was that he'd been rehired by the city police department, and introduced Wilfred to him, and so on, but the deputy was out the door before she could say a word. He didn't even *notice* her.

Maybe it was because her hair was different. Last time Mr. Earp saw her, she was still in braids. Belle was wearing her hair up now and with Wilfred at her side, she might have looked like a young matron. Maybe Mr. Earp thought she was somebody else. Even so, you'd have thought he'd tip his hat at least.

Not being noticed was an unusual experience for the Belle of Dodge City. On one hand, it was humbling; on the other, a considerable relief, for she had been *relentlessly* reminded since turning thirteen that the entire Wright family would be judged by her dress and her comportment, and that her own future depended on her behavior.

Even with wealth and beauty to give her an edge, her mother had told her repeatedly, Belle was going to have a hard time attracting a suitable husband, living here in Dodge. There weren't a lot of gentlemen to choose from, and Belle wasn't getting any younger. "When I was fifteen," her mother had reminded Belle just this very morning, for what *must* have been the seven hundred and thirty-fifth time in the past two years, "I was already married with two babies!"

As though that were enviable, Belle thought. As though Alice Wright simply couldn't *wait* for her daughter to repeat her mistakes.

"Yes, Mother," Belle said in her Humble and Obedient voice. "I suppose I am being too picky." If preferring not to be repulsed by one's husband counts as picky. "If it's all right with you, Mother, I'd like to take Wilfred to see Dr. Holliday about that tooth. May I do that, please? With your permission?"

"Don't try that fakery on me," her mother snapped.

"What fakery, Mother?"

"You're just like your father," Alice Wright said, knowing that nothing could insult her daughter more. "Yes. Take the boy to the dentist."

This would be Belle's sixth visit to Dr. Hollidays' office. She had excellent teeth herself and had considered that a blessing until the first time she saw the dentist in the store, picking up his mail. The strange thing was that John Holliday was about the only eligible gentleman in Dodge City whom her mother *hadn't* invited to dinner, so Belle had taken it upon herself to escort each of her brothers and sisters to No. 24, Dodge House, to get their teeth checked. Dr. Holliday was always exquisitely polite, and very kind to each of the children, but it never seemed to enter his head that Belle Wright might be *interested* in him. Maybe he just thought she was being scrupulous about the children's dental health.

In any case, young Wilfred's sudden tragic need for a foster home had provided a welcome opportunity to knock once more on the dentist's door.

"Why, Miss Isabelle!" Dr. Holliday cried. "What a delightful surprise. You look a picture this mornin'." He took the gloved hand she offered and held it between both of his own. "To what do I owe the pleasure of this visit?" There was sudden frowning concern. "I do hope you yourself are not sufferin' from toothache."

"I am well, thank you, Dr. Holliday, but I've brought someone who may require your professional services," Belle told him, putting her arm around Wilfred's little shoulders.

"And who is this?" the dentist asked. "I thought I had met all your brothers . . ."

Belle drew the boy forward. "Dr. Holliday, may I present Wilfred Eberhardt? Wilfred, this is Dr. Holliday. He will help you with that tooth. Did you understand, honey? *Er hilft mit diesem Zahn.*"

"What seems to be the trouble, Mr. Eberhardt?"

Wilfred stared at his feet, so Belle answered for him. "He has a baby tooth that won't come out — the new one's growing in behind it."

"Does he speak any English at all?"

"He might understand more than he lets on," Belle said, "the way I do with German — I picked it up, just listening, from the farm families. Wilfred's people spoke nothing but

German. He might not have heard much English until last week."

"And what happened last week?"

Belle told the dentist what she knew. The immigrant family, the worn-out mother, the bereaved father. The bad weather, the growing debt. The loneliness. The suicide. The little boy leading his even littler sisters to the neighbors . . .

"God a'mighty," Dr. Holliday said softly. "Is there no one in this vast land who is not in mournin'?"

"I blame my father," Belle said, suddenly angry and glad to have someone with whom to share her indignation, a luxury she had not enjoyed since Johnnie Sanders died. "Daddy actually blocked legislation that would have provided relief to those farmers when the hoppers ate their crops. And during the drought? He did it *again.* He said if folks back East find out how bad it is in Kansas, they'll stop coming here to homestead and property values will drop. Can you believe it? He thinks he's making up for it by letting Mother and me give charity to families that go bust, but they wouldn't need charity in the first place if they hadn't been lured out here with a pack of lies about what a paradise Kansas is!"

Dr. Holliday's face was grave. "That is a disturbin' accusation, Miss Isabelle."

"It's God's honest truth, Dr. Holliday! I'm

not lying —"

"Most certainly not. I meant that I was disturbed by the accusation, not that I doubted your word —"

"Daddy always says he's a self-made man. Well, let me tell you something," Belle declared. "He thinks very highly of his creator! Why, he —" She stopped and stared. "Are you laughing at me, Dr. Holliday?"

"Not at all, Miss Isabelle. I beg pardon for givin' you that impression. It was an amusin' turn of phrase, is all. Now, if you would be so kind as to act as our interpreter, ask young Mr. Eberhardt, please, if I may have a look at the tooth that is troublin' him. Tell him that I'd like to use this little mirror to look inside his mouth."

Belle did her best, which must have been good enough. Wilfred climbed into the seat.

Dr. Holliday showed the boy the mirror and let Wilfred use it to peek around in the dentist's own mouth. Belle had seen all this before when she'd brought her sisters and brothers in, but she settled herself behind the desk in the corner of the office to watch the dentist work, while thinking, just hypothetically, of course, *Isabelle Holliday. Mrs. John Holliday. Belle Holliday . . .*

In the past two years, she had often studied the paired daguerreotypes on the mantelpiece at home: pictures taken to commemorate her parents' wedding day. No doubt about it, Alice Armstrong was a lovely child at thirteen. In Belle's opinion, her mother might have caught herself a better husband if she'd waited a year or two before settling on a man, but Alice was probably practical even as an infant. Picky, after all, requires at least one alternative to reject. A Missouri farm wasn't likely to provide even *that* much choice in the way of suitors. Bob Wright's proposal was the only one Alice was likely to get.

Gazing at her father's photograph, Belle had tried but simply could *not* imagine a beautiful little girl like Alice looking at the nineteen-year-old Bob Wright and thinking, My hero! Not with Bob's bland boyish face and his dreadful little chin, which looked so much *worse* now that he was wearing that big, full mustache! Belle could hardly stand to be in the same room with him these days, given the amount of sheer physical effort required not to cringe.

Still, there must have been *something* attractive about her father, once upon a time. Certainly, he had always been a man to make the most of an opportunity — if you could believe his own boasts, that is. Belle had caught him in so many lies, she no longer gave him the benefit of the doubt and checked every claim.

Yes, her mother had confirmed, before he turned twenty, Bob Wright *was* leading trains of forty freight wagons, delivering supplies to mining camps and railway crews and army depots on the far frontier. And before Alice turned twenty, Bob had indeed made his little bride the mother of three surviving children.

In the ordinary way of things, there might have been even *more* children by then, Belle supposed with a shudder, except that Bob was often gone for long stretches, tending to business interests scattered across Missouri, Kansas, Oklahoma, Colorado, and New Mexico.

Her father routinely offered that as praiseworthy evidence of gumption, but it also meant letting his wife fend for herself and their kids in a dirt-floored soddy with nobody but wolves and savages for neighbors. Belle's own earliest memory was of huddling with her brothers under a feather bed while their mother loaded guns for the hired hand during an Indian raid. And then there was the time they all nearly drowned, fleeing downriver by canoe during an attack . . .

What kind of man hears about something like that when he gets home, and then *leaves* again a couple of weeks later? That's what Belle wanted to know.

To her misfortune, Alice Wright always seemed to do just fine on her own, which absolved her husband of the need to stick around. He'd come home now and then, get her pregnant, light out again. And there she'd be with all those little children and a new one on the way, and no word from her husband for months at time, and no way to know if she was a widow or simply abandoned.

Like most entrepreneurs, Bob Wright was hostile to federal power and interference, but he saw no harm at all in the postwar scramble for government contracts. And don't think Belle hadn't spotted *that* hypocrisy. Land grants, mineral rights and rights-of-way, mail monopolies, Indian agencies — that was where the real money was. After the war, her father was in there with the best of them, snout in the federal trough.

From what Belle was able to patch together, her mother had hoped things would get better when the family moved to Fort Dodge after Bob got the sutler contract, but Belle was old enough to remember how gloomy and angry and cold her mother turned when they got there. Living inside the fort during the Indian wars meant there was more danger of attracting an attack by hostiles, but also more help in surviving it. So that was a mixed blessing. And having neighbors might have made a nice change, except it turned out the only other civilians at the fort were buffalo hunters passing through and the Irish girls who called themselves laundresses.

As a child, Belle found the girls' curly hair and bright dresses pretty, and their breezy manner amusing and gay. She enjoyed their songs and laughter, and liked that she was their pet, but quickly learned that her mother absolutely *despised* them and that it was wise to keep her own fascination well hidden.

Now that she was grown, she understood, of course. Whatever Bob Wright had done with such women during his long absences, it was something a wife could ignore; at Fort Dodge, the women were right *there,* mocking and obnoxious. Alice might not be eager for yet another pregnancy, but neither did she welcome the constant bitter reminders of what was going on behind her back.

A lot of things got better when they moved to Dodge City. The house Bob built for the family was an enormous improvement over their little shack at the fort. Buffalo hunters and Indians were becoming a distant memory, but the whores were *everywhere.* Laughing and lewd, or drunk and desperate. Walking the streets, browsing in the store. Leaning from second-story windows, calling out to passersby.

Alice insisted that Belle's dresses be made in dark, sober colors and expensive fabrics, to avoid her being taken for one of *them.* "You never know who might be watching, Belle," her mother told her over and over, "so you must conduct yourself as a lady at all times." Alice allowed Belle to go out only between the hours of ten and noon, so her maiden eyes would not be subject to the spectacle of open prostitution. As though Belle hadn't seen worse, back at the fort. As though she didn't know what her own father was doing over at Bessie Earp's bordello.

Since Belle's last birthday, Alice's concern for her daughter's future had bubbled into a rolling boil of desperation. "Even if we started planning a wedding tomorrow, you'd be sixteen before your first baby."

"Don't fret, Mother," Belle replied, selecting the voice of Sweet Reason. "Abraham and Sarah had a baby when she was ninety-nine, so I guess I have a few years left."

The remark earned her a slap, but it was worth it.

All year, Belle had endured a series of her mother's dreary Sunday dinners, each one a transparent job interview. A visiting banker, lumpish and self-important. A railroad man, bumptious and balding. Tommy McCarty, son of the town's doctor, who was nice enough, really, but boring. A cattleman's nephew, educated at Harvard, who could only talk about how sophisticated Boston was and how he couldn't wait to go back East.

Don't let me stop you, Belle thought. There's a train leaving in the morning.

The latest, and most persistent, in this tiresome procession was Elijah Garrett Grier, who'd been calling on the Wrights regularly for months. Eli Grier was from a prominent Connecticut family and he was a war hero, her mother told Belle before the gentleman arrived that first Sunday. Even Belle had to admit that Captain Grier had seemed like a real possibility when he rode up to the house on his beautiful Arabian mare. Slim and straight-backed, good-looking and worldly, Eli Grier was almost as old as her father, but with his well-brushed tailored uniform, and his silver captain's bars, and his tall cavalry boots all shined up, he was *quite* handsome.

And don't think he didn't know it.

During the soup course, the captain pretended not to notice that his foot was pressing against Belle's under the table or that he had brushed her hand with his when she passed the salt. By the time the roast was served, however, it wasn't entirely clear to Belle whom the captain was courting. He hardly spoke to Belle at all, preferring to discuss business with her father and to flatter her mother, who was still pretty at thirty-two and probably just *starved* for attention because Daddy was never home, what with the store, and the state congress, and his political meetings, and card games. And his women.

Belle manufactured a headache before dessert, and the captain found this an opportunity to stand and bow over her hand as though he were going to kiss it, but instead he looked into her eyes with a leer. Little lady, you're not likely to top this opportunity, that leer said. Best grab me while you can.

I'd rather be buried alive, Belle smiled back, and went to bed with a book.

"What did you think of him?" Johnnie Sanders asked her the next morning when she came into the store.

"His horse is pretty," Belle said.

"That's called damning with faint praise," Johnnie observed. He tapped an account book with his pencil. "The captain's got quite a tab here, and at Ham Bell's, too. Grier's over his head in a lot of places."

"So I'm to be a line of credit," Belle said.

"And a very pretty one," Johnnie told her, and he was so matter-of-fact about it, Belle found no reason to blush. "Course, you're an ethical person," Johnnie pointed out, "but Captain Grier might overlook a character flaw like that."

Oh, how she missed Johnnie Sanders!

Despite the lack of encouragement from Belle herself, Captain Grier was *still* coming to dinner, and *still* playing hard to get, although it should have been obvious by now that Belle did not consider him worth having, thanks all the same, and —

"Miss Isabelle?" Dr. Holliday was saying. "Miss Isabelle!"

Belle felt a tug at her sleeve and looked down to see Wilfred standing at her side.

"It is just as I thought," the dentist told her. "Sometimes a permanent tooth erupts just behind a milk tooth whose root doesn't absorb on schedule. Tell young Mr. Eberhardt, please, that I believe nature will take care of it in a few days. If it remains a source of discomfort to him, bring him on back. I will help things along."

Belle gave Wilfred the good news, and the little boy smiled shyly.

"Well," she said, trying not to hope that Wilfred *would* experience enough discomfort to justify another visit, "we'll be on our way then. Thank you, Dr. Holliday . . ." She stopped, for the dentist looked as though he were thinking something over, and her heart gave a little lurch.

"Miss Isabelle," he said tentatively, "I wonder if you would act as our interpreter a little while longer? I would like to say something else — something personal — to the boy."

Which *was* a disappointment because Belle had been thinking that Dr. Holliday might ask to call on her. Naturally, she agreed to translate and was surprised when the dentist braced against his desk and lowered himself carefully onto one knee so he could look Wilfred in the eye.

"This is a terrible world," he told the child, "full of tragedy and sorrow. You have been thrust into manhood too early, but your first thought was to protect your womenfolk. That, sir, is a mark of nobility."

He glanced up at Belle, who added Dr.

Holliday's definition of nobility to the list of indictments against her father, and then told Wilfred what the dentist said. She did not know all the words, so she substituted "sadness" for "tragedy and sorrow," and told Wilfred that he was a good boy to take care of his sisters.

Within the hour, when she got home, Belle would dash upstairs to her bedroom, retrieve her diary from its secret place in a drawer beneath her underthings, and write in a looping girlish script, *I knew that Wilfred was grieving, but I did not truly understand how Alone he must have felt until this very morning when Dr. Holliday laid a kind hand on Wilfred's shoulder and told us about the day his own dear Mother died. It was so Sad! That poor man! That poor little boy! I nearly wept!*

Indeed, by the time she had finished translating the story of Dr. Holliday's loss for Wilfred, mere interest had ripened into full-blown infatuation, and Belle was blinking away tears as she watched the dentist struggle to his feet. Of course, if it had been her father who moved so awkwardly or coughed so often, the girl would have been annoyed and disgusted, but since it was Dr. Holliday, she didn't mind the cough at all, and his lameness seemed romantic, and she wondered if he had been wounded in the war. Then he made a joke about not turning Catholic because he'd never be able to get off his knees the third time the congregation dropped a curtsy to the Lord, which made her laugh. She was thrilled by Dr. Holliday's magnanimity when he refused payment for the consultation, and flattered when he said that seein' her pretty self on a fine mornin' like this was all the compensation he required, and touched when he said that it had been an honor to meet young Wilfred.

He did ask if Belle would be so kind as to take a letter to her father's store and post it for him, which she was *more* than happy to do, and she offered to bring back any mail that might be waiting for him. He thanked her but said he ought to get out into the sunshine more and that he would probably walk down later on when she decided. That was she'd help her father straighten up the stock that afternoon, just in case Dr. Holliday did come by the store.

Watching him while he sat at his desk to address the envelope, Belle made up her mind to say something that she'd been thinking for some time now.

"It was *wonderful* — what you did for Johnnie Sanders."

Dr. Holliday looked up.

"I heard that the wake was a *great* success," Belle said. "I wanted to attend Johnnie's funeral, but Daddy wouldn't let me out of the house until it was all over. Daddy always talks about how important gumption is, but

Johnnie was the smartest, hardest-working young man in this town, and yet Daddy didn't even like for me to *speak* to Johnnie when he was working at the store. All Johnnie Sanders ever needed was somebody to give him a chance and he'd have made his fortune, but Daddy acted as though just lending a book to a nice boy like that would simply *ruin* my reputation! You treat everyone with respect, Dr. Holliday, even China Joe. I admire that *very* much."

Dr. Holliday looked at her as though he were truly surprised by what he was hearing. "You are too kind," he said with soft conviction. "I do not merit your admiration, Miss Isabelle."

He was such a gracious, modest person — shy about accepting her praise, not full of himself the way cattlemen and railroad tycoons and army officers were.

Being a gentleman, Dr. Holliday walked Belle and Wilfred to the door and wished them a good day. Outside, Wilfred saw the Riney boys and they ran off to play. Belle watched the children absently for a little while, then went on home, where she spent a short time in her room, wrote a few lines in her diary, and left the house again, surprising her father when she showed up at the store and volunteered to work that afternoon.

Bob was always glad to have Belle behind the counter. Cowboys bought a lot more merchandise when a pretty girl was writing their orders down. Usually, he worried about the drovers flirting with Belle, but not that day. She seemed as cool and remote as snow on a mountaintop, and maybe a little distracted, though her father put it down to a young person's ordinary self-absorption and didn't give it another thought.

Belle herself would never tell a soul that she had spent the afternoon of June 10, 1878, dreamily cataloging a dozen different reasons why it would be *perfectly* proper for a young lady to extend a dinner invitation to a *fine* gentleman like Dr. Holliday without asking her mother's permission beforehand.

Nor would she ever reveal why, at four-fifteen that afternoon, she left her father's store in tears.

After seeing Isabelle Wright and Wilfred Eberhardt to the door of the hotel, John Henry Holliday returned to his office to tidy up before leaving for the day. When his instruments were dried and put away, he checked the supply of ether and wrote a reminder to himself about reordering brushes. Then he locked up and turned the card on the office door over to read: *J. H. Holliday, D.D.S. In case of emergency, inquire at the front desk, Dodge House.*

"Morning, Doc. Hot one today," Deacon Cox predicted when the dentist passed through the hotel lobby.

"I fear you are correct, sir," Doc replied. "We could use some rain."

On his way upstairs, John Henry made a mental note to inquire about moving to a smaller room now that Kate was gone. Perhaps farther toward the back of the hotel, away from the street noise, and on the ground floor, so he could avoid the climb. He'd make Mr. Jau happy and ask for something with a nine in the number, and no fours or sevens.

"When do you sleep?" Father von Angensperg had inquired, and John Henry had an answer now. After office hours, he returned to his room and slept through the heat of the day. At eight or nine in the evening, he would rise, dress, have something to eat. Unless Tom McCarty called upon him for help with a surgery, he worked the tables through the night.

At dawn, he washed up, changed his linen and his shirt, had a light meal, and opened No. 24. Patients were most likely to arrive early in the day, after a night when a tooth had given them a sample of hell sufficient to overcome their fear of dentistry. If no one showed up, he passed the time reading, writing letters, or napping in the reclining chair. It was not ideal, but it felt good to establish a routine, if not a practice.

His initial weeks in Dodge had been busy, for the most miserable cases came in to be treated as soon as they heard a dentist was in town, even before he was officially in practice. Since then things had slowed down considerably, and this morning was typical, which is to say, he had made no money at all.

Take Morgan's brother, for example. Wyatt was missing teeth and had a mouthful of caries, but the odds were about seventeen to one that the man would become a patient before a toothache got so bad that he was ready to kill or die. Even then, he'd most likely agree to the minimum, putting off the rest of the work until there was nothing to do but yank the crumbling wreckage out of his jaw and hope that infection did not go on to kill the poor soul outright.

Then there was that pathetic little Eberhardt child . . . John Henry Holliday could only hope he was never so desperate for income that he'd find it possible to charge an orphan twenty-five cents to pull a baby tooth.

Maybe Kate was right. This was an exercise in futility.

He pushed the thought from his mind, and pushed Kate from his mind as well, for he was done with her, he was sure of that. Miss Kate was not without redeeming qualities, but six months with her suddenly seemed symptomatic of every bad move he'd made in the past five years, and he would not miss the commotion and disorder she brought into his life.

Kate was probably laughing at him right now, thinking him a gullible fool for letting her stalk off this morning with a carpetbag full of money. In fact, he'd known exactly what she was doing and wished her joy of it. He calculated his capital loss at just under nine hundred dollars and reckoned that generous pay for six months of services rendered, considering that it was on top of room and board, not to mention the wardrobe and dental care he had provided.

His conscience was clear as he opened the door to their room — his now, quiet and empty. He felt free to make what he could of himself here in Dodge, and thought briefly of Belle Wright as he hung up clothes and straightened the belongings Kate had flung about in the maelstrom of her departure.

He would ask Jau Dong-Sing to deliver Kate's detritus to Bessie's house as soon as possible. What Kate did next was none of his affair. She could leave town and get a fresh start someplace new, or she could drink the money up and go back to work for Bessie Earp.

Either way, we're even, John Henry thought as he undressed. She is still a whore, but she is better off than when we met.

"A necessary evil." Bessie Earp had heard that hackneyed phrase all her life, and it made her want to spit. Well, which is it? she always wanted to ask. Can something necessary be evil? Can something evil be necessary?

Without prostitutes, Necessity claimed, the filthy impulses and ungovernable desires of men would have no other target than respectable women, for prostitution drains away the sins of Christian society, as a sewer carries filth from a city.

Well, then, Bessie wondered, why not treat the girls who do Necessity's ugly work with some respect? Why not give them the small dignity of a ditch digger or a street sweeper?

Because, Evil replied, their own lust is to blame for their degradation. They are unredeemed sinners, these soiled doves, these fallen women. They are drunkards and drug fiends. As long as they ply their dirty trade, their wages will be ill treatment, appalling disease, and short, unhappy lives.

If the doves are soiled, who dirtied them? That's what Bessie wished someone would ask. If the women have fallen, who pushed them? But reformers would go just this far and no farther: lament the sin, but ask no questions.

And so in every city in America, a corrupt farce played out before a respectable audience eager for cautionary tales of female depravity. The police arrested the girls and marched them down public avenues to be stared at by jeering crowds of nice people. Judges levied fines and sent the girls out penniless, with no way to pay for their next meal except go back to whoring. Politicians railed against unrepentant wickedness to win votes. And later that night, all of the bastards — cops, judges, and pols — were in the house, winking and jovial, collecting their cut of the brothel income and taking some out in trade.

"No harm done, right, Bessie? There's an election coming up. Gotta put on a show for the rubes."

Who could you complain to? To what court did you bring your suit when the judge beat the girl? Who'd jail the extortionist if the chief of police said it was legal for the house to sell liquor one week, drank with your girls the next, and arrested you for it the third? How do you change the laws when the johns can vote but the girls can't?

"Honey," Bessie's mamma used to say, "politicians and judges and coppers are money-grubbing thieves. They'll screw you, and rob you, and win elections for doing it, but there's no way around them. Smile and pay the sonsabitches off."

The sheer shameless duplicity drove Bessie to fury, but there's no one more pragmatic than a whore. Bessie had learned the facts of life at her mamma's knee, and the facts were these. Men like to fuck. If they have to, they'll pay to do it. Women like to eat. If they have to, they'll fuck to earn their bread.

In the 1840s, when Bessie's mother went

into business for herself, Nashville was pleased to call itself the Athens of the South, for all its early industries were lofty ones: publishing, education, religion. Soon, however, railroads converged on the city. A new suspension bridge linked the region's agricultural lands with markets in the North. Paddle wheelers by the hundreds steamed up and down the Cumberland River, each carrying moneyed men. And in the center of the action sat Smokey Row. Handy to the waterfront and the tracks. An easy walk, downhill, for senators and congressmen.

When Nashville fell in '62, a hundred thousand Yankee soldiers came to occupy the city. Within months, miserable Southern prostitutes had accomplished what gallant Southern soldiers never did: the complete destruction of an invading Northern army. Smokey Row put a third of the occupiers into hospitals with syphilis and gonorrhea, but when the Yankees tried to expel the girls, each hooker's place was immediately filled by two new women willing to trade the certainty of starvation for a high probability of disease and early death. Finally a Union provost marshal got fed up with high-minded hand-wringing over the Necessary Evil and instituted a system of licensed prostitution.

And that, by God, made it safer for everyone.

Each week, Nashville's working girls kept

an appointment at a quiet office in a secluded part of town. One by one, they went into an examination room that had good light, a nice bed, a table, and all the necessary appliances for a private examination. If a girl showed the slightest sign of disease, she was sent to a well-run hospital, where she was treated by an army doctor, provided with decent clothing, and given instructions in hygiene and comportment. When she was clean, inside and out, a medical officer declared her fit for duty and she was given a certificate to present to customers. Disease rates plunged and stayed low for the rest of the war. The system even made a profit, its whole expense covered by the girls' weekly license fee of fifty cents apiece.

The Yankees went home after Appomattox. Smokey Row went back to business as usual. By then, Bessie's mother had died and Bessie herself had married James Earp, a Yankee boy who'd first laid eyes on Bess when she was hanging out laundry in the courtyard of Hospital Eleven. James might have been looking down on her from a second-story window in Hospital Fifteen, but that was the only way he looked down on her. They were both being treated for the same thing, and James Earp was no hypocrite.

And no matter what anybody thought or said, he was no pimp, either.

Even after he and Bessie married, she ran

the house, for James was an easygoing, broad-minded man who nearly always deferred to Bessie's commercial judgment. That said, it was his idea to head west in '65, out where there was no law to make criminals of Bessie and the Nashville girls they took with them.

James had no real use of his left arm, for his shoulder had been shot to kindling during the war, but he could still run the bar and he had a nice way of keeping things peaceful in the house. No matter where they went, Bessie kept back money to pay doctors for exams, and set a room or two aside for girls who shouldn't be working. Local johns appreciated knowing that they wouldn't carry the pox or clap home to their wives, and they paid extra for the peace of mind. James made sure that Bessie's place got a town's best transient traffic, too, politely directing filthy miners and stinking cowhands elsewhere, but welcoming visiting industrialists and cattlemen.

When things got civilized enough for politicians to rail against vice, Bess filled envelopes with cash and smiled when she handed them over, while James made plans to move on to the next boomtown. Wherever James and Bessie opened shop, two or three of his brothers were on the police force. If things got rowdier than James could manage, there was always some signal that would bring Morg or Virgil in fast to settle things down. Even

Wyatt came running, although after he got religion, he hardly ever looked Bessie in the eye anymore and left the house again as soon as he was able.

Into this smoothly running business, one woman came and went like the goddess Discord: unpredictable, disruptive, exhausting. Kate Harony, Kate Fisher, Katie Elder . . . Who knew what her real name was? In Wichita and Ellsworth, she had worked for Bessie; here in Dodge, she just used a room in the house and gave Bess a percentage of her income from private clients. Kate was good company when she was sober and lent tone to the proceedings, for she was able to speak to eastern businessmen with charm and poise, and to wealthy foreigners in their own languages. Katie could be sharp-tongued, but some men found that exciting, and they asked for her, special. Trouble was, she drank when she was bored or scared, and picked fights when she was drunk. Bessie wouldn't have put up with Kate's behavior in anyone else, but James had always liked the girl. There was something underneath her snappish belligerence that made him feel protective and tolerant.

"She's gonna get us in real trouble this time," Bessie had whispered when Kate showed up at the house that morning. "Talk to her, James. I can't do it."

James kissed his wife's forehead and patted

her behind. "You ain't so tough as you make out," he said, but even he waited to speak to Kate until the liquor wore off. Sometimes it's better to strike when the iron is cold.

When he found her at three that afternoon, she was sitting, slumped, at the kitchen table, aching head in her hands. James poured coffee for them both and sat down across from her. "Katie," he said quietly, "Bess says your carpetbag is full of money. Where'd you get all that cash, honey?"

She wouldn't look at him, which was as good as a confession.

"It's Doc Holliday's, isn't it," he said.

"Most of it," she admitted. "Not all."

"There's an election coming up," James told her, sitting back. "Reform's looking to slap a bunch of vice laws on us here. Dodge has been good to us, Kate. We're trying to keep a lid on things. If Holliday asks Morg to press charges, George Hoover will say we're harboring thieves."

"Doc won't press no charges," she muttered. "He ain't that kind."

James stood and went to the stove and checked the flame, adding some small wood to bring it up a little. "You want something to eat?" he asked over his good shoulder. "How 'bout I fix you some eggs?"

She shrugged, but nodded.

"Bacon?" he asked. "Toast?"

She made a face. "Just eggs."

He scrambled half a dozen and poured them into a fry pan with some bacon grease. While they sputtered and sizzled, he set bread and jam on the table for himself. When the eggs were done, he spooned them onto two plates and sat down again with Kate. They ate in silence, but when she was finished with her meal, James spoke again.

"Look at me, Katie." He waited until she did. "Does Holliday ever beat you?"

She shook her head slightly and looked away.

"He don't pimp you neither," James pointed out. "You said yourself: he'd just as soon you quit."

"I make my own way, goddammit! Nobody keeps me."

"I know that, honey. Still . . . My opinion?" he asked. "Doc Holliday's probably the best thing ever happened to you. Tell me I'm wrong, and I'll listen."

James stood and cleared the dishes off the table. He did the washing up, too, because he could hold plates steady with the bad side and scrub with the good one. He liked feeling competent with small tasks like that.

When he heard Kate snuffle, he put a wet plate on the rack and came over to plant a kiss on her head. "Go back to him, honey. Treat him good. You won't be sorry."

"Maybe," she muttered, wiping her nose on

the back of her hand. "Maybe," she said. "I guess."

Three years later, after the gunfight at the O.K. Corral, barricaded against a lynch mob in a Tombstone hotel with his brothers and Doc Holliday, James Earp would look back on that conversation with Katie and think, All this is my fault.

There was plenty of blame to go around, but James was right. If he hadn't talked Kate into going back to Doc, that damn street fight in Tombstone never would have happened. Wyatt only got mixed up with Ike Clanton after Kate got mad at Doc one night and then got drunk enough to tell Sheriff Behan that Doc was in on the stagecoach robbery that touched the whole thing off. Her story was horseshit of the highest order, and as soon as she sobered up, she took it back. But by then? It didn't matter. There was already bad blood between Wyatt and Behan over that Marcus girl. Kate's accusation drew Wyatt and Morg and Virgil in on Doc's side. Before you knew it, bullets were flying and five men were bleeding in the dirt, and everything was on its way straight to hell.

A year after that, James would have even more to reproach himself with, for the aftermath was his fault, too. He would piece everything together during those awful hours after Morg's funeral, listening to his mother weep.

Virgil newly crippled, worse off than James himself.

Poor young Morgan, cold in his grave.

Wyatt and Doc, fugitives from the law, wanted for killing the bastards who murdered Morg.

All of it, James would think, numb and silent. *All of it is my fault.*

The irony is that Big Nose Kate had a reputation for meddling and for bossing other people around, but if James Earp hadn't stuck *his* big nose into something that was none of his business back in Dodge, Kate would have done all right for herself. She was attractive, resourceful, and ruthless, and she did indeed make her own way all her long life, beholden to no one to the end of her days.

And Doc? Well, none of them could have known it, but absent James Earp's well-intentioned interference in his life, Dr. John Henry Holliday would have dropped by Bob Wright's store to pick up his mail on the afternoon of June 10, 1878, and Miss Isabelle Wright would have been waiting for him, behind the counter.

"Dr. Holliday, we are having dinner next Sunday at two," Belle would have said. "I wonder . . . would you care to join us?"

That was the fork in the road.

That was when everything might have changed.

Decisions — genuine, deliberate decisions — were never John Henry Holliday's strong suit. In youth, he'd sought the advice and consent of his large family. In manhood, poor health and a poor economy had dictated his plans, such as they were.

Things happened. He reacted. Sometimes he took a rebellious pride in the cold-blooded courage of certain unconsidered deeds; just as often, he repented of his rashness afterward. There is, for example, nothing quite like lying in a widening pool of your own blood to make you reconsider the wisdom of challenging bad-tempered men with easy access to firearms.

For all his private discipline and the countless hours of practice he devoted to the mastery of useful skills, John Henry had been borne along by *ad hoc*-ery and happenstance since leaving Atlanta. If questioned, he might even have admitted that part of Kate's allure was her fearless decisiveness, which left no room for doubt or second-guessing.

"We should go to Dodge," she said. "That's where the money is."

So. Here he was. In Dodge.

Standing in Wright's General Outfitting on June 10, with a letter from Martha Anne, a copy of *Harper's Weekly,* and an intriguingly large envelope from the St. Francis Mission piled on the counter before him, John Henry would not have accepted Isabelle Wright's invitation immediately, for he would have known that it was extended under a serious misapprehension.

Belle was a Yankee girl. That clouded her judgment in matters of character. Yankees were customarily rude to their inferiors, a fact John Henry found shocking and bewildering while he lived in Philadelphia. In the North, he discovered, courtesy was considered a barometer of genuine esteem; for any decently brought-up Southerner, good manners were simply habitual. Belle Wright undoubtedly believed that his courtesy to Johnnie Sanders and China Joe stemmed from an admirable democratic conviction that they were every bit as good as he was. In reality, he thought himself no better than they: a significant distinction. It was not a surfeit of brotherly love that informed John Henry Holliday's egalitarianism. It was an acute awareness of the depths of disgrace into which he himself had fallen.

And in any case, it was one thing for a man

like himself to befriend Johnnie Sanders; it was altogether another for a young white girl to do so. Indeed, he felt more rather than less respect for Bob Wright, knowing that the man was keeping a close watch on his daughter.

Whatever Miss Isabelle Wright thought, Dr. John Henry Holliday was not oblivious to her interest in him. He had grown up in the company of genteel Southern women schooled from the cradle in the art of flattery and concealment; Belle, by comparison, could be read like an illustrated children's story. And yet . . . She was clear-eyed enough to see Johnnie Sanders for what he was. Perhaps she was not entirely wrong about John Henry's own character. At the very least, she was offering him an opportunity to live up to a lady's illusions.

Upon reflection, he'd have realized that he wanted to try.

Yes, she was young. And, yes, he suspected that she had learned all her manners by reading Miss Austen's books, but she had spirit, and living in Dodge as Belle did, she was familiar with the life to which John Henry and his lungs seemed to be adapting.

Martha Anne, by contrast, seemed less and less worldly as time went by, her letters increasingly concerned with the godly and the incorporeal . . .

Decide, he would have told himself, standing in Bob Wright's store while Belle gazed at him with level brown eyes, waiting for his response. Spunk up, and make your move.

Besides, it's only dinner.

"Why, Miss Isabelle, what a charmin' idea," he'd have said. "You are very kind to extend the invitation. It will be my pleasure."

The following Sunday, from the moment he arrived, John Henry would have felt at home. Mrs. Wright's parlor, with its velvet draperies and little nests of mahogany tables and gilt mirrors and cabinets for curios and porcelain figurines, was very like that of his Aunt Mary Anne's back in Jonesboro before the war. Even more evocative: Alice Wright's household, like his Aunt Permelia's, was densely populated by a lively gang of children, homemade and fostered, mixed thoroughly and well.

Before they sat down to dinner, John Henry would have teased Belle's brothers and sisters, and drawn out the Eberhardt girls. He'd have treated young Wilfred like an old friend, inquiring after that tooth, which had indeed come out on Friday. And though the dentist's dinner conversation would have captivated Alice and impressed Bob, John Henry's eyes would have found Belle's when they shared a small, skeptical reaction to her father's *Aw, shucks, I'm just a country boy* act, or enjoyed a smiling amusement at how easily little boys' laughter can be provoked.

After their meal, there would have been

music, for Mrs. Wright had ordered in a fine new rosewood piano from St. Louis that spring. Belle would certainly have noticed how frequently Dr. Holliday's glance fell upon the instrument. "None of us can play," she'd have confided quietly. "I suspect Mother bought it to annoy Mrs. Hoover."

"Why not just hang a sign in the parlor?" John Henry would have whispered. "It could say, 'Dodge is not as savage as it seems.' "

"More economical," Belle would have agreed, straight-faced. "And we wouldn't have to dust it."

Seeing the young people standing side by side at the piano, Mrs. Wright would have asked, "Dr. Holliday, do you play?" And John Henry would have turned to reply, "Yes, ma'am. Yes, ma'am, I do."

"Nice to know somebody can," Bob would have muttered — the first crack in his carapace of resolute pleasantness, for he suspected that Alice had bought that damn thing to annoy him, not Margaret Hoover. "Sit down! Sit down!" he'd have cried heartily. "Give us a tune then, Doc."

It wouldn't have taken much persuasion. He hadn't played in nearly a year, but he often found his hands resting on a table, silently fingering the piece that was running through his mind, and that constituted a sort of mental practice. Settling himself at the keyboard, he'd have checked the tuning —

and made the boys shout with envy and admiration — by ripping though the dazzling arpeggio that introduced the *Emperor*. That was flashy but a good warm-up, and if he crunched a few notes, no one in that room would have noticed.

He'd have begun with the Fantasie Impromptu to show off for the children and because he'd been thinking of Chopin since Father von Angensperg's visit. Next, for the grown-ups, a shift in mood and tempo: the B-flat Minor Nocturne, with its slow, watery, tidal movement, like dawn on the Georgia coast. To keep the boys interested, he'd follow with the Polonaise in F-sharp Minor, which began with a bang but floated toward a lovely quiet conclusion that always seemed to lead him — lost by then, no longer aware of anything but the music — into the Waltz in A Minor, graceful and willowy and almost unbearably sad . . .

Moved and amazed, Belle and her mother would have exchanged glances, each slightly shaken by how sure she was. For the first time in months and months, they'd have been united in a shared conviction. *Yes. Yes, this is the one.* This soft-spoken, refined gentleman, with his shy, crooked smile and sly, dry humor, who was so good with children.

In her bed that night, Belle — already girlishly in love — would have remembered every word Dr. Holliday had said and imagined all that remained unspoken. Over the next few weeks, she'd become increasingly aware of how much he yearned for a home, a family, quiet companionship, and gentle affection. That deepening understanding would have placed the two of them on a more equal footing, despite the differences in their backgrounds and their ages.

When they were alone after Doc paid a call, Bob and Alice Wright would've talked about the younger couple. In doing so, they'd have rediscovered a little of the intimacy that had been missing for so long, for no matter what their adolescent daughter thought, there was indeed a time when they were in love, and each silently regretted the accumulation of resentment and grievance that had come between them. Bob's visits to Bessie Earp's establishment would have become less frequent. Dinner invitations to Captain Grier might well have ceased.

When the time came, Bob and Alice would have given their blessing to Belle and her young man wholeheartedly. The wedding would certainly have been the most splendid in Dodge City's short history, with local guests from both sides of Front Street and a few Kansas congressmen in attendance as well, along with relatives from Missouri and Georgia.

A year or so later, at the advanced age of seventeen, Belle would have made Bob and

Alice grandparents at long last. But while there is every reason to imagine that Dr. and Mrs. John Holliday would have enjoyed a few genuinely good years together, their happiness could not have lasted long, for Belle had lived all her short days amid soldiers, buffalo hunters, railroad laborers, drovers, hookers, and drunks, among whom consumption was as ordinary as venereal disease and as untreatable as measles, whooping cough, and typhoid. Her enviable alabaster skin and delicate, slender beauty at fifteen were in fact the earliest signs of the tuberculosis that would carry her off at twenty-one. Had she and John Henry married, Dodge Citians would have shaken their heads and spoken sadly about the double tragedy when — two years after Belle's passing — Doc Holliday was laid to rest beside his wife in Prairie Grove Cemetery, not far from Johnnie Sanders' grave.

The couple's small orphaned children would remember their handsome young parents only vaguely. A generation later, John Henry Holliday and Isabelle Wright Holliday would exist only as entries in an obscure genealogy: an unremarkable Kansas dentist and the wife who had — like many women of their time — preceded her husband in death.

So. There you are. Nothing could have changed the commonplace calamity that would end those two lives — together or apart — no matter what they did or didn't do in 1878. The Fates had seen to that.

On the whole, however, things might have turned out better if James Earp hadn't intervened in something that was none of his affair. He meant no harm, of course. Helpful people never do. James and Bessie were happy; it was natural for him to think that Doc and Kate could be happy, too.

This much is sure. If Kate hadn't gone back to Doc Holliday on the afternoon of June 10, 1878, you never would have heard of him. You wouldn't know the names of Wyatt Earp or any of his brothers. The Clantons and McLaurys would be utterly forgotten, and Tombstone would be nothing more than an Arizona ghost town with an ironic name.

Too late now.

Unaware of the road he did not take, John Henry Holliday had instead returned to his hotel room after office hours that day, undressed to his linen, piled up a few pillows, and lay down, moving carefully so as not to upset his chest. Not quite ready for sleep, he leafed through a new dental supply catalog and was pleased to note that the barber chair he'd bought was far less expensive than the new Morrison Dentist's Model with the reclining mechanism. Turning the page, he saw an advertisement for a motor-driven dental drill that his cousin Robert had recently recommended and was startled by its price.

Bless his heart, he thought. Robert must be doing well.

John Henry himself was still using a foot-pedal model, but it occurred to him then that if he hired little Wilfred Eberhardt to work the drive, it would provide the boy with a small income and save his own energy for the skilled labor.

He laid the catalog aside and, for a time, simply appreciated the quiet in his room. He was alone but not lonely. Kate's absence was a relief, he decided, not a deprivation. He was, he believed, no longer prone to the paralyzing bouts of homesickness that used to overwhelm him, when the yearning for all he had lost was so powerful that his only defense was to hold himself still until the sorrow washed through him and left him empty again.

The heat was building under the roof of the hotel, but the air was dry and not so hard on him as the murderous swelter of a Southern summer. He closed his eyes and listened to the strangely lulling concert that Dodge in daylight produced. The brassy bellow of cattle, the timpani of hooves. A cello section of bees buzzing in the hotel eaves. The steady percussion of hammers: carpenters shingling the roof of a little house going up on a brand-new street extending north from Front.

Tap tap tap BANG! Tap tap tap BANG . . .

. . . The rolling thunder of artillery, the pop and crackle of small-arms fire. Wilson's voice: "A'lanna's burnin', Mr. John! They're in Jonesboro —" And Chainey's: "They'll come here next, Mr. John!" But Mamma is too sick to move, and he has to stand them off, and he can hear the harsh Yankee voices, the crude, vile language — how can they speak so with ladies near? He is firing and firing — all by himself now. Who'll load the guns if Wilson and Chainey have run off? There's no one else to save her, and the bullets are gone. "Use a rock, son," Robert yells, but there aren't any rocks and —

"Ce n'est qu'un rêve. Je suis ici, mon amour. It's only a dream. Wake up, Doc. *Je suis ici. Je ne vais pas te quitter."*

Kate was there, her arm over him, her small, soft, living body stretched along his back, her voice low and sure.

"It's just that goddam dream again. Wake up, Doc. Wake up."

She was glad she'd arrived at their hotel room in time, pleased to help him as he fought his way out of the nightmare, happy to cradle him during those first awful moments when eviscerating grief seemed briefly fresh.

"It's over now," she told him again and again. "I'm here, Doc. I won't leave you."

331

She had forgotten by then that she had not left him, that she had been thrown out. She had no memory of being told not to come back. She knew how to calm him after the dream, how to steady him while he coughed until his throat was raw and his chest burned. She knew how much bourbon was enough to help him catch his breath, and she knew how to make him forget, for a time, his mother's illness and his own.

Afterward, she always asked, "I'm a good woman to you, ain't I, Doc?" He always agreed. When he fell asleep again, she felt the satisfaction of a job well done.

"Oh! I stopped by Wright's for you," she told him when they were getting dressed for the evening. "There's a new *Harper's,* and something from that priest."

Kate didn't mention the letter from Martha Anne because she'd thrown it away. It was for Doc's own good. He was always bad-tempered and gloomy when that girl wrote to him. Nor did she comment on the look she got from that little Wright bitch when Kate identified herself as Mrs. Holliday and asked for Doc's mail.

Frowning, Doc took the large brown envelope from Alexander von Angensperg and opened it carefully. "How thoughtful," he said quietly, and held up the score to Brahms' Second Symphony.

He was still studying it when Kate left. She tended to go out earlier than he did, to look for the night's best game. She did so that evening serene in the knowledge that she could leave Doc Holliday anytime she pleased, and that he would always take her back.

Three of a Kind

When Wyatt left the dentist's office on the morning of June 10, he had every intention of asking Bat Masterson about Doc Holliday's suspicion that Johnnie Sanders had been robbed before he died. That said, the notion of figuring out who'd killed the boy never crossed Wyatt's mind.

Dead Negroes were a dime a dozen after Reconstruction, and ever since the Little Bighorn, the U.S. Army had been busy making "good Indians" out of as many native men, women, and children as the cavalry could round up and shoot. After what happened to Mr. and Mrs. Sanders back in Wichita, Wyatt simply wasn't all that surprised by their son's death. The sad truth was that a half-Indian colored kid like Johnnie was asking to get killed by standing there in his own skin, minding his own business.

Course, Johnnie wasn't minding his *own* business, and Wyatt bitterly regretted the part he'd played in the boy's demise. Still, even if

Doc Holliday was right about what happened, whoever clubbed the kid was long gone. What Wyatt wanted to know was, what happened to the money?

Maybe *that* night's take had been stolen, but the dentist thought the boy had cleared $1,800 just since the end of April. Johnnie started dealing back in October. There might be twice that much somewhere. Three times, even!

If Wyatt could find that money, Roxana would be within reach. He could enter her and Dick in the rest of the summer's races, and pay James back out of the winnings. Breed Roxana to Dick in the fall and next year, he'd have a colt and some kind of decent future back in sight.

So he wanted to find out why Bat thought Johnnie Sanders' death was an accident. Except Bat was out of town, doing something for the county probably, and by the time Wyatt had established that, a fight broke out in broad daylight just outside the Bon Ton and shots were fired. Morg and Jack and Chuck and Stauber and Charlie came running, straight out of bed and still wearing long johns. Then half a dozen soldiers from Fort Dodge decided to mix in, just for the hell of it, evidently; Wyatt never did work out whose side they were on. Even Fat Larry came lumbering out of the jail and bashed a few brawlers before he had to sit down and hold his chest. The whole business ended up taking the rest of the afternoon. By the time it was over, Wyatt was back on night duty, looking at three straight shifts with no sleep and no extra pay for his trouble, apart from his cut of the fines.

By dawn the next day, he was so whipped he couldn't think straight, and that was probably why he was stupid enough to show up at Bessie's back door with a filthy, drunk brunette clutching an oilskin.

Bessie couldn't believe what she was seeing. The girl was a two-bit streetwalker so low, she couldn't even afford the rent on a crib — just throw that greasy oilskin on the dirt and let the cowboys ride.

"What do you call yourself?" Bessie asked the girl.

"Mattie," the girl mumbled. "Mattie Blaylock."

"How long you been working, Mattie?"

"Since November."

"Of 1867," Bessie muttered. She shot a hard look at Wyatt, who suddenly found his shoes interesting. "You sit down here for a minute, Mattie," Bessie said before yelling, "James! Your brother brought us a girl."

Drying his hands on a bar towel, James stepped outside and took it all in. The hooker, slumped against the back stairs. Bessie, tight-faced, arms crossed. Wyatt, miserable.

"I'm sorry, James. I caught a *vaquero* trying

to cut her," Wyatt told him. "I threw him in jail, but she keeps following me, and . . . I didn't know what else to do."

"Wyatt," Bessie whispered fiercely, "your brother and I run a clean house —"

"I'm not saying give her a job!" Wyatt dug into his pocket and handed over some crumpled bills. "Just let her sleep here?"

"*Here?* She's probably got fleas! Not to mention —"

James put his good arm around his wife's shoulders. "I'll take care of this, honey. Go on up to bed. Wyatt, there's bread and jam in the kitchen. Get yourself something to eat. I'll be back soon."

Pulling her shawl tight, Bessie gave Wyatt one last mean look and left without another word. Murmuring encouragement, James got the girl on her feet and steered her off toward China Joe's, still holding that nasty oilcloth to her bosom.

Wyatt watched them go, his mind blank. He was past thinking, but even if he'd just spent a week taking a rest cure, he wouldn't have known what to do about Mattie Blaylock. Anything with men or horses, Wyatt handled it, but women? Well, Doc Holliday was right about that much. It was a comfort and a support to have his brothers near. Women were James' job, and he was good at it.

After a few muddled moments, Wyatt went

inside simply because James had told him to, and because he liked bread and jam.

For a while he stood dumbly in the whorehouse kitchen, glad none of the girls had come in to see what was going on. There were mirrors all over the place in Bessie's, and he caught sight of himself in the one hung above the sink. Listening hard for footsteps, he decided it was safe and lifted his upper lip in something like a smile. Wincing at what he saw, he sat down heavily.

The Frowner, his mother called him. Well, it was that or look like an idiot.

Hell. What difference did it make after all these years? He was used to things the way they were. He could hardly imagine what it might be like to laugh or smile freely. On the other hand, there was the awful memory of the tooth that went bad in '73 while he was hunting buffalo . . .

They say you forget pain, but Wyatt sure as hell hadn't forgotten being so desperate to make it stop, he came close to putting the barrel of a pistol to the tooth and shooting it out of his mouth. In the end, he let Ed Masterson hammer it out, using part of an elk horn as a chisel and a pistol butt for a mallet. If Doc Holliday could prevent *that* from ever happening again, it would be worth any amount of money.

Which was why, a little at a time, Wyatt was talking himself into a plan that would let him pay James back and pay the dentist, too.

Fat Larry didn't see any harm in city deputies working two jobs, and the saloons liked having a badge in the house. John Stauber and Chuck Trask were both dealing faro part-time, and they were making a good buck. Wyatt thought that was kind of wrong — a lawman could cheat all he wanted, bash anyone who caught him at it, and say it was for disturbing the peace. But there was no rule said you had to cheat. Drunks generally did their own losing.

With his mind just about made up, Wyatt tried to summon the gumption to fry a couple of eggs but decided to rest his eyes for a few minutes. Next thing he knew, James was back and it was full daylight.

"I took her over to China Joe's," James told him. "When she's clean, she can come back here and sleep off whatever she's using. Joe thinks it might be opium. I think laudanum, more like."

"Thanks, James."

"Soon as she sobers up, she's back out on the street, Wyatt. Bessie's not gonna let her work here. You eat anything?"

"Too tired." He pushed himself to his feet and made himself say what he'd been thinking before he dozed off. "Listen, James. About the money I owe you —"

"Forget it."

"No! I'm gonna pay you back. I don't want

trouble with Bessie over it. Dog Kelley's looking for a part-time faro dealer. He offered me a job. It's two bucks an hour, plus ten percent commission, and I won't need a bank." James looked at him, not saying anything. Finally, Wyatt answered the question his brother wouldn't ask. "Just 'cause they're serving liquor don't mean I got to drink it."

James shrugged with the shoulder that still worked, but his eyes were narrow. "I guess," he said. "If you say so, Wyatt."

Wyatt caught up with Bat Masterson a couple of nights later. The whole conversation got off on the wrong foot, and it was mostly Wyatt's fault.

Bat was coming out of the Iowa House, where he was keeping his latest girl. Even at a distance and in a crowd like the one on Front Street, there was no mistaking the sheriff of Ford County. He looked like that Irish clown fella, the one who wore yellow pants and purple shirts and a red tie. "Bat," Wyatt called, genuinely puzzled, "why in hell do you dress like that?"

"Jesus, Wyatt! Lower your voice," Bat said, looking around to see who else had heard. "Just because you don't care about clothes don't mean the rest of us have to look bad."

"Where've you been? I've been looking for you —"

"Well, you found me now. And anyways, I

don't answer to you anymore. What do you want?"

"I want my money," Wyatt said bluntly, annoyed by Bat's tone. "There's eighteen hundred dollars —"

"*What?* Did you bet on Concannon? Jesus! What kinda odds did you get?"

"What are you talking about? Who's Concannon?"

"Nobody. Forget it," Bat snapped. "So I don't owe you eighteen hundred dollars?"

"I didn't say you did."

Now both of them were confused. Wyatt shook his head and held up a hand. "All right. Just listen: Johnnie Sanders might've been robbed the night he was murdered —"

"Who said he was murdered? He just got —"

"He was at least eighteen hundred bucks to the good and —"

"Who told you that?"

"What difference does it make? Was anybody flashing a lot of cash after the fire?"

"No. Maybe. I don't know!" Bat cried. "You know what it's like around here, Wyatt. Somebody's always flashing a lot of cash. Anyways, it was a long time ago."

"Three years is a long time, Bat. Three weeks ain't. You check his room after? Was there anything there?"

"We didn't find any money, that's for sure. Maybe he was carrying it and it got burned up in the fire."

"Some of it would have been in coin."

"Well, we didn't find any puddles of silver, I can tell you that much! Look, Wyatt, you know yourself the Elephant Barn was a fire just waiting to happen. I told Ham and told him —"

"That's another thing. What was Johnnie doing in that barn?"

Bat blinked. "Hell if I know." But he was ashamed and looked it. He also knew that once Wyatt got hold of something, he wasn't about to let it go. The best policy was to own up. "I'll be honest with you, Wyatt. I didn't really pay all that much attention. It was inside city limits. It was Fat Larry's problem, not mine."

"So what were you doing there?"

"Larry was out of town and Morg asked me. I did what I could, but it wasn't my jurisdiction. Jesus, what's got you all stirred up about this now?"

"That dentist said there was an *ante-mortem* blow to the head and —"

"Hell," Bat said, dismissing this information with a wave. "Holliday's always talking about his aunties. Half the time he don't make any sense at all —"

"*Ante-mortem,* Bat. It's legal. It means 'before death.' "

Young Sheriff Masterson made an honest if brief effort to grasp the implications of what he'd just been told, but the effort failed to yield any conceptual breakthroughs. In 1878, Bat was, after all, just a modestly educated twenty-four-year-old kid who'd won a county-wide popularity contest by three votes. He had read one fewer law book than Wyatt himself. And, in any case, it would be nearly a century before proper police procedure for handling crimes went much beyond (1) arrest a suspect within a few hours and (2) beat a confession out of the bastard.

"Well, hell," Bat cried. "Before? After? What difference does it make? The kid was dead when we got there. Dead is dead! And anyways, I wouldn't believe Holliday if he told me sugar's sweet and Kansas is flat. He is a quarrelsome drunk and a card sharp — I saw him damn near blow the head off a cattleman myself! He's been run out of every town he ever lived in. He didn't tell you that, I guess! Do you know why Holliday was in Texas?" Bat demanded. "Do you know why he had to leave Georgia?"

Wyatt had heard some of it before, down in Fort Griffin, but Bat's indictment went on for some time. When he finished, the sheriff of Ford County had taken back the moral high ground.

"Half the bad men in Texas are Georgia night riders on the run," he told Wyatt. "Why, that rebel sonofabitch probably killed Johnnie Sanders himself! That's why he's telling you

343

this cock-and-bull story about robbery and eighteen hundred dollars. He's playing you for a fool, Wyatt! He acts like he's real polite, but he's laughing up his sleeve at all of us. Ask him about those niggers he killed back in Georgia. Why, he's killed so many men, he don't even count the greasers down in Texas! Go on, Wyatt. Ask him about that!"

When Wyatt found the dentist, Holliday was sitting alone in Delmonico's, a set of half-dealt dummy hands arrayed before him on the table. It was getting late for the supper trade. There were only a few people in the restaurant. Nora was taking an order from a salesman going over his account book in the corner. A couple of cattlemen were working some figures in the back.

Wyatt stood in front of him. "How much is true, Doc?"

Holliday looked up. "Evenin', Wyatt." He frowned. "How much of what is true?"

"The stories about you. The rumors. What Bat says."

"You will have to be more specific, sir," the dentist said peaceably. "Sheriff Masterson, in my observation, is a man much given to chat and loose talk. Who knows what lurid tales he's spreadin'?"

"He says you're wanted in Dallas and Denver and Atlanta for murders. He says you gutted a gambler in a knife fight out in

California. He says you gunned down three Negroes back in Georgia, and that's why you came west. He says you've killed so many men, you don't even count Mexicans."

Holliday was a poker player. His reaction might have been an elaborate pantomime, meant to throw an opponent off, though it appeared genuine enough. The dentist stared, openmouthed, and shook his head, eyes wide. He started on a laugh, but it got tangled up in a cough. He fished out a handkerchief to hold over his mouth and then just sat there, waiting to see what his lungs decided. Finally he cleared his throat and put the handkerchief back in his pocket.

"Well, now," he said softly. "Seems that the cup of my iniquity overflows! If I am such a bad man, I wonder why Sheriff Masterson has not arrested me for my manifold misdeeds? Ought to be some sort of reward offered, wouldn't you think?"

Which was a good point.

Doc took a careful sip of bourbon. "The dust this time of day," he said in explanation and set the glass down so carefully, it was all the more startling when he rose without warning.

There it was: a feline suddenness that could make you think he'd pull a knife and slice you dead, just like Bat said. Alarmed, the salesman quickly gathered his things and left. The cattlemen sat back and watched, ready

345

for whatever might happen.

Wyatt felt the calm come over him. *Try it,* he thought.

"We are of a height," the dentist observed. "Six feet?"

Wyatt's eyes narrowed. "Near enough."

Doc stepped back a pace and took in the physique that had controlled six-hitch freight teams from the age of seventeen. The wood-cutter's shoulders. The thighs solid with saddle muscle. "I would wager that you have fifty, sixty pounds on me," he said judiciously. "How much do you weigh, Wyatt? Hundred and ninety, maybe? Two hundred?"

"About that. What diff—"

Doc sat carefully, gathered the deck, and shuffled. "I was never big," he said, begin-ning another round of dummies, "but since this illness took hold, I haven't been able to keep any weight on. Doesn't matter what I eat."

He went around again with deft efficiency. Ten of clubs, flush developing. A second nine. Seven, possible straight. "I don't believe you are gettin' enough rest, Wyatt. You look tired. Please. Have a seat."

Wyatt pulled out a chair, irritated. The cattlemen got bored and went back to their negotiations.

"Let us consider the plight of the rattle-snake," Doc suggested softly, eyes on the cards. "The rattlesnake is feared and loathed, and yet he has no claws, no legs. He does not look for fights and gives fair warning if he is threatened, but if he is attacked, he cannot flee. All he has is his mouth . . ."

Partly, it was the fancy way he talked. Partly, it was the slow, slurry sound of Georgia. Mostly, it was just that the dentist didn't think like anybody else. Wyatt looked away and back again. "I don't know what in hell you're talking about, Doc."

"Reputation, reputation, reputation," Doc recited, slapping out cards one by one. *"It is idle and most false, oft got without merit and lost without deservin'."* He looked up. "You ever take a beatin', Wyatt?" Doc turned away, coughed hard once, and cleared his throat again. "I don't mean take a sucker punch. I mean, did you ever lie on the dirt and think, Why, this big, ignorant sonofabitch is about to kick me to death. I will die in this jerkwater town, just for bein' able to count." The slate-blue gaze came up: steady and humorless. "Ever take a beatin' like that?"

"Not . . . for a long time."

Doc's brows rose at that. "Ever been shot?" he asked next.

"No."

"I was. Last year. A quarrel over cards — which I did *not* start," Doc emphasized, his voice rising momentarily. "No one expected me to live, myself included. I make a narrow target, but if a bullet comes my way? Chances

347

are, it'll hit something important. So I do what I can to make myself a less invitin' mark."

He dealt again. "There's the flush busted," he observed. "You may not have noticed it, Wyatt, but the sheriff of Ford County is a shockin' gossip. Why, you tell Bat Masterson any kind of story at all and no matter how foolish it is, you can just about depend on it bein' all around town before dawn." Doc looked up, as though reminded of something. "Is it true, I wonder, what they say about you and Michael O'Rourke? Word is, you faced down a lynch mob and saved his sorry neck for a proper execution." Doc's voice, always soft, became even quieter. "Or was it your brother Virgil did that?"

There was just the slightest of tells, but Doc saw it.

"Well, now," Doc said reasonably. "Easy mistake to make, you Earp boys lookin' so much alike. Still, a reputation can be a useful thing. Odds are better for all you boys if you don't argue the details. What Virgil does gives you an edge. What you do gives Morgan one."

Another card.

"You still considerin' that dental work I recommended?" Doc asked. "No rush, of course, although at least four of your remaining teeth are doomed, and I'd appreciate the business. I am a damn fine dentist, if I say so myself, but I fear Miss Kate is right. There is no money in it out here. Poker, by contrast, can be a good and honest livin'. Takes nerve, not muscle."

He studied the hands.

"My edge is that I can count," he said quietly, "whereas the men I play against are rarely overburdened by education." He laid a seven on the nines. "No help," he said, "but sometimes a pair of nines is all you need . . . This will not fill," he predicted, and added a jack to the eight-high straight. "See? Busted."

Another card, and he paused, eyes on Wyatt's own. When John Henry Holliday spoke again, his voice was almost too soft to hear, and there was no bravado to be seen or heard.

"I killed a man in Denison. It was awful. He wanted me *dead*, Wyatt. He went for his gun and — Everyone agreed it was self-defense. The charges were dropped. You can wire and ask. Those boys back in Georgia? Nobody got hurt. It was just pups, barkin' at one another. I have paid fines for gamblin'. That is the extent of my trouble with the law. I have never set foot in California, let alone San Francisco! Which means," he whispered fiercely, "Sheriff Masterson made that up out of whole cloth, and he is a contemptible slanderin' sonofabitch! As for the rest of it: I have Mexican and black *kin*, Wyatt. They were fostered but so was I, and they count no less than blood with me!"

Doc looked out the restaurant window, toward the tracks. He was trembling, as some men will when they have been very angry, or very frightened.

Presently, the dentist took as deep a breath as he could and let it out slowly. Cool again, he said, "I myself do not believe that it is cheatin' to calculate odds by takin' note of cards layin' in plain view on a table. Do you believe that is cheatin', Wyatt?"

Wyatt shook his head: No. Of course not.

"And yet," Doc said, "when some men lose to me, they reckon it theft, and when such men believe they have been cheated, they are not inclined to express their dismay with a well-turned phrase."

The cattlemen completed their business and rose to go, tipping their hats to Nora as they left. With the door open, you could hear the competing pianos, the drunken shouted threats, the raucous singing across the tracks.

That was when Doc looked Wyatt in the eye and dropped his voice again. "So, while I may not be quite as fearsome as I sometimes make out, if you were to noise that around . . . ?"

Morgan's age, Wyatt thought, but built like young Warren was at sixteen. All bone, no beef. Sickly. Scared.

Wyatt nodded. Some of the tension went out of Doc's face.

"Thank you, Wyatt," he said graciously. "I

'preciate your delicacy in the matter." Back in control, the Georgian gathered up the deck. Tapped it into alignment. Tucked it into a breast pocket. "Naturally," he added, ever so softly, "you and all your fine brothers may rely equally upon my own discretion."

It might have been a threat. Hard to tell.

"You'll excuse me?" Doc inquired courteously. "I am off to spend another evenin' in the temples of unreason. Like everybody else in this godforsaken wilderness, I need to make a livin'."

Snake-slender and casual in fresh-pressed linen the color of cream, John Henry Holliday pushed himself to his feet — slowly this time — performed a slight bow, and left Delmonico's.

Wyatt watched him saunter off across the tracks.

The sunset beyond shone vermilion through the dust.

Next morning, Wyatt sent out the wires. All his queries were answered by the end of the week.

"No outstanding warrants in Texas, Colorado, or Georgia," he told Morgan over pancakes and bacon. "He's clean."

"Told you he was quality," Morg said. "What about — ?"

"The police never heard of him in San Francisco."

"Well, hell, if he did what Bat said —"

"There'd be something on the books."

"So Bat just —"

"Looks like it." Wyatt sat back and stared out the kitchen window of the little frame house he and Morgan had started renting. "Morg, did you see what happened when Ed Masterson was killed?"

"Hell, yes. I was coming out of the Lady Gay. Ed was rousting drunks at the Lone Star, and one of them — Jack Wagner, his name was — he up and pulled a gun. Gut shot, point-blank. Ed didn't have a chance."

"Who got Wagner?"

"Ed. He didn't die right away. He was on the ground, but he got his pistol out and put three bullets into Wagner. Ed died about half an hour later. Wagner died the next day."

Wyatt snorted. "Bat told me he killed the man who got his brother."

Morg's eyes widened. "Well, Bat shot *at* Wagner, but he was way down by the billiard parlor when Ed got it." Morgan shook his head as though to clear it. "I guess maybe Bat could have hit Wagner, but the odds're against it — Bat was coming on at a dead run."

For a time they both sat there, taking it in.

"What's that?" Wyatt asked then, lifting his chin toward the book Morg had propped against the sugar bowl.

Morg put a finger in his place and showed

352

Wyatt the spine. "It's not what I expected," Morg admitted, "but it's good."

"*Crime and Punishment . . .* 'Bout time you read a law book."

"No, it's a story, but it's not like anything I ever read before."

And it wasn't easy, either. There were a shitload of words he had to look up or ask Doc about. Not just foreign ones like *dvornik* or *batuchka,* either. *Hypochondria. Subterfuge. Torpor.* And, damn, the names! Raskolnikoff. Lebeziatnikoff. Amalia Fedorovna Lippevechzel. Who in hell could get his mouth around words like that? Even Doc had trouble with a lot of them, and sometimes they asked Kate about how to say something.

"Don't worry about the names," Doc advised. "Just read. People are people, in St. Petersburg or Dodge."

So Morg kept on, and Doc was right. The people in the book were all familiar. Drunks, prostitutes, politicians, policemen. Rich and poor, side by side. Men who beat horses and men who beat women. Good women gone bad. Bad women who weren't so terrible when you got to know them.

"It's like you can listen inside everybody's mind," Morg told Wyatt. "You can hear them think in this story. The fella it's about — Raskolnikoff? I can't work out if he's got a fever or if he's plain crazy, but his thinking's all mixed up. And you find out about people's lives, and how they got that way. I was about ready to turn temperance by page thirty."

"Wouldn't hurt you none." Wyatt finished his coffee and stood. "Tell Fat Larry I'll be a few minutes late."

Deacon Cox wasn't behind the desk at Dodge House, so Wyatt went down to Doc's office and then upstairs to check his room on the second floor. No one answered the knocks. He tried Delmonico's next, and found the dentist having dinner there, with his woman practically in his lap. When the whore saw Wyatt through the window, she sat up straight and looked like she wanted to spit.

Wyatt stepped inside. "Doc, I need a word."

"Bring with thee airs from heaven or blasts from hell?" the dentist inquired warily. "If you have come to accuse me of some new crime, sir, you may do so in front of my companion. If I am to be locked up, she will consult an attorney on my behalf."

"No, it's nothing like that. Everything you said checked out."

"I am pleased to hear it," Doc said tightly.

"Could we go outside?"

Doc got to his feet and turned to Kate. "If you will excuse us, darlin'?"

They left the restaurant. Wyatt waited for the passersby to clear the boardwalk before he said, "Look, Doc, I'm sorry about the other day."

"You were doin' your job. Let us put it behind us."

"Yeah. Good. Anyways . . . About my teeth. I have other debts," Wyatt said. "Could you take two dollars a week for fifteen weeks? I want to do all of it."

The dentist seemed surprised, then pleased. "A wise decision," he said warmly, "and one you won't regret. Come by my office after your shift. Bring your brother Morgan, too, if you will. I'll need to take a few measurements from his front teeth. Say eight o'clock tomorrow mornin'?"

Wyatt nodded and looked away. Needing something always bothered him, even if it was dentistry. He noticed Kate, still sitting at the table, glaring at him through the plate glass. What'd I ever do to her? he wondered.

"Didn't expect to see you two back together," he said.

"Miss Kate is possessed of a passionate Hungarian nature," Doc murmured. "Our reunions are compensation for her occasional lapses in good taste."

Just then, a burst of laughter from across the tracks took their attention. Bat Masterson was telling some story to his cronies, using his gold-topped walking stick to mime a rifle. The men around him were loudly appreciative.

Eyes narrowed against another brilliant sunset, Wyatt said nothing for a time, watching pink light flash off Bat's fancy chromed Colts. Even at this distance, you could see the stone in his cravat sparkle.

"Doc, if you don't mind me asking, how much did that diamond of yours cost?"

"I haven't the slightest idea." Doc's fingers went to the stickpin he always wore. "It was a gift from someone dear to me. I will die before I part with it," he said. "But I take your meanin'. Sheriff Masterson appears to be prosperin' in public service. You hear he just bought a half interest in the Lone Star Dance Hall? Now, what do you suppose that must have cost?"

For a time, Wyatt stood silently, watching Bat. "Thanks, Doc," he said before walking on. "I'll stop by after work, like you said."

Kate came outside, her scowl aimed at Wyatt's broad back. "I don't trust him," she said. She was making a cigarette: licking the edge of the tissue paper, sealing the tobacco in. "He don't drink. He goes to church! Never trust a lawman who goes to church."

"Why, Miss Kate, you are philosophical this evenin'."

Doc scratched a match against the rough wood of a hitching rail and lit her cigarette. Kate inhaled deeply and blew out a plume of smoke.

"You shouldn't trust him neither, Doc. He's no good."

"I believe you have misjudged the gentleman, but I shall certainly take your opinion under consideration."

"Buy me a drink, Doc. I need a drink."

"My pleasure, darlin'."

She took the cigarette out of her mouth and reached up, placing it between Doc's lips, her eyes on his, with the flat, challenging stare he was coming to appreciate. He drew in carefully, but still choked slightly on the smoke.

"Where's the money tonight?" he asked.

"The Saratoga," she said as they strolled down Front, arm in arm, the boardwalk hollow-sounding beneath their feet. "You feeling lucky, Doc?"

"Always, darlin', when you are at my side."

He rarely heard from Martha Anne these days, and Georgia was very far away.

Reform, he thought, just might be overrated.

"So Raskolnikoff was planning to kill that old lady all along?" Morgan asked. "He planned it up ahead of time, like it was a bank robbery?"

"That is my readin' of the affair, yes," Doc said.

Morgan shook his head. In his experience, killings were the result of momentary fury, or drunken foolishness, or plain clumsiness even. Thinking a murder through was so cold-blooded . . . "Must be like hanging a man," he mused. "That's awful."

Doc was measuring the gap where Wyatt's front teeth would have been, if Morgan had done as he was told and picked those berries instead of sneaking up to the barn with a book.

"That's all I need from you, Wyatt," Doc said after he wrote the numbers down and made some notes to himself. "I'll get the rest from Morgan."

"And you think somebody planned up killing Johnnie like that?" Morgan asked, swapping places with his brother in Doc's barber chair.

"Well, now, it might not have been so thought out. More a matter of a sore loser decidin' to get his money back, I imagine."

"Get him into the barn for some reason, then bash him," Wyatt said.

"Set fire to the barn," Morg said. "Make it look like an accident."

"That is my guess," Doc confirmed. "Open."

For a while, Doc poked around, measuring things. When he had what he needed, he sat at the desk and began to sketch Morg's front teeth. The drawing was remarkable, down to tiny little bumps along the bottom edge of the teeth that Morgan had never noticed.

"Mamelons," Doc told him. "From the Greek: small rounded mounds. Same root as 'mammary,'" he said, cupping his hands in front of his chest.

Morgan laughed. Then it struck him. "Is that where 'mamma' comes from?"

"Or vice versa . . . The dental structures wear to a straight edge as you age. Yours are still visible. I expect Wyatt's would be as well. I am requestin' replacements that match."

Wyatt asked, "When can we get started?"

"Gettin' eager? I can begin the repair work tomorrow." Doc added the diagram to an envelope addressed to Robert Holliday, D.D.S., and handed it to Morgan. "Mail this for me, son."

Morg got a kick out of how Doc called him son even though Morg was actually a few months older.

"Heat taking the starch out of you, old man?" Morg asked him.

"Morgan, I am flourishin'," Doc said, but the dentist looked pasty this morning. It was pretty close in the office, and Doc went to stand by the window, leaning his bony hips against the sill and resting one hand high on the frame. "How does that horse of yours run in this weather, Wyatt?"

The Fourth of July race was coming up. Everybody was handicapping the entries.

"He'll do," Wyatt said. "Nothing seems to bother Dick."

Morgan snickered.

"Always rises to the occasion," Doc suggested, slate-blue eyes angelic.

Wyatt frowned, suspicious. "What's funny?"

Morgan glanced at Doc and started to laugh. "Dick Nail 'Er," he said, sniggering. "Jesus, Wyatt, don't you — ?"

"Hush up, Morgan," Doc said severely. He lifted his chin and added piously, "Your brother is a pure soul."

Morgan crinkled up laughing like he used to when he was a kid, and all the brothers were crammed into an attic bedroom, and Virgil farted loud enough to wake Warren up.

"Pay that pup no mind, Wyatt." Doc remained straight-faced, but he was struggling now. "It's a fine name," he said. "For a stallion."

"You plan to stud Dick out?" Morgan asked, sobering momentarily.

Doc started to choke. Morgan broke up again. Pretty soon, the pair of them were giggling like eight-year-olds. Wyatt felt like the only grown-up in the room.

Then he got it.

"Wait . . ." he said, his face going slack. "No!" he protested, mortified. "That's not what — Oh, hell. He was named when I got him!"

Morgan wailed, and Doc was headed into a serious coughing fit.

"Anyways, I thought it was N-A-Y-L—" Wyatt started, but somehow bringing spelling into the matter just made things funnier. "Go on," he told them, annoyed. "Enjoy yourselves, youngsters. Just don't bet against him

360

on the Fourth."

By then Doc was laughing and coughing so hard, he couldn't stand on his own anymore, and Morg was trying to hold him up but not very well. When Wyatt finally gave in and started to laugh, he didn't even bother putting a hand over his mouth, and once he joined them, the other two were helpless. Doc's knees gave out, and Morg dropped him. Before long, all three of them were breathless and exhausted, and Doc wasn't the only one wiping tears from his eyes, which is why it took Morg so long to ask, "Jeez, Doc! Are you — ?"

Doc nodded, grinning through the pain. "I'm all right," he insisted, and his eyes were shining, but he was wet-faced and white, sitting on the floor of his office, pushing against his chest with both hands. "I cannot remember the last time I laughed like that," he moaned. "Now I remember why. Oh, Christ, that hurts!"

Hand on the doorknob, Wyatt asked, "Should I get Doc McCarty?"

The dentist shook his head but gestured toward the bottle of bourbon he kept on his desk. Morgan poured him a drink. Doc tossed it back, closed his eyes against the burn, and held up the glass again. It felt like a long time before he wiped his face on a sleeve and let Morgan help him to his feet. Wyatt pulled the desk chair out. Doc sat for a time, elbows on the table, head in his hands.

"You sure about McCarty?" Wyatt asked. "What's wrong, Doc?"

"Nothin'. Adhesions tearin'."

Wyatt looked at Morg, who shrugged. Doc didn't seem alarmed, so they just waited until he sat back in the chair.

"Morgan," he said, "I haven't seen a look like that since Cousin George came to visit me in Texas! You are very kind to be so concerned." His voice was hoarse but cheerful enough, and his color was better. "Healthy lungs move smoothly, like this," he told them, sliding one palm over the other. "Mine are stuck to the chest cavity. Fibrous bands form, like ropes." He interlaced his fingers. "When I cough or laugh or — God *help* me, when I sneeze — the fibers rip." He jerked his fingers apart. "It's like breathin' razor blades."

Wyatt winced and Morgan shuddered.

"You get used to it," Doc said casually, and swore there was no harm done, and no, thanks, he didn't need any help getting up to his room — he'd be fine unless Miss Kate shot him on sight for working late again.

All three of them had been up since the prior afternoon and they were, by now, well and truly tired. The brothers got ready to leave. Wyatt counted out his first week's payment, and that brought him back to the missing money.

"Seems to me, whoever bashed Johnnie

only woulda just got whatever he was carrying that night," he said, as Doc accepted the coins. "If you're right about what happened, there's eighteen hundred dollars should still be around somewheres, but Bat said there wasn't any money in Johnnie's room."

"Maybe his winnings're still sitting in Bob Wright's safe," Morgan suggested, and that reminded Doc of something.

"Wyatt, nobody seems to know where Johnnie got his bank, but I think Isabelle Wright may have backed him. If her father found out she was sneakin' money to Johnnie Sanders, there'd have been hell to pay, and I doubt that Miss Isabelle would be the one to pay it."

Morgan straightened. "You know . . . There were some books in Johnnie's room with Belle Wright's name in them. If he was seeing her on the sly —"

"No," Wyatt said.

Morg and Doc looked at him.

"Well, could be they was seeing each other," he admitted, "but Belle Wright didn't stake him."

Morgan frowned, but Doc worked it out sooner.

"Never play poker, Wyatt," he said quietly. "You are an open book."

Morgan's mouth dropped open. "Wyatt? But — where'd *you* get the money?"

Wyatt swallowed. "Borrowed it from James

and Bessie."

"Why?"

"Doesn't matter anymore."

"Oh. Oh, Wyatt," Doc said, figuring the rest out. "You poor soul . . ."

For the past few nights, he had taken note of Wyatt's technique over at the Alhambra, where the deputy now sat in when the regular dealer needed a break. Wyatt's hands were big and that could be an advantage, but at his best he would never be as deft as Johnnie had been, for he was not as flexible in the wrist or as smooth on the pull. Still, the mechanics were the same, and now there was no question.

"You taught that boy to play," Doc said.

"It was just something to take his mind off his parents," Wyatt told them. "I didn't know what else to do! Nobody else wanted him, and he kept crying . . . Faro's easy to learn and he just took to it! When he showed up in Dodge, he made a little extra money — sitting in, you know? Then, last winter . . . I banked him."

Morg looked stunned, and Doc's eyes were full of bleak compassion.

Wyatt's face was stiff. "I just wish —"

He couldn't finish, but he didn't have to. Usually it was his brother Morgan who could complete any thought. This time it was John Henry Holliday.

"Yes," Doc said. "Yes, indeed. But it's too late now."

▪ ▪ ▪ ▪

FOURTH HAND

▪ ▪ ▪ ▪

SIDE BETS

James was moving from table to table in the house saloon, collecting glasses on a tray, wiping up beer slops in the midmorning lull. He hadn't done the count yet, but the night's take promised to be good. The town was hopping, what with the Fourth of July festivities and midseason cattlemen splashing cash around.

"He's a Southerner!" Bessie was saying, as though that clarified everything. She could see the look of exasperation on Kate's face. "James, you explain it."

Deftly delivering the clinking tray, one-handed, to the bar, he came over to stand next to Bessie's chair. "Southerners out here? They're like wandering Jews, Katie. They're lonesome for a place they can't be anymore. Even if they was to go back, everything's different now. Wouldn't be home — not how they remember it, anyways."

Bessie reached up to slide her arms around her husband's thickening waist and laid her head against his belly. "You're gettin' fat and bald but, honey, you ain't so bad for a Yankee." She sighed and looked into the middle distance. "Sometimes I think I'll flat die for want of peonies and roses and sweet gum trees . . . Course, they're all gone, back in Nashville. Dug up to clear ground for vegetables during the siege. Or cut down for firewood."

"Doc ain't no Jew," Kate said thoughtfully. She lifted her feet onto the chair opposite her. "He could've cleaned up at a game last night, but he just wasn't interested. Sometimes I think he don't cares about money at all . . . He's stupid about it, almost."

"That's Southern, too," Bessie told her wryly. "Are his people planters, Kate? Mercy! Planters was the worst. Proud as Lucifer! Always in debt, always on the edge, but they still wanted the best of everything —"

That was when Kate figured it out.

"Aristocrats!" she said with a tone of bemused disdain that brought her father's voice back as though he were standing behind her in the room. "Aristocrats!" he'd cry, throwing up his hands in defeat, unable to make sense of a phenomenon that science was helpless to explain. He was called upon nearly every day to treat aristocratic stomach pains and headaches and nervous disorders. In Dr. Michael Harony's opinion, most of those ills were a direct result of the strain

370

that comes from living beyond one's means, as were the habits of gambling all night in hope of making a quick killing, and drinking in the morning to dull the fear of bankruptcy. "They spend like royalty on households and horses and hunts, on clothes and lavish parties and balls. Then they sneak out of their mansions to avoid bill collectors and insult their creditors in the street. It's absurd!"

By the time Mária Katarina was thirteen, her father had already refused her to a Mexican grandee and a minor Austrian duke, each of whom had inquired about his eldest daughter's hand, and both of whom kept making excuses about paying Dr. Harony for medical services rendered.

"If a man can't pay me," his daughter overheard him say in the rapid Magyar her parents thought she didn't understand, "he can't pay his tailor, his groom, his cook, or his butler. He's mortgaged to the neck on everything he has. By God, he won't use my money to service his debt and drag my daughter into the bargain!"

"What will become of the girl if you refuse every man at court?" Madame Harony demanded, for the notion of being mother to a duchess had been rather dazzling.

"I haven't refused every man at court," Dr. Harony pointed out, "just two of them, both wastrels, and both —" He lowered his voice and whispered into his wife's ear a bit of medical information calculated to end the conversation. Certainly nobody in the household ever mentioned *those* two names again.

Not long after that conversation, the question of marriage to an aristocrat was rendered moot. The glorious reign of His Imperial and Royal Highness Archduke Maximilian of Austria — Prince of Hungary and Bohemia, by the grace of God: Maximiliamo Primero, Emperor of Mexico — proved to be somewhat shorter than the list of his accumulated titles.

His court physician was warned to flee Mexico City by a loyal servant just before the volleys of revolutionary firing squads began echoing off palace walls. The Haronys escaped the bloodbath, but it took every jewel, every silver peso, every last centavo they possessed to flee northward, across thousands of kilometers of wilderness, to a place called Davenport, Iowa. There were other Hungarians in Davenport, Dr. Harony assured his wife and daughters. They would, he promised, find shelter with that community. And indeed, they did, briefly, but the destitute family's luck continued to crumble . . .

Now Mária Katarina Harony was just plain Kate, sitting in a Dodge City bordello after a long night, asking a madam and a barkeep for advice about the very sort of improvident petty aristocrat her father had despised.

Full circle, she thought. *Plus ça change, plus*

c'est la même chose.

She was frankly mystified by how Doc ever managed to take care of himself before she'd taken him in hand. He had inherited property in Georgia when his mother died but sold it to support himself after he came west. That cash was long gone. He never heard from his father; if the old man had anything, the bitch stepmother would get it all. Doc's uncle was pretty well off, but John Stiles Holliday had boys of his own. There might be a bequest someday, though probably nothing big. So Doc was on his own, same as Kate, but that didn't seem to matter. He always stayed in the best room at the best hotel in town. He was vain about his clothing and ordered imported English suits through a haberdasher in Atlanta. Doc wanted Kate to look good, too, and bought her French dresses and silk underthings and pretty shoes. Kate herself would have been happier with cheaper clothes and more jewelry. You could sell jewelry.

Doc acted like she was asking him to walk naked down Front Street whenever Kate attempted to economize. That damn wake had cost far more than it needed to, but Doc would spend himself into penury rather than give the slightest public hint that he cared about money.

It was Kate who kept them eating when things got thin. And if that had made a Jew of her, well, so be it! Jews weren't the only ones liable to be beaten and robbed and run out of town at any moment, without being able to go to the police. You never really owned anything but the clothes you stood up in. If you knew what was what, you made damn sure there was money sewn into seams, or gems hidden in hems —

"Katie!" James repeated. "You going to the parade?" he asked when he had her attention. "I can't get Bessie to come."

"It's bad enough gettin' squeezed for *donations* by every damn politician in town," Bessie said. "Watchin' Yankees march down Front Street, wavin' their damn flags, bangin' their damn drums, and playin' 'The Battle Hymn of the *God*-dam Republic' is more than I can stomach — Oh, James, no," she wailed suddenly. "You ain't really gonna wear that!"

"Course I am!" James said, shrugging into a ragged blue jacket that was moth-eaten and crusty with old bloodstains. "It's Fourth of July, honey!"

"I keep throwin' that damn thing out," Bessie told Kate, "but he keeps findin' it and bringin' it back in." Bess shuddered. "It's like a woman savin' the sheets she gave birth on, for Lord's sake!"

"Come on, Bess!" James urged. "You and Kate can make fun of George Hoover, and blow kisses to Bob Wright, and cheer when I march by."

"No, sir, I am goin' to bed." Bessie groaned

and got to her feet. "You two go on. Keep each other out of trouble!"

She watched them leave, Kate fitting nicely under James's good arm, which was draped casually over the little Hungarian's shoulders. Bessie wondered sometimes about James and Kate . . . It wouldn't have bothered her, of course. There were times when James got randy and Bessie'd simply had *enough* and wanted her body to herself for a few hours. It was only fair when James turned to one of the girls, but he and Kate seemed close in a different way. He treated her more like she was his baby sister Adelia, and Kate was more at ease with James than she was with other men. They seemed to understand each other, and Bessie was glad, for not many people understood her husband.

James was as hardheaded and stubborn as any of the Earps and — Lord! — he could be sarcastic! But there was a real sweetness to that man: a special sort of gentleness that you see sometimes in people who've been hurt bad but who don't want revenge.

When he left Nashville for the front in '63, Bessie never expected to see James again, and she went back to work without giving him a second thought. Then one day his brother Virgil showed up at the house with the news that James had been wounded and was likely dying. He kept asking Virg to go see if Bessie would come visit. It was little enough to do, so she went.

"Arm's no good, honey," James whispered with the ghost of a grin, "but I bet the rest of me'll work fine!"

To her own astonishment, Bessie burst into tears.

She'd seen a lot of ruined boys by then, but somehow this one got under her skin. She went to the hospital as often as she could get away from the business, expecting each visit would be the last. James held on, though, week after week, and then he started to gain. Early in the spring of '64, he asked Bessie to marry him.

"James, you know what I do," she protested.

"Yes," he said. "Yes, I do, honey. You give a lot of boys some real good memories before they die."

That was James all over. He saw something honorable in her work. He believed Bessie herself to be decent and good. In spite of everything, maybe even because of it, he respected her.

Which was why, in 1878, Mrs. James Cooksey Earp was one of a bare handful of lawfully married women living in downtown Dodge. That was also why, she supposed, both Margaret Hoover and Alice Wright — wives of the two richest men in Dodge — found it possible to speak to her.

Odd, but it was Alice who was more open about it. Alice Wright was a strange one: a small, pretty, reserved woman who made herself noticeable in a group only by her silence. Bessie had seen her around town, of course, and over at Bob's store, but then one day, Mrs. Wright walked right in the front door of the brothel and asked to speak to Bessie in private. Oh, Lord, Bess thought. She's gonna ask me to refuse Bob courtesy of the house.

Alice took the offered seat in Bessie's office, folded her hands into her lap in a composed and determined manner. Head up, eyes level, she said, "I would like to learn how to stop a baby from coming, Mrs. Earp. I expect you know how that works."

When she got over her shock, Bessie asked how far along Alice was. Alice said she wasn't pregnant. She just didn't want any more children. So Bessie gave her the best recipe she had, which was "four ounces of shredded cotton root in a gallon of water. Boil it down to a pint. Drink half a cup every couple of hours as soon as you're late. It'll bring on bleedin' in a day or so." And from that day on, Mrs. Wright and Mrs. Earp had a remarkably cordial relationship. They weren't friends exactly — Alice Wright didn't seem to be friends with anybody, really — but they spoke pleasantly to each other at Bob's store, in front of everybody. And every month, Alice gave Bessie a triumphant little smile.

Maggie Carnahan, by contrast, was apt to

cut Bessie dead in public now that she was Mrs. George Hoover. Bessie had never quite decided if Maggie's snubs were insulting or pathetic or simply funny. Like Bessie's mamma used to say, "There's no worse snob in the world than a planter's house nigger," and Maggie Carnahan was Black Irish.

Even before she married, Maggie had set great store by the appearance of respectability. Fresh off the boat from Belfast, she went to work with a cousin who was a lady's maid in New York City. To this day, Maggie clung to the standards set by three months' strict training in The Way Things Ought To Be Done, though the job itself didn't last, for the crash of '73 bankrupted the New Yorkers Maggie had worked for.

Things went from bad to worse for the girl as she moved west, town by town. By the end of '75 Maggie had fetched up in Dodge City, where Bessie gave her a job. That's how George and Maggie met.

Big George didn't seem bothered by his little wife's past. "Can't reform unless you were a sinner first," he'd declare to anyone who'd listen. Maggie would cringe and look away when he said that. By Maggie's lights, a fallen woman started out lower on the ladder to righteousness than a saloon owner who'd rotted customers' stomachs by the thousands. In Bessie's opinion, the most admirable thing about George Hoover was that he didn't see a lot of moral distance between selling flesh and selling snakehead liquor. "Vice is vice," George always said. "One part of hell is as hot as the next parcel over."

What got Bessie riled was the way George sent his wife around to collect "campaign contributions." Maggie hated being used as a bagman, and George must have known how it embarrassed her. (Eddie Foy thought that was particularly funny. "Imagine it! An Irish whore, by way of New York and Chicago, dismayed by political corruption.") Maggie worked hard to make what she was doing seem nicer, and her latest cover was asking for a donation to the City Beautification Fund.

George had added a big glass garden room to their house last year, and that had inspired Maggie's notion of putting flower boxes all around the Dodge City train station to give newcomers a better first impression of the town. Making that Ulster accent seem cultured wasn't easy, but Maggie did her level best to sound like a lady from New York when she put the bite on.

"Can't you just picture it? Flowers make such a difference!" she told Bessie. "If each business donates enough for a flower box, think how pretty it will look! It's a nice way to show civic pride, then, isn't it."

It's a nice way to wring cash out of every saloon and brothel owner in Dodge, Bessie thought, but she gave generously anyway. Big George was letting it be known that if Dodge went Reform in the next election, he might be persuaded to tolerate a vice zone south of the tracks, as long as the north side of Front was cleaned up and kept quiet. And Bessie felt sure George Hoover was keeping track of precisely how many "flower boxes" had been donated and by whom.

Unbuttoning her shirtwaist, she peeked through her bedroom window's lace curtain and watched Chalkie Beeson's brass band getting into position. After the parade, there'd be pie-eating contests, a greased-pig chase, and a full slate of horse races. Women were auctioning off baked goods and quilts to raise money for a school. In the evening, there was going to be an ice cream social with dancing, and fireworks after dark.

The town was getting civilized, and Bessie knew what that meant: time to think about moving again. Just last week, a letter from Virgil came, saying there were rumors of a big silver strike in Arizona, down near the Mexican border. That had James and Wyatt and Morgan all talking about how maybe they should go south in the autumn.

Unlacing her corset, rolling off her stockings, unpinning her hair, Mrs. James C. Earp looked around the cozy, private room she kept aside just for herself and her husband, with its carved walnut bedstead, its pretty curtains and Turkey carpet, and the framed steel-cut engravings of Grecian ruins that reminded her of Nashville.

Dammit, she thought, sliding under the sheet. I just got the wallpaper up.

The blare of trumpets, the shrill of piccolos, and the thud of drums were clearly audible on the second floor of Dodge House, as was the nearly constant crackle of fireworks and the flat *bang!* of random pistol shots, but the noise outside didn't disturb John Henry Holliday's sleep. It just made him sigh and give up trying to get any.

The hoorah had begun before midnight, about the same time the police force was rather belatedly informed that gunfire within town limits was legal on the Fourth. Wyatt was furious when he found out. Public order would be set back by a good three weeks. There was, however, nothing he could do about it, apart from insisting that his men stay on duty for the next thirty-six hours to keep anarchy at bay.

All night long, Texas visitors to Dodge took full advantage of their temporary immunity from prosecution, shooting out lights and breaking windows. They seemed evenly divided regarding the 102nd birthday of the Union so recently preserved at the cost of so many lives and such destruction. About half viewed the Glorious Fourth as an occasion for sullen, resentful drinking followed by fist-fights; the rest considered it a good excuse to get loaded and look for someone to beat up. Tired of the gladiatorial drunkenness, Doc had cashed out of an uninteresting game and gone to bed, where he had remained wide awake ever since.

Even without the noise outside, sleep would have eluded him, for Wyatt would be starting treatment soon.

This was the part of dentistry that John Henry Holliday liked most. Planning procedures step by step. Rehearsing the entire session in his mind, moment by moment, to minimize the time a patient spent under ether. By nature, he was inclined to begin with the most difficult aspect of any work so he could truthfully promise his patient, "Today was the worst. It'll be easier from now on." When he had a full practice back in Atlanta, however, he discovered that it was good policy to inquire into the patient's own preference in the matter.

"If there is good news and bad news," he'd ask, "which would you rather hear first?"

"Bad," Wyatt had answered, without hesitation. "Get it over."

So Doc would begin on the right side of the mandibular arch, which was seriously degraded. Start with the extraction. Once that hopeless molar was pulled, excavate the decay in the occlusal surfaces of the other two, drilling to find clean dentin. He preferred to use gold foil for the fillings, but that was like working with flakes of ash; his cough being what it was, the best technique was beyond him now. Silver amalgam would be good enough.

Most dentists would have pulled those bad bicuspids without hesitation; the interproximal surfaces were severely hourglassed. On the other hand, the gingival bone seemed to be intact. He hated to give up on firmly rooted dentition, but he just couldn't see a way to save those two . . .

Just past noon, when he was nearly asleep at last, the solution came to him. Suddenly and fully awake, he sat up, coughed for a while, threw on a shirt and trousers, and hurried downstairs to No. 24. There he composed a detailed outline of a novel dental procedure that would involve yoking the bicuspids together with a gold collar, for structural strength, to be combined with a variation on a cantilevered pontic. He added two diagrams — occlusal and lingual — to illustrate the idea, then rolled himself a cigarette and settled back to review what he had written, making several changes to clarify the description.

If the procedure worked as he anticipated, he decided, he would submit an article to *Dental Cosmos.* A publication like that would be a genuine contribution to the profession.

And it would please Uncle John no end.

Wyatt's case had presented a variety of interesting clinical challenges, but the real satisfaction would come a few days after the patient's final session. With his gums healing and the trauma behind him, Wyatt would begin to realize how much his teeth had bothered him all his life, how much pain he'd come to accept as normal. He'd eat better, feel better than he had in years. He'd also be able to say more than a few words in a row without thinking of his missing teeth. Occasionally those few words might be addressed to someone with dental trouble: "Go see Doc Holliday."

By all accounts, Wyatt Earp was as honest a lawman as you could find in Kansas — admittedly, not a high bar to clear. Still, if he told people that Doc Holliday was good at his job, it would count for a lot. And that was as close to advertising as a dentist could come, for the A.D.A. prohibited anything beyond the simple announcement of the opening of his office. He had no legitimate competitors in the region, but like all credentialed dental surgeons, he was up against charlatans who roamed the countryside in colorfully decorated wagons emblazoned with signs that proclaimed the driver to be a "Painless Dentist."

These shameless frauds were — in all fairness to them — vicious, destructive scoundrels, and John Henry Holliday hated them, individually and as a class, with a pure and unwavering flame.

They would drive into town and attract a crowd with a drummer's patter, offering to demonstrate their skill by extracting a tooth free of charge for the first person brave enough to volunteer. An accomplice — usually a woman — would act frightened and hesitant but come forward complaining of toothache. In a snap and with a flourish, a horse molar would be held aloft, like the rabbit pulled from a magician's hat. Proclaiming herself completely free of discomfort of any kind, the woman would urge others to approach and pay in advance to have their teeth ripped out with pliers. Howling victims were ridiculed. "Why, what a big baby you are! That little lady didn't make a peep!" Half an hour later, the butcher and his girlfriend would leave town before the infections set in, the patients died, and their survivors developed a lifelong horror of dentistry.

It was truly remarkable that Wyatt had decided to go all in. Aside from the expense and the anxiety of extensive dental work, there was the plain trust required to believe that a dentist wouldn't recommend procedures simply to jack up his fees. In Wyatt's case, it was easier to list the teeth that *didn't* need care, and John Henry was gratified that the deputy believed in his professional integrity —

"Why ain't you in bed?"

He looked up.

Kate was standing in the office doorway, small fists on her hips, ready to do battle. "You said you was tired. You said you was going to bed."

"No . . ." Doc said slowly. "I *believe* what I said was —"

She stalked in and put her hand on his forehead. "You're hot," she told him.

"It's July, darlin'."

"You look like shit."

"Miss Kate, I declare!" he cried, fluttering his eyelashes. "You are such a flirt!"

"China Joe took in seams again," she said, daring him to deny it.

"Jau Dong-Sing is a reprehensible gossip," he muttered, lowering his eyes to the papers on his desk, "and I shall speak to him about —"

"You're losing weight — I can feel it! I don't need no goddam Chinaman to tell me that. We lost money last night. Your game's off," she told him. She dug a hand into her purse and held up ninety dollars. "Do you understand how hard I work to make this much?"

"I have *never* asked you to —"

"No, but you keep eating —"

"Not much, I don't."

"Goddammit, Doc! One of us has to have some business sense, or we'll both be out in the street!"

He sat back in his chair, arms folded across his chest: a tall, thin, offended version of her small, round, furious self.

"What's the best a dentist can make in a year?" she demanded. "In a real city, with a big practice! Sixteen hundred? Two grand? Doc, you can win that in an *hour!* When you're rested, when you pay attention —"

"Darlin', if my income is insufficient to satisfy you, you are free to depart at your earliest convenience!"

"Damn you, I don't want to leave! I just want to understand why in hell you bother with this!"

"Why?"

"Yes! Why?" She grabbed the papers on his desk and waved the crumpled notes at the chair, and the drill, and the cabinet of instruments. "This office, all this equipment — it ain't never going to pay! Why do you keep spending money and trying to be a goddam dentist when you could —"

"Because," he said, astonished that he had to say it, "I can relieve sufferin'."

She stared at him, mouth open.

He stared back, dumbfounded by her surprise.

"Kate . . . People die in *misery* for want of a dentist's care! I bother with all this because

I can relieve sufferin'. I can improve lives. Sometimes I can even save them." He stood and reached over to take the treatment plan out of her hand, flattening the notes against the surface of his desk. When he spoke again, his voice was quiet and tense. "There is nobody for five hundred miles able to do what I can for patients who trust me enough to let me treat them. I am good at my work. I am proud of my profession. And I will thank you not to belittle it."

For the moment, the argument was suspended, the two of them glaring at each other. In the silence, they became aware again of the noise outside. Gunfire. Strings of small firecrackers crackling. The cheers of drunken spectators egging on a fight.

Kate dropped her eyes first. Seeing his notes, with their careful drawings and orderly numbered paragraphs, she asked, "Who's that for?"

"Wyatt."

"He'll never pay you," she said dismissively.

"He already is," Doc said tightly. "Two dollars a week."

"For crissakes, Doc, that ain't even ante!"

"Kate, the discussion is closed."

"You know he bet everything he's got on that race this afternoon?"

Doc looked up warily and saw the smug expression of a handicapper with inside information. He had money on that race

himself. So did Morg. The odds on Dick
Naylor were twenty-seven to one, last time
he checked.

"He's going to forfeit," Kate said with satisfaction.

This was news, and she could see it.

"That big stupid hick didn't think it out,"
she said. "The whole town is filled with
Texans trying to kill each other. Listen to
them out there! He ain't never going to get
away from work long enough to ride — Dammit, Doc, where are you going?"

Things happened. He reacted. He didn't
intend to defy Kate or shake off her angry
solicitude. In quieter moments, he was
touched when she nagged him about taking
better care of himself, even if her motives
were a good deal less than pure. That said, by
the time he left the hotel and plunged into
the roiling crowd outside, he had forgotten
her.

Dick Naylor was entered in the quarter
mile.

Post to post, no more than thirty seconds.

The entire population of Ford County appeared to be in town for the festivities, and
those nine hundred locals had been joined by
upwards of three thousand cowboys. Temperance ladies from Wichita were marching
through this throng, holding up neatly let-
tered placards meant to warn illiterate drov-

ers of the dangers of Demon Rum, while an unknown number of freelance pickpockets and sneak thieves, exported by the City of St. Louis, worked the crowd. Farm families made their way through the crush in open wagons driven by stiff-faced German fathers trying not to provoke an anti-immigrant riot by running over singing, shouting, belligerent Texans. Scandalized German mothers did their inadequate best to shield the eyes of gleefully curious German children from the spectacle of Irish streetwalkers hawking their commodities as shamelessly as the Jewish drummers who offered notions and patent medicines at makeshift tables along the teeming length of Front Street. And all the while, Mr. Jau's two assistant laundrymen busily sold Chinese firecrackers to idiots who lit the fuses and tossed them under the bellies of horses, just to see the animals go berserk and bolt through town, scattering the citizenry.

Battling through the swarm, Doc scanned faces, hoping to spot Wyatt or Morgan. When ten minutes failed to yield sight of a single lawman, he decided to put the von Angensperg Principle into effect: skip permission and ask forgiveness later. He had to get to the barn, saddle Dick, and ride to the racetrack by three, and he was running out of time. If anyone at the track argued, he'd say Wyatt sent him, and deal with the consequences later.

Tired of the buffeting and shoving, he decided to try for one of the alleys and moved to the edge of the street. He had just reached the boardwalk when a chair crashed through the Comique Theater's front window.

Ducking low, off balance, he raised his arms against the shower of glass. A moment later, he was spun around and knocked to the ground when thirty-some wild-eyed Texas boys boiled out of the building. He was still struggling to find his footing when he heard Eddie Foy shout, "Doc! I'm coming!"

Minnowing through the mob with lithe acrobatic dispatch, Eddie arrived at his side, hauled him onto his feet, and pulled him backward until the two of them were flattened against the wall of the theater. Once there, they had no thought except to stay out of the brawl.

The Texans were screaming for blood, a quantity of which was already streaming from the head of a limp German fiddler — and if he wasn't already dead, he would be soon, for the cowboy on top of him was pretty clearly set on opening the fiddler's throat. "When I tell you to play 'Yaller Rose,' " the kid was yelling, "you by God play 'Yaller Rose,' you damn Dutch sonofabitch!"

Wyatt appeared. Calm and workmanlike, he elbowed his way toward the middle of the mob where the German lay. With a spare economy of movement, Wyatt lifted the heavy-hilted knife up and out of the Texan's raised hand and brought the butt end down sharply on its owner's head.

The motion was so quick and so effective that things got quiet, and everyone could hear Wyatt say, "You're under arrest for assault and disorderly conduct," as though he were remarking on the weather. Kinda hot today. Looks like rain.

He'd reached down to pull the assailant upright and haul him off to jail when one Texan — out of thirty — *one* approached to object.

Wyatt dropped the unconscious Texan and straightened with a look of contempt so plain and powerful, the drover took a step back.

"Hey!" the drover said, trying for bluster. "Hold it right there, law-dog!"

"Why?" Wyatt asked. "You wanna get your sister to help?"

There were snickers.

Embarrassed, the Texan stammered, "H-hey! Hey! You can't —"

Wyatt slapped him hard. One cheek, the other.

"Yes," he said. "I can."

"Jesus, Mary, and Joseph," Eddie whispered, pale under his freckles. "They'll kill him sure."

"No," Doc said softly. "No. They won't."

And he had no idea why he was so certain, except . . . it was as though Wyatt knew something that the other man didn't. Or maybe he knew something *about* the other man, who was ashamed of it. Yes! And whatever that *something* was, both of them were agreed as to its significance.

If there was any doubt about what would happen next, the roar of a shotgun ended it. Morgan Earp's voice sang out nearby. Within seconds, Charlie Bassett, John Stauber, Chuck Trask, Jack Brown, and Bat Masterson arrived, running. Crouched, shotguns shouldered, they pushed through to Wyatt and wheeled to form a cordon around him, backing the mob away.

"Wanna go get your sister?" Morg laughed as he took his place next to his brother. "Jesus, Wyatt, you sounded just like Pa —"

"Shut up," Wyatt snapped.

Morgan's face went slack, and he looked like he'd been backhanded.

What was that about? Doc wondered.

"Sorry," Wyatt said briefly. "See to the fiddler."

Morgan knelt at the German's side. "Still breathing," he reported. "Stauber, fetch Doc McCarty!"

Drawn by the noise and the excitement, the crowd was getting bigger by the moment, and the buzz of comment became louder when people noticed which Texan Wyatt Earp had just arrested. The kid was sitting on the ground, one leg out straight in front of him, the other crumpled beneath him, a circumstance he'd lament when he sobered up. He looked like any of a thousand beardless boys in town that day, but the spur he'd landed on when Wyatt dumped him was heavy silver. His boots were custom-made, and the hat lying in the dirt nearby was an expensive Stetson.

Word got around fast. Dog Kelley and Bob Wright showed up on Doc McCarty's heels.

"That's Billy Driskill," Bob said. "Wyatt, wait! You can't —"

Wyatt had the kid by the ear, but he was looking at Dog Kelley. "I told you when I started: I don't care who it is. He breaks the law, I'm taking him in."

"Dog," Bob Wright said, his voice low and urgent, "that's Jesse Driskill's nephew. His uncle's worth millions to the city! You're the mayor — do something!"

"C'mon, Wyatt," Dog pleaded. "Be reasonable!"

"You want my badge back?" Wyatt asked.

"You'll get mine, too," Morg said over his shoulder.

Stauber and Charlie and all the others looked to Morg, and nodded. One by one, every man on the Dodge City police force told Dog, "Mine, too," ready to back Wyatt's play, even though none of them was sure yet what in hell was going on.

Doc McCarty was kneeling on the dirt by

394

then, examining the bleeding fiddler. Dog came closer and asked, "How bad is he?"

"He's young," the doctor said. "He'll live."

"Well, then," Dog said, clapping his hands once. "No harm done!"

Wyatt shook his head mulishly. "There's got to be one law for everybody, Dog."

"Yeah, but — Wyatt, he's —"

"No, sir," Wyatt insisted. "There can't be one law for rich Texans and another law for broke Texans, and another law for Negroes, and another one for Chinamen, and squaws, and Irishmen, and whores, and another one for everybody else. I can't parse it that way, Dog! I am not that smart! There's got to be one law for everybody, or I can't do this job. You want my badge or not?"

Dog glanced at Morgan, who acknowledged the look with a shrug and a nod and a sigh: Yeah, I know what you're thinking . . .

It was boneheaded and contrary, and maybe someday Wyatt would learn the ways of the world and how to go along with things he couldn't change, but not today. Today he was going to take that rich kid in or get fired for trying.

That was when Bob Wright — conciliatory and earnest — approached Wyatt to have a quiet word with him, except Dog Kelley stepped between them.

"Tell you what, Wyatt," Dog said quickly. "We'll take the kid straight to court and let him pay the fine. Everybody wins."

"Wyatt, if it's the arrest fee you're thinking of," Bob said, reaching into his own pocket, "let's see if we can't work something out —"

"Bad move," Doc murmured to Eddie.

"Bob, no!" Mayor Kelley moaned. "He don't mean it, Wyatt. Not like that —"

"Morg," Wyatt called so everyone in the crowd could hear him. "Arrest this man. He is attempting to bribe an officer of the law."

"Mr. Wright," Morgan said, "I'm sorry, but I'm taking you in."

"F'crissakes, Wyatt," Dog cried. "Morgan, no!"

"You want my badge, Mayor?" Morg asked, fingers on his star.

Dog threw up his hands in defeat. "This will not end well," he warned the Earps, but there was nothing more he could say. Bob Wright was standing right there, his face as blank as an egg, malice rising off him like a stink.

The boy on the ground was conscious enough now to respond to the pain in his ear when Wyatt tugged at it. Getting to his feet blearily, Billy Driskill let himself be led to jail, right behind the only man in Dodge almost as rich as his Uncle Jesse.

"Go on, now," Bat Masterson ordered the crowd. "Show's over. Break it up."

Slowly the crowd dispersed, leaving Dog Kelley and China Joe standing together on the street.

Jau Dong-Sing crossed his arms over his chest and shook his head, the way any American would. "Wyatt Earp one big damn dumb son a bitch," he muttered.

"A remark like that is a good way for a Chink to get himself lynched," Dog warned before he walked away, "but I ain't gonna tell you that you're wrong."

Stone-faced and determined to deliver both prisoners to a cell, Wyatt came about halfway to breaking the jaw of a tall, thin, unshaven man standing between him and the jailhouse door. Morg had time to say, "That's Doc! Don't hit him!" But something had already made Wyatt pull his fist back. A thoughtfulness, maybe. A look of appraisal that didn't quite match the man's coatless shirt and rumpled trousers.

The dentist, too, seemed distracted by events, though sheer force of habit made him say "Afternoon," to Bob Wright, as though the merchant weren't being hauled in on a bribery charge.

"It's after two," Doc told Wyatt.

Wyatt's forehead furrowed. "Did I have an appointment today?"

"No! The race! Three o'clock?"

Wyatt glanced at the sun. "Hell. Forgot all about it."

"Let me ride for you."

"In the race, you mean?" Wyatt had never seen Doc Holliday ride anything. "You sure?"

"Would I make the offer if I were not capable?" Doc cried. "What does a man have to do to be taken at his word in this town? Do I have to shoot someone? Because I am makin' a list! Yes, damn you, I am sure!"

"Well, I ain't," the Driskill kid mumbled, swaying a bit but watching Doc, who was coughing now. "You don' look too good, mister."

"Shut up. Nobody asked you," Wyatt said, still gripping the kid's ear. But he was inclined to agree with the boy, and Doc must have seen that.

"I can do this, Wyatt," the dentist insisted. "It's a short race."

"Dick don't know you, Doc. He's not an easy horse —"

"Let me try! He won't finish better if you keep him in the stall," Doc pointed out. "And he'll be carryin' less than he's used to."

"Tha's an a'vantage," young Driskill agreed. Like anybody gave a shit.

"All right," Wyatt told Doc finally, not because he thought it was a good idea but because he couldn't make himself say no to what he saw in the skinny Georgian's shining eyes. "If you can get him saddled, give it a try."

Doc nodded and set off for the stable.

"Watch out!" Wyatt called. "He bites!"

Without looking back, Doc raised a hand in acknowledgment.

"Don't hit him for it!" Wyatt yelled.

Doc turned and stared, motionless, while the crowd moved around him.

"Hell," Wyatt sighed. He already regretted what he'd just said and expected to be told off for it. "What kinda blankety-blank idiot do you take me for?" Doc would ask him. "Are you sayin' I'm a mean, stupid, s.o.b. who'd hit a horse for bein' nervy?"

Instead, what Wyatt saw was the long, slow emergence of something that began in John Henry Holliday's eyes and lifted the high, flat planes of his cheeks just before his mouth dropped open into the biggest, happiest smile Wyatt had ever seen on that boy's face.

"I knew you'd say that!" Doc hollered back joyously and, coughing, he disappeared into the crowd.

There are many reasons a horse will bite. In the wild, stallions bite during contests for a harem. Boss mares do so to enforce discipline within a herd. Sometimes it's just in a horse's nature to be mouthy, the way a retrieving dog is born with the urge to carry things around. Even a good-tempered saddle horse might snap when startled by an abrupt or careless motion. *Mend your ways,* such a horse is warning, and a human had best pay heed. It's not good judgment to pick a fight with something that can tear the muscles clean off your bones.

"Watch how he holds his head," young Robert Holliday counseled the first time he took his little cousin to the Fayetteville stable to meet Robert's new gelding. "See the tail? If you know what you're lookin' at, you can read a horse like one of your damn books."

Standing on an upturned bucket so he could see into the stall, John Henry knew exactly what he was looking at: the homeliest pony he'd laid eyes on by the tender age of eight, and if nature had produced another who could take the title away, he had not seen evidence of the achievement in all the years since.

Snickers the little horse was unkindly named, in recognition of the response his appearance provoked. He was a dirty white with flecks of black that looked like dried mud missed by a careless groom. Against that grayish mediocrity, the gelding's pink-rimmed eyes seemed as bloodshot as a drunkard's. His unloveliness might have been forgiven had it not been for a protruding and slightly wobbly lower lip that made the poor animal look addled.

"Nothin' wrong with this horse wasn't wrong with the fool who rode him," said Robert.

Faced with inconsistent expectations, defeated by unreasonable demands, Snickers would stand still, looking confused. He'd been beaten for his prior owner's failures, and having learned to fear men, the gelding no longer waited for meanness to be made manifest. Walk by his stall too quickly or too slowly or too carelessly and, like as not, he'd snake his neck out at you and clamp his teeth on whatever he could catch hold of.

"Hittin' a horse is plain stupid, John Henry. There's no excuse for it," Robert declared with the serene instructive confidence of a ten-year-old boy who's made a careful study of a single subject and knows all there is to know about it. "Horses are mirrors. They'll show you back whatever you show them. Watch a man with a horse, and you'll see what's inside his own self."

What the stable hands had, inside and out, was an entirely rational eye-rolling fright. They were scared to death of Snickers. John Henry clearly remembered the worried gray-haired uncle who'd set aside a muck shovel and hurried over to warn young Marse Robert not to let his little cousin John go near that crazy damn horse. Looking back now, he realized, there was irony to be discovered. The old man knew exactly who'd be blamed and beaten if a white child was bitten. It sure as hell wasn't Snickers.

By contrast, what Robert Holliday had inside, even at the age of ten, was a master's unconscious self-assurance, along with a basic decency that made him patient with a small, shy cousin who still talked funny. Robert had stepped toward Snickers, speaking low and friendly, not a bit scared, even when the pony tossed his head.

"Hey, now," Robert said, quiet and firm and kind. "Hey, now. Settle down, you."

That was the voice John Henry Holliday heard as he approached Dick Naylor's stall. Part of him wanted to look at his watch again, to see how much time he had to get out to the track before the race began, but he could almost feel Robert at his side, saying, *Hey, now. Settle down. Take it slow or he'll make you pay.*

At the sound of unfamiliar footsteps in the aisle, Dick faced around and blew a wary snort, halfway between curiosity and fright. There was no answering exhalation in the barn. That would be a source of concern to the horse, who was down in the last stall, away from the corrals where the cowboys' mounts were penned.

Standing a few yards away, John Henry let Dick take a good look at him before asking sympathetically, "Y'all by your lonesome in here? Where'd all your friends go? Off havin' a fine time at the fair, I expect, and here you are with nobody for company."

He reached into a bucket of carrots hanging on a hook nearby, allowing it to clank a bit against the wall so Dick would recognize the sound. He put a couple of carrots in his pocket, keeping another in the palm of his hand, and waited to see how Dick would take this turn of events.

The horse backed away, nostrils flaring, ears flicking in all directions. Tense and ready to shy, he stretched out his neck, measuring the distance to the stranger's hand.

"That's right: you don't know me, but you'd like this carrot, wouldn't you . . . Wyatt sends you his best, but he is fully occupied at the moment, diggin' his political grave. Aurelius on the plains: one law for everyone!" John Henry marveled. "Your master is a stubborn, sanctimonious Republican jackass, but I admire his principles."

Dick lifted a hoof and hit at the stall gate.

"No, sir," John Henry said firmly. "I will not be pawed at, thank you very much! But you want what I have . . . You got decisions to make, son."

Irritated by flies, a horse will shake his head, or wag it, or jerk it up and back. Irritated by humans, the same moves in rapid succession can signal equine exasperation.

"Mind your manners," John Henry warned softly, "or I will eat this carrot myself — see if I don't."

At last, there was the long, low, guttural nicker he was waiting for, used by horses to greet one another, heard by humans at feeding time.

"There you go," John Henry said warmly. He stepped closer and held his hand waist-high to make Dick lower his head and relax, letting the horse nuzzle the carrot from his palm. "That's right," he said, his voice low and friendly and calm. "I am not Wyatt, but I am a man with a carrot. Can't be too bad, can I? Oh, you found that one, too, did you? No, no, no — let me take it out of the pocket. Rip the worsted, and we'll get what-for from Mr. Jau . . ."

Lured with a third carrot, Dick let himself be led out into the aisle, stood still for a cross-tie, and even let the stranger examine his mouth, which was a hardened mass of scar tissue.

"Look at that," John Henry muttered. "Some heartless goddam sonofabitch did you a disservice, and may he rot in hell for it!"

Dick shifted uneasily.

The damage was old and not superficially abraded. Wyatt must have been using a bridle without a metal bit.

"Well, Dick, you have fallen into better hands now, and that is your good fortune. What do you think, son? Ready to return the favor? Shall we go show this burg who owns the fastest quarter-miler in Ford County?"

Dick tossed his head in response, beginning to get keyed up, and just as well, for they'd be racing soon. Running his hand along the horse's flank, John Henry retreated down the

405

aisle toward the central tack room.

Standing in the dim and shadowy light, he scanned the racks and pegs, trying to decide which saddle was Wyatt's. "That's got to be it," he murmured when he spotted one that was unadorned and worn at the edges but well cared for, with a soft-nose hackamore slung over its pommel. He had just gathered himself to hoist forty pounds of leather and iron off the rack when someone out in the aisle walked past the tack room door.

Motionless, John Henry listened.

Dick Naylor gave a low, troubled snort.

Everybody knew Dick was supposed to run today. Thousands of dollars were riding on the quarter, and there were dozens of ways to meddle with a horse and ruin his chances. It was too late for some, but others were quick. Shove a piece of sponge up the animal's nostril to impede his breathing. Hit a shin and lame the leg before a bruise could rise. Jam something into the frog of a hoof.

Heart hammering, John Henry lowered the saddle back onto the rack, careful not to let the stirrups clank. Like anyone else in town, he could have carried guns legally that day, but he'd left Dodge House in a rush. His pistol was back at the hotel, behind the front desk. The Philadelphia Deringer in his pocket was only good at card-table distances.

Hoping he could make it through the next fifteen seconds without coughing, he slid a throwing knife out of the sheath in his left boot, stepped toward the tack room door, and leaned carefully into the aisle.

"Back away from that horse!" he ordered. "Do it! *Now!*"

Kate turned and glared, offended, over her shoulder. "How dare you speak to me like —"

Dropping the knife, he rushed at her, shoving her hard and holding her down when they crashed to the floor.

The hooves just missed their heads. Dick squealed and got ready to let fly again.

Doc grabbed Kate's arm and dragged her backward, scrambling down the aisle, pulling her crabwise away from the horse.

"God a'mighty!" he cried when they were out of range. "Are you hurt?"

She was sitting on the floor, looking like a five-year-old smacked across the face and still too stunned to weep. "Are you crazy?" she cried. "God damn you, look what you did to my dress! Why did you —"

"Never mind the dress! You were about to be kicked halfway to Colorado." Doc got to his feet and did his best to help Kate up, although it was not completely clear who was helping whom because he was coughing now. "Are you hurt?"

"Yes! No! I don't know! What're you doing in here?" she demanded, rubbing an elbow. "I been looking everywhere, and Wyatt

wouldn't tell me nothing, that stupid sonofabitch —"

Dick stamped and snorted. Doc left Kate
to settle the animal down. That was when she
started to cry. It was the shock. And the fall.
And anger that Doc seemed more worried
about the horse than about her. He understood all that, but there was so little time left!

When she saw the saddle, she figured out
what he was doing, and then she was like a
terrier: nipping at his heels, yapping at him,
getting in his way. He paused just long
enough to lean over and kiss her on the
mouth, but that didn't even slow her down.

He lost his grip trying to sling the saddle
onto Dick's back, and when he dropped it,
he rounded on Kate, shouting, "For the love
of God — get out of my road!"

It was a mistake. Producing that much
volume set off a coughing fit so bad, it left
him bent over, hands on his knees, staring at
the floor and gasping like a catfish on a
riverbank.

"You see?" she cried, weeping and frantic.
"You see? Do you want to die? Are you trying to kill yourself? You can't —"

The chest pain was searing. He had nothing left for courtesy.

"God damn you, woman! Shut up!"

And Kate did because Doc never spoke to
her like that, never spoke to anyone like that.
She could see that he was truly angry, and

his anger frightened her more than that of any man she'd ever been with, not because he might beat her — who cared a damn about that? — but because he might send her away.

Cold to her core, she held her breath, watching him catch his, and she wailed in pain when he straightened cautiously and said the words she feared most.

"Darlin', I can't live this way anymore."

He wouldn't look at her. She knew what that meant. He was done with her. Panicking, she started to beg, to promise, to swear that she'd be good, but he shook his head. It was over — she *knew* it — and nothing she said now would make any difference. The horse pranced and pulled at the cross-ties while she sobbed — great, gulping, terrified sobs. He'll go to that goddam horse, not me! Kate thought furiously, and she *hated* Doc for that, so blind with tears that she almost didn't notice when he came close enough to take her in his arms and hold her while she wept.

"Hush, now," he was saying softly, over and over. "Hush, now. Hush."

When at last she quieted, he took a step back, wiped her cheeks with his palms, and pulled a handkerchief from his pocket and made her blow her nose.

All the things she's lost, he was thinking, and what she has is me.

"Darlin'," he said judiciously, "I believe the

time has come for us to define the terms of our association. I am a slender reed to lean upon, but —"

"You ain't — ? I don't have to — ?"

"No," he said. "No, but if this's goin' to work, you have to promise me —"

"I will, Doc! Whatever you say! I won't argue no more —"

"Kate! Hush up, and listen!"

Her dazzling aqua eyes were as red-rimmed as poor old Snickers', wet and frightened and fastened on his own. She snuffled in snot and wiped her nose on the back of her hand as a child might, waiting to hear what John Henry Holliday had never told her, what he had never told anyone.

"Kate," he began, "I know this disease inside and out —"

He couldn't.

Couldn't speak of the cadaver he'd dissected, about the way a chance glance at his own body could bring a vision of that tubercular pauper back to him. Couldn't bear to tell how memories of his mother's last hours would sometimes grip and shake him, like a dog killing a rat . . .

"Kate," he said finally, "I know what is waiting for me at the end of this road. I am askin' you to believe me: I am in no hurry to arrive at my destination. I know you're scared, darlin'. I'm scared, too." He looked away. "Christ, I am so damn *tired* of bein' scared . . ."

Dick Naylor snorted and pawed. Doc went to him and ran a hand down his back, murmuring. The horse quieted, and Doc spoke again, softly and without turning. "A few weeks ago, we buried a fine young man. If there were any justice on earth, Johnnie Sanders would have outlived me, and this wretched world might have been better for his presence in it. Well, none of us knows how much time we have, but I know this," he said, looking now at Kate. "I do not want to spend another *minute* of whatever I have left bein' scared. I can't carry the fear anymore. Not mine. Not yours. I have to lay that burden down."

He was silent for a time, but when he came to Kate and took both of her hands in his own, he was calmer and more sure of himself than he had been in a long time.

"This is what I am prepared to offer," he said. "I will be good to you, Kate, but if you want to stay with me, you have to let me do as much as I can, whenever I can for as long as I can. And both of us have to quit bein' scared. Will you promise me that?"

For the rest of her long life, Mária Katarina Harony would remember standing in Hamilton Bell's New Famous Elephant Barn on the Fourth of July in 1878, looking up at Doc Holliday. She would remember how quiet it was. She would remember dust dancing in

411

shafts of light filtering through narrow gaps in the barn's roof. She would remember how thin Doc looked — even then, when he was forty-five pounds heavier than he would be when he died. She would remember wondering if she had ever before seen his eyes so devoid of humor and irony. She would remember his hands, strong and steady and gentle, holding her own.

She would never understand the man himself but, that afternoon, she understood this much at least: she understood what Doc needed from her, and from anyone who was to be his friend. Her English was inadequate to express it. The austerity of Latin was best. *Visus virium:* the presumption of strength. And . . . respect, as well, for the courage it took to produce that illusion.

"Nec spe, nec metu," she said. Without hope, without fear.

"Athena," he murmured, kissing her forehead, holding her close. "That's my girl. That's my sweet, brave, Hungarian warrior . . ."

She watched, silent, while he finished tacking up and slipped the cross-ties off and led the horse out of the barn. She had never seen him ride in the six months they'd been together. They'd always traveled by stage or railway. Light and quick, he swung up into the saddle — a motion completed between one breath and the next — and held the reins

412

with relaxed assurance.

"L'audace, l'audace, toujours l'audace!" he declared with that charming, crooked grin of his. "Wish me luck, darlin'!"

She smiled damply and nodded. He reined over and the horse moved off, their partnership a fluid rhythm, full of grace and joy.

Tout casse, tout passe, tout lasse, she thought. "*Ne meurs pas, mon amour,* don't die," she whispered, but she lifted her voice to call, *"Bonne chance!"* and started walking toward the fairgrounds, to meet him after the race.

Short horse races, the events were called — not because the horses were short but because the distances were. If you happened to be looking the other way, the contest could be over before you turned your head. Even so, huge bets often rode on the outcome. John Henry Holliday had grown up hearing stories of entire plantations won and lost that way.

And yet there were no fixed rules for such races. Time and place might be determined in advance, though they were just as likely to be "Here and now." The distance to be run? From this rock to that tree — anywhere from fifty yards to five-eighths of a mile. Who would ride? The owner, some kid, a jockey. How would the race begin? Starter's gun, tap and go, ask and answer. Who'll judge the finish? And how will disputes be settled? Frequently with fists; occasionally with pistols.

On the frontier, the short-race horses themselves were not pampered, fragile Thoroughbreds but ordinary working animals, ridden by the men who depended on them daily. They were saddle horses, stock horses, cutting horses — descended from wild Spanish barbs, lost army mounts, and Indian ponies. What they had in common was early speed: an explosive start and the heart to run full-on in a straightaway competition that distilled the excitement of a longer race's home stretch into half a minute of purified, ecstatic, screaming emotion.

The times were getting shorter. Twenty-four seconds flat in an eighty-rod race was no longer uncommon. Breeders were beginning to produce heavily muscled, powerfully built animals that could break like an arrow from a bow and beat the earth with such force they seemed invincible — until some boy on a random-bred thirteen-year-old gelding with a barrel chest showed up for his first race and won it going away, stunning the favorite and ruining punters who by-God never saw *that* coming.

And *that* was what made it interesting.

There were four minutes left when Doc Holliday got to the line, and there might have been an argument about him riding Wyatt's horse, except that Mayor Kelley was as busy as Deputy Earp, and Dog had sent word from town to let substitutes act as jockeys.

Odds were adjusted to account for the weight Dick Naylor carried. A flurry of additional betting took place.

The track was dry, the race a measured quarter mile, with no heats to thin the field. The posts were taped.

A crowd of bettors — farmers, cowboys, townsmen — lined the distance. Fourteen horses were maneuvered into position.

Behind the line, a gun was raised.

And fired.

Fourteen horses: from a standing start to top speed in three strides. From a resting heart rate of thirty beats per minute to a brutal bastinado of four beats per second. Deep chests and massive hindquarters powering legs like the spokes of a wheel. Each hoof making separate contact with the ground, taking the animal's full weight for a fraction of a second in a rumbling cavalry charge, streaking toward the finish —

Fifteen seconds into the race, there were five horses out in front of the favorite, Michigan Jim, with Dick Naylor in seventh. Nineteen seconds. Jim and Dick were neck and neck, as the rest of the field began to fade and fall back. Three seconds more, and it was Michigan Jim in the lead, with Dick Naylor gaining, no more than a nose behind.

John Henry would have no memory of the moment he was thrown.

Later he would recall sailing grandly through the air, time slowing strangely until he crashed onto the ground and lay there, stunned, the air slammed out of his cheesy lungs, while the Fates and nearly thirteen thousand pounds of horseflesh wheeled and danced and hammered the ground around him. Weirdly tranquil, he thought, I should protect my hands. But he could not move, not even enough to draw his arms closer to his body. And anyway it didn't matter. He'd be killed in a moment or two.

Good, he thought, for it did not seem like such a bad end to be trampled to death on a sunny afternoon after twenty-seven glorious seconds on a racetrack.

Through the ringing in his ears, he heard Kate screaming in the distance and was sorry for her. Then he was surrounded by men waving the horses off, while somebody gripped him under the arms and dragged him off the track. Presently, his reflexes took over and he rolled onto his hands and knees, heart lurching, stomach heaving, collapsed lungs sucking wind.

Kate was kneeling at his side by then — almost as breathless as he was himself, having run as far as the horses — but she was neither weeping nor cursing him for a stupid, reckless, idiotic selfish bastard.

Good girl, he thought.

Eventually he got enough breath back to

cough, and gasp, and cough some more, and finally to speak. All he asked was "Did we win?"

James Earp was at the track and saw what happened, watching in wonder as Kate took charge of the aftermath. James himself found a rider to catch and cool off his brother's horse and lead Dick back to the stable, but it was Kate who arranged with a German to take the three of them into town in a wagon, stopping at Doc McCarty's on the way back to Dodge House.

When Doc Holliday and Kate were settled in their hotel room, James went home, spoke to the cashier and the floor maid to make sure everything was running smoothly. He settled a dispute with a customer over a bill and asked several of the day girls to stay on for overnight business. Finally, quietly, he went in to Bessie, meaning to take a nap for a few hours. The fireworks weren't until ten.

"How'd the race go, honey?" his wife asked sleepily. "Did Wyatt win?"

"No, but his horse crossed the line second. Doc Holliday was riding most of the time."

Bessie rolled over, rising on an elbow. "Most of the time?"

"Yeah, well, there was considerable discussion about that." James had unbuttoned his shirt partway and paused to pull it one-handed over his head and then down off the arm he couldn't raise. "No question about the winner. Michigan Jim at two to one, with Dick Naylor just behind him, and a bay named Creepin' Moses in third."

James climbed into bed, tuckered out.

Bessie was wide awake now. "So? What happened?"

" 'Bout two strides before the ribbon, some damn hound comes out of nowhere and crosses the track just beyond the finish line. One of Dog Kelley's coursers. Saw a rabbit or something, poking its head up in the infield, I guess."

"Mercy!"

"Yes, ma'am! It was a mess. Dick checked up and Doc went flying."

"Was he hurt?"

"Not as much as you'd think, seeing him hit the ground. I expected he was killed or broke his fool neck, but he just got the wind knocked out of him. He's scraped up pretty good and he'll be hobbling for a week, but McCarty says nothing's broke. Chalkie ruled Doc was still in the saddle when Dick crossed the line. Even the man who came in third thought so. Dick paid nine to one to place."

"Kate must've been beside herself."

"She was at first, but she got a grip pretty quick. Handled it real well."

Lying back, Bessie said thoughtfully, "I think they're going to stay together."

"Yeah," James said. "Me, too."

■ ■ ■ ■

"You bet against me?" Wyatt asked Morg later that night, still trying to understand how he himself had lost money while Doc and Morgan had come out ahead.

"We didn't bet against you. We *hedged* our bets," Morg said. "Kate says they've been doing that on French racetracks for years. You take a hundred dollars and divide it. Twenty to win at long odds, right? Then make a couple of side bets, shorter. Thirty bucks to come in second or better, fifty to come in third or better. Unless the horse is out of the money, there's a payoff. If he wins, you do real well."

It made sense. Wyatt just wished he'd heard of the system before the race. He'd put everything he had on Dick to win, and lost it all.

The brightest stars were visible. The first experimental fireworks were being shot off. This could turn into the quietest part of the night or the most dangerous.

"You seen Doc Holliday yet?" Wyatt asked.

Morg shook his head. "Kate's not letting anybody visit."

"She told me to go to hell, that's for sure." Wyatt wasn't scared of Kate, exactly, but she'd taken a dislike to him for some reason. No sense in stirring things up. "If you see her leave Dodge House," Wyatt said, "lemme know."

The night shift at Bessie's was wild, and James sent word to Kate just after eleven: We need more girls — can you help us out? Morgan told Wyatt that when their paths crossed just after midnight.

Wyatt took a break a while later and went up to Doc's room. There was a light showing from under the door, so he knocked softly. The answering "Yes?" was immediate, if weak.

Wyatt stuck his head inside. "Hey, Doc," he said quietly. "How're you doing?"

"Like Cousin Robert used to say: if you didn't get hurt, you weren't havin' fun." His voice was hoarse but he seemed cheery enough. "Not supposed to talk. C'mon in! Sit down! How's that German fiddler?"

"Back playing at the Commie-Q already." In fact, the fiddler looked better than Doc, who was sitting in bed, propped on pillows, his face all beat up from where he hit the ground.

"Press charges?" Doc asked.

"No. Somebody got to him. The Driskill kid got off with a fine for disturbing the peace. Bob Wright walked, too. Misunderstanding, the judge said."

"Pity. Trial would've been entertainin'. Rest of the town?"

"Mayhem. No murder. So far."

"Wyatt, you are good at your job. Everyone'll go home in the mornin'." Doc sounded respectful, but reassuring, too. The dentist closed the book on his lap and rolled onto an elbow to cough into a handkerchief. "Put that lamp out, will you?" he asked. "I fear I do not bear close inspection."

Wyatt didn't argue the point. Without his shirt and vest and coat and cravat to bulk him up some and make him look dignified, you could see how bony and young Doc was, besides being banged up from the fall. Still, bad as he looked, and coughing about every third word, the dentist was eager to tell Wyatt about the race, explaining about the lope out to the field to avoid a forfeit, and saying how well Dick did, despite having some of the race wrung out of him before he got to the track.

"How was he in the pack?" Wyatt asked. "He snap at anybody?"

"No, sir. All business. Hadn't been for that damned dog — I should have you press charges against the greyhound —"

Doc cursed for a while, coughing, and getting fed up with the interruptions. When the handkerchief was soggy, he tossed it into a basin on the floor. "Move those over closer, will you?" he asked, motioning toward a pile of clean cloths, but then he went right back to the race.

This was why Kate didn't want any visitors, Wyatt realized. Doc couldn't help himself. If there was somebody around, he'd talk. When he talked, he got cranked up. That brought on the cough, and then those things in his chest would rip. The boy's eyes were watering now, but still shining in the moonlight as he told about the finish.

All heart, Wyatt thought.

"I swear: two more strides, we'd've taken the lead," Doc was saying. "Didn't use a quirt on him, either —" The coughing got really bad this time, and when it was done, Doc looked exhausted. "Not supposed to talk," he reminded himself, whispering again. "He's a wonderful horse, Wyatt. I'm sorry we didn't do better for you."

"Hell, Doc. Wasn't your fault."

"He had a lot left at the end. You thought about longer races?"

"Well, not for him . . ."

Maybe it was the darkness. Maybe it was because Doc admired Dick and showed it, so open and boyish like that. Partly it was just to shut Doc up before he made himself cough again. Whatever the reasons, Wyatt found himself telling about the morning he first saw that mare Roxana, and how he once hoped to breed her to Dick.

Doc lay back to listen. Sure enough, the cough quieted. After a time, he shut his eyes, but his face was alight while Wyatt talked about the colts he'd expected from the pair. Milers, quick to break, like Dick, but with

Roxana's stamina to go distance at speed. Caught up, Wyatt went on to tell about how he thought of quitting the law because he kept getting laid off anyways, no matter how hard he worked, and about how he wanted to buy a piece of land and raise fine horses, but the mare's owner wanted two grand. Even dealing faro part-time, Wyatt was never gonna put that kind of cash together, so who was he fooling?

Doc's smile had faded by then, and Wyatt figured he was probably asleep, which is why, without really meaning to, he started to tell Doc about that deal with Johnnie Sanders. It was a way to get the matter off his chest somehow, without anybody really knowing. Except Doc was still listening, not sleeping, and he already knew what Wyatt was going to say, the way Morg so often did.

"That's why you staked him," Doc said softly. "You were goin' to buy Roxana."

"I didn't mean for Johnnie — I never would have —"

"Not your fault," Doc said. After a while he added, "I'd've done the same."

It didn't occur to Wyatt to ask that night if Doc meant he'd have staked Johnnie same as Wyatt, or played for Wyatt same as Johnnie.

Suddenly Wyatt needed to go back to work. Needed to get out of that sickroom, and away from everything he'd just told Doc.

"I should let you rest," he said, standing.

"Can I get you anything before I go?"

"Thank you, no." Doc's eyes opened. "Wait! Been meanin' to ask . . . How much's the rent on that cottage of yours?"

"Eight bucks a month. Me 'n' Morg were splitting it, but —" He didn't know what to say.

"You need your privacy now," Doc supplied, eyes closing again.

"Morg, too. He and that girl Lou took the house next door."

"Who's the landlord?"

"George Hoover."

"Well, ask 'bout the other one . . . that's almost finished, will you?"

Wyatt promised he would, and Doc mumbled something about them being neighbors soon, and reminded Wyatt to brush his teeth, but by then he was barely awake.

The rest of the night was mostly uneventful. Wyatt made his report to Fat Larry at dawn and trudged home, the three-shift duty over at last.

Mattie Blaylock was asleep, but when he crawled into bed, she woke up and put her arms around his neck.

"Aw, hell," he said wearily, and got up out of bed again.

"What's the matter, Wyatt?" Mattie asked anxiously. "I do something wrong?"

"Forgot to brush my teeth," he said.

■ ■ ■ ■

When Kate got back from Bessie's in the morning, Doc was scabby and pale under his bruises, but he was sitting at the table, practicing with a deck: split, square, pivot.

She looked at him, brows up.

"A heavenly sleep . . . did suddenly steep . . . in balm my bosom's pain," he recited.

Kate took off her hat and tossed it on the bureau before lifting the half-empty bottle at his elbow.

"I'm fine," he insisted, putting some strength behind his voice. "Sore is all."

The basin in the corner was filled with sodden handkerchiefs. Most were stained pink. The ones at the bottom of the pile were darker.

"Temporary," he told her. "I hit the ground hard. Bound to be some minor blood vessels torn."

"McCarty told you to stay in bed," she reminded him.

"Trust not the physician! His antidotes are poison, and he slays! Tom McCarty doesn't know one damn thing about tuberculosis that I didn't tell him my own self." He cut the cards and showed her the nine of clubs. "How much have I got in that carpetbag of yours?"

"Six hundred and change." She sat on the bed to unbutton her shoes.

"Does that count what I won on Dick yesterday?"

She nodded. "But not what I just made."

They had sworn off fear, but the fall was sobering. Last night, when the bleeding was worst, they'd agreed that she should keep her earnings separate. It was a matter of pride for Doc, and he wanted her to save something. Just in case.

"We can shave forty-eight dollars a month off expenses if we rent a house instead of livin' here," he said. Divvy, tumble, riffle . . . "I don't suppose you can cook."

Pulling off a shoe, she looked up. "You had slaves. We had servants."

"Fair enough."

Riffle, arch, release . . . He cut again, right-handed. Nine of diamonds.

"Grier," he said after a time, watching her undress.

"Not worth it. Word is the family's cut him off —" Doc was staring. *"D'accord,"* she said with a shrug. "When?"

"Get me some easy work first. I'd like to take four thousand into the room."

"Scared money don't win," she agreed, arranging pillows against the headboard. She climbed into the bed and laid her head back. "What've you got against Grier anyway?"

"It's a family matter."

"Don't be mysterious with me. It's tedious. He get some cousin pregnant?"

426

"Oh, nothin' so melodramatic. The captain's family is the front half of Grier and Cook Carriage Company, up in Connecticut. My father ordered a buggy from them, just before the war. I helped pick it out. Model Number Thirty-three . . . Had a lever for raisin' and lowerin' the top from the inside. One hundred and sixty dollars. Cash. Paid in advance." Hands now lax in his lap, he looked out the window. "The war broke out before the buggy was delivered. Grier and Cook started makin' gun carriages for the Northern army."

"Smart move," Kate remarked. "There's money, and then there's *money*."

"I imagine they did well for themselves." Shuffling again, he cut left-handed. Nine of hearts. "Anyway, Eli Grier was stationed in Atlanta during the occupation. My mother — You have to understand: Sherman's men stole whatever wasn't nailed down or red-hot, and they wrecked the rest. Took a Yankee dollar to buy a few damn radishes in those days, and nobody had hard currency anyway. We were all hungry, but Mamma was just wastin' to nothin'."

"A hundred and sixty federal dollars would have been a fortune."

"Indeed, but my father wasn't willin' to swallow his pride and ask for the money back," Doc said, voice soft with unattenuated bitterness. "Probably had his second wife all picked out by then . . . So Uncle John went to Captain Grier to ask if our family's payment might be refunded. Grier promised he would arrange for the money to be returned."

"And it wasn't."

"Not a penny." There was a long silence before Doc said, "He forgot all about it, most likely. A man with a bad conscience would have remembered my uncle's name."

Your mother would have died anyway, Kate thought, but she wasn't going to say so. She watched the cards dance in his hands. When he cut the deck again, she cried, "Wait! Nine of spades?"

He showed her the card. She laughed, low and cynical.

"And I thought you didn't cheat!"

"I don't!" There was a sly, crooked smile. "But I could."

"Anybody but me sees you do that, you'll get yourself shot again," she warned. "Bring me a drink, will you?"

He set the deck aside, poured, and stood carefully. "Nectar for Calypso," he said, handing her the glass. "We are a little short on ambrosia just now."

She sat up in bed, and slugged the bourbon down, closing her eyes to feel the liquor's warmth and forget about the night. Doc slid in behind her and began to rub her neck. She leaned forward, bracing against the mattress, surrendering to the sensation as he worked

428

his way down her back.

"Sternocleidomastoideus . . . splenius . . . rhomboidei, major and minor," he said, thumbs pressing. "Has anyone ever told you what a lovely trapezius you have?"

She snorted. "We're lucky Texans take off their spurs."

"Barbarians, to a man . . . These latissimi dorsi are unquestionably the most beautiful I have ever laid eyes on."

She smiled, eyes closed. "You're mad."

"That's the rumor . . . Sweet Jesus! Just look at you!" he murmured. "Round and soft as a ripe peach . . . Lie back."

"Mon dieu," she whispered after a time. *"C'est merveilleux!"*

"My hand skills have always been considered exemplary."

She giggled.

"I can stop if you're too tired," he offered.

"Stop, and I'll shoot you myself."

"I wonder what the odds are," he mused. The numbers seemed to come to him from nowhere. "Eight to five," he decided. "Against."

"Against what?"

"Me dyin' of consumption 'fore another bullet finds me."

She twisted around and looked at him, eyes serious. "Don't talk like that, Doc."

"No hope, no fear," he said with a grin,

kissing her with each word. "And I am not . . . dead . . . yet."

CHINAMAN'S CHANCE

Every Wednesday, Jau Dong-Sing went to the post office in Wright's General Outfitting to mail a letter and a few dollars to his father in Kwantung. Since arriving in San Francisco back in 1859, Dong-Sing had written each week. He nearly always sent money, too.

In the beginning, he hoped to elicit a reply. *My health is good but I am lonely,* he wrote. *I yearn for news of home.* Though he would not have said as much, Dong-Sing desired to be acknowledged for his contributions to his family's well-being. He also wished to be re-assured that the money he sent had not been stolen during its long journey from America to his family's village in China.

Letters from home were rare. Paper and ink and postage were too expensive for his family to buy often. When Dong-Sing did receive news, it was never happy or encouraging. *Your uncle died. The crop is poor. My joints are stiff and I suffer at night. Everyone is hungry. Yes, we received the dollars. Send more next time.*

And Dong-Sing did.

He had prospered in America. It didn't take much capital to establish a laundry, and you could make good money if you worked hard. When Dong-Sing moved to Dodge City, in '75, he built a shack near the river using scrap lumber. With a total cash outlay of $5.47, he bought kettles, and washtubs, a stove and irons. Then he went from saloon to saloon to announce in the only English words he knew, "I wash! Two bits!"

By the end of his first week, he had doubled his investment. At full capacity, he could clean and press forty pieces of clothing a day. He charged twenty-five cents per garment, which was less than the Irish washerwomen at the fort wanted, and his skill in ironing was unsurpassed. Pretty soon everybody preferred China Joe's washing. His business grew and grew. Now there was plenty of hotel trade, which added bed linens to his work. Families were moving into town, too. Ladies like Mrs. Hoover and Mrs. Wright didn't do their own washing anymore.

I already have two helpers and it is time to hire more, he would write home this week. *Tell two strong boys in our village if they come to San Francisco, I will hire them and bring them to Dodge.*

It seemed crazy to import laborers from so far away, but white people wouldn't work for a Chinaman, and Americans were too lazy anyway. Doing laundry was arduous. You had to haul water and stoke the fire with cow chips, all day long. Sheets and clothing were rubbed with yellow soap on ribbed-tin scrubbing boards, then dumped into giant tubs of boiling water and stirred with a big wooden paddle. Heavy, hot, sopping-wet cloth had to be lifted, wrung, hung to dry, and ironed. Even with his helpers, at the end of the day Dong-Sing was too worn out to speak or eat.

In the mornings, though, when he was fresh, he planned letters in his mind as he worked. *When you do laundry for people, you learn things about them. You know the size and shape of your customers. You know their habits. You know what people eat and drink from what they spill. You know who is so poor he must have his clothing mended again and again. You know who is so careless of money he leaves coins in his pockets.*

Don't keep the coins, his father would advise. You will be called a thief and punished.

Dong-Sing knew that, and he had always returned the money. Some Americans thought he was such a dumb Chink bastard, he didn't know enough to keep the cash. Others admired his scrupulous honesty.

Big George Hoover had to have a pair of panels put into the side seams of his shirts and vests to make the buttons close around his belly. He is going to run for mayor again.

Who is Big George Hoover? Dong-Sing's father would wonder, but he would think, If he is fat, he must be rich. Make friends with him. Get on his good side.

Dong-Sing didn't need a letter from his father to tell him that.

George Hoover was one of the men who left money in his pocket the first time he brought clothes to China Joe. Mr. Hoover was impressed by Dong-Sing's honesty. The investment of a few coins — returned instead of kept — had paid off handsomely. Soon Big George would build a bank right down the street from Wright's General Outfitting; he had warned China Joe about Bob Wright's bad accounting practices even before Johnnie Sanders was killed.

Knowing things about people is not the same as understanding them, Dong-Sing would admit in the letter he planned to send next Wednesday. Americans simply didn't make a lot of sense to Jau Dong-Sing. In China, a smart but poor boy like Johnnie Sanders could have studied hard and taken the civil service test to become a bureaucrat. Everyone would have been glad to know him. In China, if a rich man needed a favor, he could go to the bureaucrat who used to be poor and say, "Hey, my good friend! Nice to see you doing so well! I got a problem with some business dealings. Can you help me out?" In America, when Johnnie Sanders tried to better himself, he was killed.

In America, it is dangerous for a colored man to have money, so I pretend I am poor, Jau Dong-Sing wrote when the nigger boy was found. *I keep my money with George Hoover, and not in Bob Wright's safe.*

Why don't you join a *tong?* his father must have wondered.

Certainly, that would have been Dong-Sing's preference, but it took twelve men to make a *tong.* There were only four Chinese in all of Kansas, too few to club together for investments.

Dong-Sing was still a little nervous about doing business with George Hoover, but so far the arrangement was working out well. It was George Hoover's suggestion that he and Jau Dong-Sing enter into a silent partnership to build small rental houses up on Military Road. Already they had three, with plans to build a fourth. Nobody knew the capital was China Joe's, and that's the way Dong-Sing wanted it. *Big George orders the wood and supervises the carpenters so white men do not become envious of my wealth,* he wrote in his mind.

Renting to Wyatt and Morgan Earp was Big George's idea, too. He pointed out that they were Republicans and Methodists, and Wyatt was Reform like George. Dong-Sing appreciated that the Earps didn't get drunk and break things, but he didn't like the idea of taking the Reform side against Mayor Kelley and Bob Wright and a hotel owner like Deacon Cox. After Wyatt arrested Bob, Dong-Sing got even more nervous about the factions. The Earps might lose their jobs. Then Dong-Sing would have no tenants for two houses.

"You say yes to Doc," Dong-Sing insisted, even though George didn't like how much Doc drank. "He good tenant! You say yes!"

Doc likes noodles now. He is a friend who helps me with English, Dong-Sing planned to write soon. *Everyone says I sound like him when I talk, and I am proud. I have not told Doc that I am his landlord. I don't think he would mind renting from a Chinaman, but he might tell Kate and she cannot be trusted. Last week they had another fight. Doc told me to take Kate's things to Bessie's house, but I made an excuse and waited. Kate always returns and Doc always takes her back.*

Who is Doc? His father would wonder. Who is Kate? Who is Bessie?

When you do laundry for people, you know who sleeps alone and who has taken a lover. You know who is pregnant and who is not. You observe the coming and going of semen and blood, Dong-Sing thought. You can read in these stains the stories of people who hardly notice you and never speak when they pass you in the street.

Dong-Sing was shocked when he realized that Mattie Blaylock was Wyatt's girl. Dong-Sing had used Mattie himself a few times because she was so cheap, and because he wanted to see what a white woman was like down there.

Working on the wrong side of the tracks, Jau Dong-Sing had plenty of opportunity to observe the flesh trade, and it confused him. In China, good fathers had the right — the duty, even — to sell a daughter in order to feed the rest of the family. In America, daughters ran away from their fathers and whored to feed themselves alone. In China, when a wife grew old and unattractive, a rich man would take a concubine or two into his household. Here, rich men used the same girls as any lousy young cowherd who stank of dung and sweat. George Hoover had married a prostitute, and Doc was a gentleman but lived with Kate, even though she still sold herself.

The news about Wyatt and Mattie is all over town now. Everyone thinks this is a good joke, Dong-Sing wrote in his mind. *Wyatt is embarrassed, but he has been a long time without a woman.*

Wyatt didn't even recognize Mattie Blaylock when he saw her a few days after dropping her off at Bessie's that night. She was clean, and her hair looked nice, and her eyes were clear. She was wearing a different dress, too.

China Joe had traded it to her for a ride, but Wyatt didn't know that. There was a lot Wyatt didn't know, including why his sister-in-law wouldn't give Mattie a job. He figured that out when he caught a dose off the girl, though it would remain a lifelong mystery to him why he never fathered a child except with Urilla. Mattie herself would never tell Wyatt how she got the idea of coming to him that first morning, either. ("Idiot. Just move in with him!" Big Nose Kate had said. "A man like that won't throw you out.") All Wyatt knew was Mattie showed up at the house one morning after he got off work.

"Bessie told me you paid for my whole night," she said. "I'll work it off."

"You don't have to do that," he told her.

"Don't take what I don't earn," she said, head up. "I'll pay it off in cash if you give me some time, but I'd rather do it this way. James says you're widowed. I reckon you loved a girl once, you won't be mean to one now."

There didn't seem to be a good way to tell her no. It helped that she didn't look anything like Urilla. Mattie was dark-haired, and sturdy, and didn't seem likely to get sick, though later on he found out she had bad headaches with her monthlies.

After his first time with her, he couldn't hardly think about anything else. With the long drought over, he welcomed her when she came back the next day. He got bul-lyragged about it a lot, but he got bullyragged about not doing it, too, so he ignored the laughing, and the jokes, and the snide re-marks. A few extra cowboys got bashed for mouthing off. Otherwise, he kept his temper.

James was merciless. It was rich: Wyatt be-ing with a whore after he was so uppity about Bessie, whose husband was, James pointed out with immense satisfaction, lawfully *mar-ried* to the woman he lived with, unlike some brothers he could name.

And Wyatt wasn't the only Earp living in sin, James noted. Virgil had left his wife to fight in the war. Afterward, he let her think he was dead but hadn't divorced her, which meant he couldn't marry that little Allie he was with, down in Arizona. And now Morg and Lou were shacked up, too, because Lou was a Mormon and her parents refused to let her marry a Methodist.

Morg had started calling Lou his wife anyhow, and in his opinion, Wyatt ought to be satisfied with what passed for marriage in Kansas.

"Mattie's not such a bad person," Morg said one morning when he and Wyatt were over visiting Doc. "You know, if things had gone a little different, even Lou might have wound up a whole lot worse than a dance hall girl."

"Say what you will about Mormons," Doc

murmured, lying in bed but paying attention. "They are very fine dancers."

Doc had been up and around right after the fall on the Fourth, carrying things to the rented house and helping Kate fix the place up the way she wanted it. It was too much, too soon. Tom McCarty diagnosed overexcitement and ordered him back to bed for a few days. The rest was doing him good, but Doc enjoyed having visitors, no matter what Kate or Doc McCarty thought, so Morg and Wyatt stopped by a lot.

"How long ago did Urilla die, Wyatt?" Morgan pressed. "Is it nine years now?"

"Eight," Wyatt said, halfway between stubborn and sad. "I promised to love her all my life, Morg. I meant to keep my word."

That shut Morgan up, but Doc's eyes opened and he gazed at Wyatt for a long time.

"What?" Wyatt asked, a little unnerved by the way Doc was looking at him.

"That is your ghost life, Wyatt," Doc told him, and closed his eyes again. "That is the life you might have had. This is the life you've got."

Eddie Foy's favorite girl, Verelda, was pregnant last month, Dong-Sing wrote on Wednesday. *Eddie doesn't know that she got rid of the baby.*

Dong-Sing's father would wonder, Who is Eddie? Who is Verelda? Why does my son tell me such things? Or maybe he wouldn't

440

wonder at all. Maybe he didn't even read Dong-Sing's letters because they had become incomprehensible as the years passed. Maybe he just took the money and sold the paper the letter was written on.

It was hard for Dong-Sing to keep in mind what his father would understand. It was difficult even to remember what his father looked like. Children who were babies when Dong-Sing left Kwantung must be grown by now — married, with children of their own. Dong-Sing himself had noticed some gray hairs recently and realized that he was getting old. He had waited a long time for a bride, but his family never sent one, and now it was illegal to bring Chinese women into America.

I fear I will never have sons, he wrote to his father when the law was passed, in '75. *All the Chinese in Kansas are men. I will be no one's ancestor.*

The only women in Dodge who would have Dong-Sing were whores who worked in the cribs behind the saloons. Even black ones charged him a lot, and they all did extra things to ensure that they would not have a yellow baby.

Whatever you worship will consume you, Dong-Sing wrote one week. *Bob Wright worships money. Wyatt Earp worships justice. Eddie Foy worships applause. Doc worships home*

441

and family, as I do. How will this consume us?

In China, family was everything. In America, most people were all by themselves and liked it that way. Doc was alone, but he cared about his cousins and aunts and uncles. Without them he was almost as lonely as Dong-Sing himself. So Doc adopted friends to be his family. Dong-Sing understood that, of course. Just last year, he had adopted his nephew Shai-Kwan and set him up in business in Wichita to ensure that someone would light a joss stick for Jau Dong-Sing when he was gone, and sweep his grave on Ching-Ming Day. What puzzled Dong-Sing was why Doc chose such low-class people to be his friends, instead of cultivating influential or well-connected persons.

Sometimes Doc walked out to the cemetery to stand alone at the grave of Johnnie Sanders and clean it up a little. This was unwise, for the nigger boy's life was one of misfortune and bad luck. His spirit could only be malevolent.

I have warned Doc about the danger, but he does not believe that an uneasy spirit can make a person sick. To Dong-Sing, the truth was there to be read in the stained handkerchiefs and the sour smell of Doc's shirts and bedsheets. *Belle Wright goes out to that grave, too,* Dong-Sing noted. *She has started to cough sometimes, just like Doc. I liked Johnnie Sanders when he was alive, but his spirit is angry and dangerous.*

Maybe he is bringing bad luck to Wyatt Earp, too, Dong-Sing thought.

That would explain a lot.

Wyatt wasn't really sure how he and Mattie wound up living together. After she worked off her debt, she told him that she'd have to go back to the street. He was sorry for her, but that didn't mean he wanted her to stay with him.

Trouble was, when Lou and Morg moved to their own place next door, Wyatt was alone in the house and didn't have that excuse anymore.

"Mattie," he said, feeling awful about it, "I don't even have a dog."

"You could have one now, Wyatt. I could take care of it," Mattie told him. "I could take care of you. I can clean, and I know how to cook. You wouldn't have to eat at restaurants all the time. You could have home cooking."

He didn't want a dog. And he liked eating in restaurants. He liked that the waitresses knew what he wanted and brought it to the table without him asking. He liked staring out the window while he ate, keeping an eye on things while the people around him made conversation. He enjoyed the way Morg and Doc teased each other like brothers when Doc was feeling good. When they talked about what they read in books, he liked to listen without the need to say anything.

He liked being alone in crowds. He liked keeping watch, walking the beat, knowing what was buttoned up and where trouble was brewing. He liked the last hour of the night, when the drunks had passed out and the card games were over and the sun was coming up. He liked how the feel of the city changed. The south side, sleeping its night off. The north side, waking up to open its shops and stores.

On duty, he held himself responsible to every citizen of Dodge and gave their town his whole attention. Minute by minute, all night long, he was alert — as ready as Dick was, waiting for the starter's gun. When his shift was over, he felt he'd earned the sense of belonging only to himself.

For a few days after Morg and Lou moved, he lived alone and liked it. When he opened the door to the tiny rented house, he liked the silence inside. He liked that everything he owned — little as it was — was right where he left it. He liked the way he could pick up the threads of his simple life and ease back into unobserved solitude. He liked going to bed without having spoken a word to anyone, and he liked to sleep, dreamlessly, alone.

He hated how everyone noticed now when he got off work. He hated the leering, the joshing. "How's married life?" everybody asked. He'd answer, "Well, it ain't *all* bad," and that's exactly what he meant, but there'd be more laughs, as if he'd told a joke. He hated that everybody was paying attention to him.

When he got home, there'd be a meal on the table and Mattie would be waiting for him, watching his face with those big sad eyes, like a dog expecting to get kicked but helpless to leave its master. If he was late, she'd blame him for making her worry and complained about how the meal was spoiled, though he really didn't notice that the food was worse.

She wasn't a terrible cook, but she made him stuff he didn't much like, and it hurt her feelings if he didn't eat it all. Her coffee was awful and he started putting milk in it, on top of the sugar, to kill the taste some. If they went out, he had to remember to put milk in his coffee then, too, so she wouldn't know he didn't like hers. She kept the little house tidy, but he could never find anything anymore. When he asked where something was, she seemed annoyed and acted like he'd criticized her.

She was trying her best. He could see that, and he wanted to appreciate what she did. But he didn't, not really. That was the damnable misery of it: he didn't want what she had to give. It was a sadness to him, seeing how hard she tried to please him, because what would have pleased him most was if she just wasn't there.

One time, over breakfast in the Iowa House before the night shift began, Wyatt talked all this over with Doc. He thought the dentist would understand how one thing led to another, and there you were, waking up beside a woman you never would've chosen.

"Could you get rid of Kate? If you really — ?" Doc just looked at him, and Wyatt felt ashamed, but he needed to know. "I mean, this ain't anything I wanted, Doc! But I can't — I don't know . . ."

"You can't be mean enough to throw her into the street?" Doc paused to stir honey into his tea. *"Alas, poor Dido, who tried to seize with living love a heart long numbed to passion."*

Wyatt guessed that was some kind of poetry and ignored it, same as he ignored Doc's coughing. "You get used to it," Doc had said about the cough. "You can get used to anything." Including not understanding half of what Doc said.

"But Kate — she's still working," Wyatt whispered, even though they were alone at a long wooden table. "How do you — ? I mean, any man you pass on the street might've . . ."

"Ah," Doc said, lifting the cup and blowing on the tea through a slight crooked smile. "So, we are discussin' male pride now, not

446

female virtue."

"You know what I mean," Wyatt said irritably. "Why are you *with* her, Doc?"

"Wrong question," Doc said, coughing briefly.

"Well, what's the right one then?"

"Why is she with *me?*"

"Is that a joke?" Wyatt could never tell.

"You are not the only one with a ghost life, Wyatt."

For a time, holding the teacup in both hands, Doc looked out at the little stretch of Front Street visible through the restaurant window. "It's a fairy tale in reverse," he decided. "Once upon a time, there was a little girl who was raised at the imperial court of Maximilian of Mexico, surrounded by luxury and refinement. When she grew up, she was meant to become the cultured and decorative wife of a fine gentleman. A count, perhaps. Or a prince. She would have servants to supervise and a household to oversee, and children to rear in a home filled with books and art. That is the life Kate might have had, Wyatt."

When Doc's eyes came back to Wyatt's, they were as level and hard as his voice was musical and soft. "In the life she's got, about the best she can hope for is a consumptive dentist from Griffin, Georgia. The dentist, by the way, calls himself lucky to have her. Consider yourself warned, sir, and mind your tongue."

You didn't think you was so lucky the last time you two had a fight, Wyatt thought, but he nodded.

"And then," Doc went on, "there was a revolution in Mexico. In six months' time, Kate lost everything and everyone she knew. She went from Mexico City to Davenport, Iowa. Her father and mother sickened and died within weeks of each other. She was separated from her sisters and fostered by a family she'd never met before. They didn't care about her grief. Didn't speak any of the six languages she already knew. Couldn't even say her name properly. They put her to work in the daytime, and at night . . . Her foster father ruined her," Doc said with quiet venom, "and such a betrayal ought to earn that vicious sonofabitch — a place in the — very deepest — circle of hell."

He'd been fighting the cough for a while and gave in to it at last.

"So: there she was," Doc said, when he could go on. "Orphaned, pregnant, on the run, with no more than a few words of English. She found a man to marry her, but he left. The baby came early, and he died. She's been makin' her own way ever since."

Hearing it made Wyatt feel ashamed somehow, though none of it was his fault. "All these girls have some story," he said, to make it less important.

"Yes, sir! Yes, they do," Doc said, suddenly hot. "Every one of them has a story, and every story begins with a man who failed her. A husband who came home from the war, good for nothin' but drink. A father who didn't come home at all, or a stepfather who did. A brother who should have protected her. A beau who promised marriage and left when he got what he wanted, because he wouldn't marry a slut. If a girl like that has lost her way, it's — because some worthless no-account — sonofabitch left her in — the wilderness alone!"

When he was done coughing, Doc stood abruptly and dropped a dollar on the table, which was far more than he owed. Still, he didn't leave, tarrying instead to watch a crib girl make a deal with a drover out on the boardwalk right in front of them. *Misdemeanor,* Wyatt thought, and he'd have gone to arrest her, except for what Doc said next.

"They break my heart, these girls. They are so brave. Wyatt, you have to admire their nerve, at least! They go off alone into alleys and small rooms with violent, dangerous, lustful men twice their own size . . . Shall I confess my crime, Marshal?"

Wyatt looked up.

"City ordinances be damned," Doc told him. "I am never entirely disarmed. And I just play cards with the bastards."

Personally, Wyatt didn't think it took all that much nerve to lie back and let a man do what he wanted for a minute or two. The whores at his brother's place seemed to him hard and mercenary, or loose and indifferent, or silly and stupid, but he had to admit he didn't know much about any of them.

Doc Holliday was an educated and thoughtful man, so Wyatt made an effort to match up what he'd seen with what Doc said. There might be something to it, he guessed.

Later on, he asked Mattie Blaylock about her life before, and what her story was. At first she just looked at him like she couldn't decide if he was dumb or trying to trick her.

"Honest," he said. "I want to know."

"Well, they was doing it to me anyways," she told him. "Might as well get paid."

It wasn't much to go on, but he did his best to treat her like she was a lady, the way Doc treated Kate.

I sent to San Francisco for yue hua wan for Doc. I did this at my own expense, Dong-Sing thought while he worked, though he never would have written such a boastful thing to his father. *Doc was grateful. He thanked me for my generosity, but he does not want me to go to such trouble. He has asked for the pharmacist's address in San Francisco and promised to obtain the medicine for himself.*

According to the Chinese pharmacist, Doc's illness was complicated and difficult to treat. Deficiency in *yin* accounted for the cough and the frothy pink sputum, while deficiency of *yang* and damaged *Jing Luo* combined to produce a tidal fever and night sweats, but also coldness and poor appetite and general weakness.

The pharmacist sent dried milk thistle, sage, kelp, licorice, lavender, ginseng, and sorrel, to be steeped in boiling water with black tea. Jau Dong-Sing brewed the medicine up and encouraged Doc to drink it when he came by to eat noodles.

I am happy to help him, since he has always treated me with respect. I hope that he will be better soon, Dong-Sing thought, pouring more bleach into the wash water. *Sometimes his handkerchiefs are difficult to clean.*

■ ■ ■ ■

FIFTH HAND

■ ■ ■ ■

"It may have been the most vile, undrinkable, horrifyin' beverage in the history of mankind," Doc told Morgan, who felt bad for laughing so hard but couldn't help himself. "And Mr. Jau — poor soul — he is watchin' me with such eager anticipation! 'How you like dat, Doc?' he asks me. And at that very instant, I was thinkin': I sincerely believe I would rather die than choke this down three times a day . . . But I could hear my mamma's voice. Now, sugar, it was very kind of Mr. Jau, and if you can just get through the next twenty seconds without upchuckin' . . ."

For the third time in half an hour, Doc laid his dental tools on the office table and turned away to cough and curse for a while, which gave Morgan time to catch his own breath. Somehow Doc made having consumption seem funny; Morg was damned if he understood how, but when the two of them were alone like this, he ended up laughing himself blue about half the time.

He poured Doc a drink and knew to wait until Doc could answer before he asked, "You ever tried Wistar's? That's supposed to be pretty good for a cough."

"Morgan," Doc said, "I have tried them all . . . Balsam of Cherry. Borax water. Kerosene and lard. Turpentine and sugar. Calomel. Bunchberry juice. Fish liver extract. Root of pitcher plant. Everything but eye of newt — which may have been in Mr. Jau's concoction, now that I think of it." He paused to clear his throat. "Laudanum stops the cough, but it stops everything else, too. Can't work when I'm that fogged." Doc picked up his tools. "Bourbon does the job, and I tolerate it better. Light?"

Morgan lifted the lamp again and held it so there was no shadow on the denture Doc was finishing: two front teeth, cleverly linked in a gold setting.

"It's like a little sculpture," Morg marveled. "Or . . . jewelry, almost."

"Jewelry is mere adornment," Doc said, peering through a magnifying glass that was clamped into a brass stand on his desk. "This will change your brother's life in a small but significant way. If it's the last work I do, I'll die a happy dentist."

Consumption was one thing. Death was another. Morg banged the lamp down.

Doc looked up, surprised; he sobered when

he saw Morgan's face. "What?"

"You keep joking about dying, and I wish you'd quit. It's like you're trying to get used to the idea," Morg said. "Making friends with it, almost."

Doc stared, but he sounded impressed when he finally said, "Well, now, ain't you somethin'." He lifted his chin toward the lamp. Morg held it up, and Doc went back to work on the denture. "There was some bleedin' after the race," he admitted quietly, "but it wasn't arterial. And it's over. Took time for things to settle down afterward, is all."

True enough, the cough didn't sound as awful as it had right after the fall. Doc's color was better, too, but Kate said he still wasn't sleeping well, and that made him cross.

Cross ain't the half of it, Morg thought. Doc would tear into folks, sudden as a dogfight, and he was taking some real chances during card games. He swore he wasn't starting anything, but Doc's idea of "clarifyin' a point of contention" came awful close to spitting in a man's eye. "Doc," Morgan had warned a few nights ago, "you gotta be more careful. I won't always be around —" To protect you, he was going to say, but Doc cut him off and snapped, "Well, neither will I, and I am damned if I will spend my time listenin' to ungrammatical, repetitious, imbecilic nonsense without a challenge!"

Still, he was cheerful enough right now,

whistling softly while he smoothed away an almost invisible burr on the gold bezel that held the teeth.

It was interesting to watch the work, and Morg was glad to be allowed back into the office. He'd been banned after Wyatt's first appointment. Doc only let him come back today because it was the final fitting for the denture.

Wyatt didn't feel a thing when that first tooth was pulled, but Morgan still had a knot on the back of his head from where he hit the doorknob going down. When he came to, Doc was furious with him. "Dammit, Morgan, I didn't know whether to shit or go bust! There's Wyatt in the chair, and there's you on the floor, and there's the Eberhardt boy with eyes like saucers, sayin' 'I pump drill now, sir?' I can't have it, Morg — not while I've got a patient under ether. It's too dangerous!" So Mattie Blaylock came with Wyatt for the next three appointments. She was real good about things, too, cooking him soft stuff like eggs and soup for a few days after each session, while his mouth was sore.

"What is that song?" Morg asked after a while.

Doc looked up, puzzled.

"The one you were whistling."

"Was I — ?" Doc thought for a moment. "Oh! The Rondo from Beethoven's Violin Concerto."

Morgan knew what a violin was, anyways. "You play fiddle, too?"

"Not by a wide mile," Doc murmured, eyes on the mount. "When I was in dental school, I went to every concert and recital I could at the Philadelphia Academy of Music. Fell in love with that piece . . . I was studyin' the score when we were learnin' to make bridges. Comes back to me, I guess."

Must be hard on him, Morg thought, being so far from things like that. "Real pretty tune," he said.

"Indeed. You have excellent taste, Morgan." Doc put the tools down and stretched out his back, then winced suddenly, like he was snakebit. He sat still for a time, but relaxed again and went on. "Our houseboy — Wilson? — he disapproved of whistlin' somethin' fierce. Always said it was common. 'A low-class, cracker habit,' Wilson called it, but Mamma encouraged the practice when I was a boy."

"Why would she want you to do something low-class?"

"Helped me establish control over the *orbicularis oris.*" Doc gestured with a finger, circling his mouth. His hand dropped into his lap and he considered Morgan for a time, like he was deciding something. "I was born with a harelip," he said finally. "The defect was repaired when I was a baby."

Morgan couldn't help staring.

459

Doc threw his head back and stared right back, like he was daring Morg to make fun. "It is nothin' to be ashamed of," he declared.

And you could tell somehow: it was his mamma's voice Doc heard when he was saying how it was nothing to be ashamed of, but he *was* ashamed — a little, anyways. You could tell that, too.

Morg made himself stop looking at Doc's mouth. "I knew a kid once who had a harelip. I didn't know they could fix it."

"My Uncle John is a fine surgeon. You can — Oh, hell — Dammit! Some kind of — obstruction in the bronchus — I just can't seem to —"

Morg put the lamp down and waited again while the bourbon was administered and the coughing eased off. Since the fall on the Fourth, Doc had been drinking more than usual. He drank it a little at a time, though, and it didn't seem to affect him beyond helping with the cough. His eyes stayed clear and his hands were steady when he went back to work on the denture. It was such finicky work, but he seemed to have all the patience in the world, doing it. Strange, for a man who'd fly off the handle so easy, otherwise.

"I wouldn't last five minutes doing what you are," Morg said. "How can you spend so much time on something so little?"

"It's hours for me, but it'll be in Wyatt's mouth for years. The tiniest flaw will be a

460

trial to him . . . We all have different gifts, Mamma used to say. I've watched you and your brother walk straight into a mob and wondered, Where do they get the sand? I couldn't do what you do."

"You've got plenty of sand, Doc."

"Morgan," Doc said, "I am doin' my best . . . How are you and Mr. Dickens gettin' along?"

"I like him better than Dostoevsky," Morg admitted. "Oliver Twist reminds me of Wyatt when he was a kid. I liked how Oliver stands up for himself and that other kid when they was so hungry. Wyatt was like that. He cannot abide a bully. Never could, even when he was little."

"And why do you suppose that is?"

"Just his nature, I guess."

"You met Mr. Fagin yet?"

"Yeah. Ain't made up my mind about him. He's good to feed all those boys, but he's teaching them to be pickpockets, too. That don't seem right."

"But that is just what makes Fagin interestin'. Raskolnikoff, too. Fagin does his good deed with a bad purpose in mind, but the boys are still fed. Raskolnikoff kills the old woman, but he wants to use her money to improve society. As Monsieur Balzac asked, May we not do a small evil for the sake of accomplishin' a great good?"

"I don't know." Morgan frowned. "It's still

an evil."

"And yet, that seems to be the principle behind the crucifixion. Sacrifice the Son, redeem humanity . . . Hold the lamp up while you're chewing that notion over."

Morg tried, but it was too much to get his mind around. "I know what Wyatt would say. Fagin's still a fence. Raskolnikoff was a murderer and a thief. Wyatt don't care that James and Bessie run a decent house and treat their girls right. They're still whoremongers."

"And I suppose it doesn't matter that my mamma inherited her people. Or that she was a gentle mistress, taught by her elders that slavery was Athenian in its dignity and blessed by the Bible itself."

"She was still a slave owner," Morg said quietly, braced for the reaction. Doc could be real touchy about his mother.

"We are none of us born into Eden," Doc said reasonably. "World's plenty evil when we get here. Question is, what's the best way to play a bad hand? Abolitionists thought that all they had to do to right an ancient wrong was set the slaves free." He looked at Morg. "Trouble was, they didn't have a plan in the world for what came next. Cut 'em loose. That was the plan. Let 'em eat cake, I guess."

He was muttering now, eyes on the bridge. "Four years of war. Hundreds of thousands of casualties . . . All so black folks in the

South could be treated as bad as millworkers in the North! Pay as little as you can. Work 'em 'til they're too old or sick or hurt to do the job. Then cut 'em loose! Hire a starvin' Irish replacement! That's abolitionist freedom for you . . . Heartless bastards . . . 'Free the slaves' sounds good until you start wonderin' how Chainey and Wilson would make a livin' when they were already so old they couldn't do a lick of work. What was a little child like Sophie Walton supposed to do? No kin who'd care for her . . ." He looked up. "I doubt the abolitionists anticipated the Ku Klux Klan either, but here it is, makin' life worse than ever for black folks."

"The road to hell is paved with good intentions," Morg said.

"Infinitely sad, but damnably true."

Doc sat back in his chair and stared out of the window for a long time. "Bein' born is craps," he decided. He glanced at Morg and let loose that sly, lopsided smile of his. "How we live is *poker.*" Doc looked away and got thoughtful again. "Mamma played a bad hand well."

He shook the mood off and went back to work on the denture. Morgan lifted the lamp, feeling vaguely unsettled by the conversation. Naturally, Doc saw things different, being from the South. Still . . . there had been a lot of arguing about Emancipation, even in the North. Nicholas Earp was all for the war when it was to punish the secessionists. After the Proclamation, he wrote Newton and James and Virgil to quit the army and come on home. "I won't have my sons risking their necks for niggers" was what he said, but the boys stayed on and fought to the end. And Wyatt tried to join up when he was fifteen, except the old man caught him both times and dragged him home again. Somebody had to get that eighty acres of corn in.

"Doc? You think maybe it was the Klan got Johnnie Sanders?" Morg asked.

Doc stopped what he was doing. "Never thought of that . . . He was friendly with Belle Wright. Sometimes that's all it takes." He turned the idea over for a while. "No. They'd have lynched him, I imagine. And they'd want a crowd for the occasion. The Klan enjoys an audience as much as Eddie Foy." He sat still for a time, frowning. "I don't suppose you recall . . . Was that army captain — Grier, the one with the Arab mare? — was Captain Grier in town when the Elephant Barn burned down?"

Morg's face went blank. "Hell, Doc. I don't remember. Why?"

"Just curious. Johnnie might've gone into the barn to bring out that horse." Doc went back to his work and to Dickens. "So, now, what do you think about the odious Bill Sikes? There's a pure bully for you, no redemption involved."

464

Morg didn't answer. Doc looked up. "Struck a nerve, did I?"

Morgan's face had darkened, but Doc was looking past him now. "Tell me about bullies, Wyatt. I wager you have made a study of the breed."

Morg turned and wondered how long his brother had been standing in the doorway, listening.

Wyatt took off his hat and hung it on a peg. "They were beaten," he said simply. "Ninety-nine out of a hundred still are, inside. A man beats his boy, he wants a son who won't buck him. He's trying to make a coward. Mostly, it works." Face expressionless, Wyatt walked to the window and held the curtain aside, gazing back toward Iowa as he spoke. "That's why a bully will fold. You just . . . *look* at him, the way his old man did. It's not anger. It's scorn. A bully sees that look? He's nine years old again. Small and weak, like his pa wanted him. It's all he can do to keep from crying."

Doc looked at Morgan, whose eyes slid away.

"And the hundredth boy?" Doc asked Wyatt.

"We can go either way. Kill the old man, or try to become a better one." Wyatt dropped the curtain. "You ready for me?"

"Just about," Doc said. "Have a seat."

"A very natural appearance." That's what Dr.

J. H. Holliday had promised, and that's what he delivered.

It was just as well that neither Wyatt nor Morgan inquired about the provenance of the teeth themselves, for Wyatt's new ones were among the hundreds of thousands collected from battlegrounds, sorted by type and size, and made available for restorative dentistry for many years after the war. With John Henry's sketches and detailed measurements to go by, his cousin Robert had found a pair of upper centrals that matched Morgan's closely.

"It'll feel strange for a while," Doc warned, making the final adjustment, "but a couple of days from now, you'll think they were never missin'. You still need to be careful when you eat. Don't bite into apples. Slice them up like you've been doin'. And don't take up smokin' a pipe. Too much torque'll deform the mount . . . And if somebody's likely to hit you in the mouth —"

"Right! I'll be careful! Can I look now?"

"Not yet. Say 'Mississippi.' "

"Mithithi— Oh, *hell,* no!" Wyatt cried, sitting up in the chair. "Doc, thith—"

"Hush, now," Doc said. "Morgan, you laugh, and I will slap you flat. It's goin' to take some practice, Wyatt. Don't let the tip of your tongue touch the teeth. Bring it down and back, just a hair. Try it again."

"Mizzith— Hell! Mizziss—"

466

"Damn your eyes, Morgan!" Doc wheeled, coughing, and pointed to the door. "Go wait in the lobby!"

Chastened but still grinning, Morgan left the room, though he stayed in the hallway to listen, out of sight.

"Pay that pup no mind, Wyatt," Doc was saying. "Try again. Just the tip of the tongue . . . Curl the tip back a little. There you go! Yes! You're already doin' better."

This went on for about ten minutes, with time out for Doc's cough. When Wyatt was getting it right about half the time and seemed confident that he'd get the hang of it, Doc told him, "Now try 'fifty-five.' Bring your lower lip up to the teeth. Just rest the lip against them . . . Again. Good. Yes! Better! That one's easier, isn't it . . . Now try 'very vivid.' It's the same movement but voiced. Put your hand on your throat. Feel the vibration?"

"You should be in bed," Wyatt told Doc, who was coughing again.

There was a clink of glass on glass. Doc must have been pouring himself another drink. The desk chair scraped back.

"Not yet," Doc said, sounding breathless but serene. "Take a look."

Morg moved closer and peered in through the crack between the door and its frame. For a while Wyatt sat still, and Morgan found himself thinking, Poor soul — like Doc always said — poor soul, he can walk straight into a mob, but this . . .

It was about then that his own vision blurred, but Morg could hear the barber chair creak and footsteps as Wyatt got up and went to the mirror.

Blinking hard, Morgan wiped his eyes and tried to remember if he'd ever seen Wyatt look — really *look* — at himself that way. There was a small, embarrassed smile, and then a broader one . . .

In the past weeks, while Doc worked toward this moment, Morgan had often thought about how relieved and glad he'd be to see his brother made whole again. Now the moment had come at last, but it wasn't how he thought it would be. Instead of happiness, he felt a great weight of something like grief pressing on him. Sadness for all the years Wyatt's smile was gone. Anger, too, remembering how Nicholas Earp had tried to make cowards of all his sons.

It came to Morgan that Nicholas must have been a beaten boy, too, and that meant Grampa Earp was, as well. Which was no surprise, really, when Morg thought about that mean old man. How many sons were in that chain? Morgan wondered, and grief gave way to the pride he'd felt the day his brother Wyatt stood up to his first bully and put an end to a chain of vengeful, frightened, beaten boys.

Wyatt turned from the mirror. "Doc, I don't know what to th— I don't know what to say."

"Sure, you do, Wyatt: Mississippi. Fifty-five."

Morgan shifted so he could see Doc, whose eyes were filled with pleasure and satisfaction and . . . love, almost. All mixed.

"Go on, now," the dentist said softly. "Take a ride on that fine horse of yours, Wyatt, out where no one can see or listen. Practice makes perfect, y'hear?"

The men he worked with didn't notice. If anyone had asked Chuck Trask or John Stauber, for example, they might have said Wyatt was quieter than usual the next few days, or that Dick Naylor was getting an awful lot of exercise.

Women saw a difference. He seemed a little less flinty and remote, and they were glad to see him loosen a bit. Morgan's girl, Lou, told Wyatt that he looked real nice. And Mattie didn't complain when he left her alone to go out riding and work on his words. Bessie said it was money well spent and didn't give Wyatt a hard time about how he should have paid her and James back first. Kate seemed prickly about it, but even she admitted that Doc had done a remarkable job.

Mabel Riney asked straight out, "What's changed, Wyatt?" Her husband, John, was

469

sleeping off a drunk, and she was working the tollbooth while Wyatt waited around for a cattle company due to come across the river. "Something's different," she said, "but I can't make out what."

"Got my teeth fixed," he told her.

"Lemme see," Mabel said, like he was one of her sons.

He smiled, sort of, but looked away, coloring up like a boy. It was sweet, how shy he was about telling her.

"Doc Holliday done that?" she asked, impressed.

He nodded.

"How much he charge?" she asked, and whistled when he told her.

"It was a lot," Wyatt agreed, "but my teeth always used to hurt. Not anymore."

They passed the time awhile, Mabel asking things and Wyatt answering. He told her a lot about ether, which was horrible and made you think you were smothering, but then you didn't feel it when teeth were pulled or drilled, and you just had to eat soft things afterward while you healed up.

When the cowboys got to the bridge, Wyatt was all business again. Mabel took the tolls, same as usual, but started thinking about going to see the dentist herself, because she had some teeth that had been bothering her for years.

Which was why, even without an advertisement in the *Ford County Globe* or the *Dodge City Times,* Doc Holliday's business picked up quite a bit that summer. Word got around because women talk.

Eventually even Mrs. George Hoover overheard about Wyatt's teeth, though no one told her directly. Few Dodge Citians spoke to Mrs. Hoover, not even other Methodists. Whores envied and resented her. Men who'd fucked little Maggie Carnahan — before Jesus saved her and Big George married her — didn't hardly know how to act around her. And certainly, no Democrat would give Margaret Hoover the time of day.

She was used to her isolation and took a bit of pride in that evidence of her higher calling and strength of character. She had come a long way since drifting on the sea of sin and liquor that had once carried her so far from the Lord. She found it difficult to remember New York these days. She was such a greenhorn then! So foreign, so trusting.

And so much of her previous life seemed nightmarish to her, lived as it was in moonlight and in shadow.

"How old are you?" the Old Mister asked when she first came to work with her cousin.

"Thirteen, sir," she said, dropping a curtsy, just as she'd been taught.

"Old enough for a lover," he said. Then he cackled at her confusion.

471

He liked to watch while she dusted or polished or swept. In long, empty hallways and silent rooms, he would stand half-hidden in doorways, a small smile on his withered old lips.

He thought it was great fun to startle her, to make her jump. Wary, she learned to notice the musty old-man odor of stale, sweaty woolens, and cigarette smoke, and booze, and piss. Trying not to shudder, she would call out, "Morning to you, sir," just to let him know she wasn't fooled.

Sometimes he would speak in low, hushed, secret tones that she almost didn't understand — so new she was from the old country, so unfamiliar with the speech of Americans. When she could make out the words, what he said made no sense.

"When you live with me, I will love you and punish you," the Old Mister mumbled one quiet afternoon. "I will kidnap you, and you will give yourself up to me, and you will wear no clothing while you scrub floors, but I will feed you sweets . . . Here. Drink this. Go on. It's only a little."

Repulsed. Intrigued. Frightened. Intoxicated. Maggie hardly knew what she felt, except she wished she'd never left Belfast. She was so lonely, and the Old Mister was the only one who seemed to like her, and she liked the liquor. Sweet port, it was. Warming in the cold damp winter. So warming that it was possible to ignore an old man's cold, bony hands.

"Any port in a storm," Old Mister would mumble. Then he'd giggle, like he'd made a joke.

Young Missus could see what was going on between her father-in-law and the new maid, and she despised Maggie for it. "You are a wicked girl," she whispered fiercely. "You'll be punished for what you're doing with him." Young Missus could slap her and make Maggie's life a trial, but she couldn't fire her. Only the Old Mister could do that. He held the purse strings and ruled the house, and it was he who led young Maggie Carnahan to walk in lasciviousness, lusts, and excesses of wine —

All that was behind her now. Maggie Carnahan was dead. A clean new soul had risen in her place, rejoicing in Jesus. Mrs. George Hoover was a teetotal Methodist, the wife of a good man, and a rich woman — No! Better than a rich woman. She was a *lady.*

At the end of July, Margaret Hoover overheard talk about Wyatt Earp and the new dentist's work. She began to pay attention to the deputy's demeanor when she saw him at church on Sunday. It's time he did more for temperance than pray, she decided, and that afternoon she urged her husband to approach Wyatt about the convention in August.

Big George was surprised that Margaret

had thought of such a thing and was inclined to dismiss the notion, but his little wife could be remarkably insistent. Before long she had convinced him that this was a good opportunity to involve Wyatt in politics. In fact, George became so certain of the wisdom of the plan, he invited Nick Klaine along when he went to see Wyatt at the Iowa House. Which meant the newspaperman was right there taking notes for the *Dodge City Times* when the offer was made.

"Wyatt, I know you're on duty in a few minutes, so I'll get straight to the point," George started out, after saying "Afternoon" to Doc Holliday and Morgan. "The Republican Party needs men like you. You're respected, you're honest, and you can't be intimidated by the saloon interests. We'd like you to act as the Ford County representative to the party's state convention next month. This could be the year that Prohibition gets onto the Kansas platform. Yours could be the vote that puts it over the top. Now, the convention lasts two weeks, but we can get you the time off, and we'll cover your lost wages and expenses. What do you say?"

Wyatt didn't say anything at all. George's earnest smile remained unaltered, although the effort to maintain its confident brightness became somewhat more visible as the seconds ticked by. He glanced at Nick Klaine, whose pencil was poised in anticipation of Wyatt's answer. "You see, Klaine?" George cried. "This is a momentous decision and this is just the sort of judicious consideration I expected from Wyatt Earp!"

In point of fact, Wyatt was considering the offer carefully, but he was also choosing his words, still avoiding the letter *s* in front of people. "I've been dealing faro at the Alhambra, Mr. Hoover."

"We all do what we have to, to make a living, Wyatt," George pointed out smoothly, "but that doesn't mean we can't work for a better and more moral nation."

I guess, Wyatt would have said ordinarily. Instead he just shrugged, which made him seem more reluctant than he really was.

"You don't have to give me an answer right now," George said, "but representing us at the convention could lead to other things. Just think about the possibilities, is all I'm asking."

George said good day to them all and left with Nick Klaine. Wyatt looked at Morg, who said, "Why not?"

Doc sighed, and put his head in his hands, and wondered how his life had come to such a pass that he was surrounded by Republicans. "You'll need a suit," he warned Wyatt. "You can't go to Topeka dressed like that."

The idea of buying new clothes was enough to make Wyatt say, "Oh, hell, then," and brush the whole idea off.

■ ■ ■ ■

For the next couple of days, he went about his business, working on his words whenever he was alone, until the sounds came natural. Wasn't long before he was confident enough to call, "See you on Sunday," right out loud to the preacher. And he produced a sarcastic but clearly enunciated "Very funny" when Morgan played like he was going to punch him in the mouth at supper one morning.

Wyatt had done some hunting while he was out saying "Mississippi," and Mattie cooked up a pretty good venison stew. She'd invited his brothers over for a meal, but Wyatt regretted it because all Morg and James would talk about was his new teeth.

"You still ain't seen Eddie Foy's act?" Morgan cried around a mouthful of deer meat. "Well, hell, you should go! What are you waiting for?"

"I don't know, Wyatt," James said, all serious. "You smile? Somebody might die of apoplexy or something. Might cause a riot, even. You don't want to be responsible."

"James is right, Wyatt. Start slow," Morg urged. "Just hang around outside and listen for a while. Course, you'll want to alert the docs —"

"Yeah," James agreed, "you might need McCarty and Holliday, both, if your face cracks."

476

"And don't laugh!" Morg pleaded. "You laughed once already this year. Do it again, it'll be the Apocalypse for sure! We'll have the four horsemen and the rain of fire —"

They went on like that for so long, Wyatt got fed up and put off going to hear the Irishman's show just to prove they couldn't rag him into anything. After a while, though, Morg and James let up on him, and Wyatt started thinking how maybe one night he would just swing on by the Commie-Q after all.

In early August a long dry spell finally broke with a thunderstorm followed by a steady downpour that was keeping the streets quiet. There were just a few woeful horses out in the rain, heads down, tied at the rails; most men were willing to pay half a dollar to corral their animals just to keep their tack dry on the Elephant Barn's indoor racks. The saloons and dance halls were more crowded than usual because of the weather. You could hear the pianos and fiddles and hollering when you passed by the open doors. Get a few paces beyond, though, and the drumming of the rain on the galleries above the boardwalks drowned the noise out.

Around eleven, Wyatt found himself walking past the Commie-Q. He still wasn't quite ready to go inside yet, but he was willing to stand around outside the theater, just like Morg said: close enough to hear the songs and jokes.

The strange thing was, he didn't even know that he'd been avoiding the Commie-Q before he got his teeth fixed. If anybody had asked, he'd have said he didn't spend any time at the theater because there hadn't been much trouble there since he got back from chasing Dave Rudabaugh around, though Morgan said there'd been a ruckus at the beginning of the season when some drovers had threatened to lynch Eddie Foy because he was telling jokes on Texas, and they took it wrong.

According to Morg, even when those boys had a rope around his neck, Eddie kept smart-mouthing them, and they admired his nerve so much, they let him live. Word of the event had passed along the trail as the Texans drifted home, and now the Commie-Q was every cowboy's destination, along with the brothels and the gambling halls of Dodge.

Eddie's act was a lively combination of Irish step dancing and Negro hambone mixed with songs and patter. Drovers would go see the show over and over until they knew all the jokes and could yell out the punch lines with him.

"Everything in Texas is big," Eddie was hollering now. "I met a Texan with ears so big —"

"He wore his hat sidesaddle!" the cowboys yelled, laughing their heads off when Eddie

478

twisted his own hat around and crossed his eyes.

"Texans grow the biggest potatoes in the world! I told a storekeeper in Dallas, I'd like to buy a hundred pounds of potatoes. No, sir, he said —"

"I don't cut my potatoes in half for nobody!" the crowd shouted.

Wyatt thought that one was pretty good, but he didn't like some of the others.

"Any of you boys go with that blind prostitute?" Eddie asked.

"You really have to hand it to her!"

"Last night, me girl Verelda asked, Have you been screwin' around behind me back?"

"Well, who in hell did she *think* it was?" the cowboys hollered.

"They say money can't buy happiness," Eddie remarked, and three hundred whooping drunks yelled in unison, "But it'll buy Verelda!"

Which was comical at first, but then seemed kind of mean-spirited to Wyatt, after what Doc Holliday said about working girls and how brave they were. That was strange when you thought about it, because the dentist had made it possible for Wyatt to laugh at the jokes, but Doc took some of the fun out of them, too.

Eddie was singing now: "I'll take you home again, Kathleen . . ." There was nothing going on in the street, so Wyatt eased back toward the swing door to look around. Over in a corner, Doc was dealing faro, one hand sliding cards off the shoe, the other holding a handkerchief over his mouth. He was doing pretty good lately — dealing a few hours a night, getting some rest, taking patients for a few hours in the morning, sleeping through the heat of the day. That fall Doc took on the Fourth might have been a blessing in disguise. The dentist had been more sensible since then. Living regular. Working less, eating more. Even Kate seemed happier.

Bat had a poker game going in the back of the hall. His waistcoat was green and pink and yellow tonight, the brocade straining a bit over his gut. He'd be built like a barrel by the time he was thirty.

While Eddie sang in his high, sweet voice, Wyatt watched Bat, wondering how much a new suit would cost.

"If you're goin' to run against Masterson," Doc had told Wyatt a few days ago, "wear black, to make the contrast more notable. Black frock coat, white shirt, black trousers. Simple but elegant. Get some decent boots, too. And keep them polished!"

Until Doc said that about wearing black, Wyatt hadn't seriously considered running for sheriff, but that must have been what Big George meant, about how going to the Republican convention could lead to other things. So Wyatt asked Dog Kelley what he

480

thought of the idea. Dog was a Democrat, but he'd always been square with Wyatt.

"May as well run," Dog said. "Bob Wright already hates you."

What's Bob got to do with it? Wyatt wondered. Sure, Bob was sore about that arrest on the Fourth, but he got over it. Before Wyatt could ask Dog what he meant, a shotgun went off outside, and Wyatt left the Alhambra to deal with a brawl that had spilled out into the street, over by the Green Front.

Anyways, it wasn't Bob Wright who worried Wyatt. It was Bat Masterson. There was something cagey and guarded about Bat these days, like he was hiding something. It seemed unfriendly to run against him, but no question, things had cooled between them lately.

Until recently, Wyatt Earp had believed himself to be a decisive man. He used to think that once he made his mind up, that was that. Except when he told Doc he was thinking maybe he would be a delegate to the Republican convention after all, Doc laughed that wheezy laugh of his, and coughed, and shook his head.

"I declare, Wyatt," he said, "given three days, you can talk yourself into anything." Wyatt wasn't sure if that was good or bad, in Doc's opinion, but before he could argue the point, Doc said, "Tell me, Wyatt: do you consider yourself an honest man?"

Wyatt blinked. "Yeah, I guess. Sure, maybe. Anyways, what kinda question is that?" Doc could say the damnedest things.

"Ever occur to you to ask yourself why the biggest liquor wholesaler in Kansas is backin' Prohibition?"

"Henpecked, I guess," Wyatt said. And now that he was living with Mattie, he understood better how that could happen to a man. Sometimes you went along with things you'd rather not, just to be nice.

"Or Luke, sixteen nine, maybe," Wyatt added. *"Make friends with unrighteous money."* It was a text the preacher turned to when he wanted to explain why he took contributions to the building fund from men who owned saloons and brothels.

Doc sat back in his chair, eyes amused. *"Beware of good Samaritans!"* he recited. *"Walk to the right . . . Or hide thee by the roadside out of sight . . . Or greet them with the smile that villains wear."*

That was Doc. Half the time he was the smartest man Wyatt had ever met. The other half, he didn't make any sense at all. Still, the more Wyatt thought about it, the more he liked the idea of being sheriff, and it began to seem pretty likely he would win. Bat had only taken the office by three votes, last election, and more Republicans had moved into the county since then . . .

Things were getting noisy again inside the Commie-Q. Having reduced his audience to satisfying, sentimental tears with "Kathleen," Eddie Foy and the piano player were changing the mood by starting up a square dance. "Circle left! Swing your lady!" Eddie was hollering. "Now allemande right!"

The idea was to get all the Texans to dance with the bar girls so they'd make themselves thirsty and buy more drinks. Wyatt wasn't interested in a bunch of clumsy boys hopping around with trollops. That's what saved his life — because if the jokes had started up again, he'd have been listening to Eddie. He might not have turned away from the theater door and wouldn't have noticed a horseman passing by on Front Street.

The rider reined around and jogged by a second time, like he was looking for someone, and this time Wyatt paid attention. It was a kid. Too stupid to get in out of the rain, is what Wyatt was thinking when the rider turned once more, a block away.

On his third pass, the boy suddenly spurred his horse and came pounding down Front Street at a gallop and with intent. It wasn't so much that he fired his gun. It was the look on his face that told Wyatt this was more than just random hell-raising.

Before the first muzzle flash, Wyatt had time to think, He means to kill me. His own pistol was drawn before the second flash, and he settled himself to take his shot. Later, Doc would ask why in hell Wyatt hadn't taken cover. Well, the boy's horse was just a cow pony, not a cavalry mount. Wyatt knew, without words, that she'd shy or plunge or rear at the noise of the gunshot and that would spoil her rider's aim.

She made him a difficult target as well. Wyatt fired once in reply, and missed, and cursed, and splashed out into the muddy street to take a left-handed grab at the rider as the horse passed within a yard of him.

By then, the rain was done in the west and tapering off in town, but Front Street was a slough and Wyatt slipped as the horse danced sideways. All he got was a handful of tail, and he lost his grip on that.

The boy turned in his saddle to fire again, his face lit by the theater lights: stiff and scared now, but determined.

The slug hit the brim of Wyatt's hat, flipping it off into the mud.

The kid's voice broke when he shouted, "Damn!" He reined his horse around hard and dug in with his spurs, bolting for the bridge, just hoping to get out of town now, for every lawman in Dodge was in the street by then, and all of them were shooting at him.

Wyatt was following on foot, sloshing through the mire, and fell making the turn onto Bridge Street. Already down on his knees, he sat back on his haunches. The lower angle brought his target into dark relief against the sky, which was starting to lighten a little because the setting moon was beginning to show between clouds that were breaking up over Colorado. This time Wyatt aimed carefully and took a second shot, but the rider clattered on over the bridge and was gone from sight.

Bat Masterson might be a lying little weasel, but no question, he was game in a fight. He was the first out of the Commie-Q, the first after Wyatt to fire at the shooter, and the first to reach Wyatt's side now. Huffing from the run, Bat watched the rider disappear and asked, "Who in hell was that joker?"

"Never saw him before," Wyatt said.

Morg was there a moment later, with John Stauber and Chuck Trask and Charlie Bassett right behind him. Bat gave Wyatt a hand up, and then the rest of the officers were on the scene. Almost as quickly, their women appeared, holding shawls tight around their shoulders, white-faced in the watery moonlight, waiting at the edge of the street to be told whose man had been killed this time.

Morg called, "Go on home! Nobody's hit."

The women talked among themselves before going back inside, while Bat told Morg and everybody what had just happened.

"Wyatt was standing on the boardwalk out in front of the Commie-Q, and this kid comes along and opens up on him. I saw the boy through the window — looked right at Wyatt. Right *at* him! Not angry or anything, just: he had a job to do and he was by-God gonna do it."

For a time, they all stood around in the slowing drizzle, speculating on who the kid was and what he had against Wyatt, but hell! There were a hundred cowboys Wyatt had bashed or arrested, or both. Could have been any one of them. And that just counted the ones he'd dealt with in Dodge this season. Could have been somebody with a grudge left over from last year. Or from Ellsworth or Wichita, for that matter.

Wyatt didn't say much, but he never did. Finally Bat declared, "Drinks are on me! Let's get out of the rain."

They were on their way back to the Front Street boardwalk when one of the Riney kids came running over from the tollbooth.

"Mr. Earp," he called, "you hit him, sir! He's over on the south end of the bridge."

Wet and shivering, Wyatt stood in the corner of the cell while Doc McCarty examined the whimpering boy's wound. McCarty said, "I'm afraid it's mortal, son," and Wyatt closed his eyes at the news. "What's your name?" the doctor asked the kid. "Do you have kin we should notify?"

George Hoyt, he turned out to be. Crying, he told McCarty his mother's address and,

486

snuffling, he asked for a drink. Fat Larry brought in a bottle. Wyatt sat on the bunk, and lifted the boy up by the shoulders, and helped him take a good long swig, and laid him down to rest after that. For a little while, he watched Hoyt sleep.

Then he went back to work.

He knew what folks were saying when he walked his rounds that night, like nothing bad had happened. Butter wouldn't melt in Wyatt Earp's mouth. Cool as they come, ole Wyatt.

But he was shook, and bad.

Dime novelists tried to make it seem that frontier lawmen did that kind of thing all the time, but it just wasn't so — not even in towns like Dodge. Killings were nearly always one idiot shooting another; the police were hardly ever involved directly.

For Wyatt, the reaction set in while he was sitting in the mud watching Hoyt ride off over the bridge, when he still believed he'd missed his target. Before Bat arrived at his side and started talking, Wyatt was all alone, and what came to his mind was that he'd missed his sister's birthday. It was a strange thing to think, under the circumstances, but he kept coming back to it, over and over. If young George Hoyt had been a little steadier with his first shot, Adelia would always have remembered that her brother Wyatt forgot to send her a happy birthday, the year that he was killed.

Funny how much the thought bothered him.

As the night went on, Wyatt marveled that he'd been wearing a sidearm because it was so unusual for him. Ordinarily, he was just about the only sober man in town, and he counted on that for his edge. He could generally tame a troublesome drunk with a well-aimed bash across the side of the head. Carrying a weighted sap was easier than lugging a big old Colt around all night in the midsummer heat.

When he got home after his shift, he asked Mattie if she'd heard a rumor that something was going to happen. She denied it but claimed she had second sight, and said she'd had a funny feeling, so she'd handed Wyatt his gun belt before he left for work and asked him to be careful. Which was the only reason he went heeled that night: to make Mattie happy.

But if you have a gun, you're inclined to use it. And now a kid was dying.

Wyatt didn't go home right away when his shift was over. First he checked on Hoyt, who was still alive. Then he walked out toward the east end of town to watch the sun come up in a sky that had cleared overnight, and shone gold and pink this morning.

When he heard the familiar cough behind him, he did not turn. Doc Holliday's steps slowed and stopped. For a while they stood together silently.

"Now I am farther from heaven than when I was a boy," Doc said after a time. "Awful, isn't it."

To have someone look you right in the eye and to know that he intends to kill you. To hurt somebody so bad, he was going to die from what you did to him.

Wyatt asked, "Does it get easier?"

"No."

That was Doc. He didn't sugar things.

"The law can relieve a man of guilt," Doc told him quietly, "but not of his remorse."

The next day, before work, Wyatt went back to the jail to check on Hoyt again. By then the boy had been moved to the doctor's clinic, so Wyatt walked over there and sat with him awhile. Most of the time Hoyt babbled, but once he seemed lucid. He looked at Wyatt — right *at* him, like before — and said, "You seem like a nice fella. I don't know why they want you dead."

"Who?" Wyatt asked. "Who wants me dead?"

"They was gonna pay me a thousand dollars, and get the charges dropped, after."

"Who?" Wyatt asked. He never got an answer. The boy kept talking, but didn't make any sense after that.

Wyatt went to work, like usual, but for the

489

next two days he had a strange feeling of not hearing things quite right, like there was cotton in his ears, or water or something. And thoughts kept coming to him.

I could be dead instead of walking down this street.

Morg could be standing at my grave instead of joshing me about the hole in my hat.

I could be in the ground instead of drinking this coffee.

Somebody wants me dead, he'd think, and maybe that shouldn't have been such a surprise, but it was, for he was just an ordinary man doing his job, and it struck him as unreasonable that anyone would pay so much to get him killed.

Hell, he thought. Give me the grand! I'll leave.

Finally he realized he had to snap out of it before he made a mistake and let some other fool thing happen. Somebody else might get hurt.

The wire came back the day before George Hoyt died. He was wanted for cattle rustling, down near Amarillo.

Nobody in Dodge knew Hoyt personally, but the Texans in town that week clubbed together and gave the kid a big send-off. Wyatt watched the funeral procession from a small remove. A lot of the drovers looked at him like they might try something but nobody did, possibly because Morgan had rounded up Dog Kelley and Bat and Doc Holliday to stand right behind Wyatt, just in case. Even Eddie Foy stood with them.

It was Eddie's idea to go over to the Iowa House for breakfast after the burial, when the crowd had dispersed. Wyatt had been broody since the night he shot the kid, so Eddie spent the whole meal trying to make the event into a funny story, telling Dog Kelley about how he thought he was pretty agile, don't you know, until he saw Bat Masterson and Doc Holliday pancake onto the dance floor when the bullets started flying. Then Eddie told about how his brand-new eleven-dollar suit had sustained a mortal wound. When he went back to his dressing room after the shoot-out, he found three bullet holes in the suit and claimed that one was still burning.

Everyone but Eddie knew that wasn't really possible. You'd have to fire close enough to have the muzzle flare touch the cloth to make it burn, the way it did when Bat's brother Ed got shot. Still, nobody was inclined to argue the point — certainly not Bat, who appreciated that changing a few details could make for a better story.

Eddie's tale would get even better when he wrote his autobiography, in 1928. By then the theater looked like a giant block of Swiss cheese, holed by a thousand bullets fired by a dozen men. Wyatt himself never found humor in the affair. His version of the incident was grimly laconic decades later, even after his account had passed through the imagination of a biographer who often preferred well-dressed drama to bare-naked fact.

On the day of George Hoyt's funeral, Wyatt pushed his plate away, the eggs cold and his toast uneaten, and waited for Eddie to shut up. Then he told the others what young Hoyt had said about being promised $1,000 to kill him, and how Hoyt expected that the Texas warrant against him would be quashed once Wyatt was dead.

Everybody got real quiet.

"Well, that narrows it some," Morgan pointed out, after a while. "Has to be someone with a lot of cash."

"Or someone who could give that impression," Doc said.

"And clout," Eddie said, serious now, for he was a Chicago boy familiar with cutthroat politics. "You need a hell of a reach to pull strings in another state."

"Jesse Driskill, maybe?" Bat suggested. "Word is, he was plenty hot after you arrested his nephew, Wyatt."

Dog Kelley stared at Bat, giving him a chance to add a name.

Bat looked away.

He's bought, Dog thought. I wonder how . . .

"Some men never look hot, but they never forget a slight," Dog said, leaning back to dig fifty cents out of his pocket.

"Bob Wright," Morgan said.

Morg was always about two steps quicker than his brother.

Dog stood and left the change on the table to pay for his breakfast.

"Watch your back," he told Wyatt. "Next time, you won't see it comin'."

CALL

"This's a terrible hard country for women," Eddie Foy had told Alexander von Angensperg at the end of May. And it was none too easy on men, judging by recent events.

One by one, the Jesuits at St. Francis were succumbing to the toil and privation of life on the prairie. Decades of labor in the Kansas wilderness had at last weakened Father Schoenmakers' heart to such an extent that he laid down the burden of running the mission in June, and could now serve only as chaplain to the Sisters of Loretto at the Indian girls' school nearby. The loss of Schoenmakers to St. Francis was not unexpected, for his debility had steadily worsened over the years, but when a measles epidemic carried off Father Bax, along with fifteen hundred Osage on the reservation, the brawny Belgian's death was a great shock. By late June, even the vivacious and indefatigable little Italian Paul Ponziglione had been leveled by exhaustion and illness.

Which is why, in July of 1878, it had fallen to Alexander Anton Josef Maria Graf von Angensperg, S.J., to assume the summer mission circuit that Father Paul ordinarily rode, and to do so atop Alphonsus, the mule that ordinarily carried Father Paul.

Both of these experiences were humbling.

Paul Ponziglione was one of those bewildering creatures born with an extraordinary facility for languages. Since coming to Kansas from Italy a quarter century earlier, Father Paul had added English and German to his native Italian and to the French, Latin, and Greek of any educated person. He also spoke five Indian tongues fluently, and had mastered the nearly universal sign language of the plains as well.

The transparent joy with which Paul conveyed his own faith — and the Italian's personal charm — had done much to bring souls to Christ from among the Osage, the Sauk, the Pawnee, the Cherokee, and the Fox.

Even nearing sixty, the spry little priest traveled relentlessly across Kansas and southward into the Indian Territory as far as the Texas line. Like that of the saint for whom he was named, Father Paul's missionary work encompassed nascent congregations scattered throughout vast lands peopled largely by those hostile to the Faith. He had begun to reap a small but significant harvest from seeds patiently sown in his youth, and it was his policy to visit every church three times a year.

In each village, Father Paul baptized catechumens and infants or those in danger of death. He joined young couples in holy (and monogamous) matrimony, heard confessions, and celebrated the Mass. He doctored wounds as well, and danced with merrymakers, and he settled individual and public disputes. When disease and injuries took their toll, he sat by the dying and wept with the grieving.

Baptized or *Wilden,* many Indians had come to consider Paul Ponziglione a friend and a brother, or son, or uncle, or cousin, or — indeed — a father. And in the summer of '78, Alexander von Angensperg was able to take the exact measure of the reverence and affection with which Father Paul was regarded by noting the degree of distress and open dismay that greeted his own arrival.

Alexander did his garbled, halting best to reassure the Indians of various tribes that Father Paul was neither dead nor dying but merely much in need of rest. There was great relief when this understanding was reached, but that was followed by even more visible disappointment. Told that the sacraments celebrated by a different Black Robe were equally valid in heaven and on earth, the Indians displayed not so much skepticism as disgruntlement.

Arms crossed over chests.

Brows wrinkled.

Lips pursed in annoyance.

"I wanted Father Paul," the bride, or the catechumen, or the dying man would say. "Father Paul is better." And, Alexander was given to understand, he was better in all possible ways.

Father Paul spoke properly. He didn't make confusing mistakes when signing.

Father Paul brought better presents. He was more gracious in receiving gifts.

Father Paul understood how to be polite, and he knew when to make a joke. He certainly never insulted anybody by accident.

Father Paul had kinder eyes. He was friendlier and more amusing.

Father Paul knew how to dance. He was a better singer, too.

Alexander was beginning to hate Father Paul.

Alphonsus, on the other hand, was growing on him. And that, too, was a useful measure of his own lingering vanity, for — man and boy, prince and cavalry officer — Alexander Anton Josef Maria Graf von Angensperg had owned and ridden some of the finest horseflesh in Europe.

As long as he was alone on the empty plains, Alexander could appreciate the mule's easy gait, his surefootedness, and his calm. When a prairie hen whirred into the air, a horse might well have bolted, but the middle-aged Alphonsus merely flicked his long, expressive ears in worldly disdain, for horses are flighty animals who accumulate fears and superstitions with each passing year, whereas mules learn from experience, becoming more sophisticated as they mature. Day after day, Alphonsus picked his way through terrain that would have lamed a horse, traversing ravines and hillocks, negotiating the holes and mounds of vast prairie dog cities without a stumble. A horse would have weakened and grown thin as the grass grew shorter and drier, but Alphonsus remained in fine flesh on poor grazing and was ready to move on each morning. He was a sensible and reliable animal, patient and uncomplaining.

It was only when Alexander was *seen* atop this admirable beast that he felt humiliated and embarrassed. And Indians unerringly took notice.

"*Ata!* There's a man with no women to impress!"

"That horse looks pretty sick! Have you tried a sweat lodge?"

"I hope you didn't trade your gold cup for that big rabbit."

These sallies, and others like them, were considered the height of comedy. Maybe they were funnier if you spoke the language well, and if you didn't have to ask for them to be repeated over and over, in a slow and painful effort to understand exactly how you'd just been mocked — an effort the Indians found almost as funny as the mule's giant ears.

When he finally understood a joke, Alexander did his best to smile, but there was always one remark that made him blush. More mimed than spoken, it needed no translation. One of the women would look appraisingly at the mule's ears, then at Alexander's own, and ask, deadpan, "Cousins?"

Hilarity, inevitably, ensued.

Father Paul had warned that such teasing was to be expected among Indians. Paul himself put up with a lot of nose jokes, being Roman in physiognomy as well as in ancestry and faith. So Alexander soldiered on, in baking heat under a glaring sun, with no companion except Alphonsus on the long rides between each round of rejection and ridicule.

The summer and his own resolve wore away.

Alexander often prayed for patience and strength, but once, in what he suspected was the actual, factual geographic middle of absolutely nowhere, he lost all momentum and allowed the mule's pace to slow to a halt. For a time, he simply sat there, his own head the highest thing on earth as far as the eye could see in any direction, and his heart the lowest.

Perhaps, he thought, it is time to take

Schopenhauer's advice. Eat a toad first thing in the morning; the rest of the day will seem pleasurable by comparison.

Assuming he could find a toad.

Staring at the table-flat horizon, he would sometimes watch an electrical storm gather, build, break, and dissipate, often in eerie silence — the entire drama so far away that he hardly heard the thunder, though he could see the lightning. Late on one sweltering afternoon, a funnel-shaped cloud emerged from the bottom of a towering green-gray thunderhead in the distance. Lengthening, reaching toward the ground, the cyclone wobbled and spun drunkenly across the empty land, its journey as useless as his own.

He had not felt so hopeless since his days as a novice, still learning the community's ways, still doing everything he could to get thrown out — things that would have gotten him flogged in the military. "*Do* you *want* this?" the novice master demanded every time Alexander defied a superior or came to blows with one of his potential brothers in Christ.

"I want what God wants for me," Alexander would answer, stubborn, willful, and friendless.

Which simply raised the question . . .

. . . that was, at last, answered one night on the Oklahoma plains where he lay on the

500

open ground, in the rain and near the mule, probably lost and certainly despondent. To his dying day, he was not sure if he was awake or asleep or someplace in between when he heard a single word: *Timothy.*

The next morning, at first gray light, he awoke to the bland curiosity of Alphonsus, who watched, munching weeds, while Alexander rolled creakily onto his hands and knees, swatted insects away, checked his boots for scorpions, scratched a dozen new bites, took a piss, and dug a small New Testament out of his oilskin pack. He opened it to the letters of Saint Paul. Before his eyes, the text turned inside out.

Every line of Paul's praise and encouragement whispered to Alexander of the dejection and frustration that Timothy must have been reporting as he followed in the footsteps of the saint. Like Timothy, Alexander von Angensperg was ready to teach the Gospel, willing to endure hardship as a good soldier of Christ, eager to receive knowledge and understanding from God in the service of God. Like Timothy, everywhere he went, he was considered nothing more than a poor and unwelcome substitute for a man named Paul.

Over the next few days, Alexander studied and took to heart the saint's instruction to Timothy on the teaching of sound doctrine and on being an example of faith in word, conduct, love, and spirit. While Alphonsus

501

found his own way along a trail that the mule had walked three times a year for twenty years, Alexander's mind was free to compose a sermon that might lead Indian converts to see a connection between themselves and the early Church established by their beloved pastor's patron saint.

From then on, in every village, Alexander promised to convey the Indians' concern, good wishes, prayers, and love to Father Paul, just as Timothy must have promised to convey news of the Philippians and Ephesians and Colossians to Saint Paul. He stopped trying so hard to say everything correctly and learned to laugh at his own mistakes, and learned as well to enjoy the good-humored teasing that marks so much of Indian life. When he stopped talking and listened instead, he found that even the proudest and most recalcitrant of the *Wilden* believed in a spiritual reality beyond the physical, that they shared his own desire to understand and join with the sacred power alive in this world. And there were moments, now and then, when he sensed strongly the presence of the Holy Spirit amid the souls who had gathered in tiny board churches or simply stood together during the Mass under broad blue skies.

In early August, Alexander arrived at yet another indistinguishably squalid village and was taken immediately to an Indian girl of fifteen. She requested baptism from Alexander himself, rather than waiting for Father Paul, for she knew she was near death from consumption and wished to join the Church. Though her relatives were heathens, they could not deny this beloved child anything that might ease her passing. Alexander had just enough time for a brief preparation before the girl's wish could be fulfilled. Then he laid the consecrated Host on the tongue of the newly christened Mary Clare.

With that food of angels in her mouth, she breathed out her soul and was immediately united with her Creator. There was a hushed, awestruck moment before her family began to wail. She is in heaven, Alexander thought, stunned. I have witnessed a saint's death.

In the long years to come, Alexander von Angensperg would pray for Mary Clare's intercession, especially after he was transferred to the Rosebud Reservation in the 1890s. Nine of ten Lakota died of tuberculosis in those days, and each time Alexander was called to a deathbed like Mary Clare's, he prayed that she would bring about one of the three miracles he needed to present her case for canonization.

By the time Alexander had assembled his evidence, the Sacra Rituum Congregatio had already begun beatification of a young Carmelite nun known to her devotees as the Little Flower of Jesus. Like Mary Clare,

Thérèse of Lisieux had suffered from and died of tuberculosis, but the Little Flower had influential European supporters who were able to press her cause in Rome; Mary Clare had a single elderly Jesuit in South Dakota, so the petition on her behalf languished in back offices of the Vatican. But Alexander von Angensperg knew what he knew. That beautiful Indian child was in heaven. She was especially solicitous of those dying of consumption. And she could effect a cure — or at least a remission — of the disease in special circumstances.

He had seen this thrice, he believed, with his own eyes. The first time was in the summer of 1878, just outside Dodge City.

That August, after the crops were in and before the harvest began, a two-week platform convention for the Republican Party of Kansas was held in Topeka. Among the delegates was Wyatt S. Earp (occupation: policeman; residence: Dodge City, Ford County). Neatly dressed in black and wearing a decent pair of freshly polished boots, Deputy Earp was accompanied by a quiet woman whose age was difficult to guess. She was not young, but neither was she more worn than might be expected of a farmer's wife, and she was well turned out in a deep blue that complemented her hair and complexion. Wyatt would introduce her as Mattie

Earp but did not call her "my wife," for they were not married then and never would be. He let her use his name for the occasion and did not tell her to quit it afterward.

The morning Mattie and Wyatt left for Topeka, Morgan and Lou and Doc and Kate came to the Dodge depot to see them off. Morgan had been on Wyatt's back all week about letting Doc exercise Dick Naylor while Wyatt was away. Wyatt still hadn't said yes or no. He didn't want any trouble with Kate — there'd be hell to pay if anything happened — but he hated to disappoint Doc.

Morgan was giving it one last try as the warning whistle shrieked. "Come on, Wyatt! Doc knows to be careful, and I'll watch out for him."

Kate didn't say anything, but she was standing right behind Doc, where Wyatt could see her scowl and Doc couldn't.

"I don't know," Wyatt said, glancing at Kate. "What if Dick gets spooked by a coyote or something? He might throw you again, Doc. And you'd be out on the prairie —"

"I won't go far," Doc promised. "And I'll stick to trails with traffic on them. And I'll tell Morg when I'm leavin'. If I don't get back in a couple of hours, he can come lookin' for me. Did you read that *Scientific American* article I gave you?"

Doc doesn't know! Mattie realized with some surprise. Wyatt hasn't told him!

Which meant Wyatt was embarrassed that he couldn't hardly read. And *that* was the first sign she'd had that Mr. Wyatt Earp wasn't quite so perfect as he seemed. It made Mattie feel a little better about him.

She had listened while Morgan read the article to Wyatt. There was a new notion about how to cure consumption: a combination of hard exercise and cold baths was supposed to "build resistance to the illness" and give people like Doc the strength to get over it. Doc's idea was that he could take Dick Naylor out for an hour or two of riding every day while Wyatt was out of town. The horse would stay in condition for a race that was coming up at the end of the month, and Doc would have a couple of weeks to find out if he got any better. "We'll see if that punishment fits my crime" was how he put it. If the exercise didn't help or if he felt worse, he'd give it up and let Morgan take over Dick's care until Wyatt got back.

Mattie knew her place. She had no right to mix in, but Doc had been helpful to her and she wanted to take his side. The only reason she was going to Topeka was because Doc showed her how to pick out dresses and told her about table manners and things like that. Otherwise she'd have found an excuse, even though Wyatt thought she'd enjoy the excursion and claimed he really wanted her to come with him.

Mattie rarely said a word in public, and not much more in private. It took her until the train was almost ready to go before she found the nerve to touch Wyatt's elbow. "He'll break down or he'll toughen up," she said. "Let him find out which."

Everybody looked at her like she was a pig that up and flew.

Wyatt blinked a couple of times and finally said, "Oh, hell. All right, then," probably because Mattie had never asked for anything before and he didn't want to say no to her the first time. Morg grinned that big happy smile of his. Kate narrowed her eyes and glared. Doc told Wyatt he wouldn't regret it, then took Mattie's hand and kissed it like she was a lady, and leaned over to whisper, "Mattie, honey, I am in your debt."

The conductor was hollering, "Board!" by then. Wyatt tried to help Mattie up the long first step, but she told him, "I ain't crippled." She meant that she wasn't some fragile little thing that needed to be treated like a china doll, but Wyatt looked kind of hurt, so she shrugged and let him take her arm, if that's what he wanted.

Inside the car, Wyatt was going to have her sit on the aisle so she wouldn't get dirty from the ash or get holes in her clothes from the cinders. Feeling bolder, she told him, "I'd like to see," so he let her be by the window instead.

Doc was still standing on the platform when the train pulled away. Mattie gave him a little wave. He swept off his slouch hat, held it over his heart, and bowed, his shining eyes on Mattie's own.

It would have annoyed her if Wyatt did that, but somehow . . . Doc was different.

His first foray on Dick was enjoyable and uneventful. True to his word, he didn't ride far, turning back after half an hour, while he still had enough starch left to unsaddle the horse himself and brush the animal down.

The second day was harder, for he had stiffened some. The third, it was a real struggle to tack up. As he approached the Elephant Barn on the way back, he was sufficiently whipped to consider paying the oldest of the Riney boys to take care of the horse. Instead, he rested for a few minutes after dismounting. Then he managed on his own.

Things got better after that.

With some experimentation, he determined that the best time to ride was just past sunup, before the summer heat set in. By the end of the first week, he found it noticeably easier to lift the saddle from the rack, carry it to Dick Naylor's side, and settle it onto the horse's back. Even Kate had to admit that riding was good for him. He was stronger, no doubt about it. And he was hungry again — genuinely by-God *hungry.* For food. For music. For Kate.

Nights, he was content to deal faro, building up a stake for the next big poker game. Kate was relieved to see easy money accumulating, and her mood brightened as well. She kept a couple of special clients, but when she went over to James and Bessie's now, it was usually a social call. That made Doc happier.

Less anxious about his health and its consequences for her own life, Kate was able to think more clearly about his day work. It was she who suggested that Doc have the Eberhardt boy keep an eye on the office in the mornings. It wasn't necessary for Doc to sit around waiting for patients, she pointed out. If someone showed up first thing in the morning, Wilfred could run down to China Joe's and let Doc know that he should go straight to No. 24 after he cleaned up from his ride. If nobody was waiting, Doc could come home and be on call instead of sitting around in the office.

And Kate made sure that they found a better use for his time.

Mabel Riney wasn't taking any excuses on the morning of August 14, 1878. "It's your job, John," she told her husband, rousting him out of bed. "Get up and do it." And if his head pounded with every hoofbeat as drovers crossed the bridge and went back to their herds after their own long night, well, that was just too bad.

Doc Holliday rode up to the tollgate on Wyatt Earp's two-dollar horse a little past dawn. Wincing into the sun, John held out his palm and parts of some fingers to collect the toll.

Handing over two bits, the dentist looked out across the river and said in a singing kind of way, *"Boundless and bare, the lone and level sands stretch far away."* Then, in a regular voice, he said, "I'll be followin' the cattle trail south for a couple of hours, Mr. Riney. If I don't come back across the bridge by eight, you should probably ask Morgan Earp to ride out and collect my corpse for shipment back to Georgia."

Years later, after Mabel Riney was dead, when John Riney was old and toothless and a hopeless drunkard, he would let punks buy him beers while he told about the day the infamous *Doc Holliday* spoke of his bones whitening on the prairie.

"Doc got off his horse about halfway over the toll bridge, see? And he stood there at the railing, watching the river. I reckoned he was about to drown hisself because he was so sick," John would tell anybody who'd pay for a drink. "Don't do it, Doc! That's what I hollered, and I guess I saved his life that day. But y'see, that's why Doc was so fearless

510

down there in Tombstone! Because he was going to die soon anyways, so he might as well get it over with."

The funny thing was, nobody really believed that John Riney had ever met Doc Holliday, but they all believed what he said about the dentist hoping to die sooner than later. Of course, John Riney did know Doc — not well, but they had a nodding acquaintance. And Doc did speak of the possibility of dying out on the prairie south of Dodge, but it was a joke that John didn't get because he tended to take things at face value even when he hadn't been drinking most of the week, and in John's defense, Doc did make the remark straight-faced.

So John nodded solemnly and said, "Yes, sir, I'll do that."

Head throbbing, he watched the dentist start across the bridge and then dismount halfway across. John came to his own conclusions about that, for there was no way he could have known that it was Doc's birthday, or that the dentist was in fact feeling remarkably cheerful.

"Twenty-seven years old and not dead yet!" John Henry Holliday had marvelled while saddling Dick Naylor that morning. "Let's go see what's south of that bridge this mornin'," he suggested, flipping the stirrup leathers down.

Responding to his rider's high spirits, Dick

was prancing and full of himself coming out of the Elephant Barn into the cool of early morning, but the roadbed of the toll bridge was unfamiliar and Dick didn't like it much. Rather than get bucked off by a skittish horse, John Henry dismounted and spoke soothingly to the animal, letting Dick come to terms with the situation. In the meantime, the arch of the bridge provided a slight rise in perspective he enjoyed.

"Dick, if you want a hill in Kansas, you have to by-God build it yourself," he remarked.

It was a pretty morning. A thunderstorm the night before had cleared the air. Graceful in the breeze, bluestem grass rippled under a sky the color of Kate's eyes. Phlox and mallow and goldenrod added lavender and pink and yellow to the scene. Red-winged blackbirds trilled in the cattails along the river.

It was a wonder to him now that he'd once failed to appreciate the beauty of this land. The trick of it, he'd lately realized, was to pay attention to the sky as part of the landscape. The rising sun was gilding high cottony clouds from below. In a few hours, as the light shifted upward, those clouds would send amethyst and turquoise shadows racing over the emerald ground, and their sweep across the land would reveal subtle undulations in terrain that only appeared flat to the careless observer.

His own quiet contentment calmed Dick. Soon the horse felt ready to walk over the scary, hollow-sounding surface with the noisy, glittery water below, and to let his rider remount when they reached the solid ground beyond. Swinging easily onto the saddle, sitting comfortably fifteen and a half hands above the earth, gazing at the country south of the Arkansas, John Henry found himself engulfed by a sense of his own well-being. He was grateful to Kate for insisting that they come to Dodge and glad the two of them were working things out. He was pleased that he had made friends here and elated to have returned at last to a useful profession that provided him with so much satisfaction.

And — God a'mighty — to be *riding* again!

Since coming West, he had been neither well enough nor prosperous enough for long enough to consider keeping a horse to ride for pleasure. Now, with Dick Naylor beneath him, he felt himself a joyful boy once more: privileged to share in the athletic power of a large and dangerous animal willing to be controlled by the small, frail strength of a mere human being.

It came to him then that if things worked out the way he hoped, he might just buy a colt from Wyatt Earp one day. By Dick Naylor out of Roxana.

For the first time since he'd begun his practice in Atlanta at the age of twenty-one,

John Henry Holliday was beginning to think of the future as though he had a right to it. And why not? Outside, in the growing warmth and the brilliant sunshine, rocking in the rhythm of a ground-eating lope, he was aware of his body from his head to his heels and he felt *fine.*

Thirteen and a half months had passed since Henry Kahn had tried to kill him. His hip had healed slowly but fully; the scarring gave him trouble with some movements, but most days now his cane was more fashionable than functional. The pain beneath his left scapula was probably muscular; he just needed to get used to stooping over patients again. The cough was bad occasionally; he should be more careful about the things that set it off. Granted, breathing was sometimes difficult, but he expected to do better after the cattle season ended, absent the dust.

He could ride now for a good two hours at a stretch, and he felt fortunate to have lived long enough to learn that the cure for his illness might be as simple as "Go on outside and enjoy yourself, son." He wasn't so certain he'd enjoy cold baths when the weather cooled off, but for now, they were remarkably refreshing after exertion. China Joe charged less for unheated water, so that part of the therapy even saved money, which pleased Miss Kate. He was tired after the rides, but that was the whole point of the exercise, and he was sleeping so much better! He awoke restored, feeling far more rested than he had during the enforced idleness imposed by Tom McCarty after the fall on the Fourth of July.

John Henry Holliday was better in every way he could think of.

It didn't occur to him to think that better is not the same as well.

Was he fooling himself? He would not have said so. Even at twenty-two, when his diagnosis was confirmed, he was realistic. Most suffer. Everyone dies. He knew how, if not when.

Now more than ever, he was determined to cheat the Fates of entertainment, but naturally, his time would come. When it did, he believed he would accept death as Socrates had: with cool philosophical distance. He would say something funny, or profound, or loving. Then he would let life fall gracefully from his hands.

Horseshit, as James Earp would say, of the highest order.

The truth is this. On the morning of August 14, 1878, Doc Holliday believed in his own death exactly as you do — today, at this very moment. He knew that he was mortal, just as you do. Of course, you know you'll die someday, but . . . not quite the same way you know that the sun will rise tomorrow or that dropped objects fall.

The great bitch-goddess Hope sees to that.

Sit in a physician's office. Listen to a

diagnosis as bad as Doc's. Beyond the first few words, you won't hear a thing. The voice of Hope is soft but impossible to ignore. *This isn't happening,* she assures you. *There's been a mix-up with the tests.* Hope swears, *You're different. You matter.* She whispers, *Miracles happen.* She says, often quite reasonably, *New treatments are being developed all the time!* She promises, *You'll beat the odds.*

A hundred to one? A thousand to one? A million to one?

Eight to five, Hope lies.

Odds are, when your time comes, you won't even ask, "For or against?"

You'll swing up on that horse, and ride.

A week earlier, while enjoying a state of happiness as profound and unexamined as Doc's own, Alexander von Angensperg had come at last to the border of the Indian Territory. There the Great Western Trail was a wide path beaten into the grassland by millions of hooves. Trusting that it would lead him to the German farming communities of Ford County in southwestern Kansas, Alexander turned Alphonsus northward.

Pasturage improved steadily. Approaching the Arkansas River, he began to encounter cattle companies that had paused to fatten their herds before sale in Dodge. He camped with several crews overnight, but his days were spent alone until a clear mid-August morning, when he saw in the distance a coal-black dot, startling against the sunlit grass.

A lone surviving bison, he supposed, for-lornly searching for a companion. But as Alexander closed on it, the shape gradually resolved into a fine dark stallion with a slender, smiling rider. It seemed a message from God when this person called out a quote from Saint Paul.

"*Put to death that which is earthly in you: fornication, impurity, passion, evil desire, covetousness* . . . ridin' a respectable horse."

"Dr. Holliday!" Alexander cried, adding with astonished delight, "You look . . . well!"

"Very kind of you to say so, sir. I am well!" Doc declared, leaning over to offer his hand. "Keats and Shelley went to France and Italy for their cure. Kansas doesn't have the same cachet, but then I am a dentist and not a poet. What is a refined Austrian *hyparchos* like yourself doin' on an ugly mule like that?"

"The Lord's work," Alexander replied, feeling sure of it now. "That is a splendid animal you have!"

"Isn't he a daisy? *When I bestride him, I soar, I am a hawk! He trots the air; the earth sings when he touches it!*"

"Homer . . . ? No! Wait — *Henry V*!"

"Full marks!" Doc cried, reining around. "Father von Angensperg, may I present Dick

517

Naylor? A quarter-miler to be reckoned with."

"And this is Alphonsus," Alexander replied, "a mule aptly named for a saint of many virtues."

As though no time had passed since their first meeting, they tumbled into a conversation that began with Alexander's now unabashed admiration for Alphonsus and Doc's gracious admission that mules were highly prized in the South and considered superior to horses for many purposes. This led to a discussion of mule breeding, and that to horse breeding, and that to Wyatt Earp, who hoped to build a stud farm around Dick Naylor.

"I fear you have missed Wyatt again, sir," Doc told Alexander. "He's in Topeka, at the state convention of the Republican Party —" His lip curled at the words, and he added a confession dark with melodrama: "I have fallen in with evil companions."

From there, the conversation veered off toward the score for Brahms' Second Symphony, which Alexander had sent two months earlier, and that became a discussion of its orchestration. Music persisted as their topic until Dodge became visible in the distance, and Doc suggested that they have lunch together after he attended any patients that might be waiting for him. "Have you ever tried Chinese food?" Doc asked. "I have developed a taste for it, myself." It was an enthusiasm he had passed on to Morgan and Wyatt, he told the priest, and with the expansiveness that comes with recovered health, Doc had urged Jau Dong-Sing to open a restaurant on Front Street, even promising that he and Kate would invest in the venture.

"Ah . . . so Athena has rejoined you?" Alexander asked carefully.

"Adjustments made," Doc said briefly. "Compromises reached."

The couple had come to an agreement about his working hours after Doc conceded that he'd been burning the candle at both ends while getting started in Dodge. Things were going well now, and he felt sure he would one day have as large a practice as he had cared for back in Georgia. People were even coming in by train, some from as far as Wichita.

Struck by this news, Alexander asked if he might propose a short trip east. The students at St. Francis would benefit from the attention of a dentist, he told Doc. "We couldn't pay you much," the priest admitted. "Perhaps a train ticket —"

"Nonsense!" Doc cried. "I will do the work *pro bono,* of course. My Catholic cousin Martha Anne will be happy to know I am assistin' you in your work at the mission. Can you wait until October? I hate to leave Dodge during the cattle season, but I expect things to quiet down in the autumn."

Just then a black-tailed jackrabbit flashed by. Alphonsus walked steadily on, but Dick Naylor shied and danced.

"He has taken a dislike to dogs recently," Doc remarked, wheeling Dick until the horse settled. "I imagine anything crossin' his path looks fearsome now."

This reminded Alex of a cavalry charger he'd once owned. ("Valiant under cannon fire! Terrified of chickens!") The rest of the ride was passed in an amusing exchange regarding the irrationality of horses, during which Doc alluded to his participation in the Fourth of July race. ("Do tell, sir! I am agog with anticipation!" Alexander cried.) The story of the fall was alarming, but the dentist assured the priest that he had recovered fully and felt entirely well now. Certainly he looked and sounded vastly better than he had in May, when he was exhausted and a good deal paler.

"When, exactly, did your condition begin to improve?" Alexander asked. "May I guess? A fortnight ago?"

"About then. Why?"

"I am curious, only," Alexander said, giving silent thanks to Mary Clare, for he had been praying for John Henry Holliday since turning north toward Dodge. "If you come east in October, we could perhaps go to St. Louis for a few days! I understand the orchestra there is excellent."

When they reached the tollbooth, Doc insisted on paying, and insisted as well that Alphonsus should have a night of luxury at the Elephant Barn, and that Alexander himself be Doc's guest at Dodge House before continuing his circuit around Ford County. When Alexander began to thank him, Doc held up a hand.

"My pleasure, sir, but I would like to ask for something in return, if you don't object."

"Anything," Alexander said, "that is not sinful or illegal."

"Neither of those. A little more than curiosity, I should say. A little less than suspicion."

Doc outlined what he wanted. It was simple enough. Alexander was happy to oblige, but puzzled. "Why not ask about this yourself?"

"The sin of pride, I suppose," Doc said. "Such an inquiry might invite others to believe that I am hopin' to be recompensed for the expense of the wake, and that is most surely not my intent."

"Daddy? Daddy! A man just came into the store."

Bob Wright looked up from the order he was working on in the back room. It takes a fair amount to unnerve a child raised in Kansas, and a man coming into the store was not what you'd call unusual, but Belle was standing in the doorway, half-hiding herself, holding on to the jamb. It had been a long time since Bob had heard that little-girl uncertainty in her voice. His reaction was swift: grip the shotgun he kept under his desk and go directly to her side.

"What's wrong, honey?"

"Daddy," she said with quiet urgency, lifting her chin slightly toward the front door, "that man is wearing a *dress!*"

Frowning, Bob scanned the customers for someone sporting a beard and a bustle. He'd seen stranger things in his day . . . But when he spotted the gentleman in question, Bob put the shotgun away.

"Father von Angensperg!" he called, going out to the counter with his hand extended in welcome. "Nice to see you again, sir."

Belle recognized the name. It was that of Johnnie Sanders' favorite teacher at St. Francis, back in Wichita. So that's a *Jesuit,* she thought, not a crazy person!

This realization failed to make her feel a *great* deal better because everybody knew Jesuits took orders straight from the pope. Her father said that they were in league with Irish immigrants to take over the United States, which was why she wasn't allowed to attend Johnnie's funeral: because there might be some sort of papist uprising, or riot, or something. Even at the time, *that* seemed a little far-fetched, but the day of the funeral, Belle couldn't argue with a locked door, and that was exactly why she took *this* opportunity

522

to meet the man Johnnie had liked so much.

The moment her father stopped to take a breath, Belle said, "Daddy, would you introduce me to the gentleman, please?" Which he did, because there wasn't really any courteous way to get out of it.

So there she was, little old Isabelle Wright, surrounded by shirts, hats, boots, canned goods, flour barrels, hair tonic, and neckerchiefs, saying howdy-do to an international conspirator wearing a dress! And she didn't know what she might have expected such a person to be like, but it wasn't this handsome older man with his sunburned face and smiling blue eyes and *lovely* manners. She was sort of thrilled by the way he straightened and clicked his heels and took her hand like he was going to kiss it, although he didn't really — he just bowed over it and brought it close to his lips like he was *going* to — and said how pleased he was to meet her.

Except — and this might have been her imagination — there *was* something sort of strange in his expression, like he'd noticed something about her and felt concerned about it. That was disturbing, but Belle covered her confusion by telling him that Johnnie had spoken of him often.

Before she could say much more, her father cut in — so friendly in that embarrassing, fake way of his — to ask, in his heartiest voice, "What can I do for you on this fine day, sir?"

"I was wondering if I might have a minute of your time," the Jesuit said with a refined-sounding German accent. "I would like to ask a few questions about some money Johnnie Sanders might have left in your care, if that would be convenient."

Which caused Belle to prick up her ears, and don't think she didn't notice the way her father made clear that it wasn't a *bit* convenient, letting his attention be interrupted three or four times for things that one of the clerks could have done perfectly well, like quoting prices for a cowboy who wanted "a bran-new rig," and penciling a long order on some brown paper for a trail boss, and generally stalling around like anything.

Suddenly international papist conspiracies were less intriguing than her own father's odd behavior, so just to see what would happen, Belle said in her best Helpful Hannah voice, "Daddy, I'd be happy to take the gentleman into the back until you have time to speak to him." And before her father could say no, she asked the priest, "May I offer you a cup of coffee, sir?"

Well! That changed her father's mind about what would be convenient and when, because he took the priest right back into the office and closed the door behind them. But Belle was determined to find out what was going on, so she stood right by the door to listen and didn't care a *rap* if anybody saw her do it, either.

The priest's voice was pretty quiet, but her father's had a sort of carrying quality to it. Belle was familiar with some of what he was saying, so it was easy to figure out what she couldn't hear. Bob didn't know anything about any money, but allowed as how Johnnie might have booked his cash and put it in the safe without mentioning it. Bob himself used to keep all the transactions in his head, but he was out of town a lot, what with being a state representative and so on, lot of responsibilities, you see. He'd trusted Johnnie to do the books in his absence. Then the boy died in the fire just as the cattle season was picking up steam, and Father von Angensperg could see for himself how busy the store was. Bob had been more careful about accounts back when he had business partners in the old days, but since he bought out Charlie Rath and Henry Beverley, he'd gotten careless because there was nobody else to answer to, and that was why he'd hired Johnnie to take over the books in the first place.

Now, it was Belle's observation that when people gave a whole *lot* of reasons for something, it was because they were trying hard to make sure you didn't notice something else. And she was trying to figure out what her father was covering up when he said, "I haven't really looked at the account books since Johnnie passed on. What kinda figure are we talking about here, do you know?"

The answer was so startling that her father repeated it, and Belle gasped, which set off one of those coughing spells that had been giving her trouble lately. It was probably just hay fever, which doctors said now wasn't really a fever and didn't have anything to do with hay, but Belle did feel awfully warm, at night especially, and she would be glad when the first frost hit because she expected she'd feel better after the goldenrod died back.

She was still coughing when her father opened the door and frowned at her like he knew she'd been eavesdropping and didn't like it, but he couldn't say anything about it because he was still talking to the priest.

"Well, I sure don't know anything about a sum of money like that, but I'll check into it for you, and I'll let you know if I find anything out," he said. Except he had a sort of stiff look on his face that meant, *Hell will freeze solid before I tell you anything about my books, you Catholic fiend. You probably want that money for the pope.*

Belle could tell that Father von Angensperg wasn't a bit fooled either. He thanked her father for his time, though his eyes were on Belle as he spoke, and he had that look of compassionate concern again, which gave Belle the cold creeps because she didn't know as there was anything to be concerned or compassionate *about.* Personally, she thought she was the last person in Kansas anybody should feel sorry for, given that she was tolerably pretty and her daddy was indecently rich and her whole life was laid out before her like a banquet on a fine lace tablecloth, and yet . . .

Wordlessly, Alexander von Angensperg reached toward the girl's pale and pretty face. His fingers felt cool when he touched her cheek, flushed and pink.

Mary Clare's age, he was thinking. Poor child. Poor child.

"I will pray for you," he promised softly, cupping her chin in his hand.

Hope smiled.

The Fates laughed.

Belle frowned.

"Um. Thank you, sir," she said.

UNDER THE TABLE

At speed, steel wheels clicking over rail joins have a cradle's rhythm. Lulled by the heat and the train's sway, at least half the people in the second-class car were dozing. Wyatt was drowsy himself and Mattie Blaylock was sound asleep, her head drooping against his shoulder.

He was pretty sure Mattie had enjoyed going to Topeka. On balance, anyways. She liked looking in the shop windows and there were some good shows in the theaters, but she was kind of spooked by how the political people acted when Wyatt introduced her. Men would smile and tell Wyatt how he was a lucky fella to have such a lovely lady on his arm, and so on. Mattie'd just stand there without saying anything back, the suspicion plain in her face. The silence would go on until Wyatt said something like "Yes, sir. I guess I am."

First time that happened, Mattie rounded on him when they got back to their hotel room, like it was his fault when other men paid her a compliment. "I ain't lovely and I ain't no lady, and you ain't lucky to have me, and you know it!" she told him, and he couldn't tell if she was going to cry or spit. "What am I supposed to do when people say shit like that?"

Wyatt blinked. "Well," he said, trying to be helpful, "Lou says thank you."

"A man talks *nice,* he wants something," Mattie muttered.

She was pretty bitter about that. You could tell. And truth was, Wyatt did want something, but he was getting better at living with a woman again, and figured now wasn't the time.

"Nice ain't always a trick," he said, watching her undress. "You're prettier'n you think," he added, realizing that it was true just as the words were coming out of his mouth. He didn't say anything about the "lucky" part. Mattie might've noticed that, because she just looked at him hard and snorted before she turned her back to him.

Later that night, lying in bed, thinking, it struck him that Mattie's story was like Dick Naylor's. It was natural that she was nervy and suspicious. All men had ever done was ride her hard and hit her. But if a horse could change, so could a person, and Wyatt thought maybe Mattie would get used to being treated better, like Dick had. He hoped so, because Morg was right. Mattie wasn't such a bad person. She'd just been ill-used in her youth.

Sure enough, a couple of mornings after that, when they were getting ready to go out for breakfast, he noticed Mattie gazing at her reflection in the mirror. She tried a little smile then, and he could see her lips shape the words "Thank you," like she was practicing, the way he had practiced "Mississippi" and "fifty-five." Before she could catch him looking, he turned away because he didn't want to spoil it for her. He knew how different you could feel when you *saw* yourself different, and he liked that he was helping Mattie the way Doc had helped him.

That was when, without warning, a wave of feeling washed over him. It wasn't love, like he had for Urilla. Even so, it felt pretty good.

As the convention went on, Mattie started saying "Thank you" out loud when somebody said something nice to her, and then she'd glance at Wyatt and he'd nod, sort of proud of her. She still looked embarrassed, and never said more than two words if she could help it, but she started standing up a little straighter, like maybe it wasn't so bad to be noticed.

Course, nobody in Topeka knew what she used to be. As far as anyone at the convention knew, Mattie was Wyatt's real wife. And without really wanting to, Wyatt began to wonder how it would be if he and Mattie didn't go back to Dodge. Like: what if they just got on the train and stayed on it? What if they rode to the end of the rails, out in Colorado? They could get a clean start, both of them. Wyatt could quit busting heads and getting shot at. He wasn't as good as Johnnie Sanders or Doc Holliday, but he guessed he could make a living dealing faro in Denver. And Mattie could be a new person. Happier, maybe. Less afraid.

Trouble was, a lot of men in Topeka had just spent two weeks telling Wyatt he should run against Bat Masterson for sheriff of Ford County, and how the party would back him if he did. And when Bob Wright came up for reelection, they said, Wyatt ought to challenge him for representative on the Republican ticket. That's how Prohibition would get passed: one Dry representative elected at a time, until the legislature finally had enough anti-saloon men to do the right thing. But it would mean settling in Dodge for good. Which put Wyatt in mind of the train joke Eddie Foy told, where a conductor comes along the aisle and asks a drunk where he's going. "To hell, I reckon," the drunk says, and the conductor answers, "Ticket's a dollar. Get off at Dodge."

Halfway across Kansas now, listening to the chug and click of the train, Wyatt stared out the window, letting his thoughts settle some while he watched the land go by. Funny how you were traveling faster than a horse could run, and you knew you were moving, but there was no sense of the land under you. You lost the smell of grass crushed under your mount's hooves and the sound of the leather creaking beneath your hips. You couldn't really see anything small. The world was just two big slabs of color. Blue above, green below. Things got simpler.

It came down to this. If he was going to run against Bat, he needed more than suspicion. He needed a reason.

Put up or shut up, he thought.

It was early evening when the train pulled into Dodge. Lou and Morg were there to meet them but not Doc, who was laid up with a cold. Morgan wanted to go to Delmonico's for a meal, so Wyatt could tell him and Lou about the convention, but Mattie had one of her headaches starting and couldn't stand the thought of food. They stopped by Tom McCarty's pharmacy to get her a dose of laudanum; that was the only thing that kept her from throwing up until she had dry heaves. Wyatt got her home and helped her into bed, but soon as she was asleep, he left to take a walk around town.

Morgan was back on duty by then, and he figured Wyatt would want to know what had gone on while he was in Topeka.

Wyatt brushed the report off and asked instead, "Where's Bat?"

"He's not at the Lone Star?" Morg asked after a moment.

Wyatt just looked at him, like he knew Morgan was stalling for time. Which he was.

"Well, it's pretty quiet tonight," Morg said then. "Maybe he's over at the Iowa House?"

"Already checked." Wyatt glanced away before giving Morgan that hard stare that could feel like a shove. "Where's his money coming from, Morg?"

Morgan's eyes dropped. "I ain't gonna lie to you, Wyatt, but I'd rather you didn't ask —"

"Morg, are you *covering* for him?"

"Well, see, we just figured what you didn't know wouldn't —"

"Where," Wyatt said very quietly, "is he?"

Morg lasted about three seconds. "Out past Duck Creek," he said. "A little north of Howells."

In late November of 1853, when Catherine Masterson gave birth to her second son, nearly a dozen years had passed since the infamous Lilly-McCoy bare-knuckle boxing match in Hastings, New York. Even so, when her son Bat was a boy, men still spoke of that epic contest the way the Greeks and Trojans once spoke of mighty Achilles and brave Hector, in voices hushed by secondhand awe.

Homer sang of boxing matches. Vergil wrote of them. Pindar called down the blessings of

533

Zeus upon them. In paint and in marble and in bronze, on vases and in murals and with heroic statuary, ancient artisans depicted the boxer's manly beauty, with its cauliflower ears, its honorable scars and blunt, mashed nose.

For millennia, one man had squared off against another on a point of honor or simply to settle a question, here and now, once and for all. Which of us is stronger? Which more fearless and more fearsome? Which of us is the better *man?* In all that time, empires had risen and flourished and stumbled and failed. Maps of the world had been drawn and redrawn; globes had been invented. Wars and revolutions and science and industry had changed everything — but not boxing. It took the Lilly-McCoy fight to do that.

As a kid, Bat Masterson studied accounts of the match the way better-educated boys read *The Iliad.* In Bat's opinion, the fight should have been stopped in the seventy-seventh round, and he was probably right. Even then, long before it was over, McCoy was in bad shape. All the newspapermen agreed about that, and they'd recorded his condition in lascivious detail. Lips grotesquely swollen. Blackened eyes puffed to slits. Broad chest red and slimy with the blood he vomited in quick, efficient gouts during the half-minute rest between the rounds. The darling of Irish immigrants, Tom

McCoy would not concede, and swore he'd die before he'd let a fucking Englishman like Christopher Lilly best him. Cocky to the end, McCoy went 119 rounds, surviving a total of two hours and forty-one minutes until — choking on blood, blinded by it, speechless but head up and still defiant — he staggered into the ring from his corner, toed the scratch mark one last time, and fell down, stone-cold dead.

There were other fights that lasted as long or longer, fought by men as good or better, but the Lilly-McCoy event took on a larger meaning the moment Irish Tom died. Chris Lilly was forced to flee the country, skipping out ahead of a manslaughter charge. Eighteen others involved with the contest were arrested, tried, convicted, fined, and jailed.

Freelance scolds seized on boxing as a new source of indignation to fuel America's rancorous political debates. People who'd never given boxing a thought — ladies and maiden aunties, for the love of Christ! — developed *opinions* about the sport. Rather than celebrate the victor's unflagging sledgehammer power and the loser's astonishing stamina, reformers attacked Lilly as a savage beast who had transformed McCoy's face from the image of God into a loathsome ruin. The indomitable McCoy became a pitiable, doomed lamb led to the slaughter, and not the roaring, valorous, dying lion he was, refusing to be vanquished even as he was beaten.

Suddenly boxing was a thing to be loathed and done away with, like slavery and alcohol. Abolitionists rammed legislation through in state after state, until the fights were outlawed almost everywhere. "Goddam do-gooder busybodies," Bat's father always muttered whenever the subject came up, and it did so often.

Thomas Masterson was a hardworking, law-abiding man who'd never raised a hand in anger, not even against Bat, who might have benefited from a clout across the ear now and then. What Bat's father couldn't stand was reformers telling him what to do and think. Following the fights was a way to poke windbag meddlers in the eye. Tom Masterson did so with a boyish glee that he passed on to his sons, and he was not alone.

Across the country, boxing became more popular every year, for the new laws added the thrill of the illicit to the excitement of the sport. Arrangements were negotiated in secret, and word would go out: "A match tonight!" Sometimes the cops would catch wind and show up before the thing was settled, so fight promoters got craftier. Soon entire passenger trains called "Hell on Wheels" could be hired to transport the pugilists and the referees and spectators and bookies and bartenders and whores to a place nobody knew ahead of time. The train would stop in whatever isolated field took the brakeman's fancy that evening. A ring would be scraped out into the dirt with a boot heel and boxers would put up and toe the line under the stars. Prize money and crowds soared into the thousands.

Then, in 1861, the whole damn country squared off to settle a point of honor, once and for all. It would be the Lilly-McCoy fight on a continental scale: a contest between inflexible, unyielding opponents — savage, bloody, majestic, and pathetic — but not even war could slake the American thirst for bare-knuckle boxing.

Amid the wholesale slaughter of civil convulsion, there was something almost quaint and strangely decent about retail violence. This was bloodletting and brutality with agreed-upon rules, fought by volunteers, not draftees. This was barbarity, but it was barbarity committed with stylish courage, appreciated by men who might be ordered to march anonymously into annihilating cannon fire the next morning. Soldiers expected to die and be buried in impersonal heaps of maimed and mangled meat, but a man could make a name for himself in a boxing match, and be remembered.

Too young for the war, boys like Bat grew up hearing about boxers as famous as any general. Yankee Sullivan, Tom Hyer, John

Morrissey, Harry Paulson, "Bill the Butcher" Poole. Stoking interest and boosting sales by pretending to lament the outlawed sport, the popular press covered boxing as far away as Australia. When John Heenan sailed to England to battle Tom Sayers, the whole of red-blooded America cheered him on.

It was the most vicious congregation of roughs that was ever witnessed in a Christian city, Bat read, wishing fervently that he could have been there, betting, snarling, cheering, grunting with every witnessed blow, his own stomach tight in mirrored defense, his fists knotted and jabbing the air. He could imagine it all as he studied the account. *What boiled-down savagery, concentrated in so small a space! What rowdyism! What villainy!*

What fun!

Bat himself picked more than a few fights as a kid. "Bat's like a chunk of steel," his older brother, Ed, would tell folks. "Somebody's always striking a spark off him." Trouble was, Bat grew early but he stopped growing early, too. One by one, every boy he knew started to look down at him, and something about that made him even more eager to mix it up, readier than ever to teach larger, stronger, heavier kids a lesson.

Instead, he himself started learning lessons, and it wasn't long before young Bat Masterson knew two important things for sure. First off, to box well, you need more than combativeness. You need size and power, stamina and strategy. From the age of twelve, Bat was always fighting out of his class. Unless he wanted to end up like Irish Tom McCoy, dead on his feet in the 119th, he would need a way to even things up.

The second thing he knew for sure was this. Farming is a sucker's game. You can work like an ox — put everything you've got into the land — but if the weather doesn't break you, the markets will. You want to gamble with stakes like that? You're better off playing cards. You can still lose everything, but at least you don't work so damn hard for the privilege, and you by God dress up nice for the occasion.

Which is why, before he turned fifteen, he was determined to run away from home. "Ed," he told his older brother, "you can stay here and stare at a mule's ass end if you like, but me? I ain't never gonna plow another field as long as I live."

Within a few weeks of leaving, Bat was carrying a frontier equalizer: the big old Navy Colt he won off a drunk in a card game. Over the next ten years, to the line "plowboy" on his résumé, he added buffalo hunter, army scout, professional gambler, city police officer, county sheriff, and saloon owner. In 1907, when he wrote his autobiography, he would extend the list to include "genius with firearms," "a born captain of men," "generous to the last dollar." He decided to leave out "becomingly modest" and "the soul of Christian humility." That might have carried the joke too far.

Oddly, he failed to mention the central passion of his life and the one constant among the many ways he made his living: boxing. Or, more precisely, prizefighting, for matches were ever more frequently fought by professionals who had nothing against each another personally and were willing to break the law simply because the money was so good.

Bat himself never boxed as a grown man but throughout the 1880s, he would build a reputation as an expert on the Chambers-Queensberry rules. By the end of the decade, he was widely recognized as an honest and reliable referee, called upon to serve in important matches featuring boxing greats like John P. Clow and John L. Sullivan. That experience would eventually land him the best job of his life: covering sports for the *New York Sun,* where he would indulge his flair for flamboyant storytelling to his heart's content and his readers' delight until he died pen in hand, at his desk, a fat old man who'd had a hell of a good time ever since he left the farm.

Of course, his sporting knowledge and repute did not appear all at once, like Athena springing full-grown from the forehead of that divine boxing enthusiast, mighty Zeus.

Bat Masterson's apprenticeship began in Ford County, Kansas. Out past Duck Creek, a little north of Howells.

Wyatt found what he was looking for with no trouble. On a windless night in open land, the roaring of four hundred men can carry.

Astride Dick Naylor, he drew up and surveyed the scene. The ropes were pitched and respected. It cost a dollar to get in. Inside the perimeter, a crowd stood ten deep around the ring. A couple of farmwives were doing a brisk business in coffee and fried pork sandwiches; their husbands rented standing room on wagons for fifty cents. There was even a bartender selling whiskey straight from a barrel, two bits a swig.

"What's the line?" Wyatt asked a stranger.

"Nine to one, on Rowan, but I put a dollar on Hamner. He's got sand."

Bat was easy to pick out in the center of the ring, his fancy clothes giving him visibility and authority amid skinny boys clad in denim and dust. His frock coat and bowler hat had been removed, but the white of his shirtsleeves glowed in the moonlight, and the flare of torches made the gold threads of his brocade waistcoat glitter as he followed the action, eyes intent, concentration complete.

Wyatt had refereed fights up in Deadwood, and he'd done a little boxing himself. He recognized competence when he saw it. Bat was short and getting stout, but he was light on his feet, his rhythm and movement graceful and deft as the boxers shifted and fell back and came on. He showed no partiality, enforcing his rules consistently, his voice cutting through the spectators' shouts with brisk authority. His timekeeping was faultless.

The bout itself was more wrestling than boxing. The opponents were a lanky young drover and a local German boy. You could see that neither was going to do much more than bloody the other's nose. Even so, they went close to fifty rounds. When at last they'd grappled and pummeled each other into exhaustion, Bat raised the wrist of the cowboy, who'd stayed on his feet slightly longer than the farm kid. Then Bat helped the local boy up and praised him lavishly, inviting the crowd to cheer for an honorable effort.

Money changed hands with minimal grumbling. Inside the ring, Bat got both combatants to mumble "Good fight" through thick lips, their fists too cut up and swollen to allow a handshake. The crowd dispersed. The gatekeeper counted out the referee's rake and handed it over. Bat folded a substantial wad of cash into his pocket and walked toward his horse, stopping in his tracks when he caught sight of Wyatt, waiting.

"You got no jurisdiction out here, Wyatt."

"Didn't say I did."

Silence fell. Eyes on the ground, mouth

turned downward in thought, Bat tugged at his vest, smoothing the brocade. "Two idiots go at it in a bar," he proposed suddenly. "They're disturbing the peace. What do you do?"

Wyatt didn't bother answering.

"You bash them," Bat supplied with a shrug. "You don't argue. You don't explain. You don't hesitate. You bash them both, and jail them." He paused before asking, "What happens after that?"

Indifferent, Wyatt said, "None of my affair."

"That's right," Bat agreed. "That's right! It's none of your affair. You broke up the fight. The peace of the city is restored. Fines are assessed. Justice is served." Once more he paused. "But nothing is *settled*."

Letting Wyatt think that over, Bat pulled his coat off the saddle and turned away from his horse before shaking the wrinkles out.

"You lock those boys up," Bat continued informatively, "you're just giving them time to brood on insult and grievance." He shrugged into the forest green broadcloth, jerking the sleeves of his shirt down so the gold cuff links showed. "Know how many homicides we've had in Dodge, Wyatt? Just the past couple years, say."

Eyes narrow, Wyatt shook his head slightly.

"Forty-five," Bat told him, "give or take. A few were knifed, but most of them were gunned down. Ambushed in alleys. Killed on their way out of town. Shot in the back, mostly. Maybe seven had any kinda chance at all."

"You saying that's my fault?" Wyatt asked, not buying it.

"No, Wyatt, what I'm saying is, there's no harm done and quite a bit of good comes of telling idiots, 'You can settle this fair and square, but we have to take it out of town.' " Holding up his fingers, Bat began to count. "One: it saves wear and tear on the saloons. Two: I frisk the bastards for weapons before they square off. Three: when the fight's over, it's done with. I see to that! Nobody walks away humiliated, nobody wants revenge, nobody gets shot in the back a few hours later." He waited a moment before he raised a fourth finger. "Everyone goes home in the morning."

Wyatt blinked, and Bat immediately pressed his advantage.

"Is there money to be made? Hell, yes! A lot of it. And why not? My fights ain't legal, but they're by-God honest, and I earn what I get."

Wyatt looked away.

"How was Topeka?" Bat asked, for that lay between them still.

"They want me to run against you."

"I figured. You gonna?"

Wyatt lifted his chin toward where the ring had been. "How does it work?" he asked, like

544

he was just curious. "Are these your fights, Bat? Or are you just getting some of the gate? Because I'm guessing that Bob Wright's the promoter, and you're bought. If I'm wrong, then this is the only game in Ford County Bob don't have a piece of."

There was a time when Bat Masterson had idolized Wyatt Earp. They had slept side by side. They'd worked to exhaustion in sleet and snow and killing cold, hunting buffalo. They'd doctored broken fingers and sewn up gashes, and loaned money and borrowed it, and backed each other up in brawls. But *goddam* if the man didn't think he was the gold standard.

Tired of being judged, Bat snapped, "I don't owe you an accounting, Wyatt. You want to run against me? Run! But there's a lot you don't know."

Like: how elections really worked. Like: who was on his side, and who was playing him for a fool, and why. Like: how Wyatt scared folks without even knowing it because he was cold and intolerant and wouldn't bend.

"You vote for Prohibition?" Bat asked, jerking his head toward Topeka.

"Didn't pass."

"Well, thank God for that!" Bat planted meaty fists on hip bones that were already acquiring prosperity's padding. "You know what I can't figure? Why in hell would you trust a hypocrite like George Hoover and not me? What makes you think he's your friend and I'm not?"

For the first time, Wyatt looked surprised. "Friendship's got nothing to do with it, Bat!" he protested. "All I'm saying is, I never saw liquor do anybody any good, but I've seen it ruin a lot of men and —"

"Jesus, Wyatt! You can be so goddam thick! Prostitution's against the law, too. So — what? Do you think Prohibition'll stop anybody drinking? You make something against the law, people just want it more! You been to Topeka! Do you have any idea — ?"

No. He probably didn't. Wyatt wouldn't have looked for a "club" where you had to pay a membership fee for the privilege of buying overpriced rotgut. He had no notion how much money there was in illegal liquor.

Bat took a deep breath, closed his eyes a moment, and held up a hand. "All right," he said firmly. "Just do yourself this one favor before you go trying to make the whole damn state dry. Go ask your fine new dentist friend something. If Prohibition goes through, how much would Doc Holliday be willing to pay, to get what he needs for his 'cough'? You ask him, Wyatt, because that drunk's putting away a couple of quarts a day!"

Bat untied his horse, put a foot in the stirrup, and stretched for the pommel. Hopping twice, he swung up, and looked down. "You

546

gonna do something about this?" he asked, glancing back toward the trampled grass and the smoldering torches.

Wyatt's eyes stayed level, but something Bat said must have gotten through to him.

"Not my jurisdiction," he said.

Bat nodded: acknowledgment, not thanks. He gathered the reins and wheeled the horse twice. "Watch your back," he told Wyatt before he rode away. "And think hard about who your real friends are!"

Late in the summer of '78, a little epidemic swept through Dodge City. People speculated that a drummer from St. Louis brought it in on the train. It was only a cold but it was a bad one, and pretty much everybody in Dodge suffered through it before the sickness ran its course.

Wilfred Eberhardt probably caught it from one of the Riney boys, and no question: Wil was the one who gave it to Doc Holliday and Belle Wright. The boy felt awful about that. Rather than harm the two people on earth who had been kindest to him since he was orphaned, young Mr. Eberhardt would have marched his manly little self out onto the prairie and died alone, but he didn't even know he was getting sick until he sneezed right into Doc's face. That wasn't good manners, but Doc wasn't the kind to get angry with a sick child. The dentist gave Wil a nice new handkerchief, and taught him how to use it, and told him to go on home now, and come back when he was all better.

When Wilfred got in from Dr. Holliday's office, Miss Belle took one look at the boy and put him straight to bed. That was when Wil discovered that it wasn't entirely bad, being sick. Doc still paid him a dime a day. And Miss Belle brought him tea with honey and read stories to him until she got sick herself.

Isabelle Wright was genuinely fond of Wilfred, a winning child with a streak of appealing sadness under his resolve not to be a bother to anyone. In addition, of course, every moment she spent caring for the Eberhardt children did double duty, for it rubbed her father's face in what she considered his callous exploitation of the German farmers in the area. On the other hand, if Belle had known just *how* sick she was going to get, she might have asked her mother to take care of Wilfred. Not that it would have changed anything. If Belle hadn't caught the cold from Wil, she'd have gotten it from one of her own brothers, or from a customer in the store, or from somebody at church.

Being out on the open prairie for twelve weeks at a time was hardship enough without adding a sore throat, a thick head, and a dripping nose to the exercise, so it was a mercy that Alexander von Angensperg was out in the countryside while the cold was making the rounds. Most Dodge Citians were over the illness when he got back to town.

Alex was hoping to see Wyatt Earp before heading toward Wichita on the northern arc of the circuit, but when the little huddle of wooden buildings came into sight, he realized that for all its ugly, violent, noisy crudity, Dodge City had come to represent to him agreeable company and convivial conversation. Approaching the place now felt strangely like a homecoming.

He tied Alphonsus to the hitching rail in front of Dodge House, thinking to see Doc in his office between patients, but before he could go inside, he heard boots clomping along the boardwalk and a familiar voice behind him.

"Staying longer this time?" Morgan Earp called genially.

"Today only, I fear," Alexander told him, accustomed now to the way Americans omitted conversational hors d'oeuvres. "Is Wyatt back from Topeka, or have I missed him once again?"

"You caught him dead to rights this time!" Morg jerked a thumb over his shoulder in the direction of the jail. "He's just finishing the reports with Fat Larry — There he is! Hey, Wyatt, wait up! Look who's here!"

Jogging across the street, Morgan came to rest beside his brother and turned back toward the priest, grinning happily. "See,

Alex? I told you people mix us up all the time!"

And indeed they were very like in appearance. Fair, square-jawed, broad-shouldered, and lean, with hardly a hair of separation in their height. Their differences, Alexander noted, were all in their bearing. Where Morgan was amiable and open, Wyatt seemed guarded, though not unfriendly.

After a few awkward remarks about Johnnie Sanders, he and Wyatt found themselves with nothing more to say. It was Morgan who suggested that the three of them go visit Doc, who was not in his office after all. "He's been poorly," Morg explained, leading the way toward a short side street lined with a few small, neat houses set on fenced-in patches of bare ground.

"But — he looked so well when I saw him last!" Alexander said uneasily.

"Just a cold," said Wyatt.

"Yeah, bad one's been going around," added Morg. "That's my house, right there, and that's Wyatt's —"

"They're not ours," Wyatt said.

"We rent," Morg admitted easily. He gestured toward the third of five small frame dwellings. "That's where Doc and Kate live." Taking Wyatt's point, he added, "They rent, too."

Jau Dong-Sing was stepping out onto the front porch with Kate, and with the door

550

open, they could hear Doc's ugly, hacking cough.

"It's like that night and day," Morg told Alex quietly. "I don't know how Kate stands it!"

"All she has to do is listen," Wyatt said. "It's Doc who's sick."

"You Doc's guest!" China Joe cried, recognizing Alex. "Where you stay? You want bath? I bring plenty hot water. Doc, he very no good, but I bring more medicine, fix his *chi!*"

"That shit's disgusting," Kate muttered, not caring that China Joe was standing right next to her. "I can't even stay in the house when Doc drinks it." Red-eyed with sleeplessness, she glared at Alexander. "He ain't dying! He don't need no priest!"

"It's just a social call," Morg told her. "Alex is leaving for Wichita again, and —"

"Kate, you look exhausted," Alexander said softly. "This is not a good time for a visit. We'll let you and Doc get some rest —"

"Too late now!"

The voice was hoarse but cheerful. Still tying the narrow belt of a silk robe around a waist as slender as a girl's, Doc appeared in the doorway, his smile fading when he saw the open shock on von Angensperg's face.

"You make a sobering mirror, sir," he said, but he waved off Kate's worry and the priest's concern, insisting that he was fine, just a little slow to get back on his feet. Thanking Mr.

Jau for his concern and bidding him a good day, Doc urged the others to come on in and keep him company for a spell, and asked if anyone would like tea, or something stronger.

He sat down in a corner chair, breathless and white, while Kate sullenly did the honors, but perked up considerably as the conversation became livelier, for visitors always cheered him.

"I do believe I am hungry," he announced with some surprise. "First time in days! You see, darlin'?" he asked Kate, as though reminding her of some point he'd made before. "Why don't y'all go on over to Delmonico's for steak and eggs?" he suggested. "I'll make myself decent and meet you there directly."

Kate didn't argue, but it was obvious that she wanted to. Doc told her he was tired to death of being in bed and declared that it would do him a world of good to get out of the house, then shooed them all out so he could dress.

Hobbling into the restaurant nearly an hour later, he explained his limp away, saying that bed rest had aggravated an old injury. He sat down heavily, looking exhausted, but called, "Miss Nora — ?"

Then the coughing fit took over.

Around the restaurant, strangers' mouths twisted in disgust at the sound. The cough had changed, Alexander realized. It was deeper, wetter. Morgan looked away, wincing, and Kate raised her eyebrows as if to say, "See? I told you so." Presently, Nora appeared with a tray bearing Doc's usual tea and honey, along with a bottle of bourbon. Instead of a shot glass, however, she supplied Doc with a tumbler, and this he filled halfway.

With a silent, steady effort, he got it down in something under a minute, his face losing some of the tension that became noticeable only when it eased off, right before their eyes.

"Doc," Wyatt asked uneasily, "when did you start drinking that much?"

"Wyatt, I'm not drinkin' more," Doc assured him with that crooked smile of his. "I'm just pourin' less."

"I fear you have overtaxed yourself to come here," Alexander suggested, for Kate had asked them to help her keep Doc from overdoing it, and they all knew he would, given half a chance.

"You should be in bed," Morgan agreed, and not just to make Kate happier, either; but then their meals arrived at the table.

Doc talked more than he ate, and listened more than he talked, although his brief comments were good-humored and amusing. Sitting slightly behind him, Kate was silent and didn't touch her food. As soon as she thought Doc was too tired to balk, she made a signal to the priest. Alexander stood with an excuse about needing to get on the road before noon.

Doc waved to Nora and asked her to put the bill on his tab. Wyatt insisted on paying his own way, and so did Morgan. They were still working out who owed what when Isabelle Wright came into the restaurant and walked straight to their table.

All the men stood, even Doc, who would have made an honest effort to rise from his deathbed for a lady. Belle looked peaked, her nose red and raw. She only managed to say good morning to everyone, including "Mrs. Holliday," before her face took on an inward, wary, weary look and she dug quickly in her little purse for a crumpled handkerchief edged with tatting. The rattling cough came from deep within her narrow chest.

Doc pulled out a chair for her and poured a little bourbon. "Miss Isabelle," he said with quiet commiseration, "I do believe we are sufferin' from the same malady!" Alexander looked up sharply, but Doc said merely, "You have some congestion left over from that wretched cold."

Eyes watering, Belle nodded silently and sipped from the glass he'd pressed into her hand. Although she grimaced at the liquor's taste, its warmth worked quickly, and her chest felt remarkably better. "A little bronchitis," she said then, smiling wanly. "I just can't seem to shake it!"

Doc's face went slack: something about what she had just said . . . Alexander watched, waiting for the blow to land. When it did, Doc blinked once before he returned his gaze to the girl and produced a mild smile.

Unaware of his effort, Belle was still talking. "I imagine we both got the cold from Wilfred," she said, "but everyone's been coughing and sneezing." She looked at the priest then. "I heard you were back in town, sir. I wanted you to know that I went through the accounts after your visit, and I found Johnnie's money. He booked five thousand, two hundred and fifty-seven dollars over six months. He withdrew two thousand just before he died. That leaves a little over thirty-two hundred dollars. The cash is still in Daddy's safe," she said bitterly. "He probably expected to keep it."

Wyatt's mouth had dropped. Morgan's face was alight. Doc coughed, eyes bright over the cotton cloth in his hand.

Before any of them could say a word, Belle continued, "If you'll give me an address, sir, I'll send a wire transfer to St. Francis, but I don't want the money to go to that pope person —"

Suddenly silent, she held her face still. The others, even Kate, waited respectfully while Isabelle Wright fought tears, for she had spent many hours studying columns of numbers in Johnnie's terrible handwriting and had stopped often to recall his unexpected remarks, his interesting ideas and wry observations. Ten days spent in bed with a bad cold and a good book had made Belle newly aware of what a good friend Johnnie Sanders had been and of how often she still wished that the two of them could share something notable she'd just read.

Eyes brimming, Belle raised her head and straightened her back. "I think that you should use Johnnie's money to build a library for your school," she told the priest firmly. "I would be honored to donate my books to begin it."

To a man, they were stunned by Belle's notion.

The priest was delighted, naturally, and thanked her for her generosity and for her excellent suggestion. He did not notice that Morgan was crestfallen, for that cash was his brother's, but what could Wyatt say? *It's mine. I want to buy a horse.* And Doc felt punished for his pride, for he had guessed correctly and located the money but had never anticipated this. Compassion and apology mixed in his eyes, brows lifted in inquiry, he looked at Wyatt: *Do you want me to say something?*

Wyatt let out a small, hopeless breath and shook his head slightly. He stood to go, dropping two bits on the table to pay his share of the bill.

"Johnnie was a real good reader," he told

von Angensperg. "Name the liberry after him."

"It is a fine legacy for a boy who died too young," the priest said, standing to shake Wyatt's hand. "John Horse Sanders will be remembered."

■ ■ ■ ■

SIXTH HAND

■ ■ ■ ■

No Help

Kate knew his tricks. Doc would stop to have her roll him a cigarette, or pause to comment on a brawl spilling onto the street, or decide he wanted to study the clouds for signs of rain. Getting back to the house from Delmonico's took most of an hour. *You don't fool me none,* she wanted to tell him, but a presumption of strength was the only thing John Henry Holliday asked of her and that, by God, is what she gave him.

Six months of overwork had undermined him. A simple cold had damn near killed him. The chest pain was so bad, he needed laudanum to dull it. Even so, she couldn't get him into bed. Hunched in his chair, elbows on his knees, staring at the cheap floral carpet, Doc didn't even lift his head to mumble, "Kate. Please. Jus' do as I ask."

"But *why?* Is it your father's money? Doc, you don't even *like* your father!"

He shook his head slightly.

"Then why bother? Grier ain't worth your time!"

"Don' care."

"You ain't making sense," she informed him, folding her arms. "And anyways, what good is it to beat him? His credit's no good."

"Doesn' matter."

This is fever, she decided. Hoping he'd lose interest if she delayed the game, she threw up her hands. "All right! Whatever you say, but I need time to set it up."

"Get Bob Wright, too."

Her mouth dropped open. "You ain't serious," she scoffed.

Slate blue eyes rose, humorless and unblinking.

"Doc," she said cautiously, "Bob Wright's good. You can't play him! Hell, you shouldn't play at all, not like this . . ."

As his rebuttal he held out a handkerchief streaked with bright arterial red. When he spoke, his voice was soft and empty of drama. " 'S now or never, darlin'."

The argument went on, but nothing Kate said made a difference, for Doc's logic was impeccable if unspoken. It was his dispassionate clinical judgment that he would not live to see his twenty-seventh Christmas. Why hold back? What was left to him but one last grand gesture?

On the fifth of September 1878, it came down to this. Kate had made him a promise.

He held her to it.

Later she would rage at him, at his stupidity and arrogance and pride. She would swear that if she'd known what he intended, she never would have agreed to help. "Too late now" was all he'd say, but he would say it to her back, as she left him.

"I'm putting a game together," Kate told Elijah Garrett Grier in mid-September. "Stud poker. Twenty-dollar ante. No limit. You in?"

Naturally, he hesitated, for he simply didn't trust her. Twice that summer, Eli had complained to Bessie Earp about the Hungarian hooker, but Bessie only shrugged and looked at her husband.

"Katie runs her own business," James told the captain. "The house just takes a cut for laundry and the room." Kate came and went whenever she pleased, James explained, and did what she liked with whoever caught her eye. "My opinion?" James offered. "That's what customers like about her."

Maybe so, for she wasn't that pretty, and she sure as hell didn't flatter a man. Whatever the reason, Eli Grier wanted her, but the bitch just toyed with him. Once, back in July, when he thought the deal was made, she fixed him with that flat-eyed stare of hers. Breasts half-exposed by negligent lace, she leaned toward him with a feral grin, letting him breathe in her perfume and her musk, daring him to touch her. He reached out and as his fingers grazed that creamy flesh, he felt the barrel of a Deringer .36 press against the ribs above his heart.

Her voice was husky, foreign, amused. "Let's see your cash," she whispered. "For you? I cost a grand."

Then, laughing, she swirled away, silk rustling, making him watch, infuriated, as she picked another man. "For you?" she cried breezily. "Five bucks!" And off she went, not even glancing over her soft, white shoulder as she led the dazzled Texan up quiet, carpeted stairs.

"What's the matter?" she taunted Eli now. "Game too rich for you?"

It was, and he suspected that she knew it. Which is exactly why Elijah Grier said, "How about a side bet? I double my money, you're mine for a night."

"And what do I get if you lose?" she asked, delighted.

He'd left himself no path of retreat. "A grand," he said.

No woman was worth so much, but night after night, he had imagined it. What would you get from her for a thousand dollars? What could you do to her, for a thousand dollars?

"Double that," she dared.

"You're on," he said with the careless bravado that had earned him three combat commendations and two field promotions before he was twenty-three.

Kate sat back, sprawled on Bessie's upholstery. Arms flung over the crest of a settee, breasts loose and lifted, she actually seemed impressed for a moment. Then, leaning toward him, she reached over to pat his thigh sympathetically and ran her hand slowly upward.

"Tell you what," she offered, voice low. "I'll go home with the winner. If that's you?" She shrugged. "But if it's not?" She tightened her grip on him until he stopped breathing. "You'll owe me two grand."

Getting Grier was easy. So was finding a couple of cattlemen to fill out the table. The invitation to Bob Wright required something different.

"Doc wants to play you," Kate told him. "Five-card stud. No limit. Interested?"

Unbuttoning his shirt, Bob gave her one of his *Aw, shucks* looks. "Oh, I'm not much of a card player."

She laughed appreciatively, and her knowing skepticism was rewarded by his sly smile when she came over to pull the shirt down off his shoulders.

"Anyways," he said, "from what I hear, Doc Holliday's too good for me."

"Don't be so sure!" She sounded sincere because she was. "Doc don't get much real competition. It's all drunks and fools. He's tired of being sick, and he's bored. He wants a real game. That army captain with the fancy horse? He's in. Doc's got some kinda beef with him."

Bob frowned. "Eli Grier? He's courting my daughter."

Kate blinked, then smiled briefly. Later, Bob would remember that smile and the faint indulgent pity it signified.

"That's the one," she said. "I lined up a couple of other players, but Doc asked for you, special."

Most men looked better dressed; Bob was the exception, better built than you'd guess when you saw him on the street. Sure of himself in bed, and with good reason. First time around, he tried to jew her fee down. Kate told him to go to hell. "Awright," he offered, "double or nothing — if I can't make you come." To her surprise, he won the bet. He'd been one of her regulars ever since. He paid more often than not, but either way, Kate found it satisfying to see that mask of tame, inoffensive harmlessness drop like a magician's silk scarf once the bedroom door was closed.

Doc had been too damn sick to be much use to her lately; tonight, Kate found it easy to let Bob get past the professional distance she normally maintained. Which is why, laughing and out of breath, she meant it when she told him, "Your wife is a lucky woman." She almost regretted slipping the knife in, but Doc had insisted. "First you," she said. "Now Grier . . ."

God, he's good, she thought, watching. Silence was the only tell.

Eyes wide in merry astonishment, she purred, "Oh, Bob! You don't really think Grier's interested in your little girl, do you?"

He got up, keeping his back to her. Funny how men thought it was modest to stand that way. She admired the view while he dressed. Good shoulders, broad back. Power in the ass and thighs. Prosperous men generally got fat. Big George Hoover already had. Bat Masterson was getting there. Bob Wright could buy and sell them both, but he still had the body of a young freight driver. Bob had other hungers to feed.

When he'd finished with his string tie, he turned to display the perfect poker face. Mild. Amiable. No threat to anyone.

"Tell me more," he suggested, "about that poker game."

God's honest truth: Elijah Garrett Grier never meant to cuckold Bob Wright. For one thing, Eli Grier truly liked and admired Bob. And you might not think it, but they had a lot in common, though one man was a store-keeper and the other a soldier.

In long, enjoyable conversations, they had come to believe that combat and commerce presented similar challenges and drew on similar talents; the tactical brilliance Elijah Grier displayed in battle had made Bob Wright an astonishingly successful entrepreneur. Others saw risk and danger; they saw openings and opportunities. Others stood stunned in the face of shifting complexity; they cut through to solutions that seemed to arise without thought or effort. Neither was drawn to frontal assaults. Both inclined toward flanking maneuvers. With every story they exchanged, it became clearer that they were a match, each man's achievements shining a favorable light on the other's.

Bob was only three years the older, but he understood where Eli's troubles lay. "The army's running out of wars, son," he told the captain. "It's time to resign that commission! Business is in your blood, and there's money for the taking out here. You'd do well in politics, too. West Kansas will go Republican someday. A war record like yours'll be a real asset."

You have to back tactics with strategy, you see, and Bob always kept the long game in mind. One day he'd be voted out of the legislature, and it would be handy to have a son-in-law there in his stead.

When Bob Wright invited Eli to dinner that first Sunday, they both expected that the captain would be courting Bob's daughter. Who better to marry Belle than a man with

Bob's best qualities and none of his unsightliness? Eli had seen Isabelle Wright at the store, of course. Pretty, if sulky, and sometimes obnoxious. Still . . . there were a lot of advantages to marrying the Belle of Dodge, principal among them a rich father-in-law who was already talking about taking Eli on as a partner. Bob wanted to open a new store down in Texas, at the Great Western trailhead. It would make outfitting cattle companies more efficient at both ends of the season, reducing costs and attracting business.

"You put in a couple of grand yourself, we'll call it fifty-fifty," Bob told Eli, and it was a generous offer.

What Elijah Garrett Grier lacked, besides two grand to invest, was the ability to keep his eyes on the prize. Traits that made him masterly in combat — his total concentration on what lay right in front of him; the quickness with which he adjusted to changing circumstances — those were the very traits that sapped his ability to stick with a job if it took much more than an hour.

He got distracted, that was the problem. He never seemed to finish anything. And he wasn't lazy, either! If anything, he was too ambitious. He'd start something, and then somebody would ask a question, or need his help with some task he knew he could handle easily. He'd say yes to each new demand, thinking he'd get it done in a few minutes and then go back to what he'd been doing before, except three or four other things would come up, and by the end of the day, he'd have nothing to show for all his effort and no idea what had happened to the time. It was a failing as mysterious to Eli himself as it was disappointing to his family.

Despite Old Man Grier's frustration with his youngest son's shortcomings, he was furious when Elijah up and joined the army right after the attack on Fort Sumter. Mrs. Grier wept. The older Grier boys sneered and called the decision harebrained. Neighbors shrugged and shook their heads, but the laborers at the carriage factory nudged one another and speculated leeringly about why a rich kid like Eli Grier had done such a thing.

Truth was, Eli didn't have one single reason, not really. Like so many young men before and after him, he craved adventure and distinction in equal measure. He desired to be tested in some fundamental way and to be found true. But enlisting was also a way for the youngest Grier to circumvent two looming difficulties: a girl who needed marrying within the month and a gambling debt he might not have to repay if he joined the army and died gloriously in battle.

What surprised everyone, Eli included, was the sheer perfection of his temperament for war.

Cunning in combat, he would go still in the

saddle, eyes on the field, effortlessly commanding the attention of armed and mounted men. They would watch him, waiting breathlessly for the moment when his eyes lit up and he would grin, his face shining as he revealed with terse words and small gestures exactly how they would turn disadvantage into victory. Men followed that slim, spoiled, scatterbrained boy with the ancient, angry joy that warriors have felt since divine Ares lifted the first spear and made it fly. Medals and commendations accumulated. Even Old Man Grier admitted that Elijah had found his calling.

By rights, Eli should have been a colonel or even a general by now. Indeed, he had been promoted to major twice, but as decisive and effective as he was in sudden skirmishes, peace paralyzed him. Wars ended, that was the problem. Tedium set in, and that's when things went wrong.

Major Grier had been busted back to captain twice — both times for ignoring trivialities that defeated his capacity to give a good goddam. Some sonofabitch by-the-book commander would get a wild hair about inventory or payroll records. Money would be missing. Eli's careless accounting would be blamed. Last year, there'd even been suspicion that Eli had taken cash after a catastrophic card game. Only the fact that his family was rich made the accusation too absurd to pursue.

Which was fortunate, because he did occasionally borrow from the strongbox.

Well, more than occasionally, truth be told. The first time, it was only overnight. A jack-high straight flush, and the money was returned — no one the wiser, including Eli himself. The risk of being caught added welcome piquancy to the games, for every time he sat down at a poker table, he faced annihilation. Exposure and disgrace would be far worse than an honorable death in combat, but with the South whipped and with the last of the Indians penned up on reservations, only gambling offered him that perfect balance of deliverance or doom.

Until he met Bob Wright's pretty little wife, Alice.

At dinner that first Sunday, Elijah Garrett Grier made no decision to turn his back on Belle, and the trailhead store in Texas, and his own promising future. Rather, they disappeared from his mind as though they had never existed. In their stead was the mystery and challenge of Alice.

She was oblivious to his attention at first, then mystified, then skeptical. Slowly he made her believe in his interest and his admiration. At last there came a day when she turned her face to him as a rosebud to late-spring sunlight: soaking up warmth, releasing stored energy, unfolding. Coming *alive* again, after a dark and deadening winter.

Laughing, she would run like a girl, flop down next to him on a blanket warmed by summer heat, and show him what she'd carried back in her apron. Propped on an elbow, she would feed him wild blueberries and recall how she used to gather plums and grapes for jams and conserves and jellies that would bring color and sweetness to meals eaten on gray winter days. A bride so young she grew two inches after the wedding, she had faced frontier life with industry and resolve and no word of complaint about Bob's long absences. She'd birthed babies and raised children alone, and buried three all by herself. She sewed and mended and knit and washed and ironed. She baked bread and pies, and salted meat, and put up crocks of pickles. She always had a kitchen garden, and grew peas and beans, onions and pumpkins and okra, sweet corn and tomatoes and yellow squash . . .

"I was never idle when I was young," she said, her sad eyes wistful.

"You're still young," he told her, touching her cheek, but he had seen his own lost purpose in the guarded blue eyes of Alice Wright and understood her melancholy. It was not youth she missed but intensity and meaning. Bred in the Missouri backcountry to pioneer self-reliance, she had become nothing more than the principal ornament in the Honorable Robert C. Wright's grand new house: proof of his prosperity, as pointless as the dusty rosewood piano, silent in the parlor.

Now when Eli Grier sat at her table — with the children around them and not three feet from her husband — they both felt the exhilaration that comes of gambling with your very life. Behind every ordinary word exchanged, with each passing minute that sustained the pretense, hidden within all the bland courtesies, there was a shining silver wire stretched between them, vibrating with the constant delicious terror of discovery and damnation.

A whispered word. A phrase written on paper and slipped into a waiting hand. A place chosen, the time agreed upon. Excuses found, reasons given. Illicit hours stolen from duties and obligations.

She was afraid, at first. Eli's horse was familiar. Alice's movements were noted. After a time, however, it seemed plain to them that Bob must have known.

"He knows, and he doesn't care," Alice said.

There was in her voice both bitterness and elation.

"You're going to need law," Bat Masterson insisted. "First off, there's going to be enough money at that table to buy a small railway. No sense tempting thieves. Second, Holliday is dangerous as hell, but I can handle him."

Third, Eli Grier thought, the house rakes off a percentage and if the game's in the Lone Star, Sheriff Masterson is half the house.

As the date for the game drew closer, Reasons First and Second receded in significance, leaving Reason Third in high relief. There would be no cash at the table: chips only, for this was to be a gentleman's game, with all players presumed good for their losses the next day. That was lucky, since it eliminated Eli's need to acquire money for his stake. Yes, there were rumors about the dentist —

Jesus, what was his name again? Eli was awful with names. He had to be introduced three or four times before a name got a grip — yet another failing that had annoyed Eli's old man, who always bragged he never forgot a face or a name.

Anyway, the dentist was a gentleman from Atlanta, so Eli wasn't worried by Sheriff Masterson's warnings. The Grier and Cook Carriage Company had done business with Georgia's upper crust for decades. Eli himself had spent nearly two years in Atlanta after the war, serving as liaison between the army's general staff and that smoldering city's impoverished aristocrats. He was familiar with the breed, and rather fond of it.

Most of Sherman's army had truly hated Georgians — not just for the savage cruelty of slavery and for their antebellum arrogance but for the stubborn defense the state militia persisted in presenting long past the point when there was a snowball's chance in hell that they wouldn't be crushed. Every time Joe Johnston pulled back, dug in, and made yet another attempt to delay the inevitable, Sherman's men felt as though they were being forced to murder ragged skinny veterans, and gray-haired old men, and thin-faced fourteen-year-old cadets from some goddam military school. "What in hell's it gonna take to make them bastards quit?" That was the question on every Yankee tongue, and the answer was this. Nothing short of the cold, deliberate destruction of everything that stood or grew or moved between Chattanooga and Savannah.

If anything, the victors' hatred intensified after the war, for if Georgians had resisted every step toward their defeat and lost everything they'd fought for, if they starved and struggled and scratched for a living with bare white hands in scorched red earth in the years that followed their surrender, there remained to them one possession that could not be stolen, destroyed, or set alight: an unyielding and unassailable pride that had not just survived but deepened in the aftermath of conquest.

It was infuriating, the insolent malevolence in eyes that stared coldly above slight smiles. *Go ahead,* those smiles said. *Take everything of value. Burn the rest. I am still the better man.*

Unlike his brother officers, Eli understood the cool, correct courtesy and appreciated the grave, impenetrable mockery. Once, he'd thanked an Atlantan for some small deference and had been informed, with exquisite *politesse,* "A gentleman is judged by the way he treats his inferiors, sir."

The remark was, he thought, the most perfect expression of Southern hauteur he'd ever encountered. It aroused his admiration as did a well-bred horse or a fine oil painting, though most men wouldn't have gotten the joke and the rest would have been insulted.

For all his ferocity in battle, Eli Grier never took offense. Hell, nothing said to him during two years in Atlanta came close to what he used to hear at any given breakfast with his father. Southern tempers could flare to killing heights in an instant, but the anger burned out just as quickly. There was something almost sexual about that explosive release of male violence, and you did well to be aware of murderous rage lurking beneath polished gentility. In Eli's experience, however, if you were circumspect and capable of apology, you'd get along with Southerners just fine.

Sitting down at the table in the Lone Star Dance Hall and Saloon that night in late September, Elijah Garrett Grier was actually looking forward to sharing an evening with such a gentleman. At first the dentist did not disappoint. Knife-thin and pasty-pale, he had Georgia's familiar blurred and lazy accent and its casual, careless courtesy, though it was immediately apparent that he was consumptive and in considerable misery, given the way he dosed himself from a bottle delivered, without his asking, to his elbow.

"I offered Sheriff Masterson all my custom if only he and his partner were to rename the Lone Star," the dentist said with a charming, crooked grin. "I should dearly like to write home and tell my kin that I only drink in Moderation."

Eli smiled. He felt sorry for the man but certainly did not fear him. They chatted amiably, waiting for the others to arrive. It came as something of a surprise to Eli that they had met earlier that year. Eli begged pardon and confessed his debility, and was assured that no offense had been taken. It was merely a brief encounter at the Green Front back in May, the dentist told him between bouts of coughing. They had exchanged a few remarks about Roxana. No reason to recall the conversation now.

The time passed pleasantly until Bob Wright showed up. It was Bob, businesslike, who made introductions all around when the two cattlemen arrived. With self-deprecating humor, Eli told the newcomers that the odds were twenty to one that he'd be able to remember their names, admitting that he was a special kind of idiot about such things. For some reason, however, John Holliday's name finally stuck. Maybe it was the irony of a man so sick being called Doc.

The game began around midnight amid noisy conversation and raucous laughter. Bat's prophecy of trouble had attracted a number of spectators to the Lone Star that evening, and they drank in gleeful anticipation of the local outbreak of hell rumored to be imminent. Unfortunately for the Lone Star's profit, the first hours of play were disappointingly quiet. Despite the stakes, most folks drifted away to seek their entertainment elsewhere. Interest in the table was confined to the men sitting around it and to the Hungarian whore who watched the action with unwavering attention — not surprising, given the side bet she and Eli Grier had.

When Eli realized that Kate was Holliday's woman, there was a moment of unease before he lost all respect for a man who probably pimped her and certainly shared her. By that point in the game, it was apparent that Doc Holliday was neither a card sharp nor the ferocious exemplar of Southern spleen that Bat Masterson had promised. The Georgian was a decent player, but he'd been drunk when he sat down and he continued to drink as the evening progressed. Eli took pride in gambling sober and considered that the real threat was one of the cattlemen. Johnson. Or was it Johansen? Jensen, maybe. Dammit, something with a *J* . . .

And soon it didn't matter, for the cards loved Elijah Garrett Grier that night. Early on, he drew two, and filled a ten-high straight that would pay off two outstanding loans. Half an hour later, he held a pair of queens, drew three, and was astonished to find himself holding a very timely full house.

"Ladies over nines," he announced, and another bill was paid.

A while later, those three sweet nines showed up again — two dealt, one drawn. The hooker was pacing now, smoking one cigarette after another, glaring at Holliday, who was down by $1,500 and looked awful.

An hour or so later, Johnson or Johansen or Jensen, or whatever the hell his name was, slapped his final hand onto the table and stood.

"That's it for me," he declared. "Gentlemen, it's been a pleasure."

"The pleasure is all Captain Grier's," Holliday remarked affably, though Bob Wright had also taken a fair percentage of the cattleman's losses.

The Texan snorted, tossing back a drink before bidding good-bye to his opponents and three grand. Doc Holliday gathered the cards and began to shuffle, surveying the chips in front of the remaining players.

"Ovid tells us that Fortune and Venus befriend the bold," he said, "but they are fickle gods, Captain Grier. You might consider quittin' while you're ahead, sir."

"Goddammit, Doc!" Kate cried. "What are you — ?"

"Roll me a cigarette, will you, darlin'?" Doc said mildly. " 'Pears you have lost your bet with the captain. Perhaps you should retire an' prepare for the consequences."

Eli grinned, expecting Hungarian fireworks, but Kate had stopped pacing. For a few moments she watched the dentist's hands as he shuffled the cards. Divvy, tumble, riffle . . . Riffle, arch, release . . . A corner of her upper lip lifted slightly — contempt? Without another word, she pulled a small silk pouch from the carpetbag she always carried and measured tobacco from it onto a thin, fine square of paper.

"Looks like you've got more'n enough now to buy into that store we've been discussing," Bob Wright observed, staring at Eli. "About time you thought about marrying, wouldn't you say? Wonderful institution, marriage. A wife, children . . . Why, they make life worth living."

Kate choked and gave a startled laugh, shaking her head. Doc laid the deck down, slumped back in his chair, and struck a match.

"Wha's so funny, darlin'?" he asked, his

words now more slurred than blurred.

Mumuring something in French, she leaned over the table to accept the light, twisting her neck to smile with luxurious satisfaction as her breasts came within inches of Eli's face. Before she straightened, she looked the other way and kissed Bob Wright on the mouth. Then she moved behind Doc Holliday and bent to kiss his neck, before reaching around to place the lit cigarette between his lips.

"Why, thank you, darlin'," Doc said, blind as Homer to her wantonness.

He picked up the deck again, but for the third time that night, drawing in the first smoke set off a coughing fit so violent, he was nearly shaken from his chair. Bent almost double, he turned from the table, unable to go on. It was appalling, and the rest of them just sat there, not knowing what to do.

"Jesus, Doc," Kate whispered, pouring him a drink. Still coughing, he shook his head, watering eyes aimed at the floor. Then, to everyone's horror, he hawked bloody phlegm into the brass spittoon at his feet.

Revolted, and having lost better than $4,700 to Eli and Bob, the second cattleman took that opportunity to gather his remaining chips and stand. "I'm afraid I've had enough," he said.

"Not me," Doc gasped, still game. Wiping his mouth, he turned back to the table, white-faced and blue-lipped. "Evenin's hardly begun . . ."

Kate poured him another drink. Doc drained the glass she offered. Somewhat recovered, the dentist dealt. Two down, two up.

"Another three for Mr. Wright. Not much to look at, but sometimes a pair of threes is all you need. Well, now!" he cried breathlessly when a second ace appeared in front of Eli. "Fortune continues to smile on Captain Grier! You are a lucky man, sir. And . . . a queen," he said, staring. "No help for the dealer's nine."

Another round of bets. The last down cards distributed. Eli peeled up a corner of his and sat back in his chair. "Your grand. Fifteen hundred more," he told Bob Wright.

Doc folded, his face neutral when he remarked, "Too rich for me." Almost half of what he'd brought in was gone, with a little over two grand left.

"All in," Bob Wright said, pushing his chips to the center of the table. "Let's see what you have, Eli."

What Eli had should've been enough.

All night long he'd won and won and won. For crissakes, Bob was only showing a pair of threes. My God, who wouldn't have gone all in with aces full of kings?

"Four of a kind," Bob said, laying out a second pair of threes with a jack.

"Peach of a hand," Doc murmured, while

583

Kate laughed and laughed and laughed.

Bob Wright rose and looked down at Elijah Garrett Grier. "That's eighty-two hundred and change you owe me, Grier. Call it eight even," he said, his voice hard, his eyes harder. "I want the cash by noon, you contemptible sonofabitch."

"And what was our little side bet?" Kate asked Grier airily. "Oh! I remember now! I spend a night with the winner, and you?" Taking Bob's arm, Kate purred, "*You* owe *me* two grand."

"Kate, darlin', you go on along with Bob and celebrate, now," Doc urged, his voice thready. "I have a little business to do with the captain."

Drunk, sick, and nearly as stunned as Eli Grier, John Henry Holliday watched the couple leave. After a time, he cleared his throat and remarked, "Well, now. That was unexpected." Eyes unfocused, it took him a while to work it out. "Only three of us," he said to no one in particular.

Maybe Bob didn't know before, Eli was thinking, but he sure as hell knows now. Jesus, I'm in trouble . . . He looked at Holliday. "I — I'm sorry. Did you say something?"

"Three players. Pattern changed." Holliday poured himself another shot and tossed it back. "Ten grand," he said then, staring at Eli with something like sympathy. "Lotta

584

money. Haven't got it, have you."

It was not a question. Eli didn't bother to reply.

"If you will be so kind as to help me to my feet," Doc said softly, "perhaps we can both salvage some of our night's work, sir. You have a horse that I would like . . . to buy."

RAISING BLIND

The days were noticeably shorter now. This one would be agreeably warm and windless. Half past six, and the pale early-autumn sun began its rise toward a clear, high sky that few in Dodge City were in a position to appreciate; the drovers had passed out a couple of hours ago and the citizens were still home, getting dressed and eating breakfast.

Their long shadows snaking westward along Front Street, two men walked toward the resurrected Elephant Barn, its unweathered lumber still the color of fresh-cut corn bread in the morning light. They had said little since leaving the Lone Star.

Eli named a price.

Holliday countered.

"She's in foal," Eli objected.

"You're in trouble," Doc replied. "Twenty-one sixty, firm."

It was a strange number. Probably all the dentist had left, and no more than Roxana was worth. Given the sudden shift in his circumstances, Eli was already thinking about other things. How to phrase a vague telegram to his sister, for example, and how much she might be willing to wire him for an "emergency," and where he could get the rest. He had no intention of paying off the hooker, but even minus that two grand . . .

No matter how he figured it, he'd never scrape the money up by noon.

Balancing an angry cuckold's wrath against the U.S. Army's dim view of desertion, Eli began to consider Mexico. Word was, Porfirio Díaz was staffing an army . . . Yes, it was probably time to take Bob Wright's advice and resign his commission, in a manner of speaking. Past time, really. Alice was becoming tiresome and, frankly, Bob was welcome to her. She wanted so much! Attention, acknowledgment, affection. The constant demands and expectations were —

The dentist stumbled slightly, crossing the tracks. Eli caught him by the elbow and held on.

"Very kind of you, sir," Holliday said, the movement of his chest shallow and quick. "A little light-headed, I fear."

Pathetic, Eli thought, the way drunks will fool themselves.

They moved on toward the barn. Eli began to think the game through with calm detachment. After years of anticipating a bad beat, it was almost a relief to lose that big. Law of averages, he thought. Keep playing, and something like this is bound to happen. Never thought it would be Bob Wright who did the job, though. Funny how he'd thought Holliday might be the one, just on reputation alone, but the man didn't play that well, really. In fact, every time he dealt —

Eli stopped, astonished, and looked back at the dentist. "You were feeding me cards!"

"Occasionally."

"How did you do it?" Eli asked as they turned down Bridge. "I'm just curious."

"Oh . . . I am not quite so sick as I make out," Doc said carelessly, but when they got to the corral, he reached for the top rail and leaned over to spit blood. "Jesus," he whispered. "Oh, Christ."

Snapping his fingers, Eli pointed at him and said, "You switched decks while you were coughing!"

"Now and then."

"So . . . you wanted me to win until the end of the game? Yes! Let me collect the money from the table, so you could clean up! Except . . . you lost."

"That wasn't part of the plan." The dentist straightened, wincing when he pulled his shoulders back. His lips in the sunlight were nearly the color of his eyes. "Stupid mistake," he said vaguely. "Only three of us . . ."

"But you wanted Roxana? You thought I'd bet her?"

"Yes," Holliday said. "An' I was hopin' to leave some sort of legacy . . . Take care of Kate and Sophie."

Who in hell was Sophie? Eli wondered. Some other hooker, he guessed. "I had a cousin who died of consumption," he told the dentist. "Dolph used to say it felt like the inside of his chest was being scrubbed with a wire brush. Must make it hard to concentrate."

"Yes." With a visible act of will, John Henry Holliday's voice became stronger, his diction more precise, his eyes more focused. "Where is that horse of yours?"

She was in a stall about halfway down the aisle. Restless. Annoyed with him. Tossing her head and snorting when he approached. So beautiful! She took Eli's breath away, even now. Compact, high-tailed, with large, dark eyes and a broad jaw behind a small, velvety muzzle. She looked like she was made of china, but she was as tough as any mustang. Keen on patrol, Roxana had stood up well to the bitter cold and withering heat of Kansas. She could outlast every other mount at the fort, but she was hot and nervy, too, and often made life difficult in the stable.

"I'm going to miss her," Eli admitted, opening the stall door for Holliday.

The dentist approached, speaking calmly, hands low. What in hell is he going to do with a horse? Eli wondered. He'll be dead by Sunday, from the looks of him.

It came to him then that nobody knew they'd made this deal, and maybe Eli could reclaim the horse, the way he had after —

Without warning, Holliday gagged twice and twisted away, a short, sharp cough doubling him over. Startled, Roxana reared, and Eli shoved the dentist out of range before stepping in from the side to get a grip on her halter, murmuring, "Easy, easy, easy . . ." Eyes on Roxana, he warned, "You have to be careful until she knows you. She's skittish, and she's stronger than she looks —"

"Is this the way it happened?" Holliday asked softly.

Eli turned, and jerked his forehead away from a short-barreled, nickel-plated revolver. Roxana shied at the motion, moving back in the stall.

"This isn't the first time you've sold that mare to cover a gamblin' debt. Is it."

"What are you — ?"

"Lie to me," the Georgian suggested with gentle, smiling malice. "I'll shoot you where you stand."

"I don't know what you're —"

"You needed money. Johnnie Sanders knew that. He did the books for half the businesses in Dodge. He offered two grand for the horse. You agreed. He went to the safe at Bob Wright's store and met you at the barn with the cash."

"Yes, but —"

"You accepted the money and then you brained that boy, you spineless, gutless, heartless bastard."

"No!"

"You set fire to the barn, and raised the alarm, and walked away with the cash and the horse, both. Tell me I'm wrong."

"But — No, it wasn't that way at all! He — Yes! I sold the horse to him," Eli admitted, "but I didn't kill him —"

"You broke his skull and left him to die."

"*No!* Listen to me: I took the money and I went back to the saloon to pay off. When I came out, I swear, the barn was already on fire! I ran back —"

"Into a burnin' building," Holliday said, voice flat. "How courageous."

"There were men sleeping in there!"

"So you raised the alarm."

"Yes, of course!"

"You went back to Roxana's stall, and you led her out."

"I had to! She wouldn't go past the flames! I got Roxana out and helped clear the barn, and when it was all over, I took her back to the fort — just overnight! I couldn't leave her out on the street, could I? I figured I could come back in the morning and find the kid and sort it all out —"

"So you didn't see Johnnie?"

"I figured he left. I had no idea he was still in the barn —"

Holliday pulled the hammer back. Eli flinched at the quiet click.

Speaking quickly now and quietly, he said, "I swear I didn't hurt that boy. I ran back to the barn, and he was already on the ground. Roxana must have — You've seen it yourself! Look at her!" Eli cried, for the horse was showing white around her eyes. "She doesn't trust strangers and she's liable to go light on her front feet. I don't think that kid knew the first thing about horses! He probably went into the stall and she came down on him."

There *was* a curve to the fracture. It might have been the size of a hoof, but . . . "Doesn't matter," Doc insisted. "You turned his body over. You must have seen that he was still alive."

"Maybe! Yes! I don't know! I didn't look that hard! It was dark, for crissakes! The roof was caving in and —"

"So you paid your debt, you got your horse and saved the cowboys. And you left John Horse Sanders to lie there and burn."

Mouth dry, Eli tensed slightly, thinking he could —

"By all means," Holliday urged courteously. "Try it."

He's going to kill me, Eli thought. This is how I'm going to die.

"Four years of war," the Georgian said

softly, "to teach them rebs a lesson and set their darkies free! But when it came down to your horse or that boy . . . Well, hell, he was just a colored kid, and kin to no one." For an endless moment, John Henry Holliday just stood there, trembling. "God a'mighty," he said quietly. "To think we lost to trash like you."

As much as anything, it was the weight of the pistol that saved Elijah Garrett Grier's life that morning. Suddenly and utterly exhausted, Doc lowered his gun, letting it dangle at his side.

"Bob Wright knows everything," he said. "I recommend you run."

Eli nodded his entire agreement but pointed out, "I'll need a mount."

Doc glanced toward the corral. "Pick one."

"They hang horse thieves," Grier objected.

"Only if you're caught. Best hurry."

"I — The money? For Roxana?"

Slate blue eyes went wide.

Toujours l'audace! Doc said with specious admiration. "The price was twenty-one sixty. Two grand will go to Miss Kate, to clear your debt to her. I will wire the remaining one hundred and sixty to my father. Grier and Cook Carriage Company owes him the money. That leaves me with thirty-eight dollars and change. Forgive me if I am not inclined to share that with a lyin', low-life Yankee skunk. God as my witness: I should rid the world of you."

His face reduced to bone, eyes fever-bright, the not-yet-infamous Doc Holliday summoned all the strength he had left, but could not raise the gun again.

"Get out of my sight," he muttered, despairing. "Get out of Dodge. And don't come back, you soulless cur."

The oldest of John Riney's four boys generally showed up at the Elephant Barn a little before seven. Young John — Junior, everybody called him — got the job right after they moved into town, when he was eleven, and he could do the work while half asleep. You drew water for the horses in the stalls, and fed them, and mucked out the straw, and spread new, and then went on to the horses in the corral, who got less attention because the customers paid less.

Whenever Captain Grier was in town, he left Roxana at the barn, and he paid extra, which is to say he put extra on his tab. Even so, Junior always took his time getting around to Roxana because she was a bitch of a horse and he was scared of her. She seemed kind of worked up this morning, too, so truth was, he might've drug his feet a little, hoping she'd settle down. It was almost nine when he finally got to her end of the barn and saw what was bothering the animal.

If it'd been any other drunk sitting on the

floor in the corner of Roxana's stall, Junior would have just shoveled the shit out from around him, but his mother was one of Doc Holliday's patients, and Junior did not consider sitting in horse stalls to be among that gentleman's habits.

"Are you all right, Doc?" he asked, glancing at Roxana. The dentist's eyes were open but there was no answer, so Junior bent over and shook the man's shoulder some. "Dr. Holliday? You all right?"

The dentist seemed to come back from somewhere far away. His voice was weak and kind of wavery, and Junior had to lean in to hear him say, "I am fine, thank you. Very kind of you to ask."

"You don't look too good," Junior told him. "You want me to get somebody?"

"Yes. Thank you."

Junior waited, but the dentist sort of drifted off again. "Who, Doc?"

Junior was a little nervous about asking that because he expected Doc would send him for Kate. If he did, Junior planned to find his littlest brother and send Charlie to get her. Mabel Riney would wear Junior out if he went near a bad woman like Kate, but she doted on Charlie and wouldn't belt him as bad.

"Doc? Who do you want me to get?"

"Morgan," the dentist decided, after a time. Relieved, Junior asked, "Mr. Morgan over by the saddle shop, or Morgan Earp?"

"Morgan Earp. If you would be so kind."

"You bet, Doc. I'll get him." Junior looked up at the horse. "I don't think you better sit in here. That mare's dangerous."

"Yes," Doc whispered. "So I hear."

Junior leaned the shovel in the corner, and helped the dentist onto his feet, and got him out into the aisle, and kicked the stall door closed, and found a stool for Doc to sit on, and double-checked the latch on Roxana's stall, because if a horse that valuable got loose, there'd be hell to pay. Then he went off to look for Morgan Earp and found the deputy at home. Morg's girl, Lou, said that Morgan was sleeping. Junior explained about how he'd found Doc Holliday sitting like Job on a dung heap, so she got Morg up, and he dressed and came over to the barn with Junior.

Doc was still on the stool when they got back to the barn, and Mr. Earp hunkered down next to him. Junior had more work to do, but naturally he wanted to find out what was going on, so he decided to sweep up the aisle. He was real quiet about it, too, though he still didn't hear much of anything because Doc Holliday's voice was always so soft. Then Junior saw out of the corner of his eye that Doc's face was wet. That surprised him so much he stopped sweeping, and he heard Doc say, "I couldn't do it, Morg. I just

596

couldn't do it."

Mr. Earp's face got soft. "Don't worry, Doc. I won't tell nobody." The deputy stood up and looked away. "Sonofabitch probably had it coming, but you'd've hanged."

Doc kind of laughed and said something else.

Mr. Earp frowned and said, "Don't talk like that." The deputy looked thoughtful. "No point going after him. His word against yours. We wouldn't be able to prove a damn thing."

Doc lifted a hand toward Roxana and asked a question.

Mr. Earp glanced over his shoulder at the horse and said, "Not a chance, Doc. You know Wyatt."

Doc sounded stronger and more awake when he said, "Not well, but well enough. Help me up."

Leaning on his broom, Junior watched the two men as they left the barn. Doc Holliday was unsteady on his feet, and Mr. Earp was helping him quite a bit, but they were talking, heads down, all the way out to the tracks. They had just turned toward their little houses north of Front Street when Junior saw Mr. Earp stop short. Doc turned back to look at him, and the dentist was smiling now. Then Morgan gave a great shout of a laugh and put his arm around Doc Holliday's bony shoulders, and damn near lifted the dentist right off his feet.

"Now, what do you suppose that was about?" Junior asked Roxana, but she was eating and paid no mind.

The next few days were pretty lively in Dodge. On top of the usual drunk-and-disorderlies, Dora Hand got killed. People felt bad about that. She was a whore, but she sang real nice. Then Nick Klaine reported that Dull Knife and Little Wolf were headed toward Kansas with a bunch of starving Cheyenne, hoping to steal some livestock. That got everybody worked up for a while and sold a lot of newspapers, but nothing came of the scare. Then a badger burrowed under China Joe's laundry and collapsed one side of the shack, which burned down, although the new fire brigade got over there pretty quick and stopped the blaze from spreading. Eddie Foy made a funny story out of that and added it to his act. Jau Dong-Sing considered the fire good luck. He would build a new bathhouse and a better laundry, and add a cookshop. He had stoves going all the time to heat water anyway. Might as well get a big pot to boil noodles, too, and sell them the way Doc Holliday suggested.

Even with all that to talk about, the main topic of conversation in Dodge City at the end of September was how Captain Eli Grier and a good bay gelding had gone missing and how, right after that, Alice Wright took her

two youngest kids and boarded the train for
St. Louis, and how Bob Wright was making
out like it was a pure coincidence and nothing was wrong.

His daughter Isabelle was doing her best to
take over the household, though anybody
could see the girl was still feeling washed out
and sickly from that damn cold. Soon the
Belle of Dodge became Poor Little Belle. As
much as she hated the pity, Belle herself was
glad to see the end of September. It had been
a hell of a month, made worse when her
father started looking at her like he'd never
seen her before. Once he even muttered, "No
wonder you're so pretty. You're probably not
mine." He was drunk when he said it, but
still.

Wyatt Earp didn't participate in the gossip
about Alice and Eli. He wasn't exactly living
a blameless life himself these days, so there
wasn't a whole lot of room to look down on
Eli Grier or the Wrights. Which isn't to say
that Wyatt didn't take a certain amount of
secret pleasure from the notion that Bob
Wright had gotten his comeuppance. Maybe
ole Bob would pay attention to his own
troubles now, instead of going around hiring
ignorant kids like George Hoyt to shoot at
men who were just trying to do their jobs.

Of course, it had not escaped Wyatt's notice
that Roxana was still over at the Elephant
Barn. She didn't belong to the post, Wyatt

knew that much for sure. The fort commandant said she was Grier's personal mount, not government-issue. Somebody was paying her keep at the barn, but when Wyatt asked Hamilton Bell who it was, Ham said he didn't know. That seemed kind of odd, but it wasn't really any of Wyatt's business, so he didn't push it.

Like Belle Wright, Doc Holliday hadn't really gotten over that cold either and he was back in bed, trying to kick it. Wyatt noticed that Kate was splashing some cash around and seemed to be in a better mood for some reason. So it was pretty quiet next door, though Doc's cough sounded worse than ever.

Then one morning Morgan told Wyatt he was going over to see how Doc was doing, which was ordinary enough. Except Morg looked like he used to when he was a little kid and had some big secret, like he caught a toad or something and planned to scare the girls with it, but didn't dare tell Wyatt because he knew Wyatt would stop him.

Which is why Wyatt decided to sit out on the front porch for a spell before going to bed, to see what was going on.

Doc must have been feeling better because after a few minutes, he and Morgan came outside. Morg got Doc settled into the wicker rocker on the porch and pulled a shawl around the dentist's shoulders before setting off toward Front Street, grinning like an idiot.

Wyatt decided maybe he'd just go on over to Doc's and ask what in hell that was about. All Doc said was "I'm sure I haven't the slightest idea, Wyatt," but he was grinning, too, and then just sat there, rocking and looking pleased with himself, until Morg came walking back up the street.

With Roxana. Saddled.

Confused, Wyatt stood, one hand on the porch post. From behind him, he heard Doc say, "She's yours, Wyatt. A gift."

Stunned, Wyatt looked back at Doc, whose eyes were shining above a shy, sweet, crooked smile and — Well, hell. Wyatt supposed it wasn't the *worst* moment in his life. Seeing the light leave Urilla's eyes was the worst, but this came pretty close. It took him a few seconds because he hated to do it, but he said what he had to.

"I'm sorry, Doc. I can't accept anything like that."

It pained him to see Doc's reaction. The dentist looked like he'd been slapped.

"Why, you stubborn, stiff-necked, self-righteous — ! I can't believe it!" Doc cried. "And I thought you were a friend — the more fool me!"

"I told you, Doc!" Morgan tied the horse to the post by the front gate and scuffed along the walk toward the porch. "I knew he wouldn't take her."

"Doc," Wyatt pleaded, "try to understand! It was a real nice idea, but I'm sorry, it's just not right!"

Doc was almost sputtering, he was so mad. "Are you — are you actually goin' to stand there and accuse me of tryin' to *bribe* you? I won the damn animal in a card game! What in hell am I going to do with a horse like that? I can't afford to have her standin' around in the Elephant Barn, eatin' me out of house and home! I ask you for one damn favor and this is the —"

Wyatt said, "Calm down, Doc! You're gonna make yourself sick —"

Sure enough, the dentist was looking for his handkerchief now.

"All I'm askin' is that you take her off my hands! That is the rock-bottom *least* that any sort of friend would do for a sick man, but no! You are too goddam —"

"Hey, Doc! Maybe you could sell her," Morgan suggested helpfully. Digging into his pocket, he pulled out some money. "How does two dollars and fifteen cents sound?"

Doc didn't even pretend to think about it before holding out his hand for the coins. "Morgan, that sounds just about right," he said. "Help me up."

Morg offered him an arm for leverage. For a while, the two of them just stood together, side by side, watching Wyatt work out exactly which ethical issues would be rendered moot if *Morgan* owned the horse.

Doc said, "Listen close, Morg. I believe you can hear the gears grindin'."

It sounded like he was making fun, but Doc had that look on his face again: pleasure and satisfaction and affection, all mixed. And Morgan himself felt just about as fine as he had ever felt in a lifetime of feeling pretty good about things. He was proud of his older brother's earnest, boneheaded, mulish honesty; tickled that he and Doc had surprised Wyatt so completely; grateful to Doc for seeing to it that Wyatt got his dream back, even after his money had gone to build a library full of books Wyatt couldn't read if he gave each one a whole damn year.

Suddenly jubilant, Morgan couldn't keep still any longer. Giggling like a six-year-old, he did a little dance, and threw an arm around John Holliday's shoulders, and pulled him close. "Hot damn! We got him good, Doc! Look at that, will you? He's . . . Yes! Here it comes! A smile! Wyatt Earp is smiling!"

"Nice teeth," Doc remarked.

Wyatt laughed. "Should be," he said. "They cost enough."

"Somebody get Nick Klaine!" Morg yelled out at the empty street. "Stop the press! Wyatt Earp is laughing!"

Wyatt murmured, "Doc, I don't know what to say."

"Sure you do, Wyatt," Doc said softly. "Mississippi. Fifty-five. Go on, now. Take a ride on your brother's fine new horse."

Wyatt walked out to Roxana, who pranced some and shifted away, but settled as he stood talking to her quietly, letting her get to know him a little. When the time was right, he swung up and wheeled her a turn or two, until she was ready to pay attention.

He leaned forward. She gathered herself beneath him. They took off, headed north through the short grass toward a ripening wheat field, gold and copper and ocher in the mellow autumn light.

"Now, that is a sight to see," Morgan said, for it appeared that his brother was flying, as though Roxana had no legs at all but just swept along, weightless as a bird skimming the prairie. "You did good, Doc. That was a real nice thing to do."

"Yes," Doc said, sounding content. "She'll be something to remember me by."

Morgan turned and looked at him hard, but Doc's eyes were on Kate, who was walking up the street now with some groceries.

"Morgan," Doc said warily, "if Miss Kate were to ask you about Roxana? Remember: I cut the cards for the horse with Grier the other night, just after she and Bob Wright left."

TURNING THE PLAY

For Morgan, autumn had always been a special joy. Of all the Earp kids, he was the one who liked it best when the family lived close enough to a town for him to go to a regular schoolhouse in the fall. Back when the Earps lived in Iowa and Illinois, he liked how the air got crisp as an apple, and how the leaves smelled when they piled up in heaps against buildings. He liked how his mother's eyes warmed when he brought in as big an armload of wood as he could lug for the stove. Most of all, Morg liked climbing up to the attic after supper and getting into bed with a book.

He always claimed the space closest to a western window. It was colder there, but he'd pull a knitted cap down over his ears and burrow into the quilts and stick the book up to catch the dying light, reading until his hands were frozen and his eyelids were too heavy to stay open for another word. Now, of course, working nights the way he did, he didn't go to bed in the dying light, but his and Lou's bedroom window faced east. When the bright morning sun came in and hit his eyes and helped them close, he got that same feeling as he read himself to sleep.

This fall, he was working on a book called *Black Beauty* that he'd borrowed from Belle Wright. It was kind of strange because you were supposed to believe a horse was telling you the story, but it was good, too, and said a lot of true things about horses and made you think different about what you saw every day. Morgan thought Wyatt would enjoy the story if he could get past the silliness of animals talking to each other, so Morg was planning to read it aloud to Wyatt this winter when the weather closed in.

Unless him and Wyatt and James wound up moving to the Arizona Territory, that is. Morg would have to give the book back to Belle before the Earps left Dodge.

"There's no end of silver down by Bisbee and Tombstone." That's what Virgil's last letter said. The veins were so rich, the metal was right out on the surface, the way gold was in California back in '49. So Wyatt and James were talking about how if they all went down to Arizona right now, the Earps could get in on the ground floor of something big, instead of showing up a year late, when the big money was done.

Bessie wasn't real happy about the notion.

And Morg hadn't actually agreed to the plan yet, either. Lou wanted to go up to Utah to see her family again and find out if her folks had softened any about her and Morg getting married. So Morgan was caught in the middle, because he didn't want to say no to Lou but James was ready to pack, and Wyatt was edgy and restless and not inclined to what Doc called "rational argument."

For Wyatt, autumn meant the end of the cattle season, and that meant he'd be laid off again. The injustice of it ate at him, and his temper shortened with the days. Dodge was down to half a dozen herds a week, and the city had already let John Stauber and Jack Brown go. Wyatt had a big argument with Mayor Kelley over that. Sure, the number of cowboys was down, but so was the quality. These were men nobody wanted to hire, peak season, and they joined idlers who'd been fired or quit work the minute they hit town: drunks and shirkers and troublemakers who couldn't be bothered to ride back to Texas. It was no time to cut police staff, but that's what the city council wanted, so that's what happened. And then Chalkie Beeson and the other saloon owners grumbled that Wyatt was bashing extra cowboys and hauling them in on the smallest pretext so he could rack up arrest fees before the winter, but all the deputies shared that money, so it wasn't like Wyatt was making anything extra in October. He just didn't have any patience with idiots this time of year. About the only thing that cheered Wyatt up was going to the Elephant Barn to spend time with Dick and Roxana, working them in a circle corral or taking one of them out for exercise.

Every time Morgan thought about what Doc had done, he could feel himself getting a big, dumb smile on his face. Good thing, too, because it made him more tolerant when Doc got himself into trouble.

The little German kid who pumped the foot drill for Doc — Wil Eberhardt, his name was — he'd taken to keeping an eye on the dentist when Doc was gambling, even if it meant staying up all night, or sleeping in a corner of a saloon. When a bartender noticed things getting out of hand, he'd send the boy to find Morgan, and Morg would have to stop whatever he was doing and go on over and settle everyone down some. That was happening a lot lately, so Morg knew what it meant when Wil came running over around two in the morning, calling, "Mr. Earp! Come quick! There's trouble at the Lady Gay!"

Didn't take long to get to the bar. Front Street wasn't near as crowded as it had been even a couple of weeks ago, but the mood was worse. Spring carousing was celebratory and pretty good-natured; at the end of the season, knots of drunks stood around outside, passing bottles and glaring. There was more sullen defiance about the city ordinances and a greater willingness to pick fights just for the hell of it. The crib girls hated October. It was a lot more dangerous and they were more likely to get cheated, so they stole more. Usually they were too plastered to do that without getting caught and they got smacked around for it. Even at James and Bessie's, there was trouble almost every night.

So Morg figured that Doc was probably getting roughed up, but when he got to the saloon, it was quiet except for some young drover who was noodling around on the piano, trying to pick out a tune that might have been "Lorena" or maybe "Bonnie Blue Flag." Or "Buffalo Gals." Hard to tell.

Doc was just sitting at a table, playing poker. True enough, the other fellas looked pretty unhappy. Well, that's what makes it gambling, Morg thought. Not everybody gets to win.

Brows up, Morg turned back toward Wilfred, who was peeking underneath the swing doors, afraid to come inside. "Ask him," Wil mouthed, and pointed toward Kevin Ballard, who was wiping up beer slops but watching Doc and the cowboys.

"Hey, Kev," Morg said quietly. "What's the trouble?"

"Morg," the barkeep whispered, "God knows I've seen men drink, but Jesus . . .

And he keeps winning! They're going to take it out of his hide, the way he's been mouthing off at them."

Morgan approached the table, but leaned against the wall to watch the action for a while. He didn't have to listen to the muttering for long. Kevin and the Eberhardt kid were right. Doc was riding for a fall.

Pushing away from the planks, Morg scuffed over and stood across the table from Doc. "Cut your losses, boys," he told the Texans. "Go have some fun with what you got left."

Doc leaned back in his chair and stared at Morgan while the cowboys gathered up the remains of their wages. They indulged in a certain amount of unpleasant commentary about Dodge in general and about Doc in particular, but they went quietly, happy enough to quit the game while they still had money for another go at the girls.

It was a cool evening, but Doc was sweating.

"Doc, are you all right?" Morg asked. "You don't look so good." He meant it kindly, but the moment he said it, he knew Doc was going to take it wrong.

"Why, thank you, sir," Doc said, cold-eyed. "How charmin' of you to point that out. You, of course, are the very picture of rude health, which evidently entitles you to interfere with the livelihood of others, you arrogant, meddlin' sonofabitch."

Morg had heard plenty of that kind of thing come out of Doc's mouth, but this was the first time he'd been the target himself, and it was a shock to be spoken to like that. Virgil took no guff and would have cracked Doc for it. Wyatt was tolerant of back talk as long as it stayed talk; he'd have shrugged it off and walked away.

Morg sat down and glanced at the bottle on the table. It was three-quarters empty. "Hitting it pretty hard tonight," he observed.

"And precisely how is that any business of yours? Was there an election I missed?" Doc asked. "Has temperance come to west Kansas? I have not created a disturbance. Am I in violation of some new city ordinance?"

"No, Doc, but we're friends —"

"Well, get off me, then!"

Doc reached for the bottle. Morg got to it first. That alone was a sign of how much Doc had put away. Morg meant to move the bottle just out of reach, but a hand clamped over his wrist.

"Leave it," Doc warned.

Morg let loose, a little startled by how strong Doc's grip was.

Doc refilled his water glass and damn near drained it.

"Damn," Morg whispered. "Jesus . . . What's *wrong,* Doc?"

Certain that if he were to move at all —

even slightly, even to speak — everything human in him would be lost to blind, bestial, ungovernable rage, John Henry Holliday sat silently while in the coldest, most analytical part of him, he thought, If I go mad one day, it will be at a moment like this. I will put a bullet through the lung of some healthy young idiot just to watch him suffocate. There you are, I'll tell him. That's what it's like to know your last deep breath is in your past. You won't ever get enough air again. From this moment until you die, it will only get worse and worse. Bet you could use a good stiff drink now, eh, jackass?

So he let Morgan Earp wait for his answer, just as he himself waited — patiently, helplessly — until he could be sure that the liquor had taken hold, and he could feel himself inch back from the edge of the abyss. And when at last he spoke, his voice was soft and musical. "Flaubert tells us that three things are required for happiness: stupidity, selfishness, and good health. I am," he told Morgan, "an unhappy man —"

The coughing hit again, and though he was shamed by the whine that escaped him, he kept his eyes on Morg's until the fit passed. "Tuberculosis toys with its victims. It hides, and it waits, and just when we are sufficiently deluded to believe in a cure —"

"But I — I thought . . . It's just that cold, Doc. And the laudanum's helping —"

"Oh, Christ, Morg! This is not a cold! As for laudanum — God knows how Mattie can stand that poison! Usin' it is like bein' dead already."

"But you were better this summer," Morg insisted. "I thought —"

"Well, you were wrong! We both were . . ."

He had spent his entire adult life dying, trying all the while to make sense of a dozen contradictory theories about what caused his disease and how to treat it, when his own continued existence could be used to support any of them. Or all of them, or none. Because of what he'd done, or not done, or for no reason at all, the disease sometimes went into retreat, but only as a tide retreats —

He tried to think of a way to explain all that — maybe telling Morg to think of the difference between a pardon and a reprieve — but the taste of iron and salt rose again in his pharynx, and it took all he had not to gag and vomit when he swallowed the blood.

"The disease is active again," he said finally. "It is gnawing on my left lung, as a rat gnaws on cheese. Except: a rat sleeps. This never, ever lets up. Every goddam breath I take hurts, Morg. I need *that* much liquor so I can quit cryin' and leave my bed because —" he turned away and coughed, again and again, shredding adhesions, his chest aching with the effort to keep on pulling in air — "because like every other damned soul in this godforsaken hell, I still have to make a livin'.'"

His voice broke and he looked away, blinking, and for a terrible moment, Morgan thought that Doc might weep.

"I was buildin' a practice," the dentist whispered. "People were bringin' their children to me . . . I had to turn away three utterly wretched patients this week! Who will care for them now? This mornin' I had a denture like Wyatt's nearly finished for Mabel Riney. I coughed while I was adjustin' the mount. Broke it in half. Hours of work shot to hell, and nothin' to give that poor woman but her twenty-three dollars back. That'll just about clean me out. I can't make the month's rent on the office! I will have to give it up . . ."

"Where's Kate?" Morg asked softly. "She usually finds you better games —"

"She left," Doc snapped. "This morning. She found out that I am broke, and then she found greener pastures. Of course, one can hardly complain when a whore goes where the money is."

"But, Doc, all the money you paid for Roxana went to Kate!"

"I swear, Morgan: you tell her that, and I'll —"

Threat dying on his lips, Doc closed his eyes, swallowed hard, and sat trembling, left hand holding the sodden handkerchief, the right pressing hard against his chest for what felt like forever.

When at last he spoke again, it was with a bitter, quiet, hard-won precision. "When I am like this, dentistry is beyond me. So I play cards. I play cards with the most ignorant, fatuous, misbegotten clay eaters the benighted state of Texas has to offer. I *cannot* do that sober, Morgan! I have tried. The task is more than I can —"

Suddenly he was on his feet, winging his glass at the piano where the cowboy was trying to pick out "The Yellow Rose of Texas" and kept getting a note wrong.

"A-flat!" Doc shouted. "It's *A-flat!*"

"A flat *what?*" the cowboy shouted back.

"God as my witness," Doc swore, pointing at the piano, "I shall be driven to *slaughter* —"

The coughing hit again. Morgan said, "C'mon, Doc. Sit down. I'm sorry. Look, I have some money saved up, and —"

"I don't need charity! All I need is to be left alone to earn my way as best I can! And now I must go buck the tiger — which is a fool's errand — because you just busted up a poker game that I was *winnin'*, God damn you, and this time of night, faro is the only game in town that will be open to me. In future, I will take it as a personal favor if you would kindly refrain from interferin' in my affairs. Good evenin' to you, sir."

Everyone in the place watched as he left.

For a long time, Morgan sat openmouthed,

trying to think of some way to help. Nothing came to mind.

The bartender brought a whisk broom and dustpan over to the piano, and knelt to sweep up the broken glass.

Shoulda seen it coming. That's what Wyatt thought, though he heard it in his father's voice. *Walked right into it, you stupid pile of shit.*

Seven of them, waiting for him in the saloon. Bartender, gone. Off in the corner, just one man playing faro. Nobody else in the place.

He'd been warned. Twice. Dog first, then Bat. So Wyatt had started wearing a sidearm pretty regularly, and went as far as loading heavy-gauge into the shotguns behind the bars in every saloon in town. But the weeks passed. Nobody else came at him and . . . He let his guard down. He got sloppy. His shift was almost over, and he was distracted.

They had his gun before he took two steps past the door.

He'd been thinking about Mattie Blaylock, confused because it didn't start out so complicated between them. Mattie did her job and Wyatt did his, but somewhere along the line, he went off the tracks, and he was damned if he saw where. Like in Topeka, he noticed she was looking at a necklace in a store window. He went back the next morning to buy it for her, and it wasn't cheap, either, but instead of being happy, she asked, "What's this for?"

"Nothing," he said. "I thought you'd like it."

She wore it once, and it looked pretty on her, too, but after that she put it away.

Then, last night, before he left for work, he told Mattie that Big George Hoover had invited them over for dinner on Sunday. He thought Mattie would like to wear one of the dresses Doc Holliday had helped her pick out, and maybe that necklace from Topeka, but she acted like Wyatt was asking her to do something unreasonable. She looked at him like he was some kind of idiot even to think about going to dinner at the Hoovers'.

Wyatt asked if it was because Margaret Hoover used to be — well, Maggie Carnahan, and maybe that brought back bad memories or something. Mattie just shook her head like he was so stupid, it wasn't worth trying to explain it to him. Hell, he thought. I might not be the smartest man in Kansas, but I ain't *that* dumb.

Course, it turned out that was exactly how dumb he was, but at the time he was thinking that any effort to be good to Mattie seemed to ricochet back at him. She'd look suspicious and annoyed. "Why are you acting so nice?" she'd ask, like she knew he was faking. And it had just occurred to him — right when he was walking into that saloon — if you think niceness is a fraud, then maybe you think only meanness is real. So maybe Mattie would be happier if he belted her and called her a low, shameless harlot because she'd believe that, except the idea of hitting a woman —

He never finished the thought, suddenly aware that he'd just been surrounded, disarmed, and was about to be killed with his own pistol by a heavyset, middle-aged man with eyes like stones.

"I guess things're different when you're not up against a kid half your age and half your size, eh, Earp?"

I'm dead, Wyatt thought, weirdly calm, but certain this was no bluff.

"He don't look so tough now, do he, boys?" the man was saying.

There was a murmur of grinning agreement, and one of the cowboys said, "He sure don't, Mr. Driskill!"

"Are you Jesse Driskill, sir?" Wyatt asked.

There was a chorus of hoots.

"Oh, it's *sir* now! Ain't that sweet, boys? Ain't that nice and polite? No, you sonofabitch, I ain't Jesse. I'm his brother. I'm Tobias Driskill, and that was my boy you bashed, peckerhead."

A few paces behind him, a wooden chair scraped against the floor. Everyone backed off a little and left Wyatt standing alone.

Hell, he thought. Shot in the back, like Bill Hickok, and dime novelists will have the good of it.

"Think you've got enough friends to stand with you here, Tobie?" asked a honeyed Georgia voice. "Or is Achilles — alone — too many?"

"Doc? Doc Holliday?"

"Indeed, sir."

"This ain't your fight, Doc," Driskill told him.

"I beg to differ, Tobie. Deputy Earp is a patient of mine. He still owes me four dollars."

"He's worth a lot more to me dead! Hell, I'll pay you the four bucks —"

Nobody even noticed that Doc had a gun in his hand until he fired both barrels of a two-shot Deringer into the floor.

Wyatt got over the shock soonest. It was three steps to the bar. An instant later he had the shotgun in his hands.

Doc murmured, "Well, now, there's a surprise . . ."

And everyone thought he meant that he'd made them all jump, or that Wyatt Earp had just evened up the odds some, pulling a scattergun out. In point of fact, John Henry Holliday was discovering that excitement could temporarily inhibit the need to cough and make his chest pain simply . . . disappear. And in that astounding adrenaline-fueled state of grace, he spoke again, softly but fluently, his voice musical and gentle and clear.

"That is a very generous offer, Tobie, and frankly, I could use the money, but I think you'll find that Mr. Earp will decline your kindness. He is unusually scrupulous in such matters . . . Now, as it happens, I was a witness to your boy's arrest, Tobe. The youngster was in his cups, and rowdy, and in that condition he did considerable damage not only to a theater but to a German fiddler widely held to be a tolerable musician. Such persons are rare in Kansas and tend to be valued beyond what a Texan might reckon. Deputy Earp subdued your son with only as much force as was necessary to book him for assault. The young man was fined by a judge and released before midnight —"

By that time they could hear boots pounding toward them as city policemen converged on the saloon from bars all over town.

"Ah! Morgan!" Doc cried genially. "And Sheriff Masterson! Evenin', Chuck. I was just explainin' the fine points of Dodge City law enforcement to Mr. Tobias Driskill here, after he tried to jump Wyatt with this contemptible collection of illiterate, bean-eating white trash —"

With a brilliant smile, Bat stepped between Doc and the Driskill men.

"Don't mind him! He's just drunk," Bat said smoothly. "How 'bout you boys hang up your guns right over there and have a drink on me? Wyatt, I think I can straighten this out for you. Mr. Driskill, may I have a word?"

In years to come, after the gunfight in Tombstone, when the myths and lies began to accumulate, the story of that evening in Dodge would be repeated with Shakespearean advantages.

Several bars were confidently put forward as the location of the confrontation, and at least three bartenders claimed to have been eyewitnesses to the event. The man who was actually working that night never talked about it, being in no hurry to tell anyone that Tobias Driskill shoved a gun in his nose and told him to go take a piss. Which he did.

Several men later claimed to be the faro dealer Doc bucked, but only one of them admitted that he was too scared to move when the Driskill gang ordered everybody to get out. "They *might* be trouble," Doc told the dealer quietly, "but I *will* shoot you if you shut this game down while I'm ahead." And don't think Doc didn't pocket his winnings before he stepped up on Wyatt's behalf.

Eventually Tobias Driskill had not six cowhands with him but twenty-five Texas desperadoes, all taunting Wyatt Earp with guns drawn and about to mow him down in a hail of lead when — at the last possible moment — the ferocious killer *Doc Holliday* jumped up, a chromed Colt in each hand, cursing the Texans for white-livered cowards, intimidating them just long enough for Wyatt to draw his entirely legendary Ned Buntline Special. Routinely promoted to full marshal in these tales, Wyatt pistol-whipped Driskill and commanded the other Texans to "shed their hardware." A foolish cowboy raised his piece. Doc Holliday instantly shot him dead. Terrified despite overwhelming odds in their favor, the remaining two dozen Texans complied with the order to drop their weapons. Fifty revolvers were said to have been picked up from the street after Wyatt and Doc had arrested the entire gang and marched them off to the Dodge City hoosegow.

Nothing remotely like that was reported in either the *Dodge City Times* or the *Ford County Globe,* nor is there any court record of such a large number of cowboys being arrested and booked all at once — before, during, or after 1878. And yet, for the next fifty years, whenever anyone asked why he stuck with Doc Holliday long after the dentist was far more trouble than he was worth, Wyatt Earp would always give the same unadorned answer. "Doc saved my life in Dodge."

At the time, however, the whole thing was over so quickly that Wyatt only came to understand its significance during the long hours of silence he would soon spend waiting for the dentist to die, listening to a clock tick

Doc's life away.

I shoulda thanked him, Wyatt would think. *Too late, too late, too late . . .*

For instead of expressing gratitude as soon as he and Morg and Doc left the saloon, Wyatt asked, "Where'd you get that gun, Doc?"

The eastern sky was beginning to lighten. The day was going to be gray and rainy, but between the approaching dawn and the lamplight from the saloon, Morgan could see that Doc was trembling. "Come on, Wyatt. Let it go!"

"Where'd you get that gun, Doc?" Wyatt repeated.

"Morgan, you may correct me if I am wrong," Doc said, his eyes on Wyatt's, "but I believe I just saved your brother's miserable Republican hide, and he is about to arrest me for it. You have anything to say about that?"

Wyatt was right, and Morgan backed him. "It's illegal to carry firearms in town, Doc."

The dentist's hand was shaking when he offered the Deringer. "I told you before, Wyatt: I am never entirely unarmed. And a damn good thing, tonight."

Wyatt took the little pistol Doc held in the palm of his hand. "I'm sorry, Doc, but you're under —"

Before he could finish, the dentist busted out laughing —

And shouted, "Oh!" and doubled over, and staggered backward with both hands to his chest, where . . . something had just broken loose inside him, and he could feel a sharp clear focus of pain and pressure . . . but he honestly didn't care. He was still flying: still feeling the magical effects of that moment when seven men had backed away in *fear.* And it wasn't Wyatt Earp they'd feared. It was little ole John Henry Holliday, a sick, skinny dentist from Griffin by-God Georgia!

For those few enchanted minutes, he had felt strong and unafraid. And now this! This was the capper!

Straightening, throwing an arm around Wyatt, he declared, "*Nemo supra leges!* That's what I love about you, Wyatt! One law for everyone!"

"You're drunk, Doc," Wyatt said shortly, for he was embarrassed by the gesture, and Doc was starting to cough again. The sound of that right in your ear was kind of disgusting. Doc seemed to understand and moved away some, but he looked kind of strange.

"An accurate observation," he agreed, beginning to choke, "though not — not germane to our discussion —"

Just then, James showed up, wanting to know what in hell had happened. Morg started to tell him, "That Driskill kid's family showed up, but Doc . . ."

Morgan's voice trailed off.

Wyatt was staring past him toward Wright's General Outfitting, across the street. Morg turned to follow his gaze. Why is Bob Wright up so early? he wondered. Then it hit him.

"Oh, shit," he whispered. "Wyatt . . . no."

There was already a crowd. Not the hundreds of high season, but thirty or forty men drawn by Doc's gunshots, and by the abrupt departure of city deputies from saloons all over town. At first they thought maybe the Earps had some kind of beef with Doc Holliday, but then the word started to get around that a bunch of Texans had tried to kill Wyatt, and that was interesting enough to make it worthwhile to stand in the rain that was starting up, especially when Wyatt yelled, "*Bob Wright!* You want me dead, you rich sonofabitch? I'm right here!"

The merchant was at the edge of the crowd talking to somebody and kind of smirking. Bob turned at the sound of his name and stared at the deputy advancing on him. "I got no quarrel with you, Wyatt," Bob called, but there was something in his eyes . . .

"No, you'd rather pay people to do your dirty work," Wyatt said, unbuckling his gun belt, jerking the badge off his shirt, dropping them both onto the dampening dirt. "Come for me yourself, you sonofabitch!"

"All right, goddammit!" Bob agreed, pulling his own jacket off. "You're on!"

"Wyatt," Doc called, bent over, one arm

625

braced against a hitching rail. "For the love of God! Your teeth!"

Morg started forward, meaning to get between Bob and Wyatt, but Bat was on the street now, too, and gripped Morgan's arm to stop him.

"Let them settle it," Bat advised. "This has been coming since the Fourth of July."

But Morg wasn't the only one who'd seen Wyatt this angry before. James knew what could happen, too, and he was already at Wyatt's side, trying to talk sense to him.

"Give this to Doc," Wyatt said, pulling the denture out and handing it to James.

Bob took that opportunity to throw a sucker punch. It was a solid hit, but poor judgment.

"You dirty dog!" James cried, backing away. "Go ahead, Wyatt. Kill the bastard!"

All of this made for a good show and the gathering mob grew noisier as the sky lightened to a dull pewter. At first, the money was mostly on Wyatt. He was eight years younger, fifteen pounds heavier, and ablaze, his face transfigured by rage heaped up, night after night, during years of fruitless, thankless, dangerous work, protecting the lives and wealth of storekeepers and lawyers and politicians who set the price of killing a peace officer at no more than a $12 fine. But Bob Wright had advantages, too. More physical strength than anyone suspected. A slightly

626

longer reach. A deep, cold well of resentful envy and the sudden ferocious desire to take for himself everything priceless that Wyatt Earp had. The regard of other men. Respect. Loyalty, if not love.

The odds pulled even.

The rain got heavier.

The noise of the crowd dropped off.

When he figured they'd spent enough fury to be controllable, Bat stepped toward the pair, hoping he could make this into a genuine boxing match, with rounds and rests, but there was no talking to them. So he backed off.

Mud sucking at their feet, both men were staggering after half an hour, and Bob's age had begun to tell. He continued to punch at Wyatt's mouth, but every time he took a shot, he opened his own ribs, and there's a limit to how much punishment those bones can take. When Bob finally went down, he was almost too exhausted to cry out when Wyatt planted one foot and hauled off with the other, kicking with everything he had left.

"For Christ's sake, Bat, stop the fight!" Eddie Foy cried. "Sure: he's going to kill the man!"

Nobody moved. Not Bat, or Morgan, or his crippled brother James, all of them mesmerized by the stunning realization that Wyatt Earp, who never lost his temper, intended to

beat Bob Wright to death before their very
eyes.

Finally Doc Holliday pushed through the
crowd, lowered a bloody rag from his mouth,
and gripped Wyatt's shoulder so hard his
knuckles went white in the gray morning
light.

"Wyatt," he said, "stop now."

Backhanded for his trouble, Holliday reeled
and fell, bleeding from the mouth, but got
back on his feet.

"Wyatt," he said again, with that whipcrack
emphasis he could sometimes produce. "Stop
now, or it will be *murder,* and you will *hang.*"

The rain, by then, had turned the street
into a soup of horse manure, trash, and gory
mud. Mouth agape, the red haze beginning
to clear, Wyatt stumbled back from Bob's
body and fell, sitting down hard in the slop.

"What should I do?" Morg was yelling.
"Doc! Tell me what to do!"

On all fours, hands gripping the ground,
John Henry Holliday was struggling to pull
air in, but every breath meant fighting a tide
of bright red blood going the other way.

"Get McCarty," he gasped. "Keep my right
side . . . higher than the left . . . or I'll drown."

"Somebody go get Doc McCarty!" Morgan
hollered, and Chuck Trask took off running.

Prone in the mud, Bob Wright rolled over
slowly. One limb at a time, he worked himself
onto throbbing, bleeding hands and rubbery

628

knees, and paused in that position to spit blood and gather himself. With a grunt, he got one foot underneath him and then the other, and lurched upright, a forearm pressing against the fractured rib. For a while he just stood there swaying, face to the sky, letting the rain sluice over him, diluting the blood and mud and sweat. His eyes were almost closed by bruising, but he peered out through the slits of his eyelids, and spit a gob of blood, and saw Doc Holliday do the same. His vision blurred again. Wiping at his face with a shirtsleeve he managed to clear one eye long enough to take satisfaction in the damage he'd done to Wyatt Earp, who was sitting slack-jawed in the mud, watching the dentist retch up red froth.

"My God," Wyatt said. "Did I do that?"

By that time, Chuck had sprinted back with the town doctor at his heels, carrying his medical bag. Ignoring the two panting, filthy brawlers, Tom McCarty knelt in the mire at his patient's side and put his ear near, trying to make out what John Holliday was saying.

"Cavitation," the dentist gasped, after coughing out another gout of foamy blood. "Left lung . . . Hit an artery."

"All right, get him up!" Tom McCarty ordered. "Get him home, out of this rain!"

Morgan and Bat each took an arm and a leg, Morgan careful to take the ones on the right because he was taller and that would keep his side higher than Bat's.

As Doc Holliday was carried away, everyone seemed to wake up to the wet. Soon the street was all but empty, nobody left but Eddie Foy, James and Wyatt Earp, and Bob Wright.

"Yeah, Wyatt," Bob told him through pulpy lips, "*you* did that to Doc Holliday. Tha's what you're good at: breaking faces, cracking skulls. Dumb ox. 'S a wonder you got brains enough t' chew your food. 'S not *me* wants you dead, Wyatt. Who wins the nex' election if you're killed? Not me! Not saloon men, Wyatt. The *reformers* win, you dumb bastard. George Hoover wins, you stupid sonofabitch!"

Slowly, painfully, Bob walked back to his house. Eddie took off for Doc's place, hurrying to catch up with Morg and Bat. Wyatt followed James back to the bordello.

Bessie ordered him a bath. The hot water arrived quickly, though China Joe didn't leave before giving Wyatt a look of open disdain that took a lot of nerve from a Chink. Beyond thought, Wyatt soaked the mud and blood off. James came in about half an hour later with a pile of clean clothes for him to borrow.

"Here's your teeth," James said, voice neutral. "Morg's staying with Doc. Mattie Blaylock's there, too. I'm going out to find Katie. McCarty won't say it, but Morg's pretty sure Doc's dying. Kate'll want to know."

The rest of the day passed in a steady gray downpour.

Around six in the evening, Eddie Foy took Verelda and a bottle of whiskey over to Bessie's. James led them to the kitchen, where Wyatt was sitting at the table, battered and remote. The room was small, so Verelda stayed in the doorway, curious but unwilling to go all the way in. She didn't mind Morgan and she liked James, but Wyatt had always scared her.

"Our boy's still alive," Eddie reported, getting glasses down off a shelf. "Drink this," he said, pouring a shot for Wyatt. "Good for what ails you."

Wyatt stared at the glass for a few moments. Then he drank, grimacing at the burn.

"Well done," said Eddie. "I believe I'll join you. James?"

James nodded, and the three of them had a second shot before Eddie sat back in his chair.

"A man walks into a bar," he proposed, like he was onstage. "He's got a mountain lion on a leash. Man says, Bartender, do you serve politicians in this place? Why, sure, the barkeep says. There's George Hoover right over there! Man says, All right then, I'll have a whiskey, and my friend here will have George Hoover."

Wyatt looked at him and spoke for the first time since the fight. "If tha's a joke," he mumbled, thick-lipped, "I'm too dumb t' get it."

"Wyatt, I'm from Chicago," Eddie told him. "Let me explain politics to you."

He poured them all a third and leaned across the table.

"The trick of it," said Eddie, "is that you always ask, Who gains? *Cui bono?* That's how the old Romans said it. Who gets the good of it? Ed Masterson dead, killed by a drunk. Damn bad luck for poor Ed, and the citizens are outraged! A city marshal, gunned down dead on Front Street, and everyone's after asking, What's it going to take to get a little law and order around here? Then Johnnie Sanders is carried off in that fire, and sure: wasn't it Big George at the wake, buttonholing everyone in sight, noising it around that it was Demon Rum did the poor boy in? Drunks killing lawmen. Drunks setting fires. So, now, ask yourself: *cui bono* if another lawman gets killed this season? Who gains, when Dog Kelley only won by three votes last time, and the next election balanced on a pinhead, so it is! Another fine upstanding officer dead, and him a teetotal Methodist, honest as the day is long! About time somebody got tough on the saloons, don't you know . . . Vote Reform, son. Vote Reform!"

Still in the doorway, listening, Verelda

632

finally worked up the nerve to speak to Wyatt. "I don't think it was George put the price on your head," she told him. "It's just a guess, but me? I bet it was Maggie."

The men all looked at her curiously.

Emboldened, Verelda stepped closer, poured herself a drink, and slugged back the shot.

"Maggie was a bitch even before she found Jesus and swore off booze. Now she wants to be the governor's wife: Mrs. Governor George Hoover!" Verelda sang with fruity ersatz propriety, waving an imperious hand in the air. "Presiding over Dry Kansas, like the goddam queen of Sheba."

He should have slept. The fight, and then the liquor. He hadn't had a drink in years, and it should have hit him hard, but in a stand-up contest, remorse and self-loathing can battle whiskey to a draw.

It was long past dark when Bat Masterson showed up at the kitchen door. James let him in. Bessie poured him a drink. Nobody said anything when he dumped Wyatt's gun belt and star on the table. Wyatt himself barely glanced at them.

Bat shook the rain off his hat and shrugged out of his slicker. "Took a while, but I convinced Driskill his kid had it coming," Bat reported. "And I told Bob Wright I'm off his payroll. He can get somebody else to ref his goddam fights. He still swears it wasn't him put the price on your head, but now he's claiming he 'heard from somebody' the offer was only good while you were wearing a badge —"

"Horseshit," James snorted. "You could see it in his eyes, Wyatt. He wanted you dead! Why else was he out on the street at five in the morning? He wanted to make sure Driskill got you!"

"A look in somebody's eyes ain't gonna stand up in court," Bessie pointed out.

Bat leaned over and tapped Wyatt's star. "You put that on, I'll back you," he told Wyatt, choosing sides at last. "But if you need work? We can use a faro dealer at the Lone Star. Full-time. Soon as your hands heal up."

Wyatt stared at the badge for a while. Finally, stiff and sore and silent, he got up and went to the window, where he watched the rain slide down the glass.

What the Irishman said about politics made sense. Big George Hoover would have campaigned waving Wyatt's bloody shirt and he probably would have won. Maggie might well have tried to make that possible. Still . . . Tobie Driskill had a grudge, too. His brother Jesse had more than enough money to offer a bounty. They might have known George Hoyt down in Texas —

Except Bat had just admitted that he

thought it was Bob.

And James was right, too. The sons of Nicholas Earp knew what scorn looked like. Wyatt had seen contempt in Bob Wright's eyes, and felt an unleashed, vindictive malevolence in every blow that landed. He was sure of this much. If Tobie Driskill *had* killed him last night, Bob Wright would've danced on his grave.

But that could all be true, and it still might have been somebody else entirely who offered the bounty — someone who hated Wyatt's guts for reasons Wyatt himself would never know. There were a lot of men in that category. He might never find out who put the price on his head in Dodge that year.

Doesn't matter, he thought.

Humiliated, ashamed, certain Doc Holliday was dying, he was sick of it all. Sick of politics. Sick of being hated. Sick of Dodge. Sick of himself.

"Hell," he said, thick-lipped. "I quit. They're gonna fire me anyways."

James slumped in relief and shouted, "Thank God!" Then he stood up straight and declared, "To hell with 'em! This town's played out! Let's all go down to Tombstone!"

"James!" Bessie cried. "I *ain't* movin' to Arizona! Dammit, there is nothin' there but gravel and scorpions —"

"And silver and miners and *money,* honey!"

The two of them were still arguing when

635

Wyatt heard footsteps coming up the back stairs and across the porch toward the kitchen door. "That's Morgan," he said, for Morg had grown up wearing Wyatt's hand-me-down shoes, and he still kind of shuffled when he walked.

Waiting for the door to open, everybody got quiet.

This is it, they were thinking. Doc's gone.

"Wyatt?" Morg said, standing just outside so as not to drip all over Bessie's floor. "He's asking for you. Best hurry."

CASHING OUT

PLAYING FOR KEEPS

In the top drawer of Dr. Tom McCarty's desk, there was an envelope labeled *J.H.H.* Inside it was a folded sheet of heavy rag paper bearing three lines of neat, copperplate handwriting.

DR. JOHN STILES HOLLIDAY
66 FORREST
ATLANTA, GEORGIA

Beneath that, in Tom McCarty's own scrawl, was a note: *Pt requests: notify post-mortem; ship body per instructions.*

At the end of September, John Holliday had given Tom that envelope and ten dollars to cover his final expenses. "I would like to be buried next to my mother," he said, buttoning his shirt over a chest dwindled down to bone. Tom tried not to show what he was thinking, but the dentist saw the look and recited, *"Youth grows pale, and spectre-thin, and dies . . ."*

"Goddammit, John! If you would take better care of yourself, I am sure you could retard the progress of the disease. Dodge is no good for you, son. Too much dust, too much excitement! And the winters here are brutal. You need clean air and decent meals and complete rest. Now, there's a sanatorium near Las Vegas that's had some success with cases every bit as advanced as yours and —"

"How much does it cost?"

"Two hundred a month, but that's room and board and doctors and —"

"Haven't got it," John said.

They'd had discussions like this before. Tom McCarty respected John Holliday as a gentleman and a professional, but the boy was plain stupid about money, spending it like a drunken drover when he had it and then acting like it was just his fate to be poor when it was gone. As for that woman he kept . . . Well, Tom knew better than to say anything, though he'd made his opinion known: Kate was a nymphomaniac and a hysteric and a drunk who had mined John Henry Holliday like he was the Black Hills. When Tom heard Kate had taken up with Bob after Alice Wright left town, he thought, Well, she knows when the vein is played out, damn her, but John's better off without the slut. Now Kate was back again, weeping and frantic, when what the boy needed was calm, quiet care.

Mattie Blaylock was no angel, but she was the sort of stolid, unemotional woman who made a good nurse, and Tom was grateful for her help. "Mattie," Tom said, lifting his chin toward Kate, "get her out of here."

"Go on, now, darlin'. I'll be fine," John mumbled.

"John, keep quiet!" Tom ordered.

Wiping his hands on a towel, the doctor waited until Mattie had pulled Kate out into the front room, closing the door behind her. Then he sat on the bed to collect his thoughts. The room looked like the aftermath of a birth, or an abortion, or a shooting. Bloodied, muddied clothes — rags now — were heaped in the corner. John was in the chair, propped up with pillows, hunched over an enamel basin half-filled with foamy red fluid. Almost naked, slick and stinking with sweat, ribs visible from spine to sternum.

The stench of gore and necrotic lung tissue was suddenly overwhelming. Tom cracked the window open, in spite of the chilly rain. "Tell me when you get cold."

Eyes closed, John whispered, "Still hot."

That would change soon: anemia competing with fever for ascendancy.

"Well," Tom said, sitting again, "my guess is that we can rule out Rasmussen's aneurysm."

"Dead by now," John agreed. "So: Roki—"

"Rokitansky's hemorrhage, yes, I think so

641

too, and dammit, I told you not to talk! The active bleeding's stopped. That's a good sign. If you can hold your own a while longer, we can try the lycopin extract, and you'll be able to get some sleep — Oh, hell! Now what?"

Out in the front room, Kate was in full cry. They heard Mattie Blaylock tell her sharply to shut up. The door to the bedroom opened. Two of the Earp brothers looked in. Morgan again. And Wyatt, who appeared to have been hit by a train. Already distorted by bruising and cuts, his face twisted when the smell hit him.

Then he saw Doc. "My God," he said.

"You see?" Kate was yelling. "You see what you did to him, God damn you! You killed him, you lousy sonofabitch!"

At the sound of Kate's curses, John's eyes fluttered open. "Wyatt," he said, sounding pleased to see him. "Kate, darlin' . . . Don't fuss . . . Not his fault."

"John! Keep quiet!" the doctor snapped. "And Kate, if you can't stop running your mouth, I'll throw you out of this house myself. Calm down, all of you! Wyatt, I don't know what in hell Kate's yelling about, but nothing you did caused this. Bleeding episodes are not unusual in consumptives. This has been coming on for weeks — maybe months! The disease has eaten out part of his left lung. The resulting cavity impinged on an artery, but a clot has formed. For the moment, the crisis has passed, but if he starts coughing again, he could bleed to death or die of apoplexy."

Hugging herself, Kate doubled over with a little moan of fear.

"Jesus, McCarty!" Morgan cried. "He's sitting right there! He can hear you!"

"He knows what's going on as well as I do — better!" Tom said. "I'm just telling *you* people what's happening, so you will shut up, and get out, and let him rest! Am I making myself clear? Everybody! Get the hell out!"

Over the next couple of hours, the bleeding started up twice more. Kate was banished to Bessie Earp's house. Morg and Wyatt and Mattie stayed at Doc's. Around three in the morning, Chuck Trask came by to tell Tom McCarty he was needed to sew up a knife wound.

"Spurting or oozing?" Tom asked.

"Just kinda leaking," Chuck said. "Wyatt? Morg? Are you coming to work? We're real shorthanded."

"I quit," Wyatt told him. This was news to Morg, but Wyatt said, "Nothing to do with you. Go on."

So Morgan left with Chuck, but before Tom McCarty followed them, he took Mattie and Wyatt to the kitchen and showed them how to measure out four grains of dried lycopin extract and stir it into a glassful of water.

"It's effective against the cough and mildly narcotic," he told them, pulling his coat on. "When he wakes up, you make him drink a glass of the mixture, but no more than one glass every two hours. Mattie, can you write?"

She nodded and shrugged: A little.

"Well, try to keep track of when you give him a dose, so he doesn't get too much. If he's cold, cover him. If he's hot, open the window again. I don't think he'll be hungry, but I'll stop by Delmonico's and have them send over some beef broth with plenty of salt. If he asks for anything, offer that."

Mattie said she'd keep watch the rest of the night. Wyatt knew he ought to stay, but this was so much like when Urilla was dying . . . So he went home and slept at last, but poorly. He was already up and dressed when Mattie came in a few hours later.

"Kate came back after McCarty left," she told him, hanging a damp shawl up on the peg next to the door. "Morg's back, too. He's staying with Kate so she won't be alone when Doc dies."

"So, you're sure? He's . . . ?"

"Never saw anybody that sick who didn't. Why'd you quit?"

He almost said, Because you were right about George Hoover. Because my father is right and I've got shit for brains. Because I don't know who my friends are. Because I don't know who to trust anymore, except my brothers.

What came out was "Politics." Which was true enough.

For the first time since she moved in, he wished that Mattie would talk more, for his own thoughts were loud in his mind. Maybe McCarty was right. Maybe what happened to Doc wasn't Wyatt's fault, just like it wasn't really Wyatt's fault when Urilla got typhus, but it sure felt like it was, and Mattie wasn't one to tell him different.

"I'm going next door," he said.

Morg answered the knock. Kate was slumped at the table, her head in her hands, too weary to look up. Wyatt's eyes went to the bedroom where Doc lay, dead white and so motionless beneath the covers Wyatt thought that he'd been laid out. It took a moment to see that Doc was breathing in shallow little gasps, but breathing all the same.

Morg said, "If you can stay with him awhile, I'll take Kate back to Bessie's so she can get some sleep."

Probably the first time a woman ever got any sleep in that place, Wyatt thought, but he told Morg he'd sit with Doc, and that Morg should get some rest, too.

"You know about the medicine?" Morg asked.

"Yeah," Wyatt said. "Go on."

"Wyatt . . . you really quit?"

645

"Yeah," Wyatt said. "Go on."

For the rest of the day, he kept watch by himself, listening to the clock tick, dozing sometimes in the chair. Late in the afternoon, there was a short, quiet dream about Urilla, probably brought on by sitting in a sickroom like this. He was telling her, "If I made more money, I coulda done better by you," and in the dream, he felt more than heard her say, "Don't fret, Wyatt."

He woke up slowly, feeling calm. Then he saw where he was, and straightened, and winced, aware of every bruise and cut and aching joint.

Doc was awake, his face expressionless.

"You snore," he told Wyatt, sounding feeble and aggrieved.

Wyatt started to smile, but it hurt too much and he quit.

Doc seemed to gather himself to say something important, and spoke as firmly as he could, though his voice was somewhere between a whisper and a whine. "Wyatt, I cannot make you another denture. No more fights. You get that mad again, shoot the bastard. Promise me."

"I promise. How do you feel, Doc?"

Doc's eyes closed. "Anyone makin' book?"

"Luke Short was giving ten to one you wouldn't make it through the night."

It was a joke. Luke was a gambler who

wasn't even in town anymore, but Doc murmured, "Bet against me? I would've."

Wyatt made him drink a glass of water with lycopin and got him settled back down. A few minutes later, Doc roused again.

"God damn Henry Kahn," he said, sounding briefly normal. "If he'd been a better shot, he'd have saved us all a lot of trouble."

There was nothing more for a while, and Wyatt supposed Doc had fallen asleep until a tear formed in the corner of the sick man's eye and slipped sideways toward the pillow. Wyatt got a handkerchief to dry the pale, bony face. Doc's eyes opened at the touch, but he was looking at something beyond the room.

"My poor mother . . ."

This is it, Wyatt thought. When they start talking about their mother, it's over.

A few minutes later, Doc spoke again.

"Oh, Wyatt," he whispered, too breathless to sob. "This's a terrible way to die."

He said very little during the week after the hemorrhage. "What's the date?" he asked once. Told it was October 13, he said clearly, "I was supposed to go to St. Francis. Wire my regrets to Alex von Angensperg."

There was a return telegram the next day. NIL DESPERANDUM STOP 152 CHILDREN 3 PRIESTS 7 NUNS PRAYING STOP MAY I VISIT STOP

It was Morgan Earp who answered. NO VISITORS YET STOP KEEP PRAYING STOP

A routine developed. Kate and Mattie took the nights. Morgan and Wyatt split the days. Lou kept them all fed. Tom McCarty came by to check on Doc, morning and evening.

No one else was permitted into the sickroom, but China Joe appeared each afternoon with a bowl of noodles and left instructions that Doc should eat them for a long life and to fatten up. The first time that happened, Doc came close to crying again.

"How thoughtful," he said. "Thank him for me, please."

On the first of November, China Joe showed up at the door as usual, only this time he insisted on waiting until Doc was awake. Morgan offered to take a message in, but the Chinaman would not go away until he was allowed to speak to Doc personally, and when he went into the bedroom, he shut the door behind him to keep the conversation private.

Dong-Sing had heard about the rebellion of Doc's lungs, of course, and now a single glance was enough to tell him that all Doc's *yin* organs were functioning poorly. He was as white and fragile as a porcelain bowl, and you didn't have to be an herbalist to see that he was in a dangerous condition.

"Mr. Jau," Doc said softly. "How kind of you to visit."

"You no talk!" Dong-Sing ordered. Coming closer, he sat on the edge of the chair by Doc's bed. "You no worry!" He looked around the little room and waved his hand at the roof and walls. "I no charge rent."

Doc's eyes widened.

Dong-Sing held his head up proudly. "All these my house. You no tell!" Leaning close to Doc, he whispered, "That nigger boy? He rich: he dead. Teach me big damn lesson. Colored fella get rich in America, no good! George Hoover, he front man! Nobody know China Joe rich fella. So I safe."

Having unburdened himself of more English than he had ever successfully strung into a single speech, Dong-Sing took a deep breath and let it out abruptly. Then he nodded once, emphatically, like an American. *There. I said my piece, by God.*

"Kill a chicken . . ." Doc remembered. "Scare a wolf . . . ?"

"Wolf more damn smart than chicken! Me? I know what what. Now I tell George Hoover, No rent for Doc!" Dong-Sing got even quieter. "You no tell Kate! She got big mouth, tell everybody."

"You have my word, sir," Doc told him. "And my gratitude."

Jau Dong-Sing stood up and made ready to go, but Doc was looking at him with the strange intensity of the very weak, and Dong-Sing was moved to add one thing more.

"I do you big damn favor," he said, his eyes full of pride and pleasure. "This one big damn happy day for me!"

A little while later, Kate came in with a mug of beef broth. "What did the Chink want?"

Doc was looking out the window, watching a cloud move across his field of view. "Nothin'," he said, in tones of wonderment. "Nothin' at all."

She set the mug down on the dresser and helped him sit up so he could drink the broth without choking, holding the cup for him, making sure he drank it all. When he was done, she fixed the pillows and bustled around, straightening the room.

"Kate."

She stopped what she was doing and looked at him, her lovely aquamarine eyes shadowed, the skin around them spidered by fine lines of worry and fatigue.

"Viens te coucher," he said.

She frowned, the lines deepening, but he asked again, so she came to his side and lay down, nestling under his right arm, her hand cool against his chest.

"Talk to me awhile," he said. "Tell me about . . . tell me about a day when you were happy."

For a long time she was quiet, her breathing regular and deep. Poor soul, he thought. This has been hard on her . . . When he felt the chill of her tears, he said again, "Talk to me. Tell me about it."

"It was right after the baby was born. Silas was gone, that bastard." She sat up, and reached for one of his handkerchiefs, and blew her nose, and smiled briefly. "Anyway, I was working again. The baby kept crying and crying. I didn't know what to do! Nobody wants a whore with a crying baby," she said wearily. "One of the girls said, 'There's a hospital that takes charity kids. You can bring him there, and the nuns'll take him.' So we went to the hospital, and I gave the baby to one of the sisters. I knew what she was thinking, but I was so tired . . . I didn't give a damn what she thought of me. And it was such a relief. Somebody who knew about babies was going to take care of him!"

Her face was pale and scrubbed. Her fine, fair hair was pulled back artlessly. He could see the scared girl she'd been at fifteen, and the hard woman she would be at fifty.

"The other girls took me out drinking, after," she told him. "We pooled our money and bought a bottle. For the first time since I was a girl — since before we left Mexico — I was *happy.* All us girls got drunk and we laughed and laughed, and I thought, I can't remember when I was so happy! This is the happiest night of my life!"

Kate stopped and cleared her throat. Her voice was ordinary when she went on. "I went back to the hospital, a couple of days later. To visit him. One of the nuns came out. She told me the baby was dead. He died the night I left him. While I was having such a good time."

Poor child, he thought. Poor child.

The baby. Kate. Either. Both.

"You did the right thing, to bring him to the nuns," he told her. "And you were happy because that little baby stopped by to bless his mamma on his way up to heaven."

She looked at him, and barked a bitter laugh, and wept. They slept together afterward. Side by side.

All through November, whenever anyone came to sit with him, Doc would say, "Talk to me. Tell me about a day when you were happy."

In the beginning, nobody was sure that Doc was really listening. The lycopin kept him asleep a great deal of the time, but hearing people talk seemed to soothe him, and it seemed harmless enough. Eventually, Morg realized that Doc was saying that same thing to everyone. Talk to me about a day when you were happy.

"What did you tell him?" Morg asked Wyatt.

"Oh, hell," said Wyatt. "I don't know."

He had spoken of Urilla. How she was stronger than he expected, looking at her. More determined to get her way than he'd imagined when he fell in love, but good-natured and good-hearted. When he gave up trying to read the law, she didn't hold him a failure for it. The happiest day was when he found out about their baby. Urilla's eyes were shining, like she was giving him a gift.

"And getting my teeth fixed," he told Doc. "And Roxana. That was good, too."

Doc didn't say anything. He gazed at Wyatt. Just . . . waiting.

"The good of things is always kinda mixed," Wyatt said then.

Looking out the window in Doc's room, he had tried to remember Urilla's laughter, but the sound of it was lost to him. Truth was, she and the baby were gone almost before he knew he had them. And getting his new teeth reminded him of losing the real ones. And riding Roxana always made him think of Johnnie Sanders.

That was when it came to him that the only unmixed happiness he could think of was when he quit his job with the city after that fight with Bob Wright. So he told Doc that, too, and said, "I never meant to be a lawman. Stumbled into it, really. When I quit, it was a weight off."

Dealing faro was better. No politics. Just the cards and the money. Nice of Bat to give him a job like he did. Not a lot of business this time of year, but even with winter coming, there was enough going on at the Lone

Star to keep one dealer working full-time.

He was embarrassed to think so much about his own life, and embarrassed that he'd told so much to Doc. He asked Morg, "What'd you say?"

Morg got that big, boyish grin of his. "Oh, I said it was hard to name something particular. I'm happy a lot of the time. James said it was when Bessie agreed to marry him. Bessie said it was the third time James told her, 'Don't worry, honey. I'll take care of it.' First time he told her that, she didn't believe he would, but he did. The second time, she still expected him to forget or not do it, but the third time, she thought, I can count on him. I don't have to do everything myself. She said that was the first time in her whole life she believed she could count on a man. And Lou? She told Doc she's happy every morning when I get home safe from work. Isn't that sweet?"

"Mattie say anything?"

Morg hesitated. He wanted to tell Wyatt that Mattie was happy on the day Wyatt said she could stay with him, or something like that. But Wyatt could always tell when Morgan was lying.

"She's still thinking," Morg said.

"Seems kinda strange, Doc asking people to talk about things like that."

Morg thought it over. He and Doc were the same age, and Morg tried to imagine being so sick, but it was hard. When you're young and strong, it seems like you'll live forever just the way you are, but Doc probably couldn't even remember what it felt like to be healthy.

"I guess — You know how people say, Don't borrow trouble? Well," said Morgan, "I guess it's the opposite of that. Doc is borrowing happiness."

The weeks passed. The patient's color improved. His chest pain abated.

Tom McCarty eased off on the lycopin; John still managed to sleep a good deal of the time. When he sat up, he didn't cough much. The cough itself was drier. His appetite began to return.

When the dentist felt well enough to complain about being bored, McCarty partially lifted the embargo on visitors, but restricted him to no more than one a day. It was imperative that the boy not tire himself out just as he'd begun to make some gains.

Eddie Foy was the first to visit, but it was to say good-bye. His contract at the Commie-Q was over. He was going back to Chicago, where he had work lined up at a theater over Christmas and New Year's.

Isabelle Wright came by as soon as she heard it was permitted. She offered to read books to Dr. Holliday during his convales-

cence, but for some reason he wasn't willing
to let her see him. When Morgan asked why,
Doc said, "I am the ghost of Christmas yet
to come." That didn't make any sense, but
Doc wouldn't explain. "Just thank her for
me," he said. "Tell her I am not yet fit
company for a young lady."

Morgan wired Alex von Angensperg that
Doc could have visitors, and the priest arrived by train two days later. "He was real
glad to hear you were coming," Morg told
Alex as they walked to Doc's from the depot.
"He looks bad, but he's better, honest. Kate
sleeps over at my place, days. She'll be back
later. Her and Mattie and Wyatt and me take
turns with him. Don't let him get wound up.
He's not supposed to get excited."

Morgan left Alex in Doc's room. The
weather was still pretty nice, and Morg went
outside to sit on the front porch so they could
talk without him hearing. Things stayed quiet
for a while, but the conversation got louder
and more lively. Finally Morg decided he'd
best go back in and settle the two of them
down.

By that time, the priest was laughing so
hard he was almost crying, though Doc was
only smiling, propped up on a pile of pillows
and lying under a heap of quilts that Mabel
Riney brought over when she first heard that
he was sick.

"Why, hello, Morgan!" Doc said, sounding

mildly surprised to see him, like they hadn't spent damn near every day of the last six weeks together. "Father von Angensperg and I were just discussin' the vagaries of translation from Greek and Latin to English."

"We were speaking of Handel's *Messiah*," Alex told Morg.

"Which I heard for the first time when I was ten —" Doc said.

"— and the text was *He gave his back to smiters,* but Doc heard the choir wrong —"

"And I spent a very long afternoon wonderin', Now why would Jesus give his hat to spiders . . . ?"

Alex busted up laughing again. Then Morgan asked how a handle could have a messiah and the priest laughed even harder, but Doc explained about how the *Messiah* was music, and a man named Handel wrote it. Morgan told the two of them to behave themselves and not let Doc get overtired.

About half an hour later, Wyatt arrived for the afternoon shift just as Alex came back out into the front room, pulling the door closed behind him. "He's sleeping," Alex reported. "Hello, Wyatt. Good to see you again."

For a time they all spoke quietly about how ill Doc had been, how near to death.

"I hope you know how much he appreciates your care," Alex told the Earps.

"For I was sick, and you came to me," Wyatt said.

"Nah," Morgan said. "It was selfishness."

Wyatt and Alex were both surprised, but Morgan just shrugged.

"Doc doesn't have any brothers," he told Alex. "So we took him for our own."

November ended. Doc continued to make gains. Explanations varied.

Perhaps it was the prayers of Indian children that saved him.

Perhaps it was simply rest and care. And Jau Dong-Sing's noodles.

Most likely James Earp came closest to the truth.

"That's why it took us four damn years to beat them rebs," he said. "Skinny, inbred sonsabitches are tougher than they look."

Whatever the reason for his survival, by early December John Henry Holliday was laying plans to defy his doctor's orders to stay home and stay quiet. Two months cooped up in a little rented house were all that he could bear. He craved bright lights and noise, more company and livelier conversation. He became determined to celebrate the eve of his twenty-seventh Christmas by escorting Kate to a party that Bat Masterson was throwing at the Lone Star Dance Hall that night.

And nobody could talk him out of it.

Wilfred Eberhardt was paid a dime to shine the dentist's boots to a fine black gleam. Jau Dong-Sing was called upon to take in the seams of Doc's best suit. A note was sent to Wright's General Outfitting Store, ordering a burgundy cravat and a silk shirt in pale pink, to set off the newly fitted frock coat of fine dove gray wool.

Doc wanted Kate to order a gown for the party as well, but they were still living off the two grand she'd won from Eli Grier. With no money coming in, Kate was concerned about expenses. She insisted that her blue silk would do for Bat's party, but Doc would not take no for her answer and wore her to a nubbin on the topic.

On the evening of the twenty-fourth, she made him wait in the front room while she took her time getting dressed. When she emerged, she was glowing like a bride in a grass green satin that brought out the aquamarine of her eyes.

Doc got to his feet. "Sweet Jesus," he breathed. "Darlin', you are a vision, and I am a lucky man."

He helped her into her wrap and offered her his arm. They strolled toward town, stopping now and then to let him catch his breath and to gaze upward, for the west Kansas sky is black velvet on clear, cool December nights, and the Milky Way is strung across it like the diamond necklace of a crooked banker's mistress.

Turning onto Front Street, they could hear Beeson's Famous Cowboy Band and agreed that the musicians were pretty good. Chalkie had provided them with first-rate instruments and imported a decent conductor as well. Bat had rented their services for the evening.

"Is that Strauss?" Kate asked.

"Does anyone else write waltzes?"

"Oh! Speaking of Vienna! I saw Alex von Angensperg today. He came on the afternoon train."

"He stayin' longer this time?"

"Overnight at least. He's here to do midnight Mass for the Germans. He'll be at the party tonight."

Presuming that he had the strength, Kate stepped aside and let Doc open the door of the dance hall for her. They stood in the entry for a minute, letting their eyes adjust to the dazzle.

"Well, now," Doc said. "Looks like Sheriff Masterson takes the prize."

It was Bat's widely reported goal to spend more on his Christmas party than Doc Holliday had famously squandered on Johnnie Sanders' wake. By all appearances, he had achieved his ambition. The Lone Star was festive with drapery, blazing with candles and lamps, jammed with couples dancing. At dozens of tables crowded around the edges of the large main room, guests were taking full advantage of expensive booze and lavish food brought in by train from St. Louis, and made available in abundance. Hundreds of people were crammed into the place. Even the more prosperous German farmers had been invited, for they were becoming an important voting block that liked its beer and opposed the temperance reforms. Bat was courting votes.

Word got around that Doc Holliday and Kate had arrived. People started coming over to say hello to the dentist and to lie about how well he looked. Christmas Eve was a big night at the brothel, so Bessie and James were working, but Wyatt and Mattie led the way to a table where Morg's girl, Lou, was saving a couple of places for Doc and Kate. Wyatt told Kate quietly, "We got a table near the door, so you can leave easy if he gets tired," while Doc told Mattie that she looked ravishin'. Even if she wasn't sure what that word meant, Mattie could tell it was nice and said, "Thank you," with a smile.

The band started a polka. Wyatt asked Mattie if she'd like to dance.

"No," she said. "Dance with Lou."

Clapping her hands, Lou jumped up. "Thank you, Mattie — I'll just borrow him until Morg gets here! Come on, Wyatt!"

Grabbing his hand, Lou pulled Wyatt toward the dance floor. Foot tapping to the music, Doc watched them for a time. Wyatt was surprisingly light on his feet, and Lou was very good.

"We should go to Las Vegas," Kate decided.

Doc looked at her. "Las Vegas?" he said, as though she were mad, and that settled it.

"This town's played out. Ain't been a decent game since September."

"Wait five months. The cattlemen will be back."

The polka ended. Lou and Wyatt stayed on for a reel.

"How many two hundreds in fourteen hundred eighty?" Kate asked.

"A little more than seven. Why?"

"Then we still got enough money! Let's try five or six months at that sanatorium."

We, he thought.

"Are you — the goddess of parsimony — seriously suggestin' that we spend two hundred dollars a month so I can lie around listenin' to lungers cough night and day?"

"You get used to it," she told him and pointed out, *"Si finis bonus est, totum bonum erit."*

What ends well is wholly good.

Her Latin was always a treat.

"God a'mighty," he said when he noticed: "That piano's been tuned."

Kate was smiling. "Merry Christmas. I brought in a man from St. Louis. Go on! Play something."

He couldn't seem to move. "I'm out of

practice," he said.

"So? If you hit a wrong note, *ces sauvages ne sauront pas connaître la différence.*"

She watched his face, and her own softened.

"Play, Doc," she said again, more gently this time. "Play something for me, *mon amour.*"

Dodge was big enough now to need a few policemen even over the winter, though most of the saloons on the south side of the tracks were shut for lack of business this time of year. Tonight pretty much everything in town was closed, but Morgan Earp walked his rounds, checking locks and making sure nobody had decided to break in and help himself to a few bottles while everyone else was over at Bat Masterson's party.

Morg still felt strange wearing a badge when Wyatt wasn't, but Wyatt insisted he was "retired" and swore he'd never put a star on again. "It's all politics," he'd tell folks who asked why he resigned. "I'm just a faro dealer now," he'd say. Sometimes he'd add, "Money don't lie to your face." Course, everybody knew Wyatt would have been fired if he hadn't quit after his fight with Bob Wright. It was Bat who convinced the city council to keep Morgan on during the off-season. ("He tried to stop that fight. Just 'cause they look alike don't mean they're the same man. Mor-

663

gan didn't do anything wrong.") No arguing it, though. Dodge was pretty much done for the Earps. They'd be moving soon.

With Doc so sick this fall, they'd missed the good weather for traveling, but come spring, James was set on going all the way south to Tombstone. Every week there was more news about the big silver strike down there, and Bessie had finally agreed to go. For a while, Wyatt had talked of how him and Morg and Virgil could start up a stagecoach service between Prescott and the silver towns in the south of the territory, but Morg said he wasn't sure it was a good idea to compete with Wells Fargo, which was already well established in that part of the territory. So Wyatt worked all the figures again. The plan now was to stay in Dodge until Roxana foaled in the spring. In the meantime, they'd all save as much cash as they could from the brothel and Morg's salary and Wyatt's cut at the Lone Star so they'd have some capital when they arrived in Arizona and could take advantage of opportunities.

Lou came around to the move after she got a letter from her father making it plain that the family was still against her marrying a Methodist. Mattie Blaylock didn't seem to care one way or the other. Asked about going to Prescott or Tombstone, she shrugged and said, "Whatever Wyatt decides."

"I wish she'd say what she wants," Wyatt

told Morg once, but Mattie wasn't that sort.

Over at the Lone Star, a cheer went up at midnight, and everybody yelled, "Merry Christmas!" Morgan and Alex von Angensperg had talked that afternoon about meeting up at Bat's party, but now Morg figured they could walk over together when the service let out, so he drifted toward the Union Church to listen to the Catholics singing.

The songs were real pretty, even if you couldn't understand a word of what anybody said, and he could still keep an eye on Front Street while sitting on the church steps. When the doors opened, Morg got to his feet, and tipped his hat to the ladies and said "Evening" to the men, and went inside to wait while Alex took off the fancy robes he wore when he was working.

The priest had a regular suit on underneath. That surprised Morg, and he was going to ask about it when Wil Eberhardt and one of the Riney boys ran into the church, yelling, "Mr. Earp! Your brother says come quick! It's Doc Holliday!"

"What's wrong?" Morg asked. "Is he sick again?"

"Morgan, go!" Alex cried. "I'll come as soon as I can!"

The kids took off running. Morgan followed. The Famous Cowboy Band had stopped playing, and Morg pushed through the doors of the Lone Star, asking, "What's the trouble?" because everybody was standing up, like they were watching a fight or something.

Kate turned and shushed him. That was when he heard the piano.

Alexander von Angensperg was right behind him. Sounding thunderstruck, he said, "*Mein Gott* . . . It's the *Emperor*!"

Which made no sense to Morgan, but Kate looked stunned.

"Are you sure?" she asked Alex, and when he nodded, her hands went to her lips. "But that's — That's what Doc used to play for his mother . . ."

Doc? Morg thought. Except it couldn't be only him, because there were two people playing, it sounded like. He eased around until he could see better, and damn if it wasn't just Doc, all alone at the piano, his back to the crowd, and he was playing something . . . something so . . . *wonderful* that Morgan didn't even notice when Wyatt came over to stand beside him.

"Did you know he could play like that?" his brother asked.

"Hell, Wyatt," Morg murmured. "I didn't know anybody could play like that."

For he had never heard anything like it — did not know such music existed in the world — and it was hard to believe that a man *he* knew could play it with his own two hands.

There were parts of it like birdsong, and parts like rolling thunder and hard rain, and parts that glittered like fresh snow when the sun comes out and it's so cold the air takes your breath away. And parts were like a dust devil spinning past, or a cyclone on the horizon, and all of it cried out for words that he had only read in books and had never said aloud.

Glorious. Majestic. Sublime.

Everyone else — even those who'd had too much of Bat's liquor — must have felt the same, for they had all fallen silent: all of them watching Doc Holliday sway and bend and reach, as his hands flew and darted and skimmed across the keys.

When it seemed that the music had come to its end, everyone began to clap, but Alexander von Angensperg held up his hand. In a quiet, urgent voice, he told them, "Wait!" And sure enough, the music went on, but it was softer now, and simpler.

Morgan felt Lou's hand steal into his own. "Look!" she whispered.

He followed her gaze and saw Kate's face crumple, and Morg felt like crying himself, especially when Alex drew Kate toward his chest and held her like a weeping child.

Eyes closed, the priest began to sing to her, wordlessly crooning the melody that Doc played. Slowly, slowly, the notes began to rise and come together, until . . . they turned into the saddest, prettiest thing Morgan Earp had ever heard.

When the music could not have been lovelier or more moving, it changed again: first, like it wasn't sure what would come next, and then like it had made up its mind, by God, and turned itself into a sort of thrilling waltz.

Alex said something in German.

Kate wiped her face, and answered him in kind.

With his hand held high and her palm upon his wrist, a shabby Jesuit missionary led a hardened cow-town harlot to the center of a tawdry dance hall in Dodge City, Kansas. Standing taller and straighter, the priest took on the martial bearing of the cavalry officer he would have been, had the voice of the Holy Spirit not seemed so strong and so insistent. Dropping into a deep and graceful curtsy, the whore lifted her arms to him, like the imperial lady-in-waiting that she might have become, had Maximiliano Primero not been overthrown. There, before a thousand eyes, the two of them began to dance, first alone, then joined by Lou and Morgan, and then by another couple, and another, and another, until the Lone Star Dance Hall had become a grand Viennese ballroom filled with whirling dancers and swirling, sparkling music.

Ghost lives, Wyatt thought, and Mattie must have been moved as well, for she was weeping, so Wyatt took her hand.

"Mattie," he said, "would you like to dance?"

"*Yes*," she said, and then she broke his heart. "Yes, but I don't know *how!*"

So he held her instead, and they stood together, letting themselves be lifted away, carried outside themselves toward a time and place beyond their imagining as the music raced and tumbled and sailed out through the darkness toward the Kansas prairie, demanding more and more of the man who played it —

Going cold, Wyatt thought, He can't keep this up. He'll start to cough. His lungs will bleed again.

But it was Wyatt himself who could not breathe, gripped by a fear so strong, it seemed to stop the beating of his heart. Fear that this dance would end too soon. Fear that this music would be wrenched away from Doc — from all of them — before it was meant to end.

And though none of Wyatt's prayers had ever once been answered, and though he knew that his soul was not pure and his faith was not strong, and though he could not understand why God always took the best and the sweetest to his bosom and left the dregs to get meaner and worse — in spite of it all, he began to pray. *Dear Lord, please, give him time! Please, Lord, let him finish!*

But John Henry Holliday was praying too, just as earnestly and to any god who might listen. *Now. Now. Now. Take me now.*

Now: with this music beneath his hands. Now: while he was still a gentle man who might have made his mother proud. Now: while beauty could still beat back the blind and brutal disease that was eating him alive.

So he held nothing back, tempting the Fates, defying them, seducing them.

Now: as he bent into thunderous, muscular chords.

Now: as he drew back for brilliant, chiming fantasies.

Now: as he hurled his hands into the impossibly swift runs across the keyboard.

Now, now, *now,* he prayed when the music darkened and fell, and spun and caught itself, and rose again, until at last — Orpheus to his own soul — he climbed beyond Hades' grasp, beyond himself, beyond the terrifying, suffocating horror that awaited him, until exhaustion and peace had claimed him, as the music floated — softly, lightly — downward, and he let it end on the quiet chords before the final arpeggio.

Breathless and blinking like a newborn, he came back to the world around him, awakening first to rapt silence as the last notes died away, and then to applause and cheers and amazement.

"Well, did you ever!"

"I had no idea he could —"

"By God! Now, that was something!"

And he was surprised to see that sometime during the concerto, Kate had come to sit beside him on the bench, and that she was sobbing.

"*Ne meurs pas, mon amour!* Don't die on me!" she begged as he took her in his arms. "Don't die, Doc. Please, don't die."

"I am doin' my best, darlin'."

"Promise you won't leave me!"

"You have my word. Hush, now. Hush. Don't cry."

"Promise you won't leave?"

"I promise." He gave her a handkerchief.

"Liar! Everyone leaves," she muttered bitterly, and blew her nose. "Or they die."

"You have me there," he admitted. "Everybody dies."

She laid her head against that traitorous, murderous chest of his.

"Oh, Doc," she whispered, "I want to go *home.*"

"I know, darlin'."

"Take me home. Please, Doc, take me home!"

"And where is that?" he wondered. "Where is home for us now?"

Us, she thought.

She started to laugh, and wiped her eyes, and said, "Las Vegas! Please, Doc, let's try it. Just six months! Please!"

"No," he told her, though he held her close. "No, and that's final."

In late April of 1879, Dr. Robert Holliday received a note postmarked "Dodge City, Kansas."

Please forgive the long silence. I have been poorly for some time and my health remains brittle. This is to inform you that I will be moving to Las Vegas in the New Mexico Territory. I have made a place for myself in Dodge and I am sorry to leave, but the winter is severe here, perhaps worse for me than summers back in Georgia. There are hot springs near Las Vegas and a sanatorium that is the latest thing in tubercular Society. We club together and pay some quack who pretends to know what's good for us while we cough our lungs out. I don't put much stock in the enterprise, but I have a passel of children praying on me and I hate to disappoint them. Tell Martha Anne I will write soon. Give my love to the family, and tell Sophie Walton how much I miss her.
— YOUR COUSIN JOHN HENRY

■ ■ ■ ■

THE RAKE

■ ■ ■ ■

THE BITCH IN THE DECK

In 1930, the Arizona Pioneers' Home in Prescott admitted an eighty-year-old woman who called herself Mary K. Cummings. By the end of her first week, the old lady was thoroughly disliked by the entire staff. Their antipathy was returned, in spades. Imperious, opinionated, blunt, and profane, Mrs. Cummings would spend the next ten years firing off ungrammatical letters to the governor of Arizona, informing him of graft, corruption, inefficiencies, and generalized malfeasance by the employees of the Arizona Pioneers' Home and demanding an official investigation of conditions there.

The governor's replies, if any, have not survived.

Mary K. Cummings was merely the last in the old woman's impressive collection of names. The baby who began life in Hungary as María Katarina became María Catarina in Mexico, Mary Katharine in Iowa, and just plain Kate in Kansas. Her maiden surname was certainly Harony. Or perhaps Haroney. Whether she really married Silas Melvin as a pregnant teenager is unclear. She used the surname Fisher for a while and was also known as Katie Elder while a working whore in Kansas, Texas, and Arizona. Nobody ever called her Big Nose Kate to her face.

Not twice, anyway.

In her old age, Kate sometimes claimed that she had married John Henry Holliday. That was wishful thinking, though it was true that they were together, off and on, for the final nine years of his life. After Doc's death, Kate did marry a blacksmith named George Cummings; he turned out to be a mean drunk so she left the bastard, though she kept his name. Finally, at the turn of the century, she became the housekeeper for a mining man named John J. Howard. With no disrespect to the dead, we may wonder if Kate was more to him than a housekeeper, for she stayed with Mr. Howard for three decades; upon his death, in 1930, she became both executrix of his will and sole heir to his modest estate.

In 1939, a year before she died, Kate was approached by two publishers who wanted her to write a memoir about the legendary gunman *Doc Holliday*. She was surprised to find that anyone was still interested. Doc had been briefly famous, along with the Earp brothers, after the gunfight at the O.K. Corral, but nearly sixty years had passed since that half-minute shoot-out.

Doc himself and his family back in Georgia were deeply distressed by the notoriety that attached itself to his name after the events in Arizona. He moved to Colorado and he did his best to live there quietly, but his efforts to drop out of sight were only partially successful. Toward the end of his life his name was in the newspapers again when he shot a man named Billy Allen. For all Doc's reputation as a deadly pistoleer, he only wounded Allen. After he was arrested for attempted murder, John Henry Holliday's entire defense was to sit in a Leadville, Colorado, courtroom — all 122 pounds of him — coughing relentlessly. When it came time to speak, he admitted that he was destitute. In desperation, he had borrowed five dollars from Billy Allen and was unable to repay the debt on time. Allen, who outweighed Doc by fifty pounds, had declared to all who would listen that he planned to kill Doc over the matter.

"If he got hold of me, I'd have been a child in his hands," Doc said, and everyone in court could see that was true.

Sick as he was, Doc testified, he still valued his life, and so he had defended himself. After a few minutes' deliberation, the jury voted to acquit, but the trial was a sorry affair that made humiliating headlines and added misery to Doc's last months.

Thirty years later, Bat Masterson earned

Kate's everlasting contempt by pimping Doc's memory in a magazine article that portrayed the dentist as a bitter, bad-tempered drunk who killed without cause or conscience — libel that would be repeated for a hundred years. Then, in 1931, a successful posthumous biography of Wyatt Earp reminded people of Doc's part in the Tombstone gunfight. It was Wyatt's defense of Doc's good character that sent those two publishers to Kate when they heard that Doc Holliday's woman was still alive.

After some thought, Kate concluded that Doc would have been pleased if she could turn his misfortune to her advantage. She had almost signed the book contract when she found out the cheap bastards weren't going to pay her for the work, so she told the publishers to go to hell.

Nevertheless, thoughts of Doc preoccupied Kate at the end of her own long life. Of all the men she'd been with — and there must have been a thousand or more in two decades of active frontier prostitution — only John Henry Holliday remained memorable. The rest were as obvious and as easily dealt with as a phallus. Doc was different, start to finish. She never truly understood that man, but she loved him in her way.

A single letter from Kate has been preserved. Written in the last year of her life, it includes an outline of her time with Doc and an unflattering portrayal of Wyatt Earp, whom Kate considered an illiterate bumpkin. She hardly mentioned Morgan; that might seem odd, but Kate was the kind who remembered animosity more passionately than affection, and it was impossible to dislike Morgan Earp. He and Kate had forged a bond at Doc's bedside back in Dodge, and she always appreciated the way Morg could tell when his own easy strength and robust health were a comfort and a support to Doc, and when they felt like mockery and an undeserved rebuke.

That first hemorrhage was neither the last nor the worst that Doc survived, but it remained the most frightening — for Doc himself and for those who cared about him. "You get used to it," Doc always said. "You can get used to anything." Used to the gnawing pain; used to the sudden taste of iron and salt; used to the struggle to pull air in as blood from his lungs rose. After 1878, Kate and the Earps knew what to do when Doc started coughing blood and they, too, got used to the way he would rally and recover. "Cheatin' the Fates is gettin' to be a habit," Doc would say, but his cough and breathlessness worsened steadily, and each successive episode of bleeding left him weaker than before.

Please thank the children for their prayers and tell them I am not dead yet, he wrote in a letter to Alex von Angensperg after a bout of pneumonia in December of 1879. *That said, I appear to be decomposing considerably ahead of schedule. Kate finds me poor company.*

And so did everyone else.

When he was sober, intensifying pain left him sleepless and short-tempered, so he drank to get relief, and it took a lot of bourbon to do the job. When drunk, he found it difficult to govern his sly, teasing tongue. Either way — sober and snappish or drunk and droll — he was accumulating enemies. Warned, he was defiant. Kate began to feel that he was courting death and left him twice, but came back again when he asked her to join him in Tombstone.

By then liquor had begun to erode the quick wit and thoughtful intelligence that Morgan had liked so much in Doc. He, too, was worried by the chances Doc took, but no matter how difficult Doc became, Morg stuck by him. "He is a brother to me," Morg always said. That loyalty was mutual. When the Clanton and McLaury brothers faced off against the Earps at the O.K. Corral in October of 1881, John Henry Holliday stood at Morgan's side.

In Kate's opinion, the men involved in that shoot-out were spoiling for a fight and they got what they all wanted. Her account of the showdown in Tombstone is remarkable for its focus on the aftermath, when Doc retreated to their hotel room, sat on the side of their bed, and wept. He seemed stunned that what started as a misdemeanor arrest had gone so wrong, so quickly. Three men dead; Morgan and Virgil Earp badly wounded. "Doc was all broken up," Kate recalled, "and he kept saying, 'This is awful. This is just awful.' " Kate herself was worried that Wyatt and Doc would be lynched by Ike Clanton's friends.

Morg and Virgil recovered. Doc and the Earps were exonerated of wrongdoing by a judge, but Kate was right. Ike's friends weren't the kind to forgive and forget. On the night of March 18, 1882, Morgan Earp was shot in the back while playing billiards: retaliation for the deaths of the three men killed during the gunfight at the O.K. Corral.

When Morgan died in Wyatt's arms, no one — not even Virgil or James — understood the depth of Wyatt's loss or shared his grief and rage and guilt as fully as Doc Holliday. It was Doc who bought the blue suit that Morgan was buried in. And when Wyatt Earp left Tombstone to avenge his brother's murder, Doc Holliday was right beside him.

From that day forward, legend would link their names as halves of an iconic frontier friendship, but Kate knew the truth. Without Morgan to draw them together, Wyatt and Doc had little in common apart from the desire to see Morg's killers dead in the dirt. When that was accomplished, Wyatt and Doc split up and soon lost contact.

Kate was glad of that at first. She had never liked Wyatt, but with Morgan gone and the Earps scattered, the full burden of Doc's care soon settled onto her own small shoulders. That load was sometimes more than she could bear.

Doc understood why she fled and never held it against her. *Kate is gone again and it is my fault,* he wrote to Alex von Angensperg in a copperplate hand loosened by drink. *She is weary of life with a man who has been dying for years and cannot seem to finish the job. The strain of a long illness will exhaust the most compassionate.*

Despite Kate's occasional interference, John Henry had continued to correspond with his cousins, though his notes became brief and infrequent as his condition deteriorated. When Martha Anne wrote of her decision to enter the Catholic Order of the Sisters of Mercy, it made no great difference between them. Distance and time had worked their changes. Their childhood romance had long since mellowed into cousinly caring. John Henry's last letter to Sister Mary Melanie was dated May 5, 1887, and postmarked in Leadville, Colorado. *Thank you for your prayers, dear heart. I have nothing happy to report. I will be moving to Glenwood Springs when I am well enough to stand the journey.*

Mountain air may help.

If anything, Glenwood's thin air and sulfur springs hastened his decline. In September, Doc wrote to Kate, asking her to join him. She could tell from his handwriting how weak he was and came as quickly as she could. He was waiting on a bench at the stagecoach depot the afternoon she was due to arrive. Kate walked right past him.

He called her name. The effort set off a coughing fit more recognizable than the man himself. Eyes hollow, cheeks sunken, John Henry Holliday was a fragile old man at thirty-six: bent and emaciated, his fine ash-blond hair now thinned and silver-white.

He had beaten the odds before and believed that, with Kate's care, he could do it again. But there are games that cannot be won, no matter how cleverly they are played. Consumed by fever, weakened by pneumonia, undermined by alcohol and laudanum, exhausted by the violent cough that shook him day and night, John Henry Holliday died, like his mother before him, too young, after a terrible struggle with tuberculosis.

Kate was at his side.

He had wished to leave some sort of legacy but he was penniless at the end. Kate used her own savings to pay his bill at the Glenwood Springs Hotel. In memory of Doc's ruinous, reflexive openhandedness, she even gave small cash gifts to members of the hotel staff who had been especially kind to them during the last days of Doc's life.

The Deadly Dentist's malign reputation had grown larger as the man himself dwindled, but people in Glenwood Springs would remember Doc Holliday with respect. As the hotel bellhop told a reporter, "We all liked him. He bore his illness with fortitude, and he was grateful for the slightest kindness. Doc was a very fine gentleman, and he was always generous when he tipped."

It was his hands that Kate would remember.

After that autumn back in Dodge, Kate was always aware of how loose Doc's grip on life was, of how easily life could be pulled away from that frail, fierce, proud man. For years, she had feared that one day he might simply let go of life, or fling it away in a moment of disgust or despair, but to the very end, those skillful, talented, beautiful hands remained the strongest part of him. It was only as he lay dying that she understood just how much John Henry Holliday had wanted to live.

After Kate's own death in 1940, scraps of notes were found in her belongings. Several appeared to be part of what might have become a longer account of her life with Doc. *He was considered a handsome man,* she wrote. *He was a gentleman in manners to the Ladies and everyone. He was a neat dresser and saw to it that I was dressed as nicely as himself.* On another page she wrote, *Being quiet, he never hunted trouble. If he was crowded he knew how to take care of himself. He was not a Drunkard,* she insisted. *He always kept a bottle near, but when he needed something for his Pain, he would only take a small drink.*

Other notes were more philosophical. *Doc Holliday learned to live without fear the year he met me, but Hope tormented him.* And another read, *Doc was the only American I ever met who was better educated than me.* There was also the start of a letter to Sophie Walton, an elderly woman herself by then, still living with members of the Holliday family. Kate wanted to tell her that Doc always drank a toast "To Sophie" whenever he won big; the letter was never sent, probably because Kate didn't know Sophie's address.

So there is reason to believe that Kate was planning to write a memoir, though she was nearing ninety when she started and didn't get far. Perhaps she simply didn't have time to see the project through. Perhaps she found it too difficult to write in English, never her strongest language. Magyar and German were both wrong for the task. Her French and Latin were good; either might have fit her story.

Ultimately, she may have settled upon Greek. There was a short but complete essay about the derivation of the name Odysseus, which Kate translated as "One who, being wounded, wounds." And then there was this.

> O divine Poesy, goddess-daughter of Zeus!
> Help me sing the story of
> A various-minded vagabond:
> Forced by the Fates into far exile,
> Made sport of by heartless Hope
> When, all the while,
> His heart hungered for home.

> Thus sang Blind Homer of Odysseus,
> who was wily to begin with
> and made more so
> by his wanderings.
> And that was the Doc Holliday I knew.

At the bottom of the page, there was one last line in an elderly woman's wavering, spidery script.

> Calypso did the best she could.

AUTHOR'S NOTE

When Homer sang of Troy and Vergil wrote of Carthage and Rome, no one expected a bright line to divide myth from history. Arriving at the end of historical fiction today, the modern reader is likely to wonder, "How much of that was real?" In this case, the answer is: not all of it but a lot more than you might think.

To simplify the narrative in the first chapter, I have taken liberties with the details of John Henry Holliday's childhood, but the portrayal of his character and personality is firmly based on Karen Holliday Tanner's biography *Doc Holliday: A Family Portrait* (University of Oklahoma Press, Norman, 1998). A member of Doc's own family, Tanner had unprecedented access to private records and family documents, including one that recorded Sophie Walton's memories of John Henry before he went west for his health. Tanner took care to verify or debunk the many claims of murder and mayhem made against the man; her research has allowed me to write about Alice McKey Holliday's son, and not about the many fictional characters who have borne John Henry Holliday's name.

Tanner's biography also provides genealogical charts showing the relationship between John Henry's first cousin Martha Anne Holliday and the novelist Margaret Mitchell. Mitchell grew up hearing family stories about the war and later used them as background for *Gone with the Wind;* anyone familiar with Tanner's *Doc Holliday* will notice many elements of Holliday family history in the Mitchell novel.

A great deal has been written about the Earp brothers; both the quality of research and the opinions expressed vary widely. Nearly all of the literature is about Wyatt; hardly any of it deals with the Earps prior to the 1881 shoot-out in Tombstone, Arizona. For example, Casey Tefertiller's biography *Wyatt Earp: The Life Behind the Legend* (John Wiley and Sons, New York, 1997) is nearly four hundred pages long, but only its first thirty-three pages deal with Wyatt's first thirty-three years. Even less is known about his brothers prior to the gunfight at the O.K. Corral. And even *less* is known about the women the Earps lived with. Bessie Bartlett Earp may have been born in either Illinois or in New York State. I placed her in Tennessee in order to address the theme of regulated versus prohibited vice.

In my portraits of James, Wyatt, and Morgan Earp, I tried to stay as close to the facts as possible while allowing myself enough latitude to account for the seeming contradictions in their lives. For my purposes, the telling document is one that barely mentions the boys. In 1864, long before the Fighting Earps were famous, Sarah Jane Rousseau traveled from Iowa to California as part of a wagon train led by their father, Nicholas Earp. Her diary of that journey was recently published by Earl Chafin (*The Sarah Jane Rousseau Diary,* Earl Chafin Press, Riverside, California, 2002). Rousseau provided a contemporary description of Nicholas Earp as a volatile, bad-tempered, profane, and violent man who did not spare the rod. This confirmed suspicions I had already developed regarding the relationship between Nicholas and his sons.

Wyatt's fictional observation about the making of bullies rests on the insight of Edward Nolan. Eddie and his wife, Chrissie, raised their family in Belfast, Northern Ireland, during the latter half of the twentieth century, when Belfast was as dangerous as Dodge in the 1870s. Belfast boys had to be tough without inviting conflict, and Eddie taught his sons that bullies were boys who'd been beaten by their fathers. "Look at them with scorn, the way their fathers did, and they're small and powerless again, just like their fathers wanted them to be." (I do not recommend this tactic, even if you are as physically imposing as the Nolan brothers and the Earps. My advice is: *Run.*) Eddie's son Art Nolan convinced me that I should write this story. Art and his father provided endless encouragement while I worked on the novel, even as Eddie himself was facing down a lung disease as lethal as John Henry Holliday's tuberculosis. Eddie lived long enough to read the complete manuscript and to express his joy in it; I only wish I'd flown to Belfast to hand it to him. Too late now.

Wyatt Earp wasn't the only one who had trouble keeping Dodge City's shifting factions and baroque feuds straight, so I simplified Dodge City history, politics, economy, and social organization.

Details of the 1871–72 curriculum at the Pennsylvania College of Dental Surgery are accurate, as are assessments of John Henry Holliday's professional skill. I thank Dara Rogers, D.D.S., for her modern insight into nineteenth-century dental procedures. In addition, the following generously shared their areas of expertise with me.

Piano and music theory: Bob Price.

Horse and racing lore: Kristi Cetrulo; Cornelia Chapman; Lynette Hulbert; Beverley McCurdy; Mary Rose Paradis, D.V.M.; Anne Swan; Sara Tidd.

Clinical aspects of untreated pulmonary

tuberculosis and advancing respiratory disease: Nancy O'Leary, R.N.

The psychological aftermath of almost getting killed in combat: Captain Timothy Riemann, USMC.

James C. Earp's wartime service in Company F, 17th Illinois Regiment: Nathan Moran.

Indian one-liners about mules: Ray Bucko, S.J.; Peter Klink, S.J.; and Ron Kills Warrior.

Jesuit missionary history in North America: Mark Thiel; Raymond Bucko, S.J.; and Dave Myers, S.J. Father Myers is also a lawyer who checked legalisms and Latin.

Other languages: May Burl (French); Dr. Ray DeMallie (Osage); Dr. Suzanne Bach (German); Annie Ho Lucak (Chinese). I used T. E. Shaw's translation of *The Odyssey* (Oxford University Press, New York, 1956) and Robert Fagles' of *The Aeneid* (Viking Press, New York, 2006), but felt free to recast the poetry to fit Doc and Kate's interpretations.

For close reading and sensitive criticism of the story, I thank Gretchen Batton, Ellie D'Addio Behr, Ray Bucko, Kari Burkey, Rebecca Chaitin, Dick Cima, Mary Dewing, Miriam Goderich, Jennifer Hershey, Nancy O'Leary, Bob Price, Tim Riemann, Dara Rogers, Dan Russell, Vivian Singer, Kate Sweeney, Bonnie Thompson, and Jennifer Tucker.

Special thanks to Kari and Dave Burkey for a glorious experience at the KD Guest Ranch in Adamsville, Ohio. They taught me to ride with authority, and I had the time of my life learning how to pen calves!

If you have been moved by John Henry Holliday's story, please consider making a donation in his memory to one of the organizations that change lives around the world by providing free surgical correction of cleft palates and cleft lips. My husband, Don, and I have chosen the Smile Train for our own donations.

M.D.R.

ABOUT THE AUTHOR

Mary Doria Russell has studied nine languages, written five novels, and earned three degrees in anthropology. Her novels have won a number of national and international literary awards, including the Arthur C. Clarke Award, the James Tiptree, Jr. Award, and the American Library Association Readers' Choice Award. *The Sparrow* was selected as one of *Entertainment Weekly*'s ten best books of the year, and *A Thread of Grace* was nominated for a Pulitzer Prize. The daughter of a sheriff, Dr. Russell spent her academic career teaching gross anatomy at the Case Western Reserve University School of Dentistry in Cleveland, Ohio, where she still lives with her husband of forty years. She is at work on her next book.

www.MaryDoriaRussell.net